The Mill... Virgin

He has money and power –
now he is claiming her!

Three glittering, sexy romances from three
favourite Mills & Boon authors!

In March 2009 Mills & Boon bring
you two classic collections, each
featuring three favourite romances
by our bestselling authors...

THE MILLIONAIRE'S VIRGIN

Virgin for Sale by Susan Stephens
The Rich Man's Virgin
by Lindsay Armstrong
The Bedroom Assignment
by Sophie Weston

SURRENDER IN THE ARMS
OF THE SHEIKH

Exposed: The Sheikh's Mistress
by Sharon Kendrick
Stolen by the Sheikh by Trish Morey
Fit for a Sheikh by Carol Grace

The Millionaire's Virgin

VIRGIN FOR SALE
by
Susan Stephens

THE RICH MAN'S VIRGIN
by
Lindsay Armstrong

THE BEDROOM ASSIGNMENT
by
Sophie Weston

⊚™ MILLS & BOON®
Pure reading pleasure™

*Harlequin Mills & Boon Limited,
Eton House, 18-24 Paradise Road, Richmond, Surrey TW9 1SR*

THE MILLIONAIRE'S VIRGIN
© by Harlequin Enterprises II B.V./S.à.r.l 2009

Virgin for Sale, The Rich Man's Virgin and *The Bedroom Assignment*
were first published in Great Britain by Harlequin Mills & Boon
Limited in separate, single volumes.

Virgin for Sale © Susan Stephens 2005
The Rich Man's Virgin © Lindsay Armstrong 2005
The Bedroom Assignment © Sophie Weston 2002

ISBN: 978 0 263 87127 2

05-0309

*Printed and bound in Spain
by Litografia Rosés S.A., Barcelona*

VIRGIN FOR SALE

by

Susan Stephens

Susan Stephens was a professional singer who now loves nothing more than reading and writing romance. She lives in cosy chaos in a converted blacksmith's cottage in Cheshire surrounded by cats, dogs, guinea pigs, children and a very understanding husband. She loves playing the piano and singing, as well as riding, cooking and gardening and travel. When she isn't writing she's usually daydreaming about her next hero!

Don't miss Susan Stephen's exciting new novel, *The Ruthless Billionaire's Virgin*, available in May 2009 from Mills & Boon® Modern™.

For Penny…a true friend.

'YOU must leave before they come for you—'

Her mother's hands were biting into her shoulders making Lisa cry; silent tears that trickled down her cheeks unchecked, while her gaze remained locked on her mother's face.

'You must go to your father in the city.'

'My father?' Lisa's face turned suddenly fearful.

This was all the more shocking for her mother to see, because the child she called Willow had long ago learned to govern her feelings.

Lisa regained control quickly. She hated letting the mask slip. She only felt safe when no one knew what she was thinking. The mask was the shield she used to protect herself in the dangerous society in which she lived—a place where a careless glance or reckless laughter could lead to humiliating punishment in front of the whole community.

But if she was frightened of her ruthless 'family', Lisa was even more terrified of leaving her mother to their mercy. She was terrified of her father too, because he was a stranger her mother had fled from seven years before. Was her father wicked? Was that why her mother had run away? Was he even more wicked than the people who lived here?

Lisa stared fearfully at the open door. No one was allowed to close doors in the commune, let alone lock them.

'Please, Willow, please, you must go now, or they will be here.'

Her mother's voice had the desperate, pleading sound Lisa associated with horrible things, and her once beautiful eyes were bloodshot and watery. Her lips, tinged blue from the latest blows, were twisted in a grimace of desperation.

'Please, Willow—'

'Don't call me Willow. My name is Lisa…Lisa Bond.'

Hearing her mother's sob, Lisa wished she hadn't been the cause of it, and that she knew how to make her smile again. But she could only stand behind the barricades she had built in her mind, and watch her cry.

'I kept back some money from the market stall.'

Lisa looked on in horror as her mother dug inside the pocket of her flowing robe. 'But that's stealing from the community. You will be punished—'

'If you love me, you will take this and leave here.'

The coins hurt as they bit into the soft flesh of Lisa's palm. 'You'll come with me—'

'Come with you?'

For a moment, her mother's eyes brightened, but then they both heard the voices coming closer…men's voices.

'Climb through that window,' Eloisa instructed. Her voice was fierce and determined for the first, for the only time in her life. 'And don't stop running until you reach the bus depot. Here, take your father's address.' She pressed a slip of paper into Lisa's hand.

'But what about you?'

'I'll…I'll keep them here until you're far away.'

They exchanged a glance. There was no time for more. The leader of the commune had announced Lisa's initiation into womanhood that night at supper. It was an entertainment for everyone to enjoy, he said.

'My name is Lisa Bond. My name is Lisa Bond. My name is Lisa Bond.' Lisa chanted to herself as she hurtled down the pitch-black country lane. It was the only way she could block out the inner voice begging her to return to the commune and save her mother. Another, more rational voice insisted that if she did go back she would only cause her mother more pain.

When the lights of the small, local bus depot came into sight she sprinted the final few yards and launched herself onto the running board of the last bus to the city. There was no transport at the commune. She knew they couldn't get to her. At last, she was safe…

The man on board the bus took her money without comment. If he wondered at the grubby child clutching a slip of paper in a fist turned white with tension, something about the set of her mouth warned him not to intrude on her silence.

As Lisa gazed out into the darkness she was sure she could feel her mother's will urging her to turn her face to the future. And in that moment she knew for certain that somewhere deep inside her a person called Lisa Bond still existed. She would find that person, and nurture her like the seedlings she cared for in her own secret plot back at the wasteland the community called a garden. She had guarded them fiercely and controlled the weeds. In secure surroundings her plants had thrived, and so would she.

CHAPTER ONE

'SHE's here—'

Constantine Zagorakis didn't move a muscle in response to his aide's whispered aside, though his eyes darkened a little as Lisa Bond entered the room. The woman's rise to the seat of power at Bond Steel had played right into his hands. Her late father, Jack Bond, had been a difficult character; doing business with Jack's daughter promised an easier ride.

Lisa Bond had a reputation in the City for being hard. In fairness she'd had to be hard-hearted to fill the shoes of her father when he'd died. But, hard or not, she was still a woman...and women were prey to their emotions, a factor that would give him an immediate advantage.

An air of confident command hung about the chairwoman of Bond Steel as she led her directors into the boardroom. Her manner challenged him. Lisa Bond wouldn't just dance to his tune; by the time he had finished with her, she'd sing to it too.

She'd had the worst kind of childhood, but his youth had been blighted too and he'd come through. He'd make no allowances. There were only two women in the world he could trust, and Lisa Bond was neither one of them.

Bond was a woman with history. Before throwing in her lot with her father, she had lived with her mother in a place that knew no rules or boundaries. She could turn on the ice all she liked, he wasn't buying it. Beneath that front there had to be a free spirit itching to break out. He would set that spirit free *and* add her company to his portfolio at a knock-down price. Where business was concerned he had no scruples. Breaking down the opposition was Constantine's primary objective.

Like any predator, Tino sensed the change in the air as Lisa Bond walked towards him, as well as the hint of some fresh scent she wore. She was dwarfed by the men in suits flanking her, but her presence more than made up for it. Petite and trim, she had clearly chosen her dark tailored suit to create a certain impression.

She was more beautiful than her photograph suggested, with luxuriant chestnut-brown hair fixed in an immaculate chignon. Beautiful women frequently used their looks like a weapon in an attempt to disarm him, but Lisa Bond was different—and not just because she had the most compelling sea-green eyes he had ever seen. She had something more. The outcome would be the same. He would take what he wanted and walk away. A woman had betrayed him at birth; only two had won his trust since then; there would be no more.

The tabloids and the business reports all said Bond was blessed with the attributes of an alpha male mixed together with the subtle cunning of a woman. The tempting sight of her breasts leant some credence to the rumour. Had she forgotten to fasten the extra button? Or was the curve of lush breasts exposed just enough to tease another cold calculation? Either way, it was his ineluctable duty to bring her to heel.

Tino took no more than a second or two over his assessment. His senses were tuned to the highest level. Whatever happened in the meeting, he would find the key that unlocked Bond Steel's darkest secrets. Every company had them. He and his people would simply sift through the records until he found out what they were. This 'negotiation' was merely a business courtesy—a gesture that meant nothing. The moment Bond Steel's Achilles heel was uncovered he would strike.

In the role of gracious victor he might save Ms Bond's backside—he might not. That would depend on how co-operative she was. The only certainty was that he would be adding another valuable asset to Zagorakis International Inc.

While this was going on, Lisa was drawing a few fast conclusions of her own, though it was hard to think ration-ally when her back was still bristling at the unannounced arrival of Constantine Zagorakis. Her diary was planned with all the care of a military operation; she didn't like it upset. The meeting with Zagorakis Inc had been scheduled for later that morning. She had something to sell; Zagorakis Inc was always hungry. But no one had expected Constantine Zagorakis to turn up in person.

Lisa had barely had chance to sit down at her desk before her PA, Mike, had alerted her to who was in the building… Zagorakis might as well have swept through it like a fire-storm. Grown men were behaving like overexcited children at the mere mention of his presence. Fortunately, Lisa's speciality was dousing fires.

Zagorakis Inc had made an offer for one of Bond Steel's subsidiaries, a small engineering works that had done some good things in the past. The company no longer fitted her strategic vision for the core business, and the cash injection resulting from the sale could save Bond Steel.

Family-run businesses had dropped out of favour in the City, and the Bond Steel share price had taken a dive. The situation was critical. There were no other serious offers, and if she didn't nail the deal with Zagorakis she stood to lose Bond Steel, ruin the lives of those who worked for her, and face the type of humiliation that would put back the cause of women in industry a hundred years. Everything was riding on this deal.

Zagorakis Inc was cash rich and could move fast, which suited her perfectly. But that didn't explain why

Constantine Zagorakis was taking a personal interest in the deal. It was peanuts on the scale of his usual acquisitions. So, why was a world-class predator sniffing around? *Because he wanted all of Bond Steel?* That was where her suspicion dial was pointing.

When she found him staring at her, the rumour she had heard about him sprang to mind—he liked to look his prey in the eyes before devouring them. She'd laughed at the time—but now it didn't seem so funny.

She resented the Zagorakis-effect. He was like some vast power source that drew everyone's attention. A typical tycoon—he was ruthless, driven, and utterly heartless. She was no marshmallow herself, which explained the buzz in the building. This was one battle no one wanted to miss.

Some sixth sense had told him she never sat at the head of the table, but in the middle of her team. Unerringly, he had chosen to stand behind her chair as if he was already poised to take her place. And then he directed one of his minions to the seldom-used chairman's seat at the head of the table. *Who the hell did he think he was? Who was in control here?*

'Good morning, gentlemen.' She didn't need to raise her voice to command attention, though there was one dark gaze she could have done without. Zagorakis threw off sexual vibes with every move. And with treachery typical of the female body she was already longing for a slice of that high-octane maleness—something she had to get over fast.

Fortunately, she found that easy. She was Jack Bond's daughter, after all.

A bitter smile grazed Lisa's lips. Thanks to her father she had seen the depths of degradation to which a man could bring a woman. She had no intention of suffering her mother's fate, of being tossed around like some uncared for rag doll... She had to be in control.

Tino was immediately aware of the shadow dulling

Lisa's gaze. He had been anticipating a glint of challenge, or some proof of her wild nature. This new, subdued expression was a real disappointment. The hunt was spoiled before it began if the prey was wounded.

He was relieved when she quickly recovered. His imagination was in overdrive. She had probably missed an appointment at the beauty salon.

Lisa consciously relaxed her shoulder. It was dangerous to let Zagorakis see how shaken she was, but something about him reminded her of the past...

It was his presence, his strength—his overwhelming physical strength. Yes, that was it. She shook her head in a fast, instinctive gesture to close the door on those memories that were safer locked away. But for a few seconds the old film replayed in her head. The leader of the commune had been a powerful, awe-inspiring figure, but he had been an evil man, who had grown ever stronger by feeding on the insecurities of his flock.

It had been Lisa's misfortune to come to his notice when her body had started developing faster than the other girls', and she would always be grateful to her mother for helping her to run away before the obscene initiation ceremony he had planned especially for her could take place.

She glanced around quickly just to check that no one had noticed her brush with the past. No one had. They were all too busy preparing for the meeting. And now the blood was flowing freely through her veins again, and she could feel her cheeks warming up. The past would always be with her, Lisa reflected grimly. And thank goodness for it, it kept her wary, kept her safe.

'Ms Bond.'

She came to abruptly. Zagorakis was offering to shake her hand in greeting, yet all she could think was how threatening he was. She thought about her father, remembering how his icy control had proved too much for his much younger wife, causing her mother to bolt from the endless round of coffee mornings and race days to the promised freedom of the commune. Her father might have been the mainstay of every charitable committee in the area, but he had remained blind to the fact that her mother's fragile psyche had been falling to pieces in front of him...

'I'm going to be a free spirit,' her mother had said, Lisa recalled, curling her lip as she remembered their hectic flight to the commune. The only thing that was free at the commune as far as she remembered was the men's licence to have sex whenever, and with whomever, they chose. The women worked, while the men drank themselves into oblivion, only recovering in time for the next rut.

In Lisa's opinion, her mother had simply exchanged one type of savage slavery for another. Fortunately, such a thing could never happen to her. She had taken control of her life when she had escaped the commune, and no one would ever take that control away from her. If they did she always feared it would destroy her.

As Constantine Zagorakis's hand enclosed Lisa's in the customary handshake she felt a shock run right up her arm. She had thought him strong, but she'd had no idea up to that moment how powerful he was. Touching him was like touching the pelt of a sleeping lion. She could sense the power underneath. And he had the same peculiar stillness of a deadly predator, a predator poised to pounce...

'It's a pleasure to meet you,' she said, but they both knew it was a meaningless courtesy; the smile didn't even attempt to reach her eyes. The only pleasure in store for either of them was a deal that came out weighted in their favour.

Zagorakis's gaze was as hard as her own. She wished it might have been possible to learn something about him before they had met, but Constantine Zagorakis was a dark mystery of a man, a man who lived his life behind a wall of secrecy. No rumours about him had ever circulated. He was, apparently, Mr Clean, with no family that anyone knew about, no lurid sex life, no life at all outside his formidable business empire—an empire that reached into every corner of the world.

At thirty-five, Constantine Zagorakis ran one of the largest corporations on the planet. Devouring companies was his recreation of choice. But this was one business that would stick in his craw, because Bond Steel wasn't for sale. And neither was she. Lisa thought, hardening her mouth when he held her gaze. Easing her hand away from his clasp, she turned to address the room: 'Shall we sit down, gentlemen?'

And now, Zagorakis was holding out her chair like the perfect gentleman. He didn't fool her. He understood the significance of the seat of power, and was goading her with it. He had sensed how territorial she was. The fact that he could read her so accurately made her doubly cautious. 'Thank you, Mr Zagorakis.' She took her place.

'Please, call me Tino.'

'Won't you sit across from me?' Lisa indicated a place at the table, ignoring his attempt at informality. She didn't want to sit facing him, but it was better, safer to keep him in sight at all times—that way she could detect any little asides he might send to his people.

It provided her with a perfect chance to study him. His choice of outfit was nothing short of an insult: casual jacket, blue jeans, and a black, open-necked shirt—though everything was designer, she'd give him that. Still, he looked more like a buccaneer home from a raid than a suave Greek tycoon. His thick, wavy black hair was too long, and there was at least a day's worth of stubble on his face.

Her stomach gave a kick as their eyes briefly met. She didn't like his expression. Aesthetically his eyes were pleasing enough, glorious in fact, black as pitch, with lashes so long he could almost shield what he was thinking…but not quite. This was a scouting trip for Tino Zagorakis. He wasn't interested in her small engineering works. He was testing the vulnerability of the parent company, Bond Steel. He was testing *her* vulnerability.

Lisa was used to corporate raiders sniffing around. They all thought the same thing: a woman at the helm was easy pickings—their mistake. Zagorakis was no more of a threat than the rest—other than in the hot-sexual-tug department.

Businessmen she normally encountered had boardroom pallor with blubber to match, and so she had imagined him shorter, dumpier, uglier—a younger model of the grizzled old shipping tycoons. Tino Zagorakis was none of those things.

But she had to forget the man's impressive casing, and focus on the brain beneath. Bond Steel's reputation was on the firing line—not to mention her own, and from his casual approach she assumed Zagorakis thought the deal a foregone conclusion. He hadn't even troubled to shave or dress appropriately, and that showed contempt in her book.

The meeting between Bond Steel and Zagorakis Inc evolved like a polite game of tennis, with the tactical ball being passed with exaggerated politeness between the two sides. Meanwhile, Lisa concentrated her mind on the subtext: Zagorakis had identified a company he thought a good match with his own; the small portion she was prepared to sell didn't interest him; he wanted it all.

When a lull came in their discussions, he stood up. It was barely noon. 'Are you leaving so soon? I've arranged for a buffet to be laid out next door. I thought we could discuss some of the finer details.' He wasn't interested in making small talk over canapés—and it was time to lose the charm. 'We haven't finished, Mr Zagorakis—'

'I have.'

Lisa felt the blood drain out of her face. She wasn't used

to being looked at the way Zagorakis was looking at her.
She wasn't used to anyone going against her wishes. She
made the rules; everyone else lived by them—that way they
all stayed safe. But Tino Zagorakis had made it clear that
as far as he was concerned she had no rank. He would do
exactly as *he* pleased, and she could go hang. Bond Steel
was just a tasty snack…the company, the people who
worked there, counted for nothing.

'I regret I have another appointment.' He held her gaze.

Regret? Lisa didn't think so. That deep, husky voice was
pitched to make it sound as if there were some type of
understanding between them, an intimacy almost. It unsettled her, and must have unsettled her team—they had to be
wondering what was going on. Without raising his voice
Zagorakis had scored a telling point by subtly undermining
her authority. And then she saw that his eyes were hard
and calculating, and even slightly mockingly amused.

Scraping back her chair, she stood to face him. She
wasn't about to let Bond Steel be gobbled down by some
ravenous tycoon—a tycoon who thought her company was
just a set of numbers. Bond Steel wasn't a counter to be
risked. And if Zagorakis had come down from his ivory
tower to measure her, and judged her no threat, he had
miscalculated. She would defend Bond Steel to the last.

After her experience in the commune Bond Steel had
been her salvation. While other teenagers had longed for
freedom, she had craved discipline and boundaries so she
could sleep safe at night. Jack Bond had given her that.
Before she'd started to work for him he had sent her to a
school where even the rigid order had been welcome. It
had provided her with a framework within which she had
felt safe, and she had excelled. When she had returned
home she hadn't cared that her father had shown her no
favouritism; she had never expected any. Jack Bond had
only ever wanted a son, and she accepted that too. She had

worked her way up her father's company from the bottom. When he'd died, she'd taken his place thanks to sheer dint of effort. By then she had discovered the key to his success. It was nothing more than hard work and focus. Jack Bond had never allowed anything as time-wasting as emotion to stand in his way.

'Why, Ms Bond, you seem distracted.'

Those eyes—those incredible black-gold eyes—were dancing with laughter. Sucking in an angry gulp of air, Lisa felt her hands ball into fists. 'Not a bit of it, Mr Zagorakis.' Her gaze flicked over him dismissively. 'As your decision to attend this meeting was clearly last-minute, I won't keep you. I'm sure our people can arrange another time for us to meet if there are any outstanding details—'

'Shall we say dinner at nine to discuss those outstanding details?'

Lisa's cheeks flamed red. She was sure the *double entendre* was intended. In spite of her slender frame her breasts had always been regarded as her most 'outstanding' feature. And now her nipples had hardened into bullets, which, from the expression in Zagorakis's eyes, she guessed he knew.

'I'll have my chauffeur pick you up around nine at your apartment—'

'No—' Before she could say more Lisa found herself staring at an open door. 'Gentlemen, this meeting is over,' she said, quickly recovering her self-possession. 'Tomorrow morning at ten would suit me for the follow up. Arrange it for me, will you, Mike?'

By nine o' clock that evening Lisa was curled up tensely on the sofa at the penthouse she called home. Warm and pink after her bath, she was anything but relaxed. Wearing her favourite plush robe, she had the music turned down low, a crystal goblet of good burgundy on the side table next to her, and a new book just started. She had read the first page three times, and still didn't have a clue what it said.

Zagorakis's chauffeur would call round, she knew that, but still she flinched and dragged her robe a little closer when the doorbell rang. Thankfully Vera would take care of it. Vera, confidante and housekeeper, knew exactly what she had to do.

Just as Lisa had anticipated, the exchange between Vera and Zagorakis's chauffeur lasted no more than a few seconds. With a sigh of relief, she turned back to her book. But she couldn't relax… She tried changing the music. She could always find something to suit her mood amongst her vast collection of CD's… Tonight was different, tonight she had to force her fingers past the boxed sets devoted to the heavenly voice of *La Divina* Callas. The impassioned Greek-American voice of Maria Anna Sophie Cecilia Kalogeropoulos was the last thing she needed to hear. Right now anything remotely Greek was off limits. Finally, she settled for some low, smoochy jazz. The plangent wail of Miles Davis' trumpet seemed appropriate somehow.

Returning to her book, Lisa turned the pages dutifully, all the time trying to ignore the keen dark eyes and mocking smile occupying her thoughts. When the doorbell rang again she was surprised and then angry. Zagorakis had some nerve sending his chauffeur round twice in one evening. Couldn't he take a hint?

Vera answered the door, but Lisa's curiosity got the better of her. Padding barefoot across the room, she froze. The man's audacity was unbelievable. His unannounced visit to her office building had been bad enough, but this was outrageous—and Vera was having trouble getting rid of him.

'Thank you, Vera, I'll see to this.'

Lisa couldn't pretend she wasn't thankful that Vera remained hovering in the background. 'Yes?' She stared up at him. Tino Zagorakis was more casually dressed, and even more brazenly male. Without a jacket she could see how toned he was beneath his black shirt. His assessing stare was every bit as hard as she remembered.

'We arranged to have dinner tonight.'

'You arranged to have dinner tonight, *Mr* Zagorakis.'

'It's time you called me Tino.'

Oh, really? 'It's late—'

'Exactly,' he said. 'And as you pointed out, *Lisa*, we still have things to talk about.'

Lisa? When did she give him permission to use her first name? Jack Bond's first law of survival: keep everyone at a distance. *Everyone…* She relaxed minutely. He was carrying a briefcase. Of course, Zagorakis was a man who would far rather trade than indulge his carnal appetites, but she had already set up their next meeting for the following morning. She had no intention of being railroaded by him twice in one day. 'Business will have to wait until our respective teams are present.'

'If you insist.'

'I do insist. Our next meeting will be held tomorrow morning.'

'Thank you for reminding me…but we still have to eat.'

His casual shrug and the smile that accompanied it threw her, and while she was trying to figure out his angle he walked past her into the apartment.

'Like I said, *Mr* Zagorakis—' she went after him '—it's late—'

'And so I took the trouble of ordering in.' He paused mid-step to turn round and look at her. 'I didn't want to put your housekeeper to any trouble.'

And now Vera was sharing a flirtatious smile with him! What was this? A conspiracy?

In fairness, she couldn't blame Vera; the man was hot. His shirt was open far enough to show some hard, tanned chest, and his blue jeans appeared pressure-moulded to thighs of iron. And there were certain other impressive bulges below the heavy-duty belt…

'Are you sure you don't mind me coming inside?'

Lisa quickly adjusted her gaze. The only thing sure about this was that her face was heating up. 'I don't wish to appear ungrateful.'

'But?' he pressed.

'I'm tired. It's late. And I'm ready for bed.'

'So I see.'

His lips tugged up at one corner in a way that made her painfully aware that she was naked beneath her robe. The split second it took to look down to check that the robe was securely fastened was enough for his chauffeur to march past her carrying a hamper. 'Where do you think you're going?'

Zagorakis stepped forward and barred her way. 'In here?' he said, protecting his man's back by resting one arm against the doorframe of her den.

Lisa's mouth dropped open. The only thing left for her to confirm, apparently, was the venue for the picnic he had brought with him. 'You have some incredible nerve—'

'Please…no more compliments.' He held up his hands in mock defeat and she had to be prodded twice before Vera could make her presence felt.

'Hadn't you better get changed?' Vera suggested discreetly. 'You don't want him guessing you're naked under there.'

Lisa could see the sense in that. 'Stay with them, will you, Vera? I'll be back as quickly as I can.'

Jeans and a T-shirt might have been a practical choice, but smart navy trousers and a tailored white blouse made Lisa feel more in control. The sex-stripping pop socks and boring flat shoes were an inspiration, and, with her hair scraped back into a pony-tail, she was satisfied that she had done everything possible to strip anything lightweight from her appearance. A slick of clear lip-gloss was her only concession—but then she sucked it off again. No point in playing Zagorakis's game—she'd stick to her own.

The angry words she had been rehearsing all the way down from her bedroom died the moment she entered her den. The room had been transformed. Candles had been lit, and were flickering on every surface. Champagne was cooling in a bucket...and on a low table between the two sofas a platter of fresh seafood emitted a faint, salty tang. Another mouth-watering aroma said the bread in the wicker basket was still warm, and, inside a crystal bowl nestling in a dish of ice, yellow butter pats were asking to be slathered over one of the crisp, golden crusts. And she was hungry—starving, in fact, Lisa realised, praying her stomach wouldn't rumble.

'Can I tempt you?'

Transferring her gaze to Constantine Zagorakis's dark, slanting eyes, Lisa stared at him coldly.

'A few prawns, perhaps?' he murmured, reaching for a plate.

He was baiting his hook with a lot more than seafood, Lisa suspected, seeing the smile hovering around his mouth.

'What's the matter?' He put the plate down again.

Lisa had been distracted momentarily. She was sure she had just heard two sets of footsteps leaving the apartment; two voices mingling as the front door closed.

'Where are you going now?' he said.

Lisa looked down at the hand on her arm. Zagorakis released her at once. 'It's nothing,' she said. 'I must have been mistaken—'

'Mistaken?'

'I thought I heard Vera leaving.'

'Your housekeeper? You did.'

'No.' Lisa shook her head. 'Vera would have come to say goodnight to me before she left.'

'Not if she was being discreet.'

'Discreet?'

His shoulders eased in a shrug. 'It's no trouble for my chauffeur to take her home. He passes her door—'

Raising one hand, Lisa silenced him. 'Let me get this straight. *You* sent my housekeeper home?'

'It's getting late.'

'I would have called a taxi.'

'I thought I'd save you the trouble.'

'Trouble?' Trouble had come through her door at nine o' clock that morning and she hadn't got rid of him yet.

'That's all right with you, isn't it Lisa?'

Lisa? She wasn't going to let him get to her, even though he was asking one thing while his eyes were suggesting something else. She had no intention of giving him the satisfaction of seeing her shrink from the prospect of being alone with him either. 'Yes, *Tino*, that's absolutely fine with me—'

'Good.'

He seemed pleased to have got that out of the way, and then her guard must have dropped because he raised her hand to his lips and dropped a kiss on the back of it.

'I realise it's late.' He tried for contrite. 'Do you forgive me?'

Lisa snatched her hand away. 'Do you always march uninvited into other people's homes?'

His lips pressed down ruefully, *attractively*…

'I'm sorry, Lisa, I thought we had both earned some down-time.'

He was sorry? She didn't think so. But since when could someone brush a hand with his lips and set a whole body on fire?

'Don't you ever relax?' he pressed, his perceptive gaze refusing to release her.

'When I'm given the opportunity.'

'Surely you must get out of this starchy uniform of yours, and kick back once in a while?'

'Surprisingly, I tried to do that very thing this evening. I took a long, warm bath, slipped into a comfy robe, and came down here…to relax.'

'Touché,' he murmured softly.

Lisa sighed with frustration. Technically, Zagorakis was her guest—and she couldn't forget that his money could rescue her company. She couldn't afford to be too rude to him—and the food did look delicious…

'Why don't you let me choose something for you?' he suggested, picking up the plate again.

'I can manage, thank you. Really, you don't need to—' Raising her voice, she was forced to insist, 'Give me that plate.'

'Certainly.'

By the time she went to take it from him it was loaded with delicacies—but he kept his grip on it, so that she was bound to him by a too-small china plate…and when he stubbornly resisted her attempt to pull it free she could feel her cheeks start to burn. 'You really didn't need to go to all this trouble.' She tugged a little harder, refusing to give him the upper hand.

'It was my pleasure, I assure you.'

'Why exactly?'

'Perhaps you deserve a little spoiling. Perhaps we both do.'

It was hardly the answer she had been anticipating—and certainly not when it was delivered in that frank and engaging way. His eyes were so deep she was in danger of drowning in them, and they were standing far too close. The warmth of his body was curling round her like a seductive cloak and she could almost forget that, as far as Bond Steel was concerned, Constantine Zagorakis was arch enemy number one—

Breaking eye contact, she pulled away.

'Champagne?' he said pleasantly.

She was still fighting off his powerful sexual aura. But then common sense kicked in: definitely no champagne. She loved it, but she wanted to keep her wits about her. What she should do was go to the kitchen, fill a jug with iced water, and pour it over both of them. 'Thank you, I'd love a glass of champagne.'

The expression in his eyes should have brought her to her senses. She was on the point of crossing an invisible line, a line she knew she always had to stay behind. She only had to remember her mother's fate to know that she could lose everything, if she ever allowed her senses to take the lead…but she couldn't risk antagonising Tino Zagorakis. He was a formidable business opponent, and on a personal level perhaps even more dangerous…but forewarned was forearmed—and one glass of champagne couldn't hurt.

As Tino handed her the glass of champagne he lifted his own and tipped it towards her in a silent toast. She replied by walking away to perch on the edge of the room's only straight-backed chair. She needed a moment to collect herself. This encounter was something new for her. In the past men had always been happy to follow her lead, which was hardly surprising since most of her relationships were conducted in her head—she didn't have time or inclination for anything else. She liked her life the way it was—tidy, successful, and absolutely safe.

'Are you sure you're comfortable over there?'

In spite of all her good intentions, the look Tino gave her made Lisa's heart pound. If nothing else Tino Zagorakis set new standards for her fantasies. 'I'm fine, thank you.'

'More champagne?'

'Why not?' She could handle it. She could handle him too.

As he crossed the room she noticed that his movements were fluid like the big cat she had first thought him. Moving on silent feet, he reached her side before she even had time to hold out her glass.

He left her alone after that, and they ate in silence seated at opposite ends of the room, which should have been a relief. But Lisa's sensory self had taken over from the rational side of her being. The delicious food and wine slithered down her throat with dizzying speed, and the alcohol loosened her inhibitions. Some very primitive thoughts were entering her mind...just watching his mouth work as he ate was compulsive viewing; his teeth were so white and strong, his lips so firm, and mobile—

'Lisa?' He picked up on her stare. 'Would you like something more?'

As Lisa's eyes cleared she waved the bread basket away and she shook her head. 'No, thank you...that was absolutely delicious, but I couldn't eat another thing.'

'Then I think it's time we got to know each other a little better, don't you?'

CHAPTER TWO

TINO took her plate, stacking it with his on a side table. Lisa watched warily as he came towards her, and almost flinched when he was close enough to touch. But then, instead of grabbing her, he snatched hold of his briefcase and dipped inside. Bringing out some financial reports, he spread them across the low table between them.

'I think we both know you've got a few problems, Lisa—'

For a moment when his glance flicked up Lisa thought he was talking about something other than business, and blushed violently.

'I've noticed a few discrepancies here and there,' he continued. 'All easily explained, I'm sure. No doubt our respective bean-counters will soon iron things out.'

It was a relief for her mind to click back into business mode.

'Take a look at these.' He passed her some sheets. 'It's only fair that you should have sight of all my findings.'

Fair? Tino was pointing up the fact that he had uncovered a whole clutch of Bond Steel skeletons in the shortest time imaginable, in order to prepare her for a much reduced offer price, Lisa suspected. 'That's very good of you, Tino.'

She was careful to sound noncommittal. She wanted to see exactly what he had found out before showing any reaction to it.

'I'll leave the rest of these for you.' He closed his briefcase.

'You're going?'

'Not if you don't want me to.'

He had changed in a heartbeat from cold-blooded businessman to someone very different. Her pulse rate quickened in response. But this was wrong. Worse than wrong, it was dangerous.

Her gaze was drawn to his hand resting on the door…his strong, supple hand resting on the door. 'I'll see you out.' Her voice sounded distant and undecided. It was as if she were looking down at herself, or rather at the woman she might have been if her life had been different. She didn't want him to leave. The apartment would be so empty without him… She would be lonely again. Lonely but safe.

Tino had tossed a pebble into the pond and waited to see how far the ripples would travel. He had to admit he was surprised. She had capitulated rather sooner than he had imagined. Mixing business and pleasure was new to him, but for Lisa he would make an exception. He wanted Bond Steel, and he wanted Lisa Bond. Business was a game he always won, and she had become part of that game.

She thought herself strong and controlling. How strong? How controlling? He would test her boundaries and find out. His body ached for release. The thought of dominating Lisa held real appeal. It would be to her benefit too, of course. If she had the good sense to surrender he would give her the ride of her life.

As Tino caught hold of her arm Lisa snapped out of the trance. 'That's the second time you've done that,' she told him angrily, 'and I don't like it.'

'Really? Then you must forgive me,' he said in a voice that managed to be both penitent and amused.

But he didn't let her go.

And now they were close, too close, and their breath was mingling. There was no sound other than the two of them breathing. And then, perhaps by accident, the joint of his thumb brushed the side of her breast, and she sighed.

He felt her tense as he accidentally touched her when he shifted position, but that sigh was sending out a very different message. She didn't try to pull away, and now he felt the tremor running through her. He could feel it coursing right up his arm.

She wasn't jaded, and that pleased him. Her experience in the commune had only prepared her for him, heightened her capacity for pleasure… He allowed his gaze to slip to her breasts, to the full swell pressing urgently against her chaste white business shirt. He centred his attention on the taut nipples straining against the lace of her bra, and was gratified to see them harden still more beneath his interest. Lifting his head, he saw the pulse fluttering in her neck and the pink flush of desire tinting her skin. He understood her torment. He understood it and therefore would prolong it.

He was rewarded when the tip of her tongue crept out to moisten her lips. She fully expected him to kiss her. But instead he stared into her eyes, gauging her level of arousal. As he had anticipated they were almost black with desire, with just a faint rim of green remaining. She was breathing fast and the tiny gasps were making the fabric pull against the buttons on the front of her shirt. He longed to rip it off—but he wouldn't do that, because he knew she would like it too much.

She was quivering with frustration. She had never been so aroused. *She had never been aroused by a man before…* She could control most things, *all* things—so why not this? And why wouldn't he kiss her? One kiss was all she wanted, and then she would kick him out. She licked her lips, and saw his attention drawn to the full swell of her bottom lip.

Her lips were moist where she had touched them with her tongue…swollen with desire. He recognised all the signs, and, though he planned it to be this way, the sight was nearly too much for him. Dragging her close, he held her so their lips were almost touching, raising the danger level for them both.

She responded, and white-hot passion flared between them, but at the very point when he intended to pull back and teach her a lesson she stiffened and made an angry sound low in her throat. She strained against him—not with passion now, but with absolute determination to break free. He released her at once.

'Get out.' Her voice was barely above a whisper, but it contained more venom than he had ever heard. She didn't look at him. She remained frozen in place, with the back of her hand covering her mouth as if she wanted to hide it from him, wanted to hide the signs of her arousal from him. And she had been aroused, but then so had he.

'Get out,' she repeated, snapping the words at him.

In place of his surprise, Tino felt his anger beginning to rise. 'Why?' he said. 'Because I almost kissed you before you could kiss me?'

'Is that what you think?' She looked at him incredulously.

His pride was all over the place. He had never misjudged a situation so badly. 'Don't tell me you didn't want that?'

She rallied then, straightening up to confront him, her face drained of colour. 'You'll be telling me I deserved it next.'

'What? You think passion between a man and a woman is some form of punishment?' He grasped the back of his neck with his hand, and the look on his face told Lisa she was wrong about him—horribly wrong.

Straightening up, he stared at her coldly. 'I don't need these mind games, Lisa.'

'Then get out!' She made an angry gesture. 'What are you waiting for?'

'When are you going to learn that not everyone wants to dance to your tune?'

'Or yours?' Her eyes were blazing. She thought she heard him murmur something more. 'What did you say?'

'I said, you're nothing but a control freak, Lisa.' He stared straight at her so there could be no mistake.

Lisa didn't show by even a flicker that he had come closer than any man alive to proving that a lie. 'I think you'd better leave now.'

'That's the first thing you've said this evening that makes any sense.'

'What do you mean, she didn't make the meeting?'

Shifting the satellite phone to his other shoulder, Tino stared out at the clouds above Stellamaris, his private island, barely seeing the beloved contours of lush greenery, sugar sand and rock as he listened to what his right hand man was trying to tell him.

'They said she was sick—'

'Sick?'

'I don't know, Tino. I couldn't find out any more. I don't think it's serious, headache perhaps, women's problems—who the hell knows?'

'Find out for me, will you? And get back to me right away.'

'I'll do the best I can.'

Tino's voice hardened. 'That's not good enough, Andreas.'

'OK, leave it with me.'

'And, Andreas…'

'Yes?'

'Start making overtures to Clifton Steel, will you?'

'Clifton? But I thought you wanted Bond—'

Tino's voice was uncompromising. 'Just do as I ask, Andreas.'

'Yes, boss.'

He couldn't afford to feel like this about anyone, let alone Lisa Bond. Have her occupy his thoughts to the exclusion of everything else? Was he mad? After what had happened between them, professionally, he'd bury her. He would buy out Clifton *and* Bond. That would solve the problem—permanently. By the time he had finished with her she would never want to hear his name again.

Cutting the connection, Tino eased back in the leather armchair he used when he wasn't flying the jet himself. His eyes narrowed as he thought over the events of the past forty-eight hours. He had never met anyone like Lisa Bond. She had blind-sided him, slipped beneath his control. She had led him on, and then pulled back at the last moment.

But she was a woman in her late twenties, and grown women didn't behave that way. The signals they gave off were always clear. Why were Lisa's signals so misleading? Her behaviour puzzled him, and he didn't like puzzles. She was acting like a kid, a virgin, even, rather than the ball-breaking bitch everyone said she was.

And why was he still thinking about her at all? Had Lisa Bond turned his shrew-capping tactic on its head, and squirrelled her way into his limited bank of caring instincts? He had always imagined those instincts had been beaten out of him in his youth, but she had made him look at her as more than a business adversary.

He couldn't afford to go soft. With a gust of exasperation, Tino released his seat belt before the jet touched down. He was impatient to breathe the fresh clean air of Stellamaris. When Lisa Bond came back into his life he would be ready for her. And she would come back, they all did. She wanted the same thing everyone else did—his money. It always came down to that in the end.

* * *

'What do you mean, he didn't turn up?' Lisa demanded, rolling over onto her stomach in bed so that she could rest her chin on her hand.

'Just that,' Mike, her PA, assured her. 'Everyone else was here, of course—just you two were missing.'

'Don't bracket me with that man. I have no idea where Constantine Zagorakis is, but, I can assure you, he's not here with me. Make certain everyone else knows that too, will you, Mike?'

'So, what's up? You never take time off.'

That was true. Like her father, only a stretcher carting her off to hospital could get in the way of her work. Mike knew that as well as she did. But her one-to-one with Tino had left Lisa more shaken than she had expected.

'Lisa, what's happened?'

She refocused. 'Don't worry, Mike. I have a sore throat, that's all.'

'A sore throat?' He sounded unconvinced. 'I'm sorry.'

Lisa had known Mike since they were at school together. She hated lying to him. He had already brought her up to speed with what she'd missed at the meeting, and yet she felt he was holding something back. 'So, what's the gossip on the street?'

'It's more than gossip. But there's good news as well as bad.'

'Just give me the bad.' She steeled herself.

'I got a call.'

All the humour had just leached from Mike's voice, Lisa realised. 'Go on,' she pressed grimly.

'From my pal at Clifton.'

'Clifton Steel?' Mike's silence confirmed it. 'And?'

'Zagorakis Inc have asked for an initial meeting with Clifton. Apparently they're considering—'

'Their small engineering plant?' Lisa's stomach clenched with dread as she cut across him.

'No, Lisa, the whole of Clifton—'

She went cold. 'But they can't—' This time Zagorakis had really caught her out. How could anyone move that fast? 'But what about our deal with Zagorakis Inc?'

'Word is Zagorakis has gone cold on our small works. It's all or nothing for him. I heard in the last hour that he's asked his people to start courting Clifton…and, Lisa…'

'Yes?' Lisa tensed, wondering what else there could be.

'He's after us too—'

'No,' Lisa exploded, sitting bolt upright. It was everything she had been dreading. 'Bond Steel isn't for sale, Mike. I only need to sell the small works. The cash injection that will bring is all we need to set us back on our feet.'

'It may be too late.'

'We're not going to give up, and throw Bond Steel to the lions.'

'To one lion in particular, you mean?'

'Get Zagorakis on the phone.'

'Who do you want to speak to?'

'Tino, of course.'

'He doesn't speak to anyone directly.'

'He'll speak to me.'

'What if he won't?'

'Do anything you have to do to get his private number, Mike,' Lisa pressed grimly.

'It won't help you.'

'What do you mean it won't help me?'

'He took off at dawn to fly to his private island in Greece. There's no way anyone can contact him there— even his staff aren't allowed to do that. They have to wait for Zagorakis to ring them.'

'But that's ridiculous.'

'Maybe. But that's the way it is.'

'Are you sure about this?'

'Totally. I've got a friend at Clifton.'

Lisa's mind raced. 'The financial director? That tall, good-looking blond guy?'

'We're seeing each other, Lisa.'

'I guessed.' A faint smile broke through Lisa's tension. 'I hope you'll both be very happy.' That explained how Mike had learned everything so fast, and also confirmed that everything he had told her was one-hundred-per-cent accurate. And without the cash from the sale of the small works to Zagorakis Inc, she was in serious trouble.

'Shall I give you the good news now?'

'Good news? I can't believe you can have anything good to tell me after that.'

'You are fit to fly.'

'Anything but a joke.'

'This is no joke. The Bond Steel company jet has just been signed off. It's ready to go when you are.'

'Mike, that's not good news—or had you forgotten the purpose behind selling the engineering works? We can't stand more expense right now. If things get any worse than they are the jet will be the first thing that has to go.'

'Sell it by all means—but not yet, Lisa,' Mike insisted. 'Zagorakis's island is quite small. The landing strip can't take commercial airliners.'

Lisa's tense face softened abruptly. 'Mike, you're an angel! I need one clear day to prepare,' she added, thinking aloud. 'So, make sure the jet is fully fuelled and ready to fly on Sunday. Have the pilot file a flight plan for Stellamaris—'

'So, you're chasing Zagorakis?'

Mike was smart—that was why she had hired him in the first place. But after what he had told her, she was going to Stellamaris, not just to save the deal, but to nail Zagorakis to the mast. 'No, Mike,' she assured him, 'I'm chasing business.'

*   *   *

Stellamaris was beautiful. So beautiful, it made Lisa want to cry. And she never cried. Well, not since she was a child. Never in her adult life had she ever shed a tear—except on Friday morning after Mike's phone call. But those had been very different tears—Mike would have said she was having a tantrum and he would have been right. Everything within reach had been thrown at the wall. And then she had wasted another hour clearing up the mess. She never lost control. She never would again after that. What a time-wasting loss of energy that had been. *Sore throat?* Sore head was closer to the truth. Did Tino Zagorakis really think he could direct events that, not only affected her own life, but the lives of people she cared about, from his private island?

'We're nearly there, Thespinis Bond. When I turn the next corner, you will be able to see the villa.'

Then I'll close my eyes, Lisa thought, remembering to thank the kindly taxi driver. How was she going to look at Tino's ugly villa after feasting her eyes on a clear aquamarine ocean, ochre-tinted cliffs, and pale sugar sand? The fields they had passed had all been bathed in a mellow golden light, and there was a huge orange ball of a sun hanging low out to sea. She was sure Tino would live in some vast, overblown carbuncle, possibly with gold-plated walls, and certainly with a flagpole to show when he was in residence. Hideously opulent, and grotesquely vulgar, it was sure to be an eyesore after everything else she had seen on Stellamaris… Or not. 'Is this it?' she said with surprise, leaning forward in her seat.

'*Ne*, Thespinis Bond,' the taxi driver confirmed, 'this is Villa Aphrodite. Very beautiful, isn't she?'

'Yes, she is,' Lisa agreed without blinking. 'Very beautiful indeed.' Tino's villa was cloaked in white marble that shimmered peach and umber where the muted light washed over it, and even the shadows came in a tasteful shade of magenta. She imagined the walls might turn to a delicate shade of pink in the first rays of dawn… The building was large, but even without stepping inside Lisa guessed there would be rooms for formal entertaining as well as cosier rooms in which you could live in comfort all year round. The entrance would be grand and imposing, but beyond that there would be secret hideaways—a home within a palace, rather than a showpiece, as she had been dreading…*Tino's home*…

'I expect Constantine is down on the beach.'

The elderly taxi driver cut into her thoughts. The warmth and familiarity with which he spoke the name immediately rang alarm bells in Lisa's mind, reminding her that Zagorakis was a complex animal—and one she must be constantly wary of.

'Unfortunately you can't see the beach from up here.'

Half turning to her, the taxi driver reclaimed Lisa's attention, angling his shoulders while watching the road. 'Tino only arrived on Friday, so I expect he will be washing all the stresses of the city out of his mind.'

Stresses of the city? She'd give him stresses, Lisa mused grimly as her thoughts turned to her mission. If Constantine Zagorakis thought he could ditch their deal by remote control while he was enjoying a swim in the sea, he was sadly mistaken.

'It's the first thing he does when he comes home to Stellamaris,' the taxi driver continued, unaware of the tensions building in the seat behind him. 'Tino loves the ocean, like all Greeks…'

Lisa let his friendly chatter roll over her. It didn't seem possible the taxi driver was talking about the same man. Even the thought of that brute having something called a home seemed unlikely. Surely Tino Zagorakis lived out of suitcases, always restless, always searching out the next deal?

She sat back as the taxi pulled through some tall

wrought-iron gates, preparing herself with some deep steadying breaths. They were travelling slowly down a long, neatly groomed avenue lined with trees. Leading up to the grand villa, it dissected a garden bursting with flowers. In such a hot climate the irrigation alone would be a mammoth task.

'It is almost May Day—a significant day on Stellamaris. The gardens are at their best.'

Lisa met the taxi driver's gaze in the driver's mirror.

'Soon everyone will be gathering flowers to decorate their houses,' he went on. 'You are visiting Stellamaris at the most romantic time of year.'

Lisa's lips firmed. 'The villa seems to be built on top of a cliff,' she said, to distract him from a topic she had no interest in pursuing. 'How do you get down to the beach?'

'There are steps cut into the cliff face,' he explained, 'but Tino has had a funicular fitted to make it easier for his friend.'

'His friend?'

'His elderly friend.'

Constantine Zagorakis had more than one friend? That seemed unlikely.

'And here we are,' the taxi driver declared, halting at the foot of some impressive marble steps. Yanking on the handbrake, he switched off the engine.

In spite of everything she had planned—keeping a cool head, securing the deal at any price, etc—Lisa's heart was thundering. What was she doing here? What was she really doing here? She should have asked for Tino's e-mail address, and communicated with him safely on that level—impersonally.

Smoothing down her suit jacket, she paid the driver. It didn't help that she felt so hot and sticky. The tailored trouser suit she was wearing was lightweight, but not lightweight enough. She realised the fingers of one hand were biting like claws into the handle of her briefcase as she waved goodbye with the other.

She tried Mike on the mobile to let him know she had arrived safely, but there was no signal. She really was alone. Turning to stare at the impressive iron-studded door marking the entrance to Tino's home, she sucked in one more breath, and then ran up the steps.

CHAPTER THREE

LISA realized she was staring foolishly. She had been prepared for most things, but not this. Words refused to form in response to the young woman's greeting. She could only fight the rigor in her lips, and bob her head.

The girl couldn't have been much more than twenty-five, and was tall and very beautiful, with a cloud of inky-black hair that fell well below her naked shoulders. She was tanned—evenly, beautifully, naturally tanned—and she smelled fresh, like sea spray, as if she had just returned from the beach. She was wearing something floaty and diaphanous in muted shades of new-shoot green and lemon, over what might have been a bikini—it didn't feel right to look too closely—and her tiny feet were bare with bright red toenails. And Tino was standing right behind her.

Lisa sensed, rather than saw him. She didn't trust herself to look. Her head was still reeling. She wasn't taking anything in too clearly… She shouldn't care. Of course she shouldn't care… She ordered herself angrily to get her head up—to look him in the eye. When she did, she found that he was almost a head taller than his beautiful companion, and that his right hand was resting lightly on the young woman's waist.

The urge to make some angry, guttural sound at the sight of that hand—the same hand that had held her so firmly, the hand that was now resting on another woman—threatened to overwhelm her. Just when she needed all her wits about her, she was transfixed by that hand, and by Tino's proprietary air towards a young woman he was showing no inclination to introduce her to.

She took matters into her own hands 'Hi, my name's Lisa Bond. I've come to see Tino on business—'

'Arianna knows why you're here, Lisa.'

Like the woman he called Arianna, Tino was dressed casually, as if they had come up from the beach together. Lisa found herself gripped by jealousy: irrational, unwelcome, inescapable jealousy. All she could think of was the touch of his hands on her body and that for a split second before she had pushed him away she had almost lost control.

Both Arianna and Tino were so relaxed, their outfits so normal for any couple living by the sea. Tino's bronzed feet were naked, and dusted with sand, his casual shirt barely held in place by a couple of buttons. He must have dressed in a hurry... He could hold one woman so passionately in his arms it was branded on her mind, and then coolly return home to another?

Lisa calmed herself. This was business—no need to make it personal. The only way to get money into the bank fast enough to save Bond Steel was to get that money from a cash-rich company like Zagorakis Inc. Zagorakis had to buy her small engineering works. Her personal feelings were irrelevant. She wasn't going anywhere until the deal was sewn up.

She viewed the couple again, trying to work out what she was up against. There was the wrong dynamic between them for Arianna to be Tino's sister... And then she noticed Tino's bleached linen trousers were rolled up almost to his knees. The sight of his naked legs stirred some very primitive emotions inside her, not least of which was the knowledge that Arianna must know how it would feel to have those powerful legs wrapped around her—

Andreas had warned him she was coming. But this was better than he had expected. Seeing Lisa hovering uncer-

tainly on his doorstep gave him a real rush. It was time she
learned she couldn't win every battle in the boardroom, or
the bedroom.

She was thrown by the fact that he wasn't alone, and
that his companion was a beautiful young woman. Good.
That was her first lesson. She was so used to ruling the
roost at Bond Steel, she took too much for granted. No one
outside his inner circle could say if he had brothers or sis-
ters, or any family at all. Curiosity about Arianna had to
be eating her up inside; he planned to keep it that way as
long as possible.

Tino's face told Lisa very little. What was he thinking?
Chasing after him had put her on the back foot, but the
deal was too crucial to the survival of Bond Steel for her
to entrust it to a third party. Yes, of course it would have
been better for her to deal with him by mail, at a distance—
but that just wasn't her way. She never shirked a confrontation. It just hadn't occurred to her that Tino's life might
be very different from her own. She should have known
that a man like Constantine Zagorakis would never want
for female company.

She managed a smile—that encompassed both the people
facing her. 'It's very good of you to see me like this.'
Arianna smiled back, but Lisa found herself confronting a
brick wall in Tino's eyes.

Damn! Damn! Damn! She was only being nice for
Arianna's sake. This picture of domestic bliss had really
thrown her. She should have known that 'nice' didn't suit
her. She had given Tino the advantage over her right
away…

She had pictured a butler showing her into a room where
there would have been a chance to look around and draw
conclusions about the very private Constantine Zagorakis.
Those conclusions would have helped her to hone her busi-

ness strategy. There would have been time to sip a refreshing drink while she lowered the temperature in her heart to freezing just to remind herself that the idea of courting Clifton Steel must have been in his mind all the time he'd been holding her, leading her on to the point where he'd almost kissed her.

A few steadying breaths and she could feel her determination flowing back. She was over her jealousy, and ready to concentrate on rescuing the deal. On bettering him, on triumphing over the bastard!

'You're always welcome, Lisa.'

Always welcome? Was he mocking her now?

'Andreas told us to expect you.'

'It won't take long.' Lisa glanced apologetically at Arianna. She refused to see the young woman as a rival, if only because that would have meant Tino had some sort of hold over her. 'I'm staying at the Zagorakis guest house,' she added in case he should think she was looking for board and lodgings. She had the satisfaction of seeing his gaze sharpen.

'Tino, please—' Arianna touched his arm '—Lisa looks so pale. She must be tired. She's had a long journey.'

Pale and tired? Pale because she was strung out like a wire, perhaps…

'Arianna's right. Won't you come in, Lisa?'

Was the humour in his voice only apparent to her? Lisa wondered as she went past them both into the house. She would have to handle this carefully. It might be just a game to him, but she had no intention of losing Bond Steel to Tino Zagorakis.

The hallway was magnificent. It couldn't have been a more perfect setting for two such beautiful people. A plant-filled atrium stretched towards a stained glass cupola set into the roof, and where the dying rays of the sun penetrated it caused jewels of light to tremble on the floor beneath her feet.

Something made her turn and she noticed Arianna slipping away. Doubtless all Tino's women would be equally well trained. They would have to become used to coming second to his business interests.

Beneath the curve of an impressive staircase she spotted a grand piano—it surprised her if only because it wasn't there for show. The lid was raised, and there was a selection of music littering the stand, as well as the floor around the piano stool.. Bartók, Bach, Liszt and Brahms, all challenging, cerebral pieces, with a strong dose of romance in the mix...

'Are you interested in music, Lisa?'

She could feel Tino's stare burning into her back. 'Yes, I am, as it happens.'

'Does it surprise you to find music here?'

'Surprise me? No.' No one knew anything about Constantine Zagorakis, or the way he lived, but she was intrigued by the music, and felt sure it must belong to someone else. Zagorakis didn't possess the heart for music. 'Does your friend play the piano?'

'Are you talking about Arianna?'

Lisa shrugged. She didn't want him mistaking her interest for good old-fashioned female jealousy. 'Yes, I wondered if the music belonged to Arianna.'

'Arianna plays the piano occasionally—but more to learn her parts than anything else. She's an opera singer by profession.'

'I see.' Why didn't that surprise her? Was it because there was something about the dark-eyed beauty that reminded her of her idol, the late diva suprema, Maria Callas? There was the same passion and the same intensity in Arianna's expression. Was there the same heartbreak courtesy of a Greek billionaire in store for her too?

'Does Arianna do lot of travelling?' Do you travel with her? Or do you play away when she's working?

Tino made a noncommittal sound, and she wasn't about to repeat the question. And now he was holding open a door she saw led into his study. She had been so busy with her own thoughts, she hadn't realised they had arrived at their destination.

His study was cool, though surprisingly cosy. The cushions were designed to sink into, and the lighting was subtle. Two sofas were arranged either side of a large stone fireplace, but the fire wasn't lit as the weather was too warm. The windows were open and she could hear the insistent chirrup of cicadas through the slim, slatted blinds.

'Make yourself comfortable, Lisa.'

'Thank you.' She hadn't realised how weary she was, but much depended on this visit and she couldn't afford to lose concentration. She had to secure the deal. She had to save Bond Steel, whatever the personal cost. She couldn't let Tino take the company as easily as he had stolen her self-control.

He invited her to sit down.

'I'll go and get some drinks. White wine all right?'

Wine? To soften her up? She still rued the champagne she had shared with him on Thursday night. 'Just water for me, please.'

As Tino left the room Lisa knew, however well prepared she was, there were certain things she couldn't know. How far down the road was his deal with Clifton? Could she still convince Zagorakis that her small engineering works was the best option for him, and that he didn't need the aggravation of two larger companies like Bond and Clifton?

Doubt washed over her to the point where she wondered if her fighting juices were all used up—and then the door swung open and he walked in. 'Does Arianna know who you were with on Thursday night?'

'I doubt she'd be interested.'

As Tino stared at her Lisa wondered what was she doing making any of this personal—the one thing she had vowed not to do. But, however cold-bloodedly she approached the situation, a very female part of her wanted answers. Watching him open a bottle of Chablis, she wished things could have been simpler between them. If they had been she would have asked him who the hell Arianna was, and get it over with.

There was a jug of iced water on the tray as well as a bowl of fresh fruit, and there was also a plate of what looked suspiciously like home-made cookies. Lisa hadn't eaten a thing since breakfast, and now she realised how hungry she was. But how could she eat cookies when foremost in her mind was an image of Arianna playing earth mother for Tino in the kitchen?

Tino made the torture worse, biting into one of them and then uttering a deep-throated sound of pleasure. The last time she had heard him make a sound like that was when he'd almost kissed her—

'Won't you have one?' He held out the plate.

Apart from wanting to crack it over his head, no way was she going to touch it. Tino was so cool, so together, she wanted the cookies to glue his teeth together, or pull them out, or, better still, stick in his throat and choke him.

'Do try one.' He kept on watching her. 'I can assure you, they're delicious.'

'Thank you, no.' She waved them away with an impatient gesture. 'Care to tell me why you're cosying up to Clifton?'

'Ever the businesswoman, Lisa?' He shook his head as he put the plate down on the table. 'You're such fun to be with.'

'I can be.'

'Really? And when would that be?'

The verbal slap came out of nowhere. It took a moment to recover. It seemed Tino shared none of her scruples about avoiding personal issues.

'You have a proposition for me,' he prompted.

'If you're interested?'

'I'm always prepared to listen to a business proposal.'

'I hear you've gone cold on our deal and transferred your interest to Clifton Steel?'

'I'm always looking for possibilities.'

'Have you ruled out my small engineering works?'

He kept her waiting so long Lisa wondered if he'd heard the question.

'I haven't ruled anything out yet,' he said at last.

'I do have other people waiting.'

'Really? Your company's in big trouble Lisa—your share price is falling through the floor.'

'And I'll recover the situation.'

'In time?'

'Yes, if we can reach an agreement.'

'And if you go to one of these *other* companies—can they come up with the cash in time to save Bond Steel?'

'Probably not—' She didn't have the luxury of time to play cat and mouse with him. Reaching into her own brief-case, Lisa welcomed the chance to break eye contact. Tino's stare was so penetrating he made her feel naked— and she needed a clear head to do business with him. 'If you will just take a look at the figures I've been working on…'

'You've been busy—' He lifted the heavy sheaf of documents out of her hands.

Lisa watched tensely as he flicked through them, pausing occasionally to read one or other of the passages more intently. Finally laying them down on the table between them, he sat back again and folded his arms behind his head.

'You need me, Lisa.'

Her business head urged caution. There had been no other serious offers. Zagorakis Inc was cash rich. Tino could write a cheque right now if it came to it. He was the best, her only chance to save Bond Steel. 'What do you think now you've seen the numbers?'

'I'd need to study these a little longer before I give you my final answer, but—'

'OK, I'm listening.'

'Not so fast.' He straightened up, his expression hardening. 'It's me who's listening, Lisa. It's up to you to convince me that your proposal has merit.'

All the people relying on her to secure the deal flashed in front of Lisa's eyes. 'I'll give you a brief run-down of the facts—'

'No. You're not getting the point. You've come here—disturbing me on my island…at my home. This is going to be on my terms, not yours. I'll be generous. I'll give you a working week to convince me that your scheme has merit. If you're successful I'll buy your small engineering works, and bail you out. If you fail the deal is off and everything's in play: Clifton, as well as Bond Steel—'

'No. Bond Steel's not for sale.'

'If you don't deal with me—we both know it will go under.'

'So, that's it,' Lisa accused tensely. 'You're just playing with me. I don't believe you're even going to look at those figures. You'll keep me here where I'm safely out of the picture, and sit it out until Bond Steel goes down.'

'And I can pick it up for practically nothing?' He shrugged in agreement. 'You know that's good business, Lisa—and don't forget I've given you an opportunity to change my mind.'

'Five days? Five days to secure the future of my employees? You can't toy with people like that. And don't try telling me that jobs will be secure under your ownership. If you get your hands on Bond Steel, you'll strip the assets and tip people out of work without a second thought—' She shook her head. 'I was wrong about you—I thought you had some small spark of humanity, but you don't have any feelings at all, do you?'

'None.' It was true. There was very little he could get fired up about. Lisa Bond came close—but she was a page in his life he would turn very soon. He cared about his assets because they funded the project closest to his heart, and he cared about two very special and unique women. Apart from that, feelings were a luxury reserved for other people.

'I'm not staying here to listen any more to this.'

He glanced at her as she got to her feet. 'Then lose your business, Lisa.'

What alternative did she have? However much it hurt, she had to swallow her pride. She made some rapid calculations. 'I'll need internet access, and a phone that works.'

'You're in no position to dictate terms to me.'

'I have to keep in contact with my people. We work as a team.'

'Then it will be interesting for your team to see how well their leader operates without them. It's up to you, Lisa. Go home now, and the deal is off. Send the jet back without you, and there might still be a chance. We'll never know unless you stay.'

'But if you agree to purchase the company our lawyers will need to know—contracts will have to be drawn up.'

'True. So you will phone your PA now and tell him to wait to hear from Andreas, my PA.' Lifting a phone from its square black nest, Tino pushed it across the desk to her. 'Satellite,' he explained in answer to Lisa's questioning look. 'You won't get a signal for your mobile here.'

'So you're going to be the only one who can contact the outside world?'

'That's how it works. If I judge matters are coming to a head, it will be up to me to call the meeting. Now, are you going to make that call, or not?'

Right now it seemed unlikely that such a meeting would ever be called, and, if it was called, she had won. 'All right, I agree.'

He already knew the small works was profitable, but it pleased him to see how far he could push. She had set herself against him. She had made it a battle of wills. She had no idea what she had unleashed. It was his way, or no way. Always.

It was constantly at the back of his mind that if he gave the smallest concession he risked pulling a stitch that might cause his whole life to unravel. He had climbed out of the gutter; he had no intention of slipping back there.

She had to go through with it. It was that or lose the deal.

He watched her as she made the call, reassured her PA and gave him the necessary information. She handled it well. In a tight spot she was cool.

'Thank you for the call,' she said, pushing the phone back across the desk towards him.

'Where do you think you're going?'

'I'm staying at your guest house in the village.'

'There's no need to do that.'

'What do you mean?'

'You'll be staying here.'

'Here? With you at the villa?'

'There's no need to sound quite so unimpressed.'

'But Arianna—'

'Will do as I say.'

Lisa tensed with anger, and it was mostly on Arianna's

behalf. She felt no envy for the young woman now, only pity.

'That's my final offer, Lisa. Take it, or get back on your
jet and get out of here.'

That wasn't an option for her, Lisa realized; too many
people were depending on her to get this right. She couldn't
just walk away. 'All right, I'll stay. But on the understanding that we only meet for business—'

'I told you before you're in no position to make terms,
Lisa. This is my island, and I decide when and where we
hold our meetings—'

'So, I don't have any say at all?'

She didn't like that. Tough. Being nice to him for five
whole days was the most refined torture he could have de-
vised for her. 'Don't let me keep you, Lisa—' He gestured
towards the door. 'You can use the internal phones in your
suite to order any food you would like—and have it delivered to your room.'

Lisa knew her cheeks were glowing bright red with humiliation. She might have said she didn't want to socialise
with him, but she had never thought he would confine her
to her room. For a moment she wondered why he hadn't
agreed to her staying at the guest house. That way he would
have kept her out of Arianna's way... But, of course, at
Villa Aphrodite she was out of everyone's reach...
completely isolated, completely alone. 'I have to go back
to the village to collect my things. So why don't I just stay
at the guest house, as I planned?'

'That is not part of our agreement—'

'But you said five days—a working week, Tino. Today
is Sunday, so surely our negotiations won't begin until tomorrow morning?'

'It is dangerous to make presumptions in business, Lisa.
You should know that—'

Lisa's mouth hardened into an angry line as she stared

at him. So that was the way it was to be. 'I imagined you would extend the usual business courtesies.'

'And so I will from tomorrow. In the meantime, you will stay here.'

'As your prisoner?'

'Don't be ridiculous! I'm not holding you against your will. You know as well as I do that until a deal is struck we must abide by all the terms of the agreement, and not just the ones that suit us most. You have five days as my guest to convince me that I should do this deal. Hardly an ordeal, I would have thought.'

There was a gentle tap on the door, and Lisa welcomed the distraction as the study door opened, and an elderly servant walked in.

'Goodnight, Lisa.'

Her mouth fell open as Tino walked out of the room.

'May I show you to your suite, Thespinis Bond?'

Lisa softened her expression in case she scared the elderly man half to death. 'Thank you, that's very kind of you.'

'It is my pleasure, Thespinis Bond.'

His voice was gentle, and he stood back politely at the door to let her pass. How could such a man bear to work for Tino Zagorakis? Lisa wondered as she followed his elderly retainer across the hall.

The suite of rooms where she was to stay was fabulous. Taking the colours of the Greek flag as inspiration, the furnishings were mostly snowy white with the occasional highlight of cerulean. But before she had chance to properly appreciate the opulence of her surroundings, Lisa's gaze was captured by the sight of her overnight case standing at the end of the bed. Only the presence of Tino's gentle servant prevented her from turning on her heel and going to rip the head off his employer. It was obvious that whether she had agreed to stay or not, Tino had already decided that she would, and had taken it upon himself to retrieve her luggage from the guest house.

'Kirie Zagorakis thought you might prefer to eat out here alone.'

Lisa looked across the room to where the old man was smiling at her. Floor-to-ceiling white muslin curtains billowed gently in the early evening breeze, drawing her attention to the balcony beyond. It was bathed in soft light from some out-of-view lanterns, and she could see that a comfortable chair with a deeply padded cushion awaited her, as well as a dining table, ostentatiously laid out for one.

I bet he did, she thought grimly. Tino had decided she was to be cut off from the rest of the household. She smiled at her elderly companion. He was hardly to blame for his employer's machiavellian scheme. 'Thank you. That's exactly what I'd like.'

Not only had Tino made the unilateral decision that she would stay at Villa Aphrodite, he had delivered instructions to the kitchen for her supper, Lisa discovered when the elderly man showed her the buffet trolley. He must have done that when he'd left the study briefly to get them both a drink, she realised tensely.

'You have such a beautiful view from here, Thespinis Bond.'

The elderly man was pointing out across the cliff tops to where the ocean had turned coppery pink in the last rays of the sun.

'I doubt I've ever seen anything more beautiful,' Lisa said honestly. She was rewarded by the old man's smile…but then she noticed another, larger table had been laid out immediately below and a little in front of her own balcony. The edges of a white lace tablecloth were fluttering gently in the early evening breeze, and crystal and silverware were glittering in the light of flickering candles.

And now she heard the sounds of muted conversation, as well as laughter—high, tinkling laughter, as well as a lower, appreciative sound.

'Would you like to sit down now, Thespinis Bond? Shall I light the candle for you?'

Lisa turned abruptly, realising her elderly companion was still waiting for her to say something. Having struck a match, he was waiting for her permission to light a slim ivory candle. 'No, no,' she said, hurrying over to him. 'Thank you, but I think I'll wait a little. You've been very kind,' she added, seeing his crestfallen face.

Inside she was a morass of anger and humiliation, but there was no way she was going to vent her feelings on an innocent old man. It made no sense that she cared about Tino's dining arrangements, but she did—it hurt a lot. Not only had Tino chosen to dine without her, he was dining with someone else…almost certainly Arianna.

'Are you sure that is all you require from me this evening, Thespinis Bond?'

'I'm quite sure. Thank you.' Lisa smiled again, and waited until the elderly man had closed the door behind him. She would not sit obediently on her solitary perch and take the humiliation Tino had planned for her. She would feel it. Oh, yes, just as he had known, she would feel it, but she would do so in private…

Carefully loading all the supper dishes onto the trolley, Lisa rolled it towards her room. Wheeling it inside, she firmly closed the double doors behind her.

CHAPTER FOUR

LISA slept more soundly than she had expected. It had to be the sea air, she reasoned, waking slowly. Dawn was just peeping through the white muslin drapes as she stretched like a cat in the sun. At first she was reluctant to leave the warm linen sheets, but then she remembered everything that had happened the previous night.

Slipping out of bed, she padded barefoot across the cool tiled floor and opened the double doors onto the balcony. Today was Monday, the first day of her five-day trial, and she had no intention of wasting a single minute—but she could make time for this. She had guessed the view would be spectacular in daylight, but she had never imagined it could be quite so lovely.

Shading her eyes against the low-slanting sunlight, she realised the villa sat on a promontory with the ocean to three sides. The water far below the cliffs was graded in colour from a white lace frill at the shoreline to palest blue at the midline, and then on to deepest Prussian blue where the ocean floor dropped away.

The gardens surrounding the villa were equally stunning. They combined formal and informal planting with great success, and were ablaze with colour. Beyond the stone patio she could see an infinity pool. She had hoped for a pool, and was longing for a swim, but there was already someone swimming there...

Meeting up with Tino when they were both half naked was a bad idea—but hadn't the taxi driver mentioned steps leading to the beach, and even a funicular running down

56

the face of the cliff? There had to be a way she could get to the sea without walking past the pool...

Unzipping her overnight case, Lisa plucked out the bikini she had packed in the hope of snatching a few moments in the Greek sunshine. Fortunately, she had remembered to bring her flip-flops too, as well as a wrap.

The stone steps were steep and worn away in some places, and Lisa was glad of the wooden handrail fixed to the rock. When she reached the halfway point she paused to look around and catch her breath. She gazed longingly at the tracks marking the path the funicular would take. If she could have taken that route she would have been down on the shore by now, but the cabin had been too close to the swimming pool for her to risk it, and the mechanism would have alerted Tino immediately had she been foolish enough to try.

The beach formed a tempting silvery crescent, and the sea had turned to turquoise, and seemed completely flat. Fingers of cloud stretched across the brightening horizon, and the air was sweetly scented. Best of all, there was no sign of Tino, so she could relax and the new day was hers for the taking...

Jumping down onto the beach, Lisa kicked off her flip-flops and dug her toes into the damp sand. It felt wonderful against her warm skin. Tugging off her wrap, she tossed it away and ran eagerly towards the sea.

A much older woman followed Lisa's plunge into the sea with interest. The moment Lisa turned for shore she dipped down to collect the discarded wrap, and then walked down the sand to meet her.

Shaking her long chestnut hair out behind her like a banner, Lisa turned her face to the sun as she ploughed happily through the shallows. She never had time for a holiday, or even for a good swim. Feeling the sunshine on her face, and the tingle of the cool Aegean on her skin, was almost worth braving Tino's lair for—

'Yia Sou.'

Having thought she was alone, Lisa nearly jumped out of her skin at the friendly greeting. She recovered quickly, smiling her thanks as the elderly Greek woman handed over her wrap. 'Kalimera.'

'It is going to be a beautiful day,' the older woman observed, gazing up into the sky.

For you, perhaps, Lisa thought, remembering her meeting later that morning with Tino. 'Yes, it is,' she agreed politely.

'My name is Stella. I live over there in that small cottage...' The woman pointed to a quaint whitewashed building with bright blue shutters and front door, set back a little from the beach. 'I watched you swimming. You are good.'

'Thank you.'

'Won't you join me for breakfast?' Stella gazed down at the basket of freshly baked bread swinging from her arm.

Lisa's stomach rumbled on cue, and they both laughed.

'That's very kind of you.' Lisa was thankful to have found someone so friendly. Anything was preferable to eating breakfast alone on her balcony, where she knew she would only brood on the outcome of her meeting with Tino.

'We will both join you, Ya-ya.'

'Tino!' Lisa stood back as the two embraced.

Stella was clearly overjoyed to see him, but Lisa resented the fact that her own face was burning. Why was it Tino always made her feel as if she had done something wrong? It was his behaviour that was outrageous. He was wearing a sun-bleached blue vest and frayed cut-off shorts, and might as well have been naked for all the toned, bronzed flesh on show. His feet were bare, and there was a dusting of sand on his limbs as if he had found time for a swim in the sea as well as his morning workout in the pool...while she was wearing a scanty bikini beneath a filmy wrap—not her battle clothes of choice.

'Good morning, Lisa. I trust you slept well?'

'I did, thank you.' Lisa glanced at Stella, hoping she hadn't picked up the undercurrents between them.

'I have plenty of food for all of us. Come,' Stella insisted, beckoning them towards her cottage.

There was a tug of amusement at one corner of Tino's mouth, Lisa noticed as she hurried after Stella, and however she tried to mistime her stride he managed to keep in step with her. 'I suppose you just happened by?' Her tone was frosty.

'Actually, I came to see Stella.'

Lisa's curiosity flared. 'Do you know her well?'

'We've known each other for a number of years.'

'I see.'

'I doubt it.'

The murmured comment stirred her interest even more. Who was Stella? And what was her connection with the most obnoxious man on the planet?

Having reached her front door, Stella opened it and beckoned them inside.

The interior was cool and shady with slivers of sunlight slanting in through the shutters. The air smelled faintly of herbs, and, gazing around, Lisa noticed that every window ledge was lined with terracotta pots sprouting densely packed greenery. 'What a lovely home you have.'

Stella smiled, pointing to the easy chairs. 'Please, both of you sit down.'

'Are you sure I can't help you with anything?' Lisa said, ignoring this suggestion as she edged towards the kitchen door.

'No, no.' Stella was quite certain on this point. 'You two relax, and let me prepare the food. I won't take long.'

You two? Again she was bracketed with the last man on

earth she would have chosen to be paired with. Lisa would have thought the distance that existed between them would have been glaringly obvious to everyone, especially to a woman who seemed as bright and observant as Stella. Wandering across the room, she casually picked out a window seat as far away from Tino as possible. Sitting down, she stared out through the barely open shutter.

'Is that better for you?'

Lisa breathed in convulsively as Tino leaned across to open the shutters a little more for her. She could feel his warmth in every fibre of her being. And then he remained at her side so that the acute, and very troubling, awareness of him refused to fade.

'You're an early riser, Lisa.'

'I always wake at dawn on a working day.' Her voice was clipped, inviting no further conversation between them. And then, to Lisa's relief, Stella bustled back into the room carrying a loaded breakfast tray.

'Why didn't you call me to bring this in for you?' Tino demanded, crossing the room in a couple of strides to take the tray from her.

'Because you were keeping our visitor company.' Stella stared hard at him before releasing the tray, and then she turned to Lisa. 'Forgive me, Lisa, I am sure you do not want to hear us bickering.'

'You know my name?' Lisa frowned, realising she had forgotten to introduce herself. She glanced at Tino, but he was suddenly too busy unloading the breakfast tray to notice. 'I'm sorry, Stella, I should have said.' Lisa made up for her earlier lapse with a smile, 'I'm Lisa Bond. I'm here to do business with Tino.'

'Business with Tino?' Pulling a face, Stella made a fanning motion with her hand that required no translation.

'I'm sure I can handle him.' Lisa stared at him so that he could be in no doubt that she would.

'So, what are your plans today?' Stella looked between them as she piled their plates high with fresh bread and honey.

'We have a meeting.'

'I plan to take Lisa out on the boat.'

They both spoke at once, and Lisa bridled instantly. She had no intention of wasting the first of her five precious negotiating days on Tino's floating gin palace.

'And I will bring back some fresh fish for your supper,' he added to Stella.

'I shall look forward to it.' Stella clapped her hands with pleasure.

Lisa looked from one to the other. Tino was not going to ignore her. And he was not going to draw this lovely, innocent woman into some devious plan he had concocted. They had more important things to do than catch fish today. She watched angrily as he tucked into his breakfast with relish. Breaking off a crispy crust from one of the chunks of bread, he dipped it in some honey.

'No,' she said flatly.

'No?' Tino paused, bread in hand, to stare at her.

'I'm not coming with you—I have better things to do than idle my time away. I thought we both did.'

'Lisa?' Putting a hand to his chest, Tino affected an innocent expression.

'Don't you like boats?' Stella looked concerned.

'It isn't that.' Lisa hesitated. What could she say without causing an atmosphere? 'I'm just not used to doing business—'

'The Greek way?' Stella suggested helpfully.

A glance at Tino was enough to convince Lisa that he couldn't have been more pleased with the way things were turning out if he had scripted the exchange himself.

'All Greek men are fishermen at heart, Lisa,' Stella explained kindly, unaware of the tension stretching between

her visitors. 'It's better if you just go along with their way
of doing business.'

'I'm sure you're right, Stella,' Lisa said politely, not
wanting to cause offence.

'What was that? What did you say?' Tino could hardly
keep the smile off his face.

'If you'd been listening, you'd know,' Lisa said tartly,
and then froze. Stella's face was a picture, and no wonder.
She could hardly have expected her breakfast guests to start
yelling at each other.

For a moment there was an uncomfortable silence, which
Tino did nothing to break. Then, slowly turning back to his
breakfast, he dipped another piece of bread into the honey.

Lisa felt she had to say something by way of explanation
for her behaviour. 'I'm so sorry, Stella. I don't know what
came over me.'

'Think nothing of it.' Stella dismissed the moment with
a smile. 'Tempers flare high when passions are roused.'

Passions! Passions? Lisa glared at Tino. Whatever Stella
imagined, she was wrong—absolutely wrong.

'Tino has always aroused strong passions in people,'
Stella added.

She couldn't let this go on, Lisa realised, holding up her
hands in front of her. 'There's absolutely no chance of Tino
upsetting my equilibrium, Stella. It's just that—'

'It's just what, Lisa?' Tino demanded softly, unfolding
from his chair.

As Lisa's mouth opened to shoot back a reply he fed a
piece of honey-soaked crust between her lips. 'Suck on
this,' he suggested in an undertone. 'You could do with
sweetening up.'

Having no option but to chew, and then swallow, Lisa
channelled her fury into her eyes, which locked with his
fiercely.

*   *   *

Lisa had been marching along in silence since they had left the cottage, but now they were out of earshot she could speak her mind. 'I'm not going another step.'

Tino glanced back at her without slowing. 'It's not too far away now. The harbour is just over there, around the base of the cliff.'

'It's not the distance that worries me.'

'What, then?' He ground to a halt, and turned to stare at her.

'Stop this, Tino. I'm not going out on your boat. We both know you've got me over a barrel, but, if you have any decency left in you at all, you'd come back with me to the villa and hold our meeting like you promised—'

'Not now, Lisa.'

'What do you mean, not now?'

'I mean I don't want to discuss business right now?' He put his face very close so she was forced to take a step back.

'But once the deal is wrapped up we can go our separate ways,' she pointed out, 'which I know you want as much as I do.'

'Once the deal is wrapped up?' He stared at her mockingly. 'You're very sure of yourself.'

'I'm confident that I've come up with the right deal for you?'

He laughed, throwing his head back. 'So now you've got my best interests at heart? I don't think so, Lisa.'

'All right.' She was forced to hurry after him when he started down the path again. 'So we both need this deal.'

'I don't need anything from you.'

'Really? So why are your people scurrying around trying to buy up everything in sight?'

That stopped him.

'Maybe it pleases me to know that I can.'

'I'm very happy for you, but my life is rather more complicated. I have loyalties.'

'You have an overabundance of pride...and a highly inflated opinion of yourself.'

'That's rich coming from you!'

'And if the tables were turned, you'd treat me differently? No. So don't expect any leeway from me, when you'd give me none yourself.' He turned back to the path, forcing her to run after him again.

'But you gave me your word that this week would be devoted to our negotiations.'

'On my terms.' He didn't pause, or look back.

'All right.' Lisa stopped running. Resting her hands on her knees, she tried to catch her breath.

'All right, what?'

At least he had stopped. He was standing a few yards away, waiting for her to say something. She fought for control. But as she straightened up her feelings erupted. 'I suppose Arianna is happy about our little pleasure cruise?'

'Arianna isn't your concern.'

'How convenient for you.'

'Why are you worrying about Arianna?'

'Someone needs to. I feel sorry for her.'

'Why, exactly?'

'I think you know why, Tino.'

'No, I don't. I'm waiting to hear what you have to say about it.'

'All right, then... What the hell are we doing here?' She gestured around. 'We should go back to the villa and have our meeting under proper conditions. All this is far too distracting.'

'I thought that part of our agreement was that I decide when and where our meetings are held.'

'But we can't have them here.'

'Exactly.' His voice was maddeningly controlled.

'You're becoming forgetful, Lisa. I already told you that we are not holding any meetings today.'

'So, you're breaking your word?'

'I don't remember saying we wouldn't be holding any meetings this week. You shouldn't have agreed to something before you were certain of the terms.'

'Don't you dare lecture me on business etiquette. I agreed to your terms before I realised how irresponsible you were going to be.'

'Irresponsible?'

'Yes,' Lisa insisted fiercely. 'Irresponsible. Now, can we stop wasting time, and get back to the villa? I want a shower—I'm all salty. We can still get in a couple of hours of discussions before lunch... What do you think you're doing?' She glared down at the hand on her arm. 'Don't you dare touch me!'

But he was already propelling her along the path.

'I'm warning you—'

'And I'm telling you,' he fired back, dragging her in front of him to stare into her eyes. 'I make the decisions here, and today business is off the agenda. You heard me tell Stella I'd get her some fish for her supper? Well, that takes precedence over anything else.'

'You're going fishing?' Lisa demanded incredulously.

'No, Lisa—we're going fishing.'

Before Lisa could stop him he swung her off the ground, and held her so tightly she couldn't fight him off.

'If I say we're going out on the boat, we're going out on the boat,' he informed her as he strode along. 'And if I choose to take hold of your arm, I take hold of your arm. Do you understand me any better yet, Lisa?'

'I understand you're a brute—and you'd better put me down right now, or face the consequences.'

'Consequences? What consequences are those, Lisa?' His pace didn't falter. 'Are you going to set your lawyers onto my legal team? Because I strongly advise you to think twice before you do that.. unless, of course, you want to be begging me to give you a job in a couple of months' time.'

'I wouldn't expect you to give me the dirt from under your fingernails.'

'As I don't have any, you'll have to excuse me if I'm not too worried about that.'

'Are you going to put me down—or shall I scream?'

'Scream all you want.. no one will hear you.' They'll only think we're having fun. You're not going to win this one—accept it.'

Lisa kicked her legs furiously in reply. 'This isn't a joke, Tino.'

'What's your problem? Are you still worried about Arianna? Or are you more worried about being alone with me?'

Lisa gave a short, scornful laugh. 'Yes, I am worried about Arianna—but as for you?' She looked at him with disdain. 'I couldn't give a damn about you.'

Dropping her to the ground, he held her at arm's length, the tension flaring between them. 'No need to descend to the language of the gutter, young woman.'

'To describe you?' Lisa couldn't believe she was shouting. 'I'd say it's absolutely necessary.'

'And if I told you Arianna and I aren't a couple?'

'I'd be happy, relieved—for her. And I'd still want to go back to the villa. No contact between us other than for business, remember that, Tino?'

'So, we shouldn't do this, for instance...'

The breath shot out of Lisa's lungs as he dragged her close. Feelings exploded out of her. And it wasn't the fact that Tino was kissing her that went storming through her brain, it was the fact that she loved it. He felt good, better than good. Making rough, animal sounds, she moved passionately against him. But as he moulded her even closer to him she hated him—hated him for making her want him so badly it hurt, so badly her legs were giving way beneath her.

She came to her senses abruptly. Bond Steel's future depended on her, and this was how she behaved? Tino was only playing games with her, and while she was distracted his troops were swarming all over her business.

She started fighting him then. She fought his mouth, his lips, his tongue, and she grappled with his hands, making sounds of fury in her throat. But he had her bound so tightly against him, she could hardly breathe, let alone break free. And then, just when she felt she had no more fight left in her, he let her go, and stood back.

'So this is your idea of persuasion?' he said.

'It's a lot more honest than kissing you back.' Turning her face away from him, she held her forehead with her hand. 'I can't believe I'm in this position. I hate you so much.'

'No,' Tino countered steadily. 'What you hate is the way I make you lose control.'

'I know what I mean.'

'Dangerous ground, Lisa. You know what they say about hate.'

'Don't flatter yourself!'

'I don't.'

Lisa made an angry sound. 'So, I'm stuck with this for the next week?'

'If you mean me.. then, yes, you are.'

'Well, don't ever try that again,' she warned. 'And don't give me that look either. I'm warning you...I mean it, Tino.'

'Of course you do.'

Tino knew what was at stake for her, Lisa realised, and, like it or not, she was tied in to this. Tino Zagorakis held the fate of Bond Steel in the palm of his hand, and she had to play by his rules, or risk losing everything.

He stood watching her, slouched on one hip. 'Do you know what you need?' His voice had turned low and mocking.

'No, but I'm sure you're going to tell me.'

'You need someone to say no to you, Lisa—someone who can curb your headstrong ways.'

'Headstrong?' She'd never put a foot wrong in all her adult life—and no one in his right mind would call her headstrong. No one would dare. 'And I suppose you think you're man enough for the job?'

'I know I am.'

The sardonic murmur made Lisa shiver with desire. She had to fight it, fight him. 'I've had enough of this. I want to go back.'

'Not a chance,' he said flatly. 'We are going to enter into negotiations Greek style.'

'What are you talking about? Greek style?' Ancient tableaux of partly clothed men and women captured in various poses of sensual indulgence sprang into Lisa's mind. She was prepared to go a long way to secure the deal, but not that far.

'We're going to get properly acquainted before we sit round a table.'

'Properly acquainted?' Her throat squeezed tight. 'Why? I don't want to.'

'Bad luck for your company.' He shook his head.

'No—stop…wait a minute.' To Lisa's relief he stopped walking and turned around.

'So, we're agreed?' he said. 'No more talk of business today?'

She muttered two words grudgingly: 'All right.'

'That's good, Lisa.'

Did he have to make it sound as if she had achieved something monumental?

'That wasn't so hard, now, was it?'

Lisa confined herself to a glare.

'There can be no possibility of a deal until I find you more biddable.'

'Biddable?' That was too much! 'So, now you're resorting to blackmail?'

'Blackmail?' Shaking his head, Tino made a sound of disappointment with his tongue against the roof of his mouth. He was teasing her, taunting her—baiting her. 'No, not blackmail, Lisa. You see, if you respond well, I will be fair. But if you are determined to remain wilful and contrary, then you will have to be tamed.'

'Tamed? I'd like to see you try.'

'Is that a challenge, Lisa?'

And then, incredibly, before she realised what he meant to do, he had picked her up and put her over his knee! And before she could recover from that, he exclaimed, '*Theos!* You would send me mad!' And let her tumble to the ground as if her naked flesh had scorched him.

Wiping a hand over his eyes, Tino looked as if he couldn't believe what had happened. Scrambling to her feet, Lisa couldn't believe it either. She didn't know whether to rail at him, or laugh, and the longer they stood staring at each other, the more she wanted to laugh.

Tino was clearly stunned that a moment of passion had brought him to the point where he had almost put her over his knee and spanked her, while she was surprised the idea excited her so much. She had to think fast. She couldn't let this drive a wedge between them or it would be the end of the deal. 'We both need some cooling-off time.' Nervous laughter bubbled out of her, but Tino's expression stopped it dead.

What was this turning into? Tino stared at Lisa hard. He

had never come close to losing control before, but right now his senses were raging. In an ideal world, sex between them would have been fun—explosive—but the courtly dance of civilised behaviour stood between them. That and his determination to bring her to heel. But he realised now that where the thought of subduing a woman physically was anathema to him, the thought of spanking Lisa as a prelude to something else was overwhelmingly appealing.

'Are you all right?' His voice sounded gruff in his ears. 'All right?'

He braced himself for the explosion he was sure would come, but when she held his gaze her eyes were sparkling brighter than he'd ever seen them…

She wanted him.

He kept his face neutral, though right now his mind was in turmoil. He was relieved to know he hadn't frightened her, but this wasn't a game to him any more..or, if it was, the rules had just changed, because he wanted Lisa Bond more than he had ever wanted anything in his life before…and that made him deeply uneasy.

CHAPTER FIVE

FOR a few seconds the air between them crackled with intensity. It wasn't just Tino who had been carried away, Lisa realized; she had been too. The thought of a physical tussle with a man as strong as Tino ending in something that didn't involve violence was going to play on her mind for a long time to come. If she could trust a man enough…if she could trust Tino enough…if it could be safe. She'd never been with a man before, had always been so scared. Now, all she felt was aroused and very tempted.

'I'm going fishing,' Tino said brusquely, breaking into her thoughts. 'Are you coming with me, or not?'

Lisa glanced down at her salt-caked self.

'We can get some things for you down at the port.'

'Wait,' she called as he started down the path. 'What are you talking about? What things?'

He stopped, and turned around. 'Sun cream, a hat…nothing to get too excited about. Come on, then—we've wasted enough time.'

'Can we talk business on the boat?'

'You never give up, do you, Lisa?'

'No.'

He stopped so abruptly she almost bumped into him. 'Do you need forty hours to convince me?'

'Of course I don't.'

'Then what are you worried about?' He started off in the direction of the harbour again.

'I'm not worried,' she shouted after him.

'Really?' He lengthened his stride.

'Cold-blooded *son of a bitch*,' Lisa muttered as she hurried after him.

The local store stocked most essentials, and a straw hat with a wide brim was soon found for her, as well as some high factor sun cream—two bottles.

'You're very fair-skinned,' Tino said as he pressed them into her hands. 'You must use plenty.'

Lisa bobbed her head, still mutinous. Gazing out to distract herself from Tino's mannish sweep of the store, she saw his yacht towering over the local boats. At least, she presumed it must be his. It was a sleek white colossus amidst all the tiny fishing vessels. 'That's an impressive business perk,' she said when they left the shop.

'I'm glad you like it.'

He was right. She didn't need forty hours to convince him, and when would she get another opportunity to take a cruise on a billionaire's yacht? Lisa was surprised by how childishly excited she was at the prospect. She was even a little impatient when Tino stopped outside another shop and steered her inside.

At the local bakery and general food store, when greetings had been formally exchanged with the beaming host, a wicker basket, not dissimilar to the one Stella had been carrying, was handed to them over the counter.

'Our picnic,' Tino explained, taking charge of it.

'Our picnic?' Lisa frowned. Didn't billionaires carry chefs on their yachts these days?

When Tino walked straight past the gangway to the *Stellamaris Odyssey*, she halted at the foot of it.

'What now?' he grated, turning round.

'But, I thought—'

'Oh, dear—your bottom lip is trembling, Lisa.'

She probably did look like a child whose promised treat had just been snatched away—that was how she felt. 'I didn't want to go fishing in the first place,' she pointed out, pretending not to care.

'Does this look like a fishing boat?' Tino gazed up the sides of his sleek white yacht.

'No, of course not, but I thought—'

'You thought?'

He made it sound like a breakthrough.

'You insisted we must go out on your boat, Tino—'

'No one in their right minds would call the *Stellamaris Odyssey* a boat, Lisa.'

'Oh, well, excuse me! What am I supposed to know about billionaires' toys?'

'This is the woman who owns a jet talking?'

'I don't own a jet; my company owns a jet.'

'Forgive me—I understood you owned Bond Steel?'

'Most of it,' she admitted tightly.

'In my opinion a day out on a luxury yacht is nothing special. I use it for business, and for impressing clients. You don't need to be impressed, do you, Lisa?'

'No, of course not.'

'Excellent, because I've got something rather different planned for you.'

Now he *was* making her nervous…the sexual tension was still crackling. Craning her neck, Lisa tried to see past him. Whatever craft they would be using had to be here somewhere, she reasoned, but the last boat in line after the *Stellamaris Odyssey* was a modest blue and white fishing boat. 'Do you mean that?'

'What's wrong with it? Or is my poor fishing vessel not good enough for you, Your Royal Highness?' He gave her a mock bow.

Holding herself firmly in check, Lisa took one last longing look at the *Stellamaris Odyssey*.

Following her gaze, Tino smiled. 'Oh, no, Lisa, that would be far too self-indulgent. I'm sure you agree that lean and mean is the best way to do business. You do still want to do business with me?'

'Of course I do.'

'In that case, come along—the galley on the fishing boat is rather primitive, and we don't want our wine getting warm.'

It was fun. She hadn't expected that. The day she'd moved in with her father, five-star luxury had become the norm— and even a five-star norm could become boring after a while. Not like this… This was special. The sun was warm on her face, and the breeze tasted salty and fresh…

While Tino took the helm, Lisa stored their provisions in the simple galley before joining him on deck.

'I hope you found the ice. I had someone from the yacht bring it over in a bucket.'

'Don't worry—our wine is now in that bucket.' She wasn't going to let him run away with the idea that she was still disappointed. 'Are you going to tell me where we're heading, or is that still a secret?'

'No secret—somewhere special…somewhere private.'

Private? How well did he intend them to get to know each other? Lisa's heart started pumping. 'How much more private does it get? This is your island, isn't it?'

'Why don't you wait and see?'

Tino was right. The tiny cove they sailed into was completely secluded, and the only sound apart from the rolling surf was the beat of a thousand wings as birds rose in a cloud as they approached. The boat puttered in with its engine idling, and when she leaned over the side Lisa could see tiny fish swooping in vast shoals beneath them. 'Come and see this,' she called excitedly, forgetting the state of their relationship.

Cutting the engine, Tino joined her at the rail. 'We'll have to swim ashore. I can't take her in any closer.'

'What about our food?'

'I'll just drop anchor.'

Lisa turned to watch Tino pad across the deck. He looked like no businessman she'd ever seen before. The ones she was used to dealing with were somewhat lacking on the strong-tanned-leg front…and on the muscular-torso front too.

'Food?' he reminded her when he came back.

'What? Oh, yes, the food.'

'Well? Where is it?'

'In the galley.'

'So, go and get it.' He folded his arms.

It seemed compliance was her lot—for now, Lisa accepted grimly.

'There's a waterproof ice-box in the galley,' Tino called after her as she hurried off. 'Fill it up with our provisions, and then attach the rope you'll find on the shelf. When you've done that, give me a shout, and I'll carry it up.'

'I can manage.'

'I'll carry it up.'

She turned and they stared at each other unblinking.

'I'm just going to check the lobster pots to see if I have a treat to take home for Stella,' he told her steadily, 'and then I'll come down and get the ice-box and carry it up for you.'

When Tino returned he was as good as his word. Leaning over the rail, he carefully lowered the ice-box as close to the sea as the rope would allow. He let it drop the last couple of feet and then sprang onto the side-rail. 'Don't worry, I'll help you up.' Crouching down, he reached out to her.

Take his hand? Not in a million years.

'Have it your way.' He straightened up, balancing easily on the narrow rail as the boat rocked to and fro.

'You mean I've got to dive in…from up there?'

'Unless you'd rather go to the stern and climb down the steps.'

'No. This is fine for me.' Thrusting her hand into Tino's, she let him help her up.

'You'd better take this off before you try to dive in.'

Lisa gasped as he tugged off her wrap. 'That's pretty slick. How many times have you done that before?'

'Do you care?'

'No, of course not.'

Arcing away from her with a grin, he dived backwards into the sea. Breaking the surface, he shook his hair out of his eyes. 'It's your turn now, Lisa. Don't worry, I'm here to save you.'

'Why doesn't that fill me with confidence?' Lisa muttered. Closing her eyes, she didn't hesitate. If she had, she would have been forced to trudge to the stern with her tail between her legs to find the steps.

'That was quite a dive,' Tino said, steadying her as the waves buffeted them against each other.

'Well, I could hardly let you get the better of me.'

'No, indeed.'

He had already slipped the rope from the ice-box over his shoulder, she noticed, trying to avoid brushing against him.

'Are you going to make it to shore all right without me?'

'I should think I can manage.' The sooner she left him, the safer she would be!

'In that case, after you.' Pulling away a couple of strokes, he gave her room to kick out.

This was not what she had imagined when she'd left home, Lisa realised, striking out for the shore. This was the first deal she had negotiated in an aquamarine sea beneath a blazing hot sun with a man like Tino Zagorakis. All the more reason to keep her wits about her.

'You're full of surprises.'

And he did look surprised when she opened the ice-box on the beach. She had just pulled out the sun cream and now her rather squashed hat. 'I'm not a complete numb-skull, you know.' She rammed the battered hat onto her head. But as she dipped inside again to find the sun cream so did Tino, putting their faces millimetres apart.

'Would you like me to rub some cream onto your back?'

'No.' Her voice was sharper than she intended as she pulled back abruptly. 'Thank you,' she managed belatedly.

Why had it never occurred to her that they would land up on a beach together practically naked? She should at least have tied her wrap around her waist. As it was they might as well have been two castaways on their own desert island... And now she was blessed with Tino for the whole day, Tino in his customary mocking mood...

Lisa looked away to distract herself. There was an apron of pristine ivory sand, beyond which the land broke up into scrub with a shading of feathery tamarisk trees, and beneath those some gnarled, and not half so friendly, prickly juniper bushes. Wild flowers were scattered about the sand dunes where they were sitting—pink campions, violet sea-lavender...

'Do you like it here?'

'I love it. It's one of the most beautiful places I've ever seen—but then I thought that when I first saw Villa Aphrodite. You're a very lucky man.'

'Luck played no part in it.'

Lisa tensed. Tino's voice had changed. He reminded her of Jack Bond. That was exactly the sort of comment her father would have made.

They ate in silence after that, drinking sharp green wine out of pottery beakers. The olives, soaked in oil, were plump and delicious, and the shopkeeper had included some sweet fat raisins to eat with the crusty bread and goat's cheese. There was even a drawstring muslin bag containing some sugared almonds for their pudding. They reminded Lisa of other people's weddings.

'Almonds and raisins.' Loosening the string on the muslin pack, Tino tipped some of them into his hand, and then added some raisins to the mix. 'The bitter and the sweet, just like life.'

Lisa seized the opportunity. 'About Arianna…'

Lisa noticed how closed Tino's expression had become. There was definitely more to his relationship with Arianna than he was letting on. She was right to probe.

'I've told you all you need to know about Arianna.'

'You told me that she was Stella's daughter, but—'

'But what? What more do you want to know about her, Lisa?'

Not just Arianna.. *you* and Arianna. 'I'm not sure yet.'

'Yet?' He stared at her thoughtfully for a moment, and then his eyes brightened with understanding. At the same time one corner of his mouth tugged up in his trademark annoying half-smile. 'Do you think I've brought you here to pounce on you?'

'I think you've got marginally more style than that.'

'That's very kind of you—and for your information, I have known Arianna since the day she was born. If you think of her as my sister you will have the true picture.'

'That's it?' It was actually a lot more than she had expected him to tell her, and enough to set her pulse rate racing.

'That's all you're getting. Would you like some?'

'Some what?' Lisa froze, still debating the implications of a single and unattached Tino as he leaned towards her.

'Almonds and raisins.'

'Oh, yes…thank you.'

He filled their beakers with more wine.

The little she had learned about him had fuelled her curiosity, as well as her determination to keep his revelations on a roll. 'Tell me about that beautiful piano you have at Villa Aphrodite.'

On the point of handing her the beaker, he drew back. 'What do you want to know about it?'

'Do you play?'

'Yes.'

'Just "yes"?'

He shrugged. 'What more is there to know?'

She guessed he had already given her more information than he had ever given to anyone outside his inner circle, but that wasn't going to deter her from discovering more. Taking the beaker of wine from him, she said casually, 'I don't mean to probe, but—'

'If I need a private investigator,' Tino cut across her, 'I'll know who to call.'

'So you do enjoy playing the piano.'

Throwing back his head, he made a throaty, frustrated sound. 'Yes. Is that all?'

'If you'd rather not talk about it…'

'Oh, no,' he assured her sarcastically. 'I love to chat.'

'I gathered.'

'I learned to play the piano as an adult.'

Lisa went very still. 'You must be very good,' she said carefully, not wanting to push him too hard. 'Those are difficult, demanding pieces.'

'I play well enough.'

'I guess you needed a hobby.'

'You guess? Are you waiting for me to confirm or deny your guess, Lisa?'

'No, of course not—I'm sorry.'

'I always wanted to play the piano, that is all.'

'And you couldn't have lessons as a child?'

'No.' Impatience was pinging off him now. 'I couldn't have piano lessons until I paid for them myself.'

Lisa knew she was by no means the only child who had

yearned for things she couldn't have until the day she took charge of her own destiny, but something about Tino's stilted confession suggested he had wounds that ran deep. His lack of history intrigued her. Had he erased the past to hide something so terrible that even she could not imagine what it was? The thought that they might share something so intrinsic to their make-up was deeply unwelcome. It gave them a bond—a bond she didn't want to share with a man who held her company's fate in his hands; no one knew better than she how ruthless the past could make you.

'I first met Stella when I was a very small boy. She had an old piano and I loved the sound of it.'

Lifting up her head, Lisa hid her amazement. Tino had started talking about the past again, and without any prompting this time.

'Arianna was born when I was seven.'

'So, you grew up in the same neighbourhood?' *Damn, damn, damn!* Why couldn't she just learn to keep her mouth shut?

'Something like that. Shall we pack up?'

He had changed like quicksilver, and she knew that was the end of his revelations. She knew it because she recognised the same technique she always used to put up a smokescreen to hide the past. She would get nowhere pushing him now.

They travelled back with only the rhythm of the engine and the sibilance of the water streaming past the wooden boat breaking the stillness of late afternoon. Lisa could understand why Tino loved island life, and why he worked so hard to preserve his anonymity. To be able to exchange the feverish pace of the business world for the solitude of Stellamaris had to be the most precious thing he had... But still his past intrigued her. Why was it all such a secret? He had told her a little about the piano, and something about Stella and Arianna, but what else was he hiding?

Would she find out more on Stellamaris? Or would she leave the island knowing as little about Tino Zagorakis as she did now?

Glancing at him, Lisa realised that Stella was right: the Greeks did have a natural affinity with the sea. Had Tino named the island after his elderly friend? Or had Stella's parents chosen her name in tribute to their beautiful island home?

'Have you thought about dinner, Lisa?'

'Dinner?' It was the last thing on her mind. Tino had just cut the engine, and they were drifting slowly towards the mooring. She had been focused on the picturesque houses circling the quay—their Technicolor shades seemed to have been intensified by the fading light. 'I hadn't really thought about dinner. I suppose I'll eat later, on my balcony.'

'It would be a good opportunity to talk.'

'To talk?' Her heart started thundering. 'About business?'

'Of course.'

He sounded mildly impatient—and had every right to, Lisa realised. He would hardly welcome any further investigation into his life—and there was no question of them making small talk, since neither one of them was good at that.

'Well?' He was still staring at her.

'Oy, Tino! Opa! Siga…Siga!'

Hearing the warning shout, they both whipped around in time to see one of the local men gesticulating furiously.

'Theos!' Tino swung the wheel violently, narrowly avoiding a collision.

'That was close.' Lisa was still shaking with shock, but Tino had made the adjustment in time, and the fishing vessel slid neatly, if narrowly, into its berth beside the *Stel-*

lamaris Odyssey. 'I imagine that might have been an expensive mistake if you had crashed into your yacht.'

'Expensive mistake?' Tino stared at her for a moment, as if he couldn't quite believe what had happened, and then he stalked away to toss the mooring ropes to the man waiting on shore.

Straddling the deck and the shore, he looked magnificent. As the two men secured the ropes she could see how much bigger he was than the other man, but, even so, their movements were perfectly synchronised. It was as if they shared the same internal rhythm. If she had learned nothing more than this, Stellamaris was Tino's true home. But if that was so, then what drove him? What demon in Tino's past would make him leave his beautiful island home in search of new worlds to conquer, new deals to make?

She was sure now that they shared something more fundamental than business, and it was something very few people would have recognised. They both kept the past hidden, and though she didn't know what had happened to Tino yet she did know that the past had shaped them, made them both strong—but it was their weakness too.

CHAPTER SIX

ON THE walk back from the harbour Tino was lost in his own thoughts, giving Lisa all the space she needed to scroll through the events of an incredible day. Her lips were still burning from his kiss, and how was she supposed to forget that he had almost spanked her, or how aroused that had made her? What might have happened if he hadn't drawn back? Would she have lost control? Just thinking about all the possibilities was enough to excite her.

'I'll leave you now.'

Her cheeks reddened guiltily as he reclaimed her attention.

'I have to take the lobsters to Stella.' Reaching past her, he opened the garden gate.

He seemed to have forgotten the dinner invitation. 'I'll see you tomorrow morning at eight?' She spoke briskly. And when he didn't answer, she added, 'I can't let you win this by default because you never found time to listen to my proposal.'

'I don't need that kind of advantage, Lisa.'

'Let's wait until tomorrow before you get too confident?'

Tipping his head, he gave her one of his rare smiles. 'I'm looking forward to it.'

'In that case, I'll say goodnight.'

As she walked away Lisa hoped crazily that he would call her back. Almost immediately, she found she missed him… She missed walking with him, relaxing with him, talking to him… She missed everything about him—which was ridiculous. They had shared one day. But sharing was something she never did. The lack of privacy in the commune had seen to that. There had been no private space, no personal possessions. Her time there had made her selfish. She knew that. Today had been different. Today she had experienced an alternative, and found she liked it. She liked it a lot.

Opening the door to her bedroom, Lisa smiled, remembering the moment Tino had almost crashed into the harbour wall. He hadn't come out of the day unscathed either. They had both been equally distracted. Tossing her battered sunhat on the bed, she freed her hair and ran her fingers through the tangles. She would take a long, lazy bath, and forget about dangerous Greek men—she had to focus on business now.

It was a very different bathroom from the sophisticated wet room she used at the apartment. In that ultra-modern space, minimalism ruled. Tino's preferred style was traditional, as if he appreciated the history behind every object. The various jars and crystal vases were exquisite, as was the beautiful pale peach fabric covering the antique chaise longue in one corner of the room. Everything had been chosen with care, or maybe he had inherited the lot from his wealthy parents…

The commune had been littered with other people's junk. All she craved now in her life were a few highly sought after examples of modern craftsmanship—precious items, carefully selected, and then kept like museum pieces for her pleasure alone, almost as if she needed to remind herself that no one could force her to share them.

When she walked onto the balcony after her bath she was forced to dodge out of sight, seeing Tino deep in conversation with one of his gardeners. It had been foolish to walk outside wrapped in nothing but a towel, but the sunset had drawn her. The remarkable light had bathed the two men in an other-worldly glow, and even the petals of the flowers they were holding seemed lit by some spectral fire.

Then she remembered the taxi driver telling her that the May Day festivities required every house on Stellamaris to be filled with flowers. The meeting between Tino and his gardener would be something to do with that, she supposed. The gardener was probably outlining his plans, while Tino was making his selection from the available blooms.

The May Day celebrations would start on Friday. Had Tino planned this week knowing he would be too wrapped up in local festivities to spare time for their business discussions?

On this point at least, Lisa felt confident. Tino Zagorakis would never forego the chance of a business deal in favour of a local flower festival.

She would have to put her suit back on, Lisa realised, returning inside—or the trousers and shirt part of it, at least. She hadn't brought anything more with her than her swimming things, a change of underwear and tops, and her pyjamas. She had not expected to be staying longer than a couple of nights at most...

As she opened the wardrobe door Lisa exclaimed with surprise. It certainly wasn't empty now. Her initial thought was that all the beautiful outfits must belong to Arianna, but as she ran her hand along the rail she could see that they still had labels attached, as if they had been sent on approval from some high-class boutique.

She frowned, and pulled back. Was this Tino's idea? If they were meant for her, she couldn't accept them. Of course she couldn't accept them. But on the other hand, if she was staying until Friday she had to have something to wear. And she already had to pay him back for the sunhat and cream—she could just add this to the tally...

A quick call to the housekeeper confirmed they were for her. Tino had judged her dress size accurately, suggesting he had made some pretty thorough observations. Lisa felt heat flood through her, and then as she remembered the chest of drawers across the room excitement rushed through her. Nothing like this had ever happened to her.. and, surely, there couldn't be anything else?

Wrapping her fingers around the handles, she dragged a drawer open and stared inside. A sigh slowly peeled out of her. Underwear that she had only ever lusted after before was stacked—not laid, but stacked in neat piles—and arranged carefully according to colour. Of course she could easily have afforded any of it, but where clothes were concerned she was frugal. In the commune dozens of outfits had been shared around, but she had always worn the same threadbare track suit, guarding it jealously. The habit had stuck; though her clothes were no longer threadbare, she still kept her wardrobe to a minimum.

On the rare occasions when her father had pressed money into her hands so she didn't disgrace herself at a social function, she had spent as little as possible, returning the change to a man who had been as bemused by his daughter's parsimony as he had been appalled by her mother's reckless transfer of funds to the commune. Treating herself had been out of the question, wasting her father's money unthinkable, and she still kept rigid control of her finances. This abundance of luxury goods was like every birthday come at once…

It certainly beat having things sent on approval to the office, Lisa reflected ruefully as she rummaged through the drawer. Who, for goodness' sake, had time to choose briefs made of the finest flesh-coloured gossamer net? As she held them up she knew that her decision to keep some of the things was already made. She might be destined to eat dinner alone, but she was going to be dressed to kill.

She chose an elegant floor-length silk skirt in dove-grey with a matching camisole that had a toning, chiffon overshirt in shades of grey and smoky lilac. The colours were ideal for her complexion, and she wore her hair down. In one of the drawers she was stunned to find a pair of beautiful amethyst earrings in a small velvet case. She never wore jewellery, but these were gorgeous—and whoever had chosen them had exquisite taste. Maybe she would develop a taste for jewellery too, Lisa mused, viewing her reflection in the floor-length mirror.

She turned at a knock on the door, feeling rather foolish as she hurried to open it. She was dressed for an occasion, not to eat dinner alone on her balcony.

'Oh.' Lisa stared with amazement at the vast floral arrangement the maid was holding out to her.

'For you, Thespinis Bond.'

'Are you sure?'

The girl looked at her.

Of course, she was sure, Lisa realised, kicking her sluggish brain cells into action as she stood back to let the young girl into the room.

'Shall I put them over here for you, Thespinis Bond, where you can see them from the bed?' The maid hovered by an ornate console table.

'Yes, please. That's definitely the right place for them… They're magnificent.'

'They are all from the gardens here at Villa Aphrodite.'

'Oh.'

'I almost forgot, Thespinis Bond. There is a card for you.'

Taking the vellum envelope, Lisa waited until the maid had left the room before opening it. Her heart started to thump heavily as she read the firm, uncompromising script. 'I would be delighted if you could join me for dinner this evening, Tino.'

So he hadn't forgotten. Her heart was hammering like a piston. She was excited and apprehensive too. A small part of her wanted this to be the most romantic thing that had ever happened to her—that was ever likely to happen to her—but she knew she had to be wary of Tino's motives. This was all very nice, but she couldn't afford to be distracted yet again from the purpose of her visit. Was this just part of his business plan—his well-thought-out strategy to soften her up? Everyone said Tino Zagorakis would stop at nothing. Was this just another example of the tactics he was prepared to employ?

As Lisa stared at the beautiful flowers they might as well have sprouted darts all aimed in her direction. There was another discreet tap on the door, and when she opened it Lisa found the same maid hovering.

'I'm sorry to trouble you again, Thespinis Bond, but Kirie Zagorakis would like your answer now. Will you be joining him for dinner, or would you prefer to dine in your room tonight?'

'Tell him…' Lisa glanced towards the balcony where she could see the lights from the garden reflected on the stone balustrade. Whatever Tino's motives, she didn't feel like hiding in her room. 'Tell him I will be down shortly.'

She couldn't delay any longer, Lisa realized, laying her hairbrush on the dressing table. She had brushed her hair so vigorously and for so long it was springing out around her shoulders. A spritz of perfume, and a slick of lip-gloss, and she was ready…

Tino turned the moment she walked onto the balcony. It was almost as if he could sense her presence before he saw her.

'You look beautiful.'

'Thank you. You look different too,' Lisa observed dryly.

'Yes, well, I thought I might as well make an effort,' he said casually.

As they stared at each other Lisa found she was smiling. But she had to keep part of herself aloof if she was ever to stand a chance of remaining immune to Tino. He was wearing a black dinner suit that made him look more hand-some than ever—if such a thing was possible. The white, open-necked shirt was a startling contrast against his tanned skin—and she was blatantly staring at him, Lisa realised, quickly looking away.

She was so beautiful it was the easiest thing in the world to forget about business. And business was the purpose of every moment he spent with her. It was easy to forget about dinner too, and just take her to bed...

He had never felt such unbridled lust for any woman. And why should he hold back when there was no reason to do so? Time was running out, after all. And she was smiling at him—and looking as if she meant it. He was getting the hang of this wooing business. Just as he had expected, the day out on the fishing smack had thrown all her preconceptions about him into confusion. The clothes that had been flown in for her from the top Athenian de-signers had clearly delighted her, or she wouldn't be wear-ing them. The modest jewellery was a masterstroke—the amethyst earrings gleamed in the candlelight, setting off her sun-kissed skin, drawing his eye to the lustre of her hair, and making her even more beautiful for him. Next time he'd buy her emeralds to bring out the colour of her eyes.

They couldn't stand like this staring at each other for ever, Lisa realised, still smiling as she walked forward. She felt strangely bashful, but then she wasn't used to presenting herself for a man's approval. And, for some reason, what Tino thought about her appearance really did matter to her.

'You look lovely, Lisa.' Taking hold of her hand, he raised it to his lips.

At his touch a quiver ran through her, and it didn't stop there, so she pulled her hand away—too late.

He searched her face.

She stared at him and heard a little cry, and then realised that it was her own voice and that Tino had swung her into his arms.

As he strode inside the house with her all the servants seemed to have disappeared. He mounted the stairs swiftly, holding her close and safe in his arms. When they reached the top landing he shifted her weight effortlessly, and opened a door. Walking inside, he kicked it shut behind them, and lowered her to the ground in front of him, steadying her on her feet.

Gazing up, Lisa thought she saw something in Tino's eyes that mirrored her own need. Acting on impulse, she reached up and wrapped her arms around his neck. Pulling back, he stared down at her for a few moments, as if he had to confirm something.

Lisa wasn't sure which of them moved first, which of them gave in first. She only knew that she needed to feel Tino pressed up hard against her. She needed his mouth to claim hers with the same urgency she had to draw her next breath. And then they were kissing each other passionately, and she had her fingers laced through his hair, keeping him fast, pressing against him with all the hunger a lifetime of denial could produce. She heard the sounds of passion she was making, and didn't care. Nothing mattered now—all she cared about was that Tino didn't let her go, and that this time he didn't leave her unsatisfied, because now she wanted all of him, with no restrictions, no boundaries, no doubts…

They were like two lions mating, raw, primitive, desperate, hungry. There was so much sex in the air it formed a miasma around them, invading their nostrils, and sending them both hurtling off to a place where no clear thought was possible, and only sensation and hunger existed; hunger that only one act could relieve.

'I need you,' Lisa gasped as Tino lifted her into his arms.

'*Thee mou!* I need you more,' he ground out as he carried her over to the bed.

'No—don't rip it off.' She closed her hands protectively over the chiffon over-blouse, suddenly nervous, suddenly conscious of what they were about to do.

'I'll buy you another, *Thespinis mou*.'

'But I like this one.'

'Then take it off,' he instructed roughly. 'Take it off for me, *yineka mou*.'

She was panting, eyes wide. She was his equal and that made her feel safe. Slipping off the bed, Lisa undid the sash at the front and then allowed the chiffon blouse to fall. As it floated to the floor she felt no fear. There was an unspoken connection between them that for some reason made her trust him. Watching Tino take her place on the bed and then stretch out like a sleek black panther was more seduction than she could take.

'Continue,' he instructed lazily.

'No.' She stared fiercely at him. 'This is far too one-sided.'

Quirking a brow, he sat up and shrugged off his jacket.

'Get rid of it.' She could see he was as aroused as she was, and then he indicated that it was her turn now.

Slowly easing the straps of the silk camisole from her shoulders, Lisa let it drop. Then, swooping down, she took it from the floor by one finger. She was wearing nothing underneath.

'Have you no shame?' Tino murmured appreciatively.

'None.' Gazing down, Lisa saw how taut her nipples had become. They seemed to be stretching out to him to both tease and provoke his censure. Raising her head, she gazed steadily into his eyes.

'Just as I'd hoped.' He quickly opened the buttons on his shirt.

'Take it off.' Her voice was firm, and once he had

obeyed her she rewarded him, arching her back and displaying her breasts to their best advantage.

Easing back on the pillows, she noted the thrust of his arousal.

'Have *you* no shame?' she demanded softly, her voice thick with desire.

Stroking down the length of it, he looked at her. 'None…would you like me to develop some?'

'It's a little late for that, I should imagine.' Lisa found her hands were shaking as she reached for the fastening on her skirt. 'And I'll be sure to make you pay if you do.'

'I'm counting on it.'

Slipping her finger down beneath the waistband, Lisa closed her eyes as she allowed the column of silk to pool at her feet.

'And now the rest,' Tino insisted, referring to the transparent pants she was wearing.

Lisa shook her head. 'It's your turn now—'

'Who is going to make me?'

'Me.' It came out on a breath, but she couldn't move; she was transfixed by his lips, lips she wanted to feel all over her body, possessing her mouth, possessing her totally, utterly, everywhere…

Lying back on the bed, Tino caught hold of the brass rail behind his head and stretched out.

Taking her cue, Lisa picked up the chiffon over-blouse and walked to the head of the bed.

'What are you going to do with that?'

'I'm going to tie you down, and then do whatever I want with you—'

'I don't think so.'

It happened so fast. One minute she was standing there, and the next she was flat on her back on the bed staring into eyes that were blazing with desire.

'I had to save you from yourself,' Tino explained softly,

making a pretence of contrition. 'I knew how precious the top was to you. How could I let you use it to tie me up?'

Lisa gasped and writhed beneath him as he began teasing her ear lobe with his teeth. 'I'm guessing you'd buy me another?' Her words came out in a hectic whisper.

'And so I will,' he assured her. 'I'll buy you a thousand tops if you want them, but I'll never let you master me, Lisa Bond.'

'Is the missionary position all I'm good for, then?' Her lips curved with amusement as she stared into his eyes.

'Pleasure is what you're good for. But pleasure on my terms, not yours.'

Somehow she managed to slip away. 'Then there can be no pleasure for either of us.'

Reaching out, he caught her back to him. 'I decide about the levels of pleasure in this relationship.'

'Oh, you do?'

'Just answer one question. Do you want me?'

'Yes, I want you...' Lisa hesitated, and then admitted softly, 'I want you more than anything.'

Tino fought the feeling rising in his chest. This had nothing to do with emotion. He just wanted to give her more pleasure than she had ever known, pleasure she would remember for the rest of her life, pleasure that would make every other man fall short in her eyes... He concentrated his attention on the tiny pants she was wearing. He pressed his palm against her stomach and felt her quiver of desire course up his arm. She was trembling with passion and so he slipped his fingers beneath the waistband to tease her.

'Don't stop, Tino.'

She writhed beneath him. 'What are you asking me to do, Lisa? You have to tell me exactly what you want—or how can I possibly know?'

'You know what I want you to do,' she told him fiercely.

'But I have to hear it from your mouth.' He rubbed the

thumb pad of one hand roughly over the full swell of her bottom lip.

'I want you to…'

'Yes? You want me to do what to you, Lisa? You have to tell me.'

'I'm… ' She hesitated, and then she saw the change in his eyes. He was so intuitive she didn't have to explain a thing.

'You're a virgin?' He turned suddenly serious.

'Not exactly. I've just never—' She blushed red.

'What does "not exactly" mean, Lisa? You either are or you aren't a virgin. It's one of life's few absolutes.'

'I've never had sex with a man.'

'That's not so bad, is it?' Cupping her chin, he turned her to face him so she couldn't evade his stare.

'It's not that simple. I've never had time for relationships. But back at my apartment, I have a drawer full of—'

'Please—I really don't need to hear the details.' And now he smiled wickedly. 'If I do, you may convince me that all the rumours I hear are true.'

'What rumours are those?' Lisa was immediately defensive.

'That women may very soon be able to do without men altogether?'

'Why don't I believe you?' She smiled, relaxing again as he tried for a crestfallen expression.

'You don't believe I have insecurities?'

She raised a brow.

'You'd be surprised.'

'I certainly would.'

He couldn't play games any longer. He couldn't wait any longer. He had never felt like this before. Dragging her to him, he turned her, and had her beneath him in the space of a few seconds. He kissed her until he could feel her arching against him. He brought her on top of him then, so

that he could cup her bottom and stroke her the way he
was very sure she would like.

She sighed raggedly. 'You have to stop that.'

'Why?'

'Because it feels so good.'

'Then that's the only encouragement I need to continue.'

She whimpered with pleasure, helpless beneath his touch,
relishing the way he was massaging her buttocks and, in
the process, pressing her hard against his rigid erection.
'That feels so good.' A shudder of pure lust consumed
Lisa's body as she stared into Tino's eyes. 'I'd like to—'

'Like to what?'

'Continue.' She smiled against his mouth.

'In that case…' Catching hold of her wrists, he turned
her again, pinning her securely beneath him.

She had never done this with anyone. She had never
trusted anyone enough. With Tino it was different, because
she didn't feel frightened of him…and that was because
when Tino touched her, even when he held her pinned
down like this, she knew he would never forget himself, he
would never forget how vulnerable she was pitting her
strength against his. He knew how firmly to hold her, and
when to let go. He could read every nuance in her face,
and had mastered his prodigious strength so she could wrestle with him and still feel safe.

The warmth in her heart was threatening to overwhelm
her, Lisa realised, feeling her eyes fill with tears. Fire was
rushing through her limbs at the thought of making love
with him, but there was something even more compelling
building inside her… Was it tenderness? *Or could it be
love?* It was something she had never felt before, so it was
hard to be sure—and then Tino greedily seized one of her
tightly extended nipples and began to suckle, and no more
thoughts were possible…

Lisa cried out with delighted surprise, lacing her fingers

through his hair to urge him on. Why hadn't she known pleasure like this existed? Why had she never felt this way before? When Tino stopped briefly to read her face she made an angry sound, and kept on making it until he found the other nipple and suckled on that one too.

'That's better,' she approved throatily. 'I like that.'

'Oh, do you?' He lifted himself on one elbow to stare into her face. 'And do I exist solely for your pleasure now?'

She considered his question through narrowed eyes. 'I don't see why not.'

As she gazed at him he could feel her strength and her certainty. They were worthy combatants. 'Then don't you think you should take these off?'

'Let me,' she insisted, and he watched as she ripped off the fragile briefs. Her boldness excited him. The fragile briefs were as much a hindrance to her as they were to him. This was a joust between equals; each of them wanted to see how far the other would push. 'Lie down,' he murmured, aching to pleasure her. 'Lie down, and spread your legs.'

She was clearly shocked by his suggestion—but her eyes were brighter than ever, and her cheeks were flushed pink with excitement. He trailed his fingers very lightly between her legs to feel how wet she was. Closing her eyes, she groaned, and then opened them a little wider for him. When he stopped, her eyes flashed open.

'That's not fair.'

'What isn't fair?' He pulled back to look at her.

'You sound so stern.' She seemed pleased by it. Turning onto her side, she rested her chin on her elbow to stare up at him. 'You *are* stern,' she observed huskily. 'Mmm, I like that.'

'Do you?' His senses roared as he caught her meaning.

'Yes, I do.'

As she reached for his trousers he caught hold of her

wrist, stopping her. 'You're a very naughty girl, aren't you, Lisa?'

'If I'm naughty, will you punish me?' she responded teasingly.

His breath caught in his throat as she stared at him. When she looked at him like that he longed to put her over his knee just as he had on the cliff path, but this time he wouldn't stop… This time he would give her exactly what she wanted. He could see she was remembering what had almost happened there, and that it was exciting her as much as it was exciting him.

He couldn't believe what she was asking him to do; he couldn't believe how much he wanted to do it. The thought of attending to those impudent curves made his throat tighten with anticipation. She had an extremely narrow waist that emphasised the fullness of her hips, and from his vantage point her bottom appeared to be a perfect pink globe…palest pink. She was thrusting it towards him now as he stared at her, almost as if she could read his mind…and now she was writhing a little to tempt him still more. 'Are you asking me to put you over my knee?'

'Would you?'

She made it sound more like a request, than a question. 'Do you want me to, you naughty girl?'

'Maybe—if you can catch me.'

'What?'

'You don't seriously expect me to mildly submit, do you, Tino?'

'I'm not sure.' His senses flared. She was inviting him to indulge in a tussle they both knew could only have one conclusion.

'Naughty girls don't just roll over and submit.'

'Don't they?' He gave her a firm look.

'No…they're rebellious, and cunning, and—'

She shrieked as he caught hold of her, and then they

rolled over once, twice…and then they were falling… falling off the bed.

She was laughing, he saw with relief. 'Are you all right?'

'I will be soon,' she promised provocatively. 'I suppose I should be grateful that you brought me on top of you to cushion my fall… I suppose I should be relieved that your reflexes are so sharp.'

Everything was a tease now. She had moved away from him, and she was on her hands and knees, staring at him like a beautiful pussy-cat, her eyes narrowed to arrow slits of emerald. Her bottom was raised high, displayed to its best advantage. He relished the moment, sure she couldn't possibly know the effect the sight of it was having on him…but then she undulated, and even raised it a little higher, proving that she knew exactly what she was doing.

'You *are* a bad girl,' he observed huskily.

'Tino… I want it.'

She gasped as he moved quickly behind her. Kneeling on the floor, he stroked his hands lightly over her naked rump. 'Down,' he said softly.

She obeyed him at once, resting her head on her arms so that her bottom was raised as high as it could be. He dealt her several firm strokes, and had the satisfaction of hearing her call throatily for more. The next few ended in a caress that brought her very close and that was his cue to lift her to her feet. Holding her in front of him with their faces almost touching, he very slowly stroked his hands up her arms relishing the sight of the shudders coursing through her. 'I had no idea this was going to turn out to be quite so energetic, or half so dangerous.'

'Are you frightened of me, Tino?' She whispered the words against his mouth.

Even he didn't know the truth to that. She made him feel things he shouldn't be feeling… She unsettled him more than any woman he had ever known… She pushed him further than he had ever considered going with a woman before. 'More to the point,' he said, 'are you frightened of me?' He searched her eyes.

'I'm in more danger from this.'

'Oh,' he murmured softly as she cupped him through his evening trousers.

'I'm glad you understand me.'

'Oh, I do,' he assured her as he reached to undo his zip.

'Let me,' Lisa whispered.

He held his hands out to the side.

'That's better.' She held his gaze as she undressed him, and only broke it when she was forced to dip down to remove his trousers completely and toss them away. 'Now you get your reward.'

But as she reached for him he pulled away.

'Not before I give you yours.' He swept her up.

'If you insist.'

And he did...

CHAPTER SEVEN

LISA shrieked with shock and with excitement as Tino joined her. As he pulled her on top of him she dropped a kiss on his firm mouth. 'You're not going to get away from me now.'

'As I'd hoped,' he murmured. 'Shall we begin?'

'Oh, please,' she sighed, reaching for him. Now the barriers were down between them his clean male scent was all the aphrodisiac she needed. Yet still he played with her, holding her away from him, refusing her any satisfaction. Cupping her chin, he caressed the sensitive area just below her ear…but when she tried to kiss him on the mouth he made a sound of denial down low in his throat, and held her away again. She wriggled against him, wanting the touch of his hands, needing it desperately. 'You will send me crazy, teasing me like this,' she complained breathlessly.

'Not crazy, just into a deeper state of arousal,' he observed clinically.

'You sound so cold.' She laughed it off, confident that it was a figment of her imagination.

Pulling away, he lavished a look down the whole trembling length of her.

'Hold me, Tino. Touch me.'

Her words drove him. His passions had never been roused to such a level. But he must keep control…that way he would give her more pleasure than she had ever dreamed of.

'You're not making me wait any longer,' she insisted fiercely.

He caught her wrist as she reached for him, and held both her hands over her head, keeping them secure in one fist on the pillow. She didn't try to resist him. 'So, you've no more fight left in you?'

'I didn't say that—but if you use your strength there's no contest.'

He released her immediately, and she sprang to the other side of the bed, staring at him, teasing him…

'I'm a naughty girl, Tino…or had you forgotten?'

'I have not forgotten anything, Lisa.' Nor had he. He remembered Bond Steel, and how she had set herself against him. 'Before I give you what you want, you must welcome my authority.'

Seeing the change in Tino's eyes, Lisa shivered with desire. 'Can you master me?'

'Let me ask you a question, Lisa… Do you want me to pleasure you?'

'You know I do.'

'Then you must convince me that you will submit to my command.'

'Never.' The single word left her lips on a sigh…a sigh that was laced with all the temptation she could muster, and her expression tempted him on still more.

'Never?' he queried softly. 'Do you want your bottom smacking again, Lisa?'

Lisa could hardly breathe with excitement as she nodded suggestively. Her lips were moist as she gazed at him spellbound with fascination at the thought of what might lie in store for her.

She shrieked as he rolled her over his knees. The sudden impact of Tino's warm hand on her soft flesh was so good. Lisa shrieked again, and wriggled her buttocks to show her approval. The pressure of his hard thighs against her was electrifying, and he judged the spanking perfectly. She knew he meant to rouse her all the more, and he had succeeded.

His hand lingered, and his skilful fingers, warm and firm, curled around her buttocks until he nearly, so very nearly, touched her where she ached to be touched. Nothing had ever felt this good, but it still wasn't enough. 'How can you tease me like this?'

'Did I give you permission to question my actions, you naughty, naughty girl?'

With each word, Tino's hand landed firmly on the soft pink swell of Lisa's bottom until she thought she would pass out from an overdose of pleasure.

'Have you learned your lesson yet?' he demanded.

'No!' Lisa exclaimed as loud as she could when her face was muffled by the bedclothes and she was teetering on the edge of the biggest climax of her life. 'I need much more. Oh…' She sighed with pleasure as he changed his touch into a stroke.

She was moving now, rubbing herself against him, lifting her buttocks towards his hand, inviting more and more of the delicious taps. She was more aroused than she had ever been. She had needed this. It made her trust him, showed her how right it could be with the right man. She had to have him now—all of him. 'All right, all right—I submit…'

Swinging her round, Tino settled her on the soft bank of pillows. 'Say it, then.'

'Say what?'

'I, Lisa Bond…'

'I, Lisa Bond,' Lisa repeated huskily, holding his stare.

'Submit to whatever you decide will bring me most pleasure.'

'That's far too much for me to remember,' she complained, reaching for him.

'Submit,' he growled, dragging her close.

Lisa's eyes darkened as she looked at him. 'Not without a fight.'

'Of course. I would hate to disappoint you.'

And this time when Tino kissed her he denied her nothing. Just the touch of his warm, naked flesh pressing against her body drew whimpers of pleasure from her lips. His arms were strong and firm around her, and he kissed her passionately, tenderly, letting her show him what she wanted, and then responding with more skill than she could ever have imagined a man might be capable of.

'Oh, Tino, I love—'

He silenced her with another kiss, frightened of what she might say, frightened of the depth of feeling welling inside him. He wasn't supposed to feel anything outside the need to satisfy them both. He was in a hurry to lose himself in sensation and ease the pain that came with knowing he didn't deserve anything good...

'Tino?'

When she saw the expression in his eyes Lisa looked away. The emptiness was too much to bear. Looking into each other's eyes was like looking into a mirror. They were both so frightened of being hurt again, and they'd had more than enough pain as children to last them a lifetime. 'Will you make love to me now?'

He smiled slowly. She was the most desirable woman he had ever met, and she was prompting him? 'I've never had to be reminded of my duty before.'

'Your duty? And I don't want to hear about *before*.'

She was right. She was a virgin. It had to be special for her. He would make sure it was. 'I have to be sure this is what you want.'

'I am sure—and I don't think you need much prompting now.' She wrapped her hands around him.

The breath gusted out of his lungs at her touch. 'That feels so good.'

He had never taken a woman so carefully, so tenderly, or with such tightly reined in passion. Lisa's only experience had been at her own hands. He could understand it, it made perfect sense; she was always in control that way. It made him super-aware of her now, super-sensitive to her breathing, and to the look in her eyes, to the set of her mouth, and to the touch of her hands on his body. He wanted it to be perfect for her. He wanted it to be the first time that either of them had ever felt like this.

Lisa drew in a sharp breath as Tino entered her, and then softened when she felt his brief hesitation. She didn't want him to think he was hurting her and stop. The surprise at his size had been welcome, the panic over almost before it began. She had never imagined it could be like this, that any man could be so tender, that she could feel so cherished, or so safe. 'Please, Tino…please don't stop.'

Caressing her with his warm, strong hands, he did as she asked, tipping her up to meet him so that he could inhabit her completely, and then he groaned as she tightened her muscles around him, drawing him deeper still.

'Are you sure you want this?' He nuzzled her neck as she bucked beneath him.

'Yes, but more than anything I want to please you.'

'You are pleasing me,' he assured her.

He made his strokes deep and slow, relishing the sight of her passion-dampened face. He gave the greatest pleasure he could as the silken noose of her body sucked on him convulsively. He applied a little more pressure at the end of each long thrust until finally she gazed at him in disbelief.

'It's so good,' she managed breathlessly. 'Oh, please don't stop… Don't ever stop.'

Her fingernails raked across his shoulders. He barely felt the pain as he slowed the pace to keep her teetering above the abyss of intense sensation for as long as he could. But then the tension in her face, the absolute hunger in her eyes, as well as the apprehension he sensed in her as she approached pleasure beyond her understanding, proved too much for him, and with a few firm strokes he pushed her over the edge.

She cried out then, joyously, continuously, as if the powerful spasms would never end. He held her firmly and it took all his strength just to keep her in position without hurting her while he made sure that she didn't miss a single, satisfying moment of pleasure.

He calmed her afterwards with long, soothing strokes, until she stirred restlessly again. 'Aren't you satisfied yet?'

'I'll never have enough of you,' she admitted, knowing she meant that in every way.

'What else do you have in mind?'

As he teased her she drew back inwardly into her little shell of uncertainty. She wanted one thing, but Tino wanted something else. And she wanted too much. 'How about I ride you into submission?' The front she could always put in place to hide uncertainty in any given situation had really come into its own, Lisa realised, tossing her hair back provocatively.

'To the finish, if you please.'

'If you insist.'

'I do insist,' Tino assured her, swinging her on top of him.

She eased down on him slowly, and rubbed herself rhythmically against him. She was composed entirely of sensation…

'No,' he insisted softly, 'let me do that for you.'

She gasped and slumped inert as his searching fingers found her, and gently, skillfully, began to work. 'I won't be able to move a muscle if you don't stop doing that.'

'Then I shall have to stop,' he said, pretending regret, 'because I'm holding you to your promise.'

When he took his hand away she started to move again, taking him deep inside her. But then she teased him, pulling back, and making him wait—but he was having none of it, and caught her to him again. Lisa's spirit soared as Tino took control, and as their eyes met in that moment they were one. He touched her delicately, and persuasively, until she could only move convulsively in time to a rhythm of his choice until they climaxed violently together.

Sleeping in Tino's arms was almost the best part of all, Lisa realised. She had woken in the middle of the night, and now she traced the line of his lips with one finger. She gasped as he captured the tip in his mouth. 'I thought you were asleep.'

'Barely.' He narrowed his eyes to look at her. 'In fact, I need very little sleep.'

'That's good to hear.'

'Isn't it?' he said, moving behind her. He nestled close so that he could touch her while he thrust into her. He played her well, judging her responses so finely that she angled herself shamelessly, moving so that he could see everything he was doing to her in the low light seeping into the room from the lanterns outside.

'You're quite a woman,' he murmured later when they were lying twined around each other.

Lisa could only manage to mumble groggily and snuggle a little closer. She felt so safe, so content it was like returning home after an arduous journey...

'Do you know how special you are?' Tino whispered as he stroked Lisa's hair. Her breathing was so even he knew she was asleep. And it was as well she couldn't hear him saying words that would have misled them both—dangerous words...

Instinct warned him to pull back while there was still time. There was only one possible ending to this—and it was the same ending he had envisaged the day he'd walked into the Bond Steel boardroom. And she would hate him when he took the company from her…

Moonlight was streaming into the bedroom as Tino started up in bed wide awake. He had fallen asleep so deeply he could hardly believe the old nightmare had returned. Springing out of bed, he paced the floor. Halting by the window, he gazed out, seeing nothing.

How could a man admit to having nightmares? How could a man live with such images in his mind? Why wasn't his will strong enough to get rid of them?

Hearing Lisa stir, he quietly opened the doors leading onto the balcony and stepped outside. Planting his hands on the stone balustrade, he stared out towards the horizon. Stella was the closest thing he had to a friend, and even Stella Panayotakis didn't know all the things that had happened to him in the orphanage. It was better she never knew… And yet the past had made him the man he was today—it drove his every move. It had given him a private island, unimaginable wealth, and even worldwide respect— the only thing it could never give him was the capacity to love.

He glanced back inside the room where he could see Lisa's hair spread out across the pillow like a cloud. Her face, deep in sleep, was pale and trusting like a child's in the moonlight… His appetite to compete with her, to subdue her in every way, had deserted him utterly. If he had been capable of love, he would have loved Lisa Bond. But learning to love, like learning to feel, was a luxury he could never buy. And more importantly he had embarked upon a journey that no one else could share…a lifelong journey that demanded everything of him, a journey that drove him from deal to deal in the endless quest for money to fund his dream, to sustain his project…

It shamed him that he had set out to triumph over her.

Taking Bond Steel from Lisa was one victory he didn't
need…but there was something he could do to salve his
conscience. He would buy her small engineering works. He
would give her the break she so desperately needed… He
would give a little, just this once. She deserved that much—
as that was all he could give. He would send the necessary
information right away.

He would have liked to do more for her, but anything
on a personal level was out of his reach. Straightening up,
Tino stretched out his powerful limbs and turned his face
up to the stars. He was a man people envied, a man who
could buy anything he desired, but he was a man with nothing, because he had nothing to give. He had nothing to offer
Lisa other than money and sex—and she deserved someone
better than that. Someone better than him.

Lisa woke to another beautiful day. But then every day was
more beautiful than the last on Stellamaris. Stretching languorously in Tino's bed, she felt the empty space at her
side and looked around for him. The room was empty. He
would be swimming, she remembered, sighing deeply with
contentment.

Propping herself up on the soft bank of pillows, she
viewed the spacious room with interest. A mischievous
smile curved her lips. She hadn't taken it all in the previous
night, because Tino had demanded all her attention.

It was much as she might have expected: a man's
space—marble floors, state-of-the-art sound centre, plain
walls, neutral colours, and a couple of extraordinary pieces
of modern art on the walls. Hockney, Lisa realised as she
identified the vibrant images created by the British artist
from Bradford.

Tino's room. Smiling to herself, Lisa snuggled back on
the pillows. She had never felt like this before… She had
been waiting for Tino Zagorakis all her life. Even when

she closed the biggest deal, or when she remembered the day her father had handed over the reins of Bond Steel to her—nothing, *nothing* came close to the way she was feeling now, after spending the night in Tino's arms.

She had felt safe in his arms...*in a man's arms*. She had felt cherished for the first time in her life. She had felt Tino's arms around her, sometimes seeking nothing more than an affectionate hug, which had meant more to her than she could safely express without breaking down and spoiling the day with ugly comparisons.

She had never known affection; she had never known how wonderful a touch, a gesture, or just a simple look from someone who really cared for you could be. And then Tino had made love to her...really made love to her. So he really did love her a little bit, even if expressing his emotions didn't come easily to him.

And what a lover. Lisa eased her body on the bed, feeling all the unaccustomed signs of lengthy lovemaking... But they'd had fun too. She had never in her wildest dreams imagined that sex could be such fun. And they had laughed together, as much as they had desired each other, and felt a ravening hunger for each other. They had laughed together...

She laughed now, dashing away tears of sheer emotion. She had never thought of herself as an emotional person before; she'd spent all of her life hiding her emotions, pretending they didn't exist. But one night with Tino had reduced her to an emotional mess. What she felt for him was so wonderful, so unexpected, such a revelation, she didn't have a clue how she was going to handle all the feelings competing for space inside her.

Leaping out of bed, she hunted for his bathroom. Doors, doors: closets, dressing-rooms—one with nothing but casual shirts and jeans, another with suits at one end, and those see-through-fronted drawers at the other, holding goodness knew what. She was laughing again by the time she found the bathroom. As she might have expected, it was fabulous. Clad in black marble, the shower alone was big enough for a rugby team! She wouldn't waste time on a bath, though that was easily big enough for two... She had seen baths like it in magazines, but even in her own rather splendid bathroom at the villa there was nothing approaching this scale of opulence. Once she was showered, and dressed casually in cream cotton trousers and a sky-blue short-sleeved shirt, she knew exactly what she wanted to do...

What this room needs is a woman's touch, Lisa reflected as she turned full circle still fixing her hair in a casual ponytail. Flowers...flowers like the ones Tino had sent to her room, only even better than those... She would go downstairs and seek the gardener's help.

The kitchen was busy when she found the same young girl who had brought the flowers up to her room. Fortunately, Maria spotted her, and came across at once to see if she could be of help.

'These flowers are for Kirie Zagorakis,' Lisa explained, 'Could you help me with them, Maria? Do you have a vase?'

'*Malista*—of course, Thespinis Bond.' Maria glanced back to where her colleagues were hurrying about.

Lisa thought the young girl looked a little anxious. 'It seems very busy in here. Are you sure I won't get you into trouble?'

'No, I am happy to help you,' Maria assured her. 'Come over here, Thespinis Bond. You can arrange them at the sink we use for such things.'

The flowers were magnificent. Lisa had chosen them to complement the reds, orange, green and pinks of the Hockney painting. Gazing round Tino's room, she decided to set them on a low Swedish-style table opposite the picture.

Standing back to admire her handiwork, she sighed. 'Perfect.' Now all she had to do was to find Tino and spring the surprise on him. Why shouldn't men have romantic gestures made to them? She could already picture them, arms linked as she dragged him along, teasing him… He would pretend to hold back… He would be puzzled, but laughing—they would both laugh. She couldn't wait to see his face when she brought him back to his room…

Tino frowned as he cut the line. Lisa wasn't in her room. No one in the house seemed to know where she had gone. He should have woken her…but she had looked so peaceful. She would be down on the beach, he guessed, and if so it would be hours before she returned…

He rang the housekeeper, and asked her to send someone down to the beach to find Thespinis Bond for him. The kitchen was in uproar, he could hear all the hectic preparations in the background. It pleased him to know that his household was equal to any task he set them. He ran a tight ship, a successful ship; everything on Stellamaris ran like clockwork…

CHAPTER EIGHT

'LISA—'

Lisa blenched as Tino sprang to his feet.

She felt sick…sick and stupid all at once. It wasn't a feeling that crept up on her as she gazed around the room Maria had directed her to; it hit her straight in the stomach like a blow.

The men gathered around the boardroom table were all in business suits—lightweight, but formal nonetheless. Tino, of course, was dressed casually, but in his own particular style that denoted rank as well as authority. His jeans were expensive, his shirt beautifully tailored, and as always he was immaculately groomed. His thick, wavy black hair—the same glossy black hair she had laced her fingers through, moulding the scalp beneath with an urgency approaching frenzy when he had made love to her; *that hair*—was swept back from his handsome brow and was still slightly damp, as if he had only just emerged from the shower after his swim…

Everyone was staring at her…and these were hard-bitten men, her men, along with Tino's board of directors—chosen for their business acumen, not for their compassion. She was horribly exposed—without make-up, her hair casually arranged, her feet bare, her clothes simple.

To Tino's credit, he came around the table to her at once. 'Excuse us, gentlemen. I will be back with you shortly.'

Guiding her out, he closed the door behind them quietly and leaned back against it, as if to ensure they could not be followed.

Lisa managed, 'I didn't realise—' before Tino shut his eyes, as if he accepted part of the blame…as if she should have known, as if the moment she had walked into the room had been as agonising for him as it had been for her.

'No one could find you. Where the hell were you?'

'In the garden.' Her voice was shaking. 'In the kitchen, and then back in your room.'

'They must have missed you. I tried to find you, Lisa, to warn you I'd set up an emergency meeting—I sent people to find you.'

'I don't understand… What's everyone doing here?'

'You wanted this deal so badly…I thought if I brought everyone over—' He stopped and looked at a point somewhere over her head. 'I wanted to give you the best chance. My people have identified a better deal with Clifton—but you already know that.'

'Tino?' Her voice sounded small, and wounded, and Lisa hated herself for the weakness, but she wasn't in charge of her body now, or her powers of speech.

'You'd better go and get changed—'

Tino sounded so cool, so businesslike, so logical…so distant…

'I will call for coffee—it will distract them,' he said, as if he was thinking out loud. 'By the time you return, they will have forgotten. When you come back, they will have forgotten what they saw, and think only of business, of the money to be made.'

There was nothing in his eyes for her, Lisa realised. *Nothing.* Even now that he was looking straight at her, there was nothing there, nothing at all… She might have imagined what had happened between them the previous night for all the recognition there was in that stare. It was back to business. 'You're quite sure of all this, are you, Tino?' she said coldly. 'You're quite sure they will have forgotten what a fool I just made of myself?' She hardened her mouth, her face, her mind, and her heart, kicking herself back into cold, emotion-free business mode. Jack Bond was right, after all—there was no room for emotion in business.

'I'll be back in exactly a quarter of an hour,' she said briskly when Tino didn't say a word. 'I'll want to start the meeting promptly, so see the coffee is cleared away by then.'

Lisa spent the rest of that day with her head buried in figures, balance sheets and predictions. She had never welcomed them more.

Tino was right about one thing: there had been a brief tension when she'd walked back into the room. But once she was safely dressed in business armour—sharp suit, crisp white blouse, heels clacking in a steady, reassuring rhythm across the marble floor—her confidence had quickly been restored. Everyone could see that everything was back to normal: her hair neatly dressed in its customary chignon, her lips carefully outlined in peach, her make-up applied with a steady hand… Only her heart was in pieces, and that was the one thing no one could see.

Lisa had her head bent over the document under discussion and was almost caught out when everyone around her started shuffling papers. The meeting was over. She added a few last thoughts to cover for her abstraction, and then tensed when Tino had the final word…

'I would like you all to be my guests this evening at dinner. Shall we say nine o' clock, gentlemen…and Lisa?'

He didn't look at her directly. She might have been someone he had only just met, another suit who had come to Stellamaris on the same flight as the rest. She added her own half-hearted grunt to the general murmur of acceptance, and then, collecting up her things, she started to load her briefcase.

'Lisa.'

Lisa flinched even though it was only her PA, Mike, calling to her. She was a bundle of nerves on top of everything else. That was what happened when you let your guard down—everything went to pieces. She turned around smiling, mask in place—or so she thought. Mike quickly drew her out of earshot.

'Shit, Lis'! What's happened?'

Lisa stared in amazement. Mike...beautiful Mike, with his astute blue eyes, carefully shaped brows, and expensive highlights neatly sculpted to his gorgeous, gorgeous face, never swore, never called her by a pet name, even though they had known each other for years. Was it that obvious? 'Is it obvious, Mike?' she asked him in a tense whisper, glancing around.

Taking her arm, he turned her so she faced the wall, so they both did. He put his head very close to hers, and put his arm around her protectively. 'Are you OK, Lisa? Can I do anything for you?'

What was happening to her? Lisa wondered, fighting back tears. Was she falling apart? She felt a handkerchief pressed into her hands, and nodded briskly, applying it to her mascaraed eyes as cautiously as was practicable when you were mopping up a waterfall.

'No, that's fine—you keep it,' Mike said when she absent-mindedly attempted to hand the ruined silk back to him.

She made a mental note to buy him a dozen more to replace it the moment she got back home.

'Lisa!' Mike hissed imperatively out of the corner of his mouth. 'Can I do anything for you, anything at all? Can I get you out of here?'

She saw the sense in that. 'Yes, please, Mike, that would be great.'

Putting a shielding arm out in front of her face, Mike swept them both out of the room as only he could, with *élan*, with chin tipped at a formidable angle, as if he were protecting the Queen of England from unwanted attention.

'That was a great exit,' Lisa admitted shakily when they reached the drive. Taxis were pulling up ready to take the men back to the Zagorakis guest house.

'Your voice is still wobbly,' Mike observed, 'and your face is a mess.'

'Thank you for your honesty—I think.'

'Someone has to be honest with you, Lisa.'

Lisa turned to look at him. 'You're right. I value your opinion… You do know that, don't you?'

'Thank you,' he said, preening a little. 'It's always nice to hear that you do.'

'In future, I'm going to be very different.'

'Not too different, I hope.' Mike frowned. 'There is a certain kudos in being the trusted advisor of one of the most difficult women in business today.'

'Is that what they say about me?'

'Close.'

'Hmm.' Lisa nodded thoughtfully. 'Actually, Mike, there is something else you could do for me.'

'Name it,' he said frankly.

'Sit next to me tonight. I've had enough of Zagorakis's attempts to manipulate me.'

'It would be my pleasure.'

Lisa chose the most glamorous gown she could find amongst her new clothes. It was a lacy confection that fell off one shoulder, and had a short tight skirt with a flirty tail that kicked out at one side. She brushed her hair until it gleamed like silk, and applied her make-up with unusual care—too much of it…

Far too much of it, Lisa decided, staring into the mirror. She could hear her father's sneering voice; it still haunted her. 'Your mother always wore too much make-up when she was upset.'

'And I wonder why that was, Daddy?' Lisa muttered, slapping cleansing cream onto her face.

Slipping out of the dress, she left it on the floor. Pulling on her own suit trousers and her own sensible shoes, she weakened as far as a plain ivory silk shirt was concerned when it came to plundering the collection of new clothes in her wardrobe. And that was only because she knew the evening would be warm even if they were seated outside, and she couldn't bear to be stifling in a jacket—and her own white blouse had already been taken from the room to be laundered.

She collected her hair in a loose pony-tail at the nape of her neck. Nothing too frivolous; nothing that could be construed as an attempt to win anyone's attention. Face tonic to freshen up, and then some tinted moisturiser, and a slick of lip-gloss. She confined herself to a smidgen of mascara, and a spritz of perfume later she was ready—just at the moment Mike knocked on the door.

He looked fantastic, as always. Lisa felt dowdy by comparison—and clearly looked it too, from Mike's disappointed expression.

'Oh, no… No, no, no,' he exclaimed, shaking his head. 'The minute we get back home, I'm taking you in hand.'

'I look that bad?'

'You look like a sleek, beautiful leopard masquerading as a mouse.'

'As good as that?'

'Shall we?' Mike said, offering her his arm.

Tino glanced at her, and then looked away as she walked arm in arm with Mike onto the patio. The other men were already sipping drinks, and hadn't noticed her at all. Waiters were moving amongst the small gathering with canapés, and more drinks, and absolutely everyone was in dinner suits, including Tino.

'You know what?' Mike whispered in her ear.

'What?'

'You look as out of place now as you did when you walked into the boardroom earlier today. Why don't we about-turn, and I'll sort you out?'

'Are you serious?' He clearly was, Lisa realised, when Mike wheeled her away.

As she opened the door of the first wardrobe Mike threw up his hands in a paroxysm of delight.

'Designer heaven!' He flicked expertly along the rail. 'We'll take this, and this... Oh, and this.' Holding the gossamer-fine beaded and sequinned shawl up close against his Ozwald Boateng jacket, he sighed theatrically.

Closing her eyes briefly, Lisa shook her head and smiled. She wasn't going to get out of the room again until Mike had his way—she might as well give in.

'Mike, you're my fairy godmother,' Lisa exclaimed a little while later, staring transfixed at her reflection in the full-length mirror.

'Fairy godsister, please... Well, what do you think?'

'What do you think is more to the point,' Lisa said, turning around to smile at him.

'Well, that brute of a Greek isn't going to ignore you now, that's for sure,' he said with satisfaction, offering Lisa his arm.

Mike made her pause just inside the door where the light was a little brighter than on the patio. There wasn't quite an audible gasp, but there might as well have been. Every man had turned to stare.

Mike had dressed her hair high so that she looked taller than usual, and a few softening tendrils had been allowed to escape around her carefully made-up face. Mike had designed her make-up too, to complete the 'look', as he called it, with all the care he might have applied to one of his famously fabulous room settings. Her eyes were smoky, her lashes black… Her lips were full and glossy red, and there was just a hint of rouge to define her cheekbones—the end result? She looked like something out of *Vogue* or *Tatler*— anyway, quite unlike herself, Lisa decided.

She had never gone for full-on glamour in her life before, but, of course, Mike did nothing by halves. The strappy sandals he'd insisted she wear had stratospheric heels, and the dress he had chosen was cut, appropriately enough, with a nod to ancient Grecian styling. Cunningly draped, it fitted where it touched, and was extremely elegant, yet sexy— with a slit up the side to a point where Lisa felt quite a draft, especially as Mike had specifically ruled out the wearing of underwear.

Seeing Tino swallow, she rejoiced.

'Up yours, Zagorakis,' Mike murmured, showing his own feelings were somewhat less subtle.

'Mike, please,' Lisa whispered, finding a smile had crept onto her own lips. 'Gentlemen,' she said casually, dipping her head minutely to acknowledge everyone.

There was a stampede to be the first to find her a drink, a canapé, a seat if she wanted one; only Tino stood back, his face a mask she couldn't read.

The evening was delightful, the food delicious—or that would have been the press-release version, Lisa realised cynically, glancing at Tino. Having chosen a seat as far away from her as possible, he was deep in conversation with his financial director.

'I shall sulk.'

Lisa turned as Mike spoke to her.

'I've gone to all this trouble and you're staring at him like a lovesick ninny. Honestly, Lisa, if he wasn't so gorgeous, I'd be quite put out.'

'I'm sorry, Mike.' She touched his arm. 'Was I being so obvious?'

'Well, luckily for you, he didn't notice. He's far too busy talking business.'

'Time to mingle again,' she suggested.

The dinner was over, last dregs of coffee and brandy had been drunk. Mike half rose—Lisa stopped him, putting her hand on his arm. 'Mike, can I come back with you to the guest house?'

'Of course…but why?'

'Well, I've been staying here at the villa.'

'I know.'

'And now…'

Mike held his hands up to silence her. 'You don't have to say another word—as long as you're quite sure about this?'

Lisa followed Mike's gaze to where she could see Tino turning on the charm. He looked fiendishly fabulous: stronger, taller, and more interesting than any other man present, talking easily to everyone, except her. She caught a flash of white teeth as he responded to another man's comment, and then a fierce, black-eyed stare when he caught her looking at him. 'I'm absolutely sure.'

'OK, then, but we have to brave the receiving line, or whatever the opposite of that might be,' Mike informed her briskly. 'Come along, darling, everyone else is starting to leave now. You just stay with me, and I'll see you through it safely.'

There were some things even Mike couldn't fix.

'Where do you think you're going?' Tino said.

'I'm going to the guest house with Mike.'

Instead of arguing with her, Tino took hold of Mike's elbow, and drew him to one side, leaving Lisa standing alone out of earshot. And when Mike half turned to her, Tino put his hand on his arm and drew him back again to say something more. To Lisa's amazement, Mike, her right-hand man, her PA, her friend, walked away without another word, and when she tried to go after him Tino caught hold of her arm and held her back.

'What the hell do you think you're doing?' she demanded, looking down at his hand on her arm.

'I might ask you the same question,' he replied icily.

'It's clear you don't want me here, so I'm going to where I am wanted.'

'You're talking like a spoiled brat, Lisa.'

He led her back inside the house, and closed the door. 'Did you have to make such an exhibition of yourself?'

'Do you have to hold my arm so tightly?'

He released her immediately. 'You'd better come into my study and we'll talk there.'

'We've nothing to discuss.'

'So, this is the thanks I get?'

'Thanks? For what?' Lisa demanded incredulously. 'For making a fool out of me?' She tried to push past him and go outside again to find Mike, but he blocked the door.

'All this is for you, Lisa.'

'And you didn't think to tell me you had called my people over?'

'I wanted to surprise you.'

'Well, you certainly did that.'

'I tried to find you...I tried to warn you they were here, but no one knew where you were.'

Lisa smiled bitterly. 'Maybe because I was doing something for you.'

'What?'

'It really doesn't matter now.' She reached past him to the door handle. 'Let me out of here now, Tino.'

'Or what?'

'I call for the police, and tell them you're holding me against my will?'

Tino held her stare. 'On Stellamaris, I *am* the police.'

'Well, I'm happy for you. Now will you call for a taxi to take me to the guest house, or do I have to make that call?'

Seizing her arm, he marched her down the corridor towards his study. When they got inside, he slammed the door and stood with his back to it. 'Would you mind telling me what all this is about?' His angry gesture encompassed every inch of Lisa, from her beautifully coiffed hair to her shell-pink toenails peeping out of the glamorous sandals, and before she could answer he added, 'Did you have to make such a show of yourself in front of all those men?'

'Are you jealous, Tino?'

'Jealous? Of a tramp?'

Her stinging blow caught him full on the face, shooting his head back. He stared at her in total disbelief, nursing his chin.

Lisa could hardly believe what she had done. She hated violence of any sort. She despised it. And now she had sunk to the lowest level possible. It didn't matter that Tino thoroughly deserved it; nothing would ever excuse such a loss of control. 'I should never have done that.'

'You pack quite a punch.' He nursed his chin.

'That was unforgivable.' She had never lost control before, not even to the extent where she had cursed at someone. She didn't know herself any more, and she didn't like the person she had become.

'I'm sorry too.'

She looked at him.

'I shouldn't have called you those names.'

They were apologising to each other? What was happening? They had plumbed the extremes of emotion together, and now the carefully controlled Tino Zagorakis was bending towards the equally unyielding Lisa Bond?

'Stay on.'

'What?' Now she *was* astonished.

'Stay on at the Villa Aphrodite until Friday, as we agreed. We haven't finished our discussions yet—and this is a big place, Lisa. I'll keep out of your way; you keep out of mine.'

If there had only been business between them, that would have made perfect sense... And there was only business between them, Lisa reminded herself. Tino had just made that clear. So, why couldn't she stay?

But where had it all gone? Where had all the passion and tenderness gone? If this was the life expectancy of the average love affair, she could do without them. She should have known the closeness between them was only an illusion. As Jack Bond had said when he'd thrown earth on her mother's coffin: 'Any woman who expects too much out of life is destined to be disappointed.'

CHAPTER NINE

WHEN she woke the next morning Lisa lay in bed propped up on pillows, staring at the sea, knowing she would never be able to look at the ocean again without thinking about the day she spent on Tino's boat...

For that one short day they had been so close... Thinking that would last was as foolish as expecting the morning mist to hang around. They were both far too sensible to get close to anyone. She had just been swept away by the madness that affected many women from cold northern climes—she had seen another way of life, another type of man, and imagined that she could slip easily into his world.

Hearing a tap on the door, she slid out of bed. Grabbing a robe, she hurried to find the same friendly young maid standing outside.

'Would you like to take breakfast on your balcony again this morning, Thespinis Bond?'

Lisa hesitated. Why should she be confined to barracks? She had reached an accommodation with Tino. There was no reason why she shouldn't go down for breakfast. There were still a few points she wanted to discuss with him off the record before their teams joined them later. 'Would it be any trouble to you if I had my breakfast downstairs, Maria?'

'No trouble at all, Thespinis Bond. I will set a place for you on the patio right away.'

Another new outfit! It couldn't be helped, Lisa thought as she checked her appearance in the mirror. She would pay back Tino for everything she had worn, and then perhaps negotiate directly with the boutiques for the other

124

clothes and accessories. Everything was so beautiful, it was hard to let any of it go.

Lisa's heart was thumping as she walked onto the patio. It didn't matter what type of agreement she had agreed to; after all that had happened between them she still had a lot of readjusting to do.

'*Kalimera*, Lisa.'

There was no sign of Tino. Lisa didn't know whether to be relieved or not, but she was happy to see Stella Panayotakis sitting at the breakfast table... 'I didn't expect to see you today, Stella. What a lovely surprise.'

'For me too,' Stella assured her. 'Won't you join me?'

She indicated the place next to her, and Lisa saw that this was the only other place set at the table.

'Tino will not be joining us this morning,' Stella explained, seeing her glance. 'He's been called away.'

'I see...' Called away? Avoiding her after everything that had happened between them was more likely, she suspected.

'Tino didn't tell you?'

'No, and we're supposed to be holding meetings all this week.' She couldn't keep the tension out of her voice.

'I am sure Constantine would not have left the island unless it was important, Lisa.'

'I'm sure you're right, Stella. But I can't understand why he just didn't warn me. I'm sorry, Stella, I know this isn't your fault, but the issues I have come here to discuss with him are really important. And Tino is just so...unpredictable. Nothing happens without his approval.'

'Please don't get upset—and you don't need to apologise. I can see how much this means to you.' Sitting back in her chair, Stella stared at Lisa in silence for a moment. 'The people in your company are very lucky to have you for their champion, Lisa.'

Stella's endorsement only made Lisa more aware of the

responsibility she had towards her co-workers at Bond Steel. 'Do you know how I can get in touch with him? Do you know where Tino's gone, Stella?'

'I'm afraid I can't help you, Lisa.'

Can't help me, or won't help me? Lisa wondered, sensing Stella was watching her words as if she was protecting Tino for some reason.

'What time is your first meeting this morning?'

Stella's question prompted Lisa to refocus on the older woman's face. 'Ten o'clock.'

'But it's only eight o'clock. Why don't you come down to the beach with me for a stroll before you start work? You never know, Lisa—Constantine may have been in contact with his household by the time you return to the villa.'

'I'd love to come with you.' Lisa sighed.

'Then why not indulge yourself for once?'

'All right.' She smiled. It was hard not to when Stella was around.

'Shouldn't you change first?' Stella suggested, glancing at Lisa's elegant outfit.

'Will you give me five minutes?'

'Of course.'

They took the funicular down to the beach. 'It's great to be able to admire the view without picking your way down the cliff face,' Lisa admitted wryly.

'You should never do that, Lisa!' Stella warned. 'That cliff is for mountain goats, and crazy men like Tino.'

Lisa seized the opening: 'Have you known Tino for long?'

'It seems like for ever.' Stella quickly became guarded again. 'Look,' she said, pointing out to sea. 'Can you see the dolphins, Lisa?'

Stella's adroit change of subject didn't bode well for discovering facts about Tino. Her reluctance to talk about him made Lisa more certain than ever that both of them were hiding something.

When they reached the beach and the doors slid open, the first thing Lisa saw was another couple. Engrossed in each other, they were standing at the water's edge with their fingers entwined. The young woman's face turned up to her dark-haired companion was like a pale flame in the morning light. A stab of jealousy made Lisa hesitate and want to turn back. Had Tino been lying to her all along? And Stella too? No, not Stella…Stella would *never* lie to her. But she didn't want to see… She didn't want to be sure… She couldn't bear to be so cruelly disillusioned. 'I'm sorry, Stella. I should never have come down to the beach. There really isn't time… I should go back and prepare for the meeting.'

'You work too hard, Lisa. You should make a little time for yourself.'

Lisa's glance slipped back to the couple standing at the water's edge.

Misreading her interest, Stella grabbed hold of her arm, and started to lead her across the sands. 'You must meet my daughter.'

'Arianna and I have already met—briefly, at the villa when I first arrived.'

'Then let me introduce you properly,' Stella insisted, giving Lisa's arm a little tug.

It wasn't Tino! *It wasn't Tino*… As they drew closer and Lisa saw her mistake she instantly regretted her suspicions, and when Stella began the introductions she discovered that, like Arianna, Giorgio was also an opera singer, an Italian tenor of some renown. He and Arianna were due to start a week's rehearsals for a major new production at the Covent Garden Opera House in London. Of course, that was why Stella had been staying at the villa, Lisa realised.

She had wanted to give the two lovers some space, before world attention intruded on their personal lives.

'I have something to ask you, Stella.'

Lisa looked up at Arianna's handsome companion, and then looked at Stella.

'Not yet, Giorgio,' Stella warned, her eyes twinkling.

'No,' Arianna agreed. 'We must wait for Tino.'

Wait for Tino? Lisa's mouth hardened. Why did he have to be part of this? Could no deal be struck, not even a love match, without his seal of approval? Why should Arianna's happiness depend on him? She couldn't understand it. Surely Stella's approval was all that mattered?

'Arianna is right, Giorgio,' Stella said, 'You must be patient. We have to wait for Tino to return.'

With a heartfelt groan, Giorgio looked for some relief from Arianna, but she only shrugged and kissed him impulsively on the cheek. 'Waiting will make everything that much better,' she insisted.

Every mention of Tino's name was like a burr in Lisa's side. It was growing increasingly hard to hide her feelings. 'How long do you expect Tino to be away from the island, Stella?'

'He will be back when he has finished his other business.'

Arianna's face lit up with understanding. 'Ah, so Tino has gone to the—'

'Arianna!' Stella silenced her daughter with a look. 'We will talk about this later.'

Why had they all turned to stare at her now? Lisa wondered. Why was she being left out of the loop? Didn't any of them trust her? She held in her feelings, but it seemed as good a time as any to leave. 'It's been lovely meeting you, Giorgio, and seeing you again, Stella, Arianna—' she glanced apologetically at her shorts and bare feet '—but I really have to go now.'

'I guess that's not your business uniform?' Giorgio suggested.

'Next time you must share our breakfast,' Arianna offered warmly.

She had been wrong to doubt any of them, Lisa realised, but where Tino was concerned she couldn't think straight. 'I'd love to.' But there wouldn't be another time, Lisa realised, giving Stella an impulsive hug. Breaking away, she ran across the beach without glancing back.

As the funicular took her slowly up the cliff Lisa noticed the three figures were still standing in the same place waving to her, but then her vision blurred and she couldn't see them any longer.

As Lisa had suspected, the meeting soon reached a point where Tino's presence was essential. No one breathed at Zagorakis Inc without his say-so—and time was running out. 'I think we'll have to call it a day here, gentlemen.'

'My apologies everyone. I hope the meeting went OK without me?'

Lisa stared. Tino had just walked into the room as if he had never been away. 'Yes, what a shame you missed it.' She reached for her briefcase. Five days…*five lousy days*, were all they had agreed upon—and he couldn't even make it past two.

'That will be all, everyone. We will reconvene tomorrow.'

Lisa tensed as he took control, adding her own rider, 'Yes, thank you everyone.'

As the men filed out Tino pointed to the chair she had just vacated.

'The meeting is over, Tino.'

'And I want to hear what went on.'

'I'm sure one of your team will fill you in.' Picking up her briefcase, she tried to move past him.

'But I want you to tell me.'

'OK, then, shut the door.' She stayed where she was while he crossed the room to see to it. 'You couldn't even be bothered to make the meeting, so why are you so interested now in what went on?'

'My interest in the deal has never wavered.'

'Unlike your interest in our agreement?'

Leaning back on the door, he stared at her. 'Stop this, Lisa. I called the meeting, didn't I?'

'So you should have been here when it started—except you couldn't be, because you had to be somewhere else, somewhere more important.'

'I thought it was agreed that we have no hold over each other.'

'No hold over each other? So, that night we spent in bed was simply recreation for you—a little pleasure on the side? Didn't you think there might be consequences?'

'Consequences? Why should there be consequences? I took precautions.'

Lisa's face flamed red. Tino was always top of the class where practicalities were concerned. He had wanted a few guilt-free hours of pleasure, of release—it meant no more to him than that. But was she any better? She had lost control, and now she had to pay the price—but not for very much longer. 'You'll have to find someone else to fill you in on the meeting, Tino.'

He stood aside to let her pass, but as she swept past he reached out and stopped her. 'Are you coming to the dinner tonight?'

'At the fish restaurant? No—I'm going to start my packing this evening.' She stared coldly at his hand on her arm.

'Of course, you must have a lot of things to pack. Would you like me to have some extra suitcases brought to your room?'

She reddened, second-guessing his thoughts. 'I'm going

to pay you for everything. It's all—' She stopped, feeling awkward.

'Chosen with care,' he murmured sardonically.

She knew that wasn't true. Holding his gaze, she smiled faintly. They really were as bad as each other. 'I can just imagine.'

'So, we'll meet again tomorrow morning?'

This time Tino not only stood back, but held the door wide for her, and Lisa felt that deserved a little information: 'We may be able to sign before Friday—things went really well this morning.'

'I shall have to confirm that with my team.'

Wasn't her word good enough? She firmed her voice. 'And I'll be leaving the moment we sign.'

'We have an agreement.'

'An agreement you broke.'

'I'm here now.'

'That's hardly the point. You were the one who said we couldn't cherry-pick agreements.'

'I had to be somewhere else.' His mouth flattened uncompromisingly.

Secrets…always secrets. 'You can't just bend our agreement to suit yourself.'

'I'd say we've got a pretty good agreement. Didn't you say we're about to cut a deal in record time?'

'I'll see you tomorrow, Tino.'

He stood in her way.

'Do you mind?' She waited, but this time he didn't stand aside.

Closing the door, he locked it. 'What the hell do you think you're doing?'

'I have another proposition for you.'

'It's too late for that, Tino. I've got everything I could possibly want from you.'

'I don't think so,' he argued softly.

'I must have missed something.'

'What have you missed, Lisa? This?'

Before she could respond he dragged her close. She whipped her face away when he tried to kiss her.

'Let's get rid of this first.' Seizing her briefcase, he tossed it onto a chair.

'What do you think you're doing? Don't play games with me, Tino! Let me out of here right now.'

'If I thought you really wanted to leave, I'd let you go immediately.'

'You don't know what I want.' She fought him. 'I don't believe this.'

'Do you believe this?'

Holding her firm with one hand, he cupped her face with the other and brushed her mouth with his lips until he drew a ragged moan from the very depths of her soul. 'I don't think you want to leave just yet, do you, Lisa?'

She was trembling as he teased the seam of her mouth with his tongue, and then because she wanted to, because she had to, because she couldn't stop herself, she pressed herself against him, and then her mind was wiped clean of everything but the need to have sex with him.

Tino removed her tailored trousers in one easy move-ment with the cobweb-fine briefs she was wearing under them. She gasped with relief hearing the foil package rip. 'Oh, yes, please.' And burrowed her face into his chest as he lifted her…

It was the most reckless thing she had ever done. The windows were unshuttered, the drapes fully open. Anyone walking past couldn't miss what was happening inside the room. It only fuelled her excitement.

Tino lowered her down on top of the boardroom table and lifted her legs to lock them around his waist.

'This is madness.'

'Yes, isn't it?' he agreed.

He was so matter-of-fact he made her mad for him, and when his warm breath tickled her ear she shuddered uncontrollably.

'This is what you want, isn't it, Lisa? It's what we both want.'

Her eyes were growing heavy-lidded with desire. 'It's what we both need,' she agreed throatily.

'Oh, yes, we need it,' Tino murmured as he passed the tip of his erection between her legs. 'You're so wet.'

She leaned back against his arm at a better angle for him.

'You're so beautiful,' he teased, drawing back a little, 'maybe I'll just look at you instead.'

'Don't, Tino,' Lisa warned. 'I can't wait any longer.'

'In that case…'

A low moan of pleasure flowed from her lips as he eased himself into her.

'Better?'

'Much, much better,' Lisa agreed, closing her muscles around him as her voice tailed away. She felt wonderful…he completed her…

'There's no hurry…just relax, and enjoy yourself.'

He behaved as if they had all day, as if they were alone on the island! 'But if anyone should come around the back of the villa—'

'The only person who is going to come is you, and, after that, me.'

His tone was dry and amused, but Lisa detected a strand of tension. The possibility of discovery excited him, she realised. 'You have less to lose than I do if we are discovered.'

'Is that so?' He thrust deep, forcing her to collapse against him with a groan of delight.

'It's true,' she managed to gasp. 'You will be hailed as a stud, whereas I—'

'Talk far too much.'

If Tino hadn't been holding her so securely she might have slipped to the floor, Lisa realised as they both recovered from what had been a shattering climax. She was reluctant to let him go, reluctant to stand alone, reluctant to lose the warmth of his body, and the wonderful feeling of security his strength always gave her.

'Do you feel a little better now?' he teased softly, nuzzling his rough chin against her neck.

'A little better.'

'But not fully sated?'

'Are you?' She let her hands slide up his arms, relishing the feel of naked power flexing beneath her searching fingertips.

Tino smiled as he eased out of her, and then he looked past her out of the window. 'What perfect timing.' Moving in front of Lisa, he shielded her.

Then she saw the group of men heading for the beach. 'You knew,' she breathed incredulously. 'You knew they could walk past here at any moment.'

'Don't tell me the possibility of discovery didn't excite you too?'

She couldn't admit that it had.

'Do you think I got all this by being cautious?' he gestured around.

'No, I don't suppose you did.' But did she want to become part of his risk culture?

'So, Lisa—do you still want to rush back to the UK when we sign the contract?'

Truthfully, no. Even with all the warnings she'd been giving herself she still wanted him. She wanted him so badly she knew it was dangerous...out of control. 'I must reassure everyone at Bond Steel as soon as I can.' That was the perfect excuse—so why couldn't she just turn away from him and stay safe?

'You can let them know any number of ways,' Tino pointed out. 'Or you could just send Mike home with the good news. I'm sure he'd like that.'

'I'm sure he would. But why should I stay here with you?'

'Because you want to.'

She held his gaze, wondering if it was safe for her heart to beat so fast. 'You're very sure of yourself.'

'Forty-eight hours of sexual excess? Sounds tempting to me.'

As her gaze strayed to Tino's mouth Lisa knew he was right.

'It's perfect for us, Lisa—no strings, no consequences… I can't offer you the long term, and I know that's the last thing you're looking for.'

In that moment something died inside her, but something far more elemental took its place. 'I'm not sure if I should stay.'

'Yes, you are,' he said confidently. 'And just think of it—we'll be all alone when the others leave the island.'

'Except for your staff.'

'Who are well schooled in discretion. We will be able to extend our area of study into all the extremes of erotic adventure.' He smiled against her mouth. 'We're the same, you and I, Lisa; don't fight it. Looking at you is like looking in the mirror. I don't always like what I see, but at least I always know what you're thinking.'

She wanted sex with him so desperately it was like a kind of madness, but even more than that she longed to be close to him…even though she knew Tino was never going to let that happen.

'So? Give me your answer, Lisa. Do you accept my proposition?'

Gazing up at him, she saw that his warm, wonderful eyes had turned black with erotic promise.

'I accept.'

CHAPTER TEN

THRUSTING his face into his hands, Tino made a rough, animal sound as he paced his room. What was he turning into? What the hell was Lisa turning him into? Right now, he was no better than a rutting beast scenting a female ripe for sex.

And now he was blaming Lisa for his own weakness! As he stood in the centre of his study his face contorted with anger and disgust. What kind of a man did that make him? Was it Lisa's fault that he only had to look at her, or think about her, and he turned into that most primal of men—a man who could think of nothing but possession, and sex?

He couldn't think about business, or Stellamaris, or about any of his other responsibilities, because she filled his every waking moment, as well as his dreams at night. He could see no further than keeping her with him every precious second he could until they both returned to their cold, emotion-free lives. While she was in Stellamaris he could fill his eyes with every nuance and quirk in her expression, fill his nostrils with her scent, and his hands with her silky flesh… He couldn't let her go, not yet. That accounted for his preposterous scheme—an erotic adventure for the next forty-eight hours? He couldn't believe he had suggested it. And he only had because he wasn't capable of committing to anything more, and that shamed him.

They'd shared explosive sex, which accounted for an erotic adventure being the first thing that sprang into his mind, but they'd shared some tender moments too. As he remembered those now his mouth flattened with despair.

He would have done better to take her on a tour of the island. He of all people knew how dangerous it was to play with anyone's feelings—and he had no excuse; he knew she was as scarred as he was. And what? Did he want to hurt her more? The best thing he could have done for Lisa was to stay away from her for good.

In just one day more their business dealings would be concluded. Of course the deal was done. For the first time in his business career he hadn't listened to his advisors, to his own intuition, or to the bald facts as they appeared in columns of figures on the documents that lay untouched on his desk. He could see no further than the fact that Lisa's company desperately needed a cash injection from him, and that he wouldn't let her fail.

She could have had anything she wanted from him, but he knew she would only take what she needed to secure the future of her people. He had been wrong to say they were alike when he was still holding himself aloof, still keeping his true feelings hidden.

He smiled grimly, remembering all the clothes he had ordered for her. He hadn't troubled to choose them himself. Of course he hadn't. When had he ever taken time to do that—even for himself? Money bought more than fabulous clothes, and fast cars, it bought the undivided attention of top people in whatever field he chose to spread his wealth.

Delegating trivia like shopping had always worked fine for him before. He didn't care as long as there was always a clean shirt waiting, but now it wasn't enough. He wanted to choose something special for Lisa, and he wanted to do that without anyone else's interference. He wanted her to have something precious, something unique, something to remember him by.

Making a harsh noise that sounded nothing like a laugh, Tino stared at himself in the mirror, his mouth twisting with self-disgust.

'Come in, Maria.' Lisa recognised the knock on her bedroom door. She was almost ready for dinner, and it was always a pleasure to see the young girl.

'Why, Maria, you look beautiful.'

'We can never wait for anything here in Stellamaris, so the celebrations for May Day have already started in our village,' Maria explained, spreading her hands lovingly down her intricately embroidered skirt. 'We are all in national costume.'

'Well, I think you look absolutely stunning. What a wonderful heritage.'

'You look very lovely too, Thespinis Bond,' Maria said, her black eyes widening as Lisa stood up.

'Thank you, Maria. I only hope Kirie Zagorakis will think so. He bought this dress for me.' Lisa blushed, realising that she had confessed rather more than she ought to, but the jade-green chiffon, though more modest than some of the other gowns in her wardrobe, was perhaps the most beautiful dress she had ever owned, and tonight, in spite of their pact, she wanted Tino to look at her with something other than lust in his eyes.

'What's that, Maria?' Apprehension struck Lisa as she stared at the velvet box in Maria's hands.

'Kirie Zagorakis asked me to bring this to you, Thespinis Bond. He asks you to put them on for him this evening.'

Lisa frowned as she stared at the small velvet case Maria was holding out to her. Maria frowned too, sensing her unease.

'Just leave it over there.' Lisa pointed to her dressing table. She couldn't bring herself to open the small case in front of anyone, not even Maria.

As Maria did as she asked Lisa stepped forward impulsively, and took the young girl's hands between her own. 'You've been very kind to me, Maria.'

'Kind to you?' Maria looked at her with surprise, tilting

up her chin to stare into Lisa's eyes, 'Is no one else kind to you, Thespinis Bond?'

'Of course, they are, Maria.' Lisa looked away briefly. 'But you've made me feel so welcome here.'

Turning at the door, Maria smiled at her. 'I hope you have a lovely evening, Thespinis Bond.'

Lisa circled the jewellery box as if it were an asp. It was just a small box in navy-blue velvet, she told herself sensibly... A small, beautifully made box that looked as if it had come from one of the most exclusive jewellers in Athens. But how could that be possible? Had it been delivered by jet, or by helicopter? Or did Tino keep a stock of such things, just in case—perhaps increasing the value of the gift depending upon the services he had received? The blood drained from her face at the thought of the pleasure they had shared. Was this her payment for it?

Lisa looked at the jewel case again. She wanted to believe it was a spontaneous gift with no strings attached; something she could return without causing offence. She had last seen Tino five hours ago. Plenty of time for a wilful billionaire to call for his jet to go shopping...

But that wasn't Tino's way, Lisa remembered. He ordered in: designer clothes, accessories, jewels, like other men ordered pizza. The amethyst earrings had been a perfect example. Was he upping the ante now, perhaps tempting her with priceless baubles to see if he could push her into becoming the billionaire's bought woman? Exhaling tensely, she picked up the box, and checked her pale reflection one last time in the mirror.

The return of the gift, as well as the confrontation she expected to erupt between them—none of that was possible, Lisa realised as soon as she walked onto the patio. Tonight was clearly a night of celebration for Arianna and Giorgio.

She didn't need anyone to tell her that Tino had given

his permission for the two of them to marry; the joy on each of their faces told its own story.

'Lisa,' Arianna said happily, hurrying forward to draw her into the tightly knit group. 'Giorgio and I are to be married.'

'I'm so happy for you,' Lisa said sincerely. Drawing Arianna to her, she held her close for a moment. She knew Tino was standing just a few feet away. 'Giorgio,' she said, releasing Arianna, 'you're a very lucky man.'

'I know that, Lisa,' Giorgio assured her as he put a protective arm around Arianna's waist.

Tearing her gaze away from them, Lisa went next to Stella, and took both the older woman's outstretched hands in her own, 'This must be a very happy day for you.'

'This is the happiest day of my life,' Stella admitted, dragging Lisa into a bear hug. 'And now I only have one task left to complete on Cupid's behalf.'

'Which is?'

The sound of Tino's voice made Lisa tense in Stella's arms.

'Why,' Stella said, turning from Lisa to Tino, 'I would have thought that was obvious, Constantine. I still have to find someone who will marry you.'

'That is one task far better left undone,' he said softly.

Stella's noncommittal hum made them all laugh.

'Shall we sit down?' Stella suggested. Pointing to a chair, she indicated that Lisa should sit next to Tino.

Discreetly, Lisa put the small velvet case on the table between them.

'Do you want me to put them on for you?' He leaned across.

'No. I do not want you to put them on for me,' Lisa said under her breath, 'whatever *they* might be.'

'You mean you haven't looked?' His voice rose. 'You mean you haven't even opened my gift.'

Everyone was staring at them.

'Forgive me, Stella Panayotakis, Arianna, Giorgio,' he said smoothly. 'I did not mean to interrupt your conversation.'

'Is that a gift for Lisa?' Stella said happily. 'You should give it to her yourself, Tino.'

'No, no, I—'Lisa started to protest as she pushed her chair back from the table. But then she felt Tino's hand on her arm and froze. She couldn't do this. Of course she couldn't do this. She couldn't ruin Arianna's evening. 'Forgive me, everyone.' She found a laugh. 'I've never been very good at receiving gifts.'

'Perhaps that's because you haven't received enough gifts,' Stella remarked, busying herself with some olive-oil dip for her bread.

'What have you bought for Lisa, Tino?' Arianna cut in, dispelling the tension with her excitement. 'I love presents. And, Giorgio—I'm very good at receiving them.'

Everyone laughed, and then Arianna said, 'Well, aren't you going to show us what you have bought for Lisa, Tino?'

He shrugged, and flipped the catch on the jewel case.

There was a stunned silence. The perfectly matched emerald earrings were surrounded by brilliant cut diamonds.

Giorgio was the first to recover. 'Why, they're magnificent,' he said bluntly. 'I've never seen such splendid stones.'

They were everything she had been expecting, and dreading too, Lisa realised as she watched Tino pluck the earrings from their velvet nest.

'I remembered how much you loved the amethysts,' he murmured, brushing back her hair to fix one earring in place. 'And I thought these would be even better, because they will bring out the colour of your eyes.' Cupping her chin in one hand, he brought her round to face him so that Lisa had nowhere to look but straight into his.

'There…I was right,' he murmured, adjusting the second one. 'They're perfect.'

There was a spontaneous round of applause.

She knew he could see the tears building up in her eyes, and she hated herself for the weakness. It took every ounce of will-power and years of practice to hold them back. 'Thank you.' Her voice sounded so wooden. 'The earrings are lovely.'

'And now we go dancing in the village to celebrate,' Stella declared energetically.

'Will you excuse me?' Lisa pushed up from the table. 'I seem to have developed a slight headache… The flickering candles, perhaps.'

'Lisa—' Tino started to get up from the table too, and then Arianna did too.

Stella held her daughter back. 'You must be exhausted, Lisa. I know what these meetings have meant to you. Business has taken everything out of you. You need rest now…rest, and quiet.. and, goodness knows, you won't get that in the village. Tino,' Stella said, turning to him, 'see that you take care of Lisa. She must go to bed with a cup of warm milk.'

'Of course, Stella,' he murmured politely, giving her a small bow.

Was this payback time for the priceless emeralds? Lisa wondered, because, however much she wanted Tino, she could never be bought.

They both stood as still as statues until Stella, Arianna and Giorgio had gone, and then Tino turned to her. 'I'm not sure about the cup of warm milk.'

'Tino, don't.'

'What do you mean, don't?' he said, lifting his warm hands away from her shoulders.

Taking off the earrings, Lisa held them out to him. 'I don't need these.'

'No one *needs* beautiful things, but they are an expression of...'

'Of what, Tino?' Lisa said tensely. 'Possession?'

She could see he was shocked. Perhaps she had gone straight to the heart of the matter. 'Please take them back, Tino. I can't take them. If I did want some new jewellery, I would buy it for myself.'

'But it gave me such pleasure to buy them for you.'

Lisa almost smiled, but it would have been a sad smile. Tino sounded like a small child who couldn't have his own way. They were both spoiled. They spoiled themselves. They had both reached a point where they could buy anything they wanted. And none of it mattered, none of it counted for anything. They were always flailing around thinking that the next purchase would fill the gap in their hearts, but it never did. 'You bought the earrings for me? Did you pick them out yourself? Or did you make a telephone call, and have someone else do that?'

'I took the jet.' His mouth curved a little in wry appreciation of the privileged position in which he found himself.

'So, you did choose them.'

'Yes, of course I did—there's no need to sound so surprised.' Opening his fist, Tino stared down at the priceless gems nestled there. 'I thought you'd like them.'

'I do like them, but—' How could she put her thoughts into words? They were both hopeless, both so clumsy when it came to managing the simplest of human relationships—and theirs was scarcely that. They matched perfectly sexually but something inside was broken—for both of them. 'If you had wanted to give me a gift, why didn't you give me some flowers from the garden, Tino? Like you did before...that would have been lovely.'

'But I wanted to buy you something really special.'

'The flowers were special...but emerald earrings?' Lisa searched for the right words, words that would make sense to a billionaire to whom priceless emeralds would make no more dent in his bank account than another yacht. 'I feel as if you're trying to buy me, Tino—as if you're trying to pay me for my services.' She made a gesture of frustration.

'Your services?' Now he did smile. 'Please.' He held the earrings out to her again. 'Take them back as payment on account.'

'This isn't a joke, Tino.'

'I agree with you.' He lowered his voice. 'Take them, Lisa, I beg you.'

'You beg?' She shook her head. 'Put them away before you lose them, Tino. They will have to be returned. I'm sorry, but you have flown to Athens for nothing.'

'For nothing?' His mouth tugged up wickedly at one corner. 'Are you sure?'

'The earrings must be returned to the jeweller, Tino. We've both made mistakes. We're both useless when it comes to knowing what to do, how to behave in situations that don't involve business.'

'Is that what we have between us—a situation?'

'Today is Wednesday and I'm going home on Friday. Let's not make any more of this than we should...please, no more grand gestures, Tino.'

'No more flying to Athens to buy you jewellery, you mean?'

As he gazed at her she saw a glint of humour had returned to his eyes. She pulled away. 'You must be exhausted, after your journey.'

'Not too tired to want you in my bed.' He dragged her back into his arms. 'And I will have my own way on this—with or without emerald earrings, you and I have an agreement to fulfil.'

He carried her upstairs, and, shouldering open the door to his suite, took her straight to the bed.

Lisa watched as he tugged off his shirt. 'Tino, please, this doesn't feel right.'

'Why should we waste time when time is running out? We should make the most of it, don't you think?'

'I just can't do this.' Lisa tensed, expecting him to react to having his male pride badly dented, but instead he surprised her, coming to kneel at the side of the bed.

Taking her hand in his, he raised it to his forehead and closed his eyes. 'Lisa, I'm so sorry... You're right—we're both hopeless cases. Can you forgive me?' He looked up.

'You'll take the earrings back to the jeweller's?'

'If you really don't want them,' he agreed, searching her face. 'I'll do anything for you.'

Yes, but only for the duration of their agreement, Lisa thought sadly. And then Tino smiled at her, and the delicious curve of his mouth, and the laughter in his eyes, won her over.

She would have been frightened of a man like this at one time, Lisa realised, a man who could make her do anything he wanted with his strength alone, but it was the need she saw in him, the need that so perfectly matched her own that made her weaken...

He saw the change in her at once, and eased up from his knees. 'You can't resist me?' he proposed wickedly.

'Was there ever a more arrogant man on the face of this earth?'

'Not here, surely?' He looked at her wryly, and then gazed around. 'I'm standing in the middle of my own bedroom.'

'Then come to me,' Lisa suggested seductively.

Was lovemaking supposed to start with shrieks of laughter, and end like this? Lisa wondered, lying snug in Tino's arms. He had just dropped off to sleep, as well he might after the exertions of the day—and she didn't just have flying in mind, she reflected mischievously, brushing a stray lock of inky-black hair from his eyes. He moaned softly with contentment, and shifted position slightly at her side, drawing her a little closer.

'I think I love you, Tino Zagorakis.' She was safe in the knowledge that he couldn't hear her—but she did love him, Lisa realised with a jolt of happiness. He was everything to her. Tino was everything she had ever dreamed of and far more than she could ever have imagined. He made her laugh…he made sex fun and safe—and he'd found a use for the emerald earrings, though not the use the high-class jeweller would have had in mind when he'd secured the sale… If the jeweller discovered where those earrings had been clipped Tino would never be able to return them!

Burrowing her face into Tino's chest, Lisa kissed him tenderly, but she had disturbed him, and he stirred restlessly, pushing her away in his sleep.

'No…I don't want to.' He thrashed his head on the pillow.

'What don't you want to do, my love?' she said softly, tracing the line of his mouth very gently with her fingertip.

'Don't hurt me.' The words jerked out of him, muddled and indistinct.

Resting up on one elbow, Lisa stared down feeling increasingly alarmed. 'Tino? Are you asleep?' He was fast asleep, she realised, and he was held fast in the grip of some awful dream. 'Tino, please, wake up.'

Lisa's heart was thundering in her chest as Tino shook her off.

'No!' he exclaimed louder than before, jerking away from her.

'Tino!' Shaking his arm, she raised her voice, hoping to get through to him.

'Leave me… Go away… Get out of here!'

His voice, still muffled by the pillows, was barely deci-pherable. But she knew now that he wasn't speaking to her, he was still locked in the dream—and there was something horribly reminiscent of the commune about it.

But surely Tino hadn't lived in a commune? That was too much of a coincidence to swallow, and the world would have heard of it by now—as her past had been played out in the glossies and tabloids. So, what, then? From the little Lisa could unravel, she gathered someone was trying to force him to do something, and Tino was determined to fight them off.

They both had terrible secrets locked inside them like maggots waiting to destroy any chance of happiness that came their way.

'Don't!'

She recoiled from his cry, but the sound of it was so distressing she reached out anyway, braving his flailing limbs. He swore at her viciously in Greek. It was as if in his sleeping mind the language he had been using all night with her, the language of business and Shakespeare and love, had been wiped from his mind by some unspeakable wickedness from his past.

When his breathing finally steadied and he was quiet again, she curled up, nuzzling her head into the hollow between his shoulders, and wrapping her arms protectively around his waist. She lay awake long into the night won-dering if Stella knew… Did anyone know that Tino Zagorakis cried out in his sleep like a wounded child?

'Lisa?'

She held her breath as he turned over, and then she smiled in the darkness to see him returned to his normal self.

'Why are you staring at me?' he murmured so softly she had to lean closer to hear him. 'When you could be here—'

he turned her like lightning so that she found herself beneath him '—kissing me?'

'You were dreaming.'

'Of you,' he said confidently. Lifting himself on his arms, he stared down at her.

'No.' Lisa shook her head. 'Not me, Tino, you were dreaming about something else.'

She cried out—that small excited cry she always gave when he entered her. 'This—I must have been thinking of this,' he insisted, kissing her deeply as he started to move.

CHAPTER ELEVEN

THEY overslept on Thursday morning, waking twenty minutes before the meeting. There wasn't a moment to spare for a kiss, or a lingering touch, there were just shrieks of panic from Lisa, and an amused expression on Tino's face as he jumped out of her way when she scrambled for the shower.

'There's room enough for two,' he pointed out.

She bumped him out of the way when he tried to get in close, soaping herself vigorously. 'Oh, no, you don't—I know what two in a shower can lead to with you. Let's get this meeting over with, and the contract signed.'

'I'm all for that.' Stretching languorously, he pushed his hair back and turned his face towards the warm cascade.

'Doesn't anything unsettle you?' Lisa gazed at him.

'You, perhaps.'

But even as he spoke she remembered his nightmare, and wished there had been time to ask him about it. Leaving him in the shower, she snatched a towel from the heated rail. 'I'll see you at the meeting—don't keep me waiting.'

Lisa felt obliged to say something in answer to the look on Mike's face as she walked past him into the boardroom. Her hair was still wet, though she had gathered it on top of her head with a tortoiseshell comb, but there had been no time for make-up. 'I've been swimming, Mike.'

'Of course you have,' Mike said smoothly. 'Do I take it Zagorakis has been diving too?'

'I said swimming, Mike. In the sea.' Lisa was relieved when Tino chose that moment to walk into the room.

'I'm sorry to have kept you, gentlemen.'

No explanation required for his damp hair, or for the fact that Tino was fresh out of the shower. He had kept everyone waiting, and, from the almost imperceptible easing of muscles amongst his team, Lisa guessed for the first time ever.

The meeting lasted just over two hours, and then financial directors each made a closing statement. They had straightened out any remaining niggles between them.

'Are you ready to sign the contract?' Tino invited, looking directly at her.

Turning to her team, Lisa gazed enquiringly amongst them. There were no objections. 'Yes, we're ready.'

The deal was completed in seconds, and handshakes exchanged all round.

'If you would all like to follow me out onto the veranda,' Tino announced, 'we will raise a toast to the future in champagne.'

Lisa waited until the last taxi had pulled away before turning back to the house. Tino had suggested they have supper in the village that evening. She knew she should feel excited about that, and exultant about the deal, but his nightmare still haunted her—and so far there had been no chance to talk to him about it. She fully expected that he would refuse to discuss it, but she had to try—someone had to try to get behind his iron façade.

The village square was packed with people, but Lisa felt wonderfully safe with Tino's arm locked around her waist. He steered her towards a raised wooden stage in the centre of the square where a man had just removed the microphone from its stand. Silver haired, and with a magnificent moustache, he clearly commanded respect.

'Takis Theodopoulus,' Tino explained, whispering in Lisa's ear. He is one of the finest folk singers in Greece.

When he starts to sing he will explain everything you need to know about Greece and the Greeks.'

'But I won't understand him if he sings in Greek.'

'You'll understand Takis Theodopoulus.'

It was true, and when the folk singer began he tugged at her heartstrings in a way she'd never known before, and then Lisa noticed how captivated everyone else was—the music was like magic binding them together. Most people were holding white handkerchiefs aloft, and waving them in time to the beat, but then Tino tugged on her hand and she followed him back through the crowd.

'Now you can see why I love Stellamaris so much,' he said when they found a quieter spot. 'Life is good here—everyone expresses themselves so freely.'

When he held her glance Lisa knew they were both thinking the same thing; the past had robbed them of that freedom. 'Tino, there's something I really want to ask you about.'

'Not now.'

'Why?' Lisa dug in, prepared to be stubborn, but then she saw the hunger in his face.

'Because I can't wait any longer.'

'The flower shop?' She gazed around to make sure they were alone as he dragged her into the doorway. 'No, Tino…we can't possibly.'

'Why not? There's no one here. Everyone's in the village square listening to the singing.' Testing the door and finding it unlocked, he drew her inside.

Lisa inhaled deeply. She could grow dizzy from the scent of flowers alone, and it seemed exaggerated in the darkness… It was as if she were blindfolded and every one of her senses was enhanced…and then Tino was holding her close to him, and murmuring words in his own tongue against her neck.

'Are you warm enough?' he murmured, moving against her.

'Tino, we can't…not here. This is someone's business.'

He didn't tell her that every business on Stellamaris was his until the young owner was confident enough to run it by himself or herself. It wasn't the time, and there wasn't the time. He wanted her now with no waiting, and no explanation.

'Tino, please—I want to speak to you.'

'Not now.' He could feel her softening as he ran his fingers lightly down her spine. She had changed into one of the pretty summer dresses he had ordered for her, and she felt cool beneath his hands. She shivered beneath his touch, but not from cold. He glanced out towards the square. The light from a thousand candles told him there wasn't the slightest chance they would be disturbed… Making a sudden decision, he swung her into his arms. 'In here.' He shouldered open another door.

'I only hope you don't get splinters,' he said as he lowered her onto the wooden worktable. He spoke against her mouth, teasing her with his tongue, eager to taste her again.

'No chance of that,' Lisa murmured, feeling the cool green leaves give a little beneath her weight. And then her legs were locked around Tino's waist, and her tiny lace pants tied with ribbon had been removed.

'I made an excellent choice in underwear.'

'You made?'

'OK, so next time I'll choose them myself, and make sure they all tie like this. It's most convenient.'

'Tino… No…really, what if?'

He silenced her with a kiss, leaning into her as he loosened his belt. 'No more talking, Lisa,' he warned. 'You have to concentrate now… I haven't eaten yet, and we have a table booked at the taverna for ten o' clock.'

'You mean I'm on a fixed time slot?' She pulled back to look at him. 'I don't believe you.'

'Believe.'

He caught her to him as she cried out for him, bending his knees to achieve a better position as he sank deeply inside her. 'Is that good?'

'Oh, yes, yes, and a lot warmer too.'

'Central heating never fails.'

'Just make sure you don't stop,' Lisa warned in a whisper as her laughter was overtaken by a sob of delight.

Lifting her legs, Tino positioned them over his shoulders, supporting her back so she could lean at a more acute angle, affording him greater access.

'Good, so good,' Lisa groaned before giving herself over to a black velvet world of sensation.

Tino attended to her needs with a catalogue of perfectly judged thrusts, and when she felt the sudden tension in him Lisa anticipated the moment he would lose control. It drew an immediate response from her. Crying out excitedly, she felt the first wave of spasms hit them both at the same time like a tidal wave sweeping them to the brink of consciousness and back. And all the while, Tino held her firmly, timing his movements to extend the pleasure for her as long as he could.

'And now we eat,' he said when at last she had quietened.

'Not sure I've got enough strength left for that.'

'Are you all right?' He bent his knees to stare into her face.

'I don't know,' Lisa admitted honestly. 'I'm—'

'Exhausted? Sated? Contented?'

'All of those things.' She was exhausted, but she would never get enough of him—and as for contented? She would never be contented until she unravelled the mystery of his pain. Tenderly, as she might have touched a child, she traced the outline of his face with one hand. 'Tino, I—'

Catching hold of her hand, he silenced her, bringing it to his lips to kiss the tender palm. 'We must hurry, or we will lose our table.'

'I can't believe anyone would dare to give it away.' Lisa laughed as she hunted in the dark for her underwear.

'I receive no special treatment in Stellamaris—I should be offended if anyone tried to make a fuss of me.'

'Even me?'

'For you, I might make an exception.'

She melted into him as he dragged her close to kiss her deeply again. He smelled so good, warm, clean man, woody aftershave, and there was a fresh aroma rising from all the juicy greenery they had pounded. 'You should fasten your jeans before we leave,' she reminded him, smiling against his mouth.

'And have buttons attached to my shirt by tailor's thread in future.'

Lisa laughed as she smoothed down the creases in her own crushed dress. 'I'd only rip a hole in the fabric.'

Grabbing hold of her hand, he drew her towards the door.

She hung back. 'Tino, please…there's something I really want to ask you about.'

'Anything—but ask me later at the taverna after we've eaten. You've given me quite an appetite.'

But she couldn't ask him at the taverna—she couldn't break the mood. How could she bring up the subject of his nightmare when they were surrounded by dozens of people—most of whom he seemed to know? The brightly lit taverna was full, and the steady thrum of the bouzouki band contributed to a sensuous ambience. With all the children safely in bed with older guardians watching them, everyone was intent on wringing out the last bit of enjoyment from the night.

The tables were all draped with blue and white table-cloths that reached down almost to the floor. The tables had been set at a decent distance apart, allowing for privacy amidst the party atmosphere, and Lisa was soon as relaxed as everyone else, but she couldn't help wishing life could be less complicated.

'Why are you sighing?'

She looked up to find Tino's gaze locked onto her face. 'Because I'm so happy.'

'I'm not sure that was a happy sigh.'

'Your senses must be highly developed if you can ana-lyse a sigh over all this noise.'

'You have no idea just how highly developed they are.'

He frightened her with his perception; he excited her too…and as he continued to stare at her she found that, instead of curbing her hunger, the recent sex with him had only made her want him more.

'And now I do know what you're thinking,' he assured her, starting to stroke her leg beneath the tablecloth.

'Tino, no! You can't,' Lisa gasped, realising what he meant to do as his hand travelled steadily up her thigh. 'Not in here.'

'There's nothing I can't do,' he told her confidently. 'Just slide to the edge of your chair, and you'll find out.'

With his powerful calf wrapped around her own, he eas-ily nudged her thighs apart. Lisa could hardly believe what he was intent on doing to her. 'Tino, you really can't.' But his hand was already home, and his fingers had started working rhythmically, and persuasively.

When a sharp cry escaped her throat, he passed a napkin across the table to her with his free hand. 'I promised you an erotic adventure—bury your face in that if you don't want to draw attention to yourself.'

Peeping over the bunched-up linen square, Lisa found the apparent unconcern on Tino's face only aroused her all the more. He was staring out across the dance floor as if he were the most innocent man in the room, while she knew he was savouring every moment. But not half as much as she was, she realized, sliding to the very edge of her chair. 'You'll pay for this,' she promised him huskily.

'I certainly hope so. Now, concentrate. You're on another fixed time slot—the coffee will come round soon.'

After coffee Lisa danced with him, to slow, sensuous music that wrapped them both in a seductive cocoon. With her eyes closed she relished the feel of his strong, protective body pressing against hers.

'I think it's time to go,' Tino murmured at last, drawing her by the hand from the dance floor.

He was right, Lisa realized. They should go before their dancing caused comment. But as they were about to walk out of the taverna one of the other men caught hold of Tino's sleeve. Smiling broadly, the man rasped a few words to him in Greek.

Turning to her, Tino apologised. 'The men are about to dance the *Kalamatianos*. They have asked me to join them. It would be an insult to my friends if I refuse.'

Once again she was to be denied the chance to speak to him, Lisa realised with frustration, but, like their insatiable passion for each other, it would have to wait. She returned to her seat as Tino joined the other men on the dance floor.

The traditional dance was so powerful and so aggressively masculine Lisa started to find it unnerving. Glancing around the other women to reassure herself, she noticed how unconcerned they were—they were even urging on their men. But the more she watched and tried to tell herself that it was only a dance, the more the men's powerful response to the rhythm made it seem like a mating call, primal and fierce, that called for submission, and promised domination. The expression in the eyes of some of the men reminded her of men in the commune, and she shuddered as the intensity soared.

She couldn't take any more… She didn't even know that the music had stopped. As the cheering began Lisa blundered out of her seat, heading for the exit, blindly stumbling into tables and knocking her legs against the wooden struts.

'Lisa.'

She should have known Tino would come after her. He caught up with her before she reached the street. 'Let go of me!' She tried to pull away, but he was too strong for her.

'Lisa—what's wrong?' He held her close.

'Let me go, Tino.'

'You're shaking.'

'No, I'm not, I'm fine.'

'Then why are you running out on me?' Steering her outside, he pinned her against the wall, arms stiffly planted either side of her face. 'Tell me what's wrong, Lisa.' He gazed intently at her. 'Look at me.' He thumped the wall in frustration.

'Why? So you can frighten me with this?' She stared at one clenched fist pressed into the wall at the side of her face.

'What?' His face paled. 'Is that what you think of me? Is that what you think I'm trying to do to you, Lisa? No.' He turned away.

This was supposed to be about him! Lisa raged at herself inwardly. Tonight was supposed to be about Tino—not about her. What had she done? Fear made her weak…fear that, having lost control with a man for the first time in her life, she was being used for sex as her mother had been used. She would never shake it off, and Tino needed someone whole, someone untouched by shadows, someone who could help him as she never could.

'You're right,' Tino exclaimed before Lisa had chance
to express her thoughts. 'I'm no good at this—I should take
you back.' He held out his hand, and then, as if remembering how things were between them, he let it drop down
to his side again.

By the time the first fingers of dawn were edging over her
balcony Lisa had finished packing. First thing on Monday
she would ring all the boutiques and find out how much
money she owed Tino. The monotony of packing had
soothed her a little and made her see that it was better this
way. There hadn't been time to work through everything
in the past that stood between them… How could there ever
be enough time for that? The men's dance in the taverna
had been the turning point when she had realised that they
could never have a future together.

The rational part of her insisted that the dance had been
nothing more than a celebration of the men's heritage—but
when would the past rear its ugly head again? When would
it destroy them both? She had to leave Stellamaris before
that happened.

'Do you mind if I come in?'

Lisa's eyes widened with surprise to see Tino leaning
into her room from the balcony outside. 'Be my guest.' She
tried for casual, but her heart was juddering. She hadn't
expected this. It would have been easier not to see him
before she left. She still wanted him so badly it was like a
continual ache in her heart, and for that reason alone she
had to go. She couldn't hurt him; she could never hurt him,
and if she stayed she knew she would.

She waited tensely, watching him view all the debris on
her floor. There were shoeboxes and tissue paper scattered
everywhere. 'I'll pay you for everything.'

He silenced her with a gesture. 'You wanted to say something to me last night, Lisa, and we never got the chance.'

'It doesn't matter now.' She looked away, ashamed that when she'd had her chance to ask him about his nightmares she had allowed her own fears to take precedence over his. Because she loved him she had to leave before she caused him any more harm—or herself.

'I hear you're leaving around noon?'

'Yes, that's right.'

'Then why don't we have breakfast together before you leave? There's plenty of time.'

'No.' She could see he was surprised at the force of her refusal. 'I'm really not hungry.'

'You don't need to be hungry to enjoy breakfast overlooking the sea.'

'It's too early for me.'

He frowned as he studied her. 'But you always like to see the sun rising over the ocean.'

'Generally, yes. But today—well, I think it's better if we make a clean break.'

'Do you really believe that?'

As he took a step forward she could have touched him. She was sure she could feel his body heat warming her. 'I still have some clearing up to do.'

'Can't you leave that for now?'

'I can't leave the room like this.' She looked around.

'I promised Stella you would come.'

Taking a deep breath, Lisa turned away from him to stare out across the balcony. Sunrise was playing tricks with the horizon and the sea wore a pink-tinted blanket of cloud. It was like a dream. If only it could have been a dream, how much easier that would have been for all of them. But it wasn't a dream, it was all too real, and how could she leave Stellamaris without saying goodbye to Stella? Saying a final goodbye to everything that Tino was.

She couldn't refuse, Lisa realised. Tino had put her in a position where she had to share breakfast with him. She shook her head as she turned back to him. 'You play dirty, Tino.'

'Yes, I know.'

'Will you give me a few minutes to clear this up?'

'I'll give you as long as you need.'

'Fifteen minutes? Out by the pool?' She didn't expect him to catch hold of her. She didn't expect to have his heady, familiar scent invading her senses. 'Yes?' she managed faintly. 'What is it, Tino?'

He didn't say anything, he just held her, and then, as if accepting it was all over between them, he let her go and stood back.

'I'm glad things have turned out well for you in the end, Lisa.'

She made a sound as if she were agreeing with him. His breath was warm on her skin, and she knew the sound of his voice would be locked in her mind for ever.

'I'll see you down there.' She kept her tone bright, and then she waited, not daring to move a muscle until he left the room. She didn't even know that she had bitten down on her lip to keep from calling him back until she tasted the warm, salty tang of her own blood.

CHAPTER TWELVE

IT WAS the sound of the piano that drew Lisa into the shadows of at the turn of the stairs. Sitting silently on a step, she peeped through the struts to see who was playing— though in her heart she already knew. Every pianist had their own unique sound that brought something of their personality to a composition... How could she have misjudged Tino so badly? How could she have attributed the presence of the piano to anyone else... *someone with more heart*?

He was a great deal more proficient than he had pretended to be, quite remarkable, in fact, for a man who had only learned the instrument as an adult. But then Lisa guessed that Tino would have applied himself to learning the piano with the same single-minded determination he brought to everything else.

His sensitive touch drew an incredible array of sounds from the beautiful old instrument, but just as she found herself slipping away with the music he brought his hands down heavily on the keys. Recoiling at the discord, she wondered if he had seen her... She held her breath, but to her relief he left quickly in the direction of the door leading outside. She counted to a hundred before following, and it took all that time for the last ugly wave of jangling sound to disappear.

Stepping out into the fine morning light, Lisa thought the musical episode a perfect soundtrack for her affair with Tino. They were both passionate, sensitive people, but a jarring, angry chord always came between them. That was why there was no future for them together—neither of them knew how to break down the barricades they had brought with them from the past.

Her heart thundered when she saw him waiting for her. Just a tall black silhouette in the shadows, he was a man without feature or expression, a man she still didn't know in spite of all the intimacy they had shared. Shivering a little, she walked towards him. He came forward to greet her. He looked impossibly handsome, and totally assured.

'Will you come with me to meet Stella?'

'Of course.'

Just as it looked as if they might ease into a conversation, a man hurried towards them from the house.

Would they never have chance to hold a normal conversation? Lisa wondered as she stood to one side while Tino exchanged a few words with the man in Greek. He seemed pleased about something, she noticed as he turned to her.

'Will you excuse me, Lisa? I'm afraid something has come up.'

Something would always come up, she realised. 'That's fine by me. I'll go and meet Stella; don't worry.'

'I'll join you both later.'

She started to say something, but Tino was already striding away towards the house. He had recovered a lot faster than she had, Lisa reflected sadly, walking away.

'Lisa! What a lovely surprise!' Stella exclaimed, stepping out of the funicular cabin. Drawing Lisa into her arms, she drew back, and looked into her face. 'What's wrong?'

'Nothing.'

Stella shook her head in disagreement. 'I don't believe you. You're so tense. And where's Tino?' she added, looking around.

'He's been called away.'

'Ah.' Stella looked thoughtful. 'And what is this new note of resignation in your voice? Has all the fight gone out of you, Lisa?'

Lisa smiled a little. 'You think I should have rugby-tackled him to the ground?'

'You can't let him have all his own way.'

It was impossible to remain oblivious to the mischief in Stella's eyes. 'Next time,' Lisa promised without much conviction.

'So, there is to be a next time?' Stella's sharp gaze focused on her face.

'No, Stella, this is my last day on Stellamaris.'

Stella sighed as she linked arms with Lisa and drew her up the path. 'Don't be impatient with Tino, Lisa, he's a very busy man.'

'I'm not impatient.' Just disappointed, sad, and angry with myself for thinking it could be any different.

'I should think not,' Stella exclaimed, snapping her out of it. 'I am here.'

Lisa squeezed Stella's arm affectionately. She had to put Tino out of her mind, but Stella wasn't making it easy for her.

After breakfast Stella raised the subject of Tino again.

'I'm not disappointed,' Lisa lied. 'He invited me for breakfast, I just thought he might make the effort to turn up.'

'He's a good man, Lisa.'

Lisa turned her head away. She wasn't ready to hear that, not from Stella, not from someone she trusted as much as she trusted Stella. Then Stella covered her hand with her own as if she sensed her turmoil. 'Don't...' Lisa pulled her hand away. 'I might cry.'

'And if you do?' Stella demanded gently. 'What is wrong with crying, Lisa? Why are you so ashamed of your emotions?' Digging into her pocket, she pulled out a crisply laundered handkerchief and handed it over. 'Sometimes the view in Stellamaris is enough to make me cry...and sometimes my memories are enough. Other times I cry because I am so happy—like the time when Giorgio told me how much he loved Arianna. I'm not ashamed of how I feel. I rejoice in the gift of life in all its guises. And I am Greek,' she added, smiling mischievously, 'so naturally I feel things very deeply, as we Greeks do. We have a hunger for life, Lisa…a passion.'

'I have all those things inside me, Stella.' Lisa's voice was desperate. 'But I don't know how to set them free.'

Stella touched her arm. 'Then I must help you,' she said gently.

'No one can do that.'

'How many Greeks do you know?'

The expression on Stella's face forced a smile onto Lisa's lips. 'Too few, and one too many.'

'Tino?' Stella asked shrewdly. 'He's the one too many?'

'Yes,' Lisa admitted, 'though I don't really know him.'

'What do you want to know about him? Shall I tell you that he is the most wonderful man I have ever known? No? Why are you shaking your head at me, Lisa? Do you find that so hard to believe? Let me tell you a little more about Tino. He paid for Arianna to go to the music conservatoire. Without him my daughter's wonderful voice would never have been recognised. And he gave me more than I could ever tell you… Far more than money, Tino is the son I never had. The apartment block where I live when I am in Athens, and the cottage here in Stellamaris—Constantine gave them to me. He gave me the whole block of apartments, Lisa.' Stella touched her hand to her chest to express her emotion. 'And still you frown?' She shook her head.

'I just can't believe we're talking about the same man. You told me once you'd known Tino *for ever*, so you must have known his family. Can't you tell me a little about them so that I can understand him better?'

It was hard to believe how rapidly Stella's expression changed from open and friendly to completely shut.

'Tino hasn't told you about his background?'

'About his family, no.'

'Then I can't tell you either. I'm sorry, Lisa, only Tino can tell you about his past.'

And he would never do that, Lisa realised.

'I'm very sorry to have deserted you, ladies.'

'Tino.' Lisa's heart turned over as she gazed at him. 'I wasn't sure I would see you again.'

He made a casual gesture. 'They wanted me to check on something inside the house—'

'We ate breakfast without you,' Stella cut in. 'We didn't know how long you would be, Constantine.'

'And I apologise, *Ya-ya*, for not being there to greet you this morning.' Embracing Stella, Tino kissed her affectionately on both cheeks.

'Whatever took you away,' Stella said, 'I can see it was important from your face, so I will forgive you, Constantine.'

'It was important, *Ya-ya*. It was of the utmost importance.'

Lisa's stomach clenched. Why was he looking at her? 'You haven't been having second thoughts about the contract, have you?'

Tipping his head to one side, Tino smiled at her. 'I do think of some things other than business, you know.'

'But not often enough,' Stella observed tartly. 'And now, if you two will excuse me, I should like to take a walk around the gardens to be sure that your flowers are at their best for our festival tonight, Constantine.'

'Of course.' Lisa turned to her. 'The taxi driver told me that you fill your houses with flowers for May Day here on Stellamaris.'

'Not until later today,' Stella explained. 'After our siesta this afternoon there will be a procession through the village, and then when all the houses are decorated there will be a party in the village square.'

'Another party.' Lisa smiled.

'Life can be hard.' Stella shrugged. 'So we Greeks cel-ebrate whenever we can—' Reaching out, she rested her hand on Lisa's arm. 'You must make time to be happy too, Lisa.'

'Will I see you before I go?' Lisa's throat tightened.

'I'm sure we will see each other.'

When Stella smiled at her, Lisa wanted to go and throw her arms around the elderly Greek woman and beg her not to leave. It didn't make any sense, Lisa reasoned, watching Stella make her way down the path. She had stood on her own two feet since she could stand, she ran a huge and complex business, she had money and prestige, but right now all she wanted was for Stella to be her friend so she could learn all the things she didn't know or understand— all the important things, the things she had never found time for in the past.

'I'm told your suitcase is still upstairs.'

Lisa came to with a jolt. Tino couldn't have made it any plainer that he couldn't wait for her to leave. 'I'm sorry, Tino, I forgot the case. I did mean to bring it down.'

'Don't worry, I'll do that for you. Just show me where it is. Are you thinking about business again?' he said when she didn't reply.

'Actually, I was thinking about changing my life.'

'Changing your life? That's rather momentous, isn't it?'

'Yes, it is. But Stella Panayotakis talks a lot of sense… She's made me think; she's made me re-evaluate every-thing. Is Stella a relative of yours, Tino?'

'As good as.'

'Only *Ya-ya* means—'

'Grandma. Yes, I know, Lisa. About these changes…'

He held the door into the house for her. 'Tell me something about them.'

'I would never relinquish my seat on the board at Bond Steel,' Lisa began slowly, thinking aloud, 'but I have many talented people on my team and with this cash injection they will hardly need me on a daily basis. The job isn't enough for me any more.' She shrugged and flashed a wry smile at him. 'Before you ask, I don't know what I *do* want to do yet. Let's just say Stellamaris has made me greedy—and don't look so worried,' she added dryly. 'What I want, we both know you can't give me.'

'And what's that?' Tino asked as he followed her into the house.

'I want stability, a broader view on life, a long-term future to look forward to…and I don't ever want to stop working.'

'I'm very pleased to hear it.'

'I just want to make room in my life for other things.' How strange it felt to be walking up the stairs with Tino discussing her future like this as if they were two strangers whose paths had briefly crossed.

'Here we are,' he said, opening the door to her suite. 'Just show me where the suitcase is, and I'll take it down for you.'

Lisa stood transfixed on the threshold of the room. Then, walking past him, she turned full circle. 'What are these?'

'Flowers,' Tino said dryly. 'Remember? You said that flowers would be special. Don't you like them?'

'I don't know what to say.' Every surface in the room was covered in the most beautiful floral arrangements Lisa had ever seen. She wanted to believe they were for her, but she knew they couldn't be. And then she remembered. 'Of course, it's May Day.' She turned, and gave Tino a quick smile, remembering that this scene would be reproduced in every household on the island. For a moment she had imagined—Lisa shuddered, realising how close she had come to making the most terrible fool of herself. 'I'm sorry, Tino. I shouldn't be keeping you waiting like this. My suitcase is over there behind that chair.' She saw the shadow flit across his face. In these days of equality, of course, she shouldn't expect him to carry it for her. She should take it down herself. 'The flowers are really beautiful,' she said, when he didn't move. 'You have some wonderful traditions on the island.'

'Yes, we do.'

His voice was expressionless, and then she noticed that his eyes were the only part of him that did show emotion—and the look in them frightened her.

As the moment stretched on Lisa knew that she was only making things worse with her indecisiveness. What on earth was she waiting for, anyway? 'I expect my taxi will have arrived by now.' Walking past Tino, she grabbed hold of the suitcase and started for the door. Her foot had barely touched the landing when he yanked her back inside the room again.

'What do you think you are doing?' Lisa stared angrily at his hand on her arm. 'What's wrong with you, Tino?'

'What's wrong with *me*?' He slammed the door. 'This is the matter.' His furious stare embraced the room.

'The flowers?' Lisa said uncertainly, putting down her case.

'Yes! The flowers! What the hell else could I be referring to?'

'I've already said how nice they are—'

'*Nice?*' He looked away as if he needed time to compose himself, and then, staring towards the heavens, he cursed in Greek.

The fact that she had made a terrible mistake didn't come to Lisa like a thunderbolt, it was a long-drawn-out torture that dripped ice through her veins until finally it reached her heart: *the flowers were for her*... Of course they were for her! She had schooled herself always to think the worst of people. Any normal woman would have seen that immediately, the moment Tino had opened the door—the moment she'd stepped over the threshold, the moment she'd seen what he had done for her. 'Tino.' Lisa found that her throat had dried to the point where she could hardly make herself heard. 'I'm so sorry, I didn't realise...and they're so beautiful.'

'I thought this was what you wanted.' He stopped and passed a hand over his eyes as if he wanted to blot out the moment when he had decided to lay his heart at her feet so she could trample on it.

'I'm so ashamed... I thought—'

He whirled around to confront her. 'You should be ashamed. You're just like all the rest. You tell me that you don't want jewels—that flowers are what touch you the most...but when I give you flowers you are disappointed and you treat my gift with contempt.'

'Tino, please—listen to me.' Taking hold of his arm, Lisa flinched as he pulled away.

'We'd better not keep your taxi waiting.' He didn't look at her. 'If your pilot misses his slot you won't be able to leave the island tonight.'

Lisa braced herself as the jet took off, soaring high above the clouds over Stellamaris.

On the journey to the airport she had seen the flower-laden carts with children sitting on the buckboards tossing handfuls of blooms to crowds lining the streets. The car had been forced to slow, so she hadn't missed a single detail of the procession. Everyone had been in such high spirits and she had longed to be part of it...with Tino.

To make matters worse, when she'd said goodbye to Maria before leaving the villa she had learned that Tino had been up before anyone else that morning choosing flowers for her in the garden. He had carried the arrangements up to her room while she was having breakfast with Stella, not trusting anyone else to do it; that was the important matter that had delayed him.

It was as well she was leaving. She damaged everyone she cared about. Her mother had sacrificed everything for her, and Jack Bond—a man she still found it hard to call her father—had looked for a love she could never give him. She could see it all now with agonising clarity, and knew she couldn't risk causing any more harm. She cared too much for Tino to stay.. and, even had she wanted to stay, he had made it very clear that he didn't want her in his life. Business was her forte. She was good at that. She had done the deal she had set out to do. She had to be satisfied. She had to accept there were some things in life she would never master, and love was just one of them.

Seated in his study, Tino grimaced. The suspicion that he had been tricked was only boosted by the sound of Lisa's jet passing overhead.

Emotions had no part to play in business and he had made a fundamental error allowing her in. He only had to think of the flowers to know she had made a fool of him... Had she used him for sex? Or had she used sex to secure the deal? Either way this wasn't over. He couldn't just let her walk away...

This time he didn't ring the bell and wait patiently for her housekeeper to answer it, he thundered on her door with his fist, and then shouted her name through the letterbox.

'All right, all—' Lisa pressed back against the wall as Tino stalked past her. 'Nice to see you too,' she added under her breath as she followed him into her den. 'Would you like a drink?' She glanced down at her own flute of champagne, feeling the world had gone mad, or that she had fallen asleep and had to be dreaming.

'Celebrating, Lisa?'

The tone of Tino's voice soon brought her round. She had never seen him like this before. 'Could you snarl a little louder? I didn't quite hear you.'

'I said, are you celebrating, Lisa?'

It was Vera's night off, and Tino's visit seemed so unreal. It was hard to believe how much he affected her. She had to keep staring at him just to make sure she wasn't dreaming. She felt exhilarated briefly, but then caution took over, and now the expression on his face hardly invited enthusiasm. Maybe she would do better to feel intimidated…but instead of that she felt sad—sad for both of them. They were both so enmeshed in the past, so emotionally scarred, they didn't know how to express themselves other than through business. They both had so much, but where things that really mattered were concerned they had nothing.

The only way forward was to keep everything on an impersonal level, Lisa decided, as if they were in a business meeting. But first she had some apologising to do. 'I'm glad you've come.' She held open the door of her den for him. 'I've been hoping for an opportunity to say how sorry I am about the flowers.'

'The flowers?'

As Tino frowned Lisa realised her mistake. He couldn't have cared less about the flowers. He had something a lot more important on his mind—his pride, perhaps? And then she realised that she was still holding the glass of champagne in her hand, and that he was staring at it. She felt bound to explain. 'I was just drinking a toast to my new life.'

'Your new life?' He cut across her. His eyes narrowed

with suspicion. 'The last time we spoke you mentioned changes. You move fast.'

His tone was hostile, but one of them had to keep calm. 'So many questions, Tino,' she said lightly. 'Why don't you join me in a glass of champagne?'

Instead of answering, he stood vibrating with some inner conflict.

'So, why are you here?' she prompted, wanting him to say something, anything.

He shook his head, his face a rigid mask. 'You've got a nerve.'

Lisa stiffened defensively. 'What are you talking about?'

'Do you really think you can use me?'

'Use you?' All Lisa's thoughts on staying calm evaporated. 'And just how am I supposed to have used you?'

'I think you know. What was I to you, Lisa—some sort of device to excise your ghosts?'

'*My* ghosts?' She stared at him.

He stared back at her unflinching.

'Or is there something else? Don't tell me—' she held up her hand '—I forgot to sign something.' She stared accusingly at his jacket pocket. 'Well? What are you waiting for? We might as well get this over with.'

His expression turned glacial. 'Is that what you think of me?'

'I think I understand you pretty well, yes.'

'Understand me? You understand nothing about me.'

He couldn't believe this was happening. He couldn't believe she could arouse such feeling in him. They were eyeing each other like gladiators in the coliseum. There was so much passion in the room he could feel it swirling around them.

It was the last thing he had wanted, the last thing he had anticipated; emotion was his *bête noire*, something he avoided at all cost because he didn't understand it. He didn't have a strategy to deal with it. And he didn't want to understand it—something so unpredictable, so unquantifiable?

He turned away feeling frustration building inside him again. He couldn't find the words to express his feelings—and all he could be sure about was that coming to see Lisa was the worst mistake he had ever made.

'I don't know why you came here,' she threw at him.

How could he tell her when he hardly knew himself?

'I think it's better if you go now and never come back.'

Did she have someone else? The thought speared through him as she spoke. 'Is there someone else?' *Was this jealousy?*

'What?' She stared at him incredulously.

'Don't hold back on my account, Lisa. If you've got someone else here in England, just tell me.' His voice sounded hoarse. The cost of exposing his innermost thoughts to her was terrible—far worse than he had expected.

'Someone else?' As they stared at each other Lisa saw the expression in Tino's eyes change. This was not the formidable business opponent she knew, or even the confident man. Those eyes were the eyes of the child who had been locked in a nightmare, the child who had cried out to her in the night. For just those few seconds it was as if all the barricades Tino had raised against the world and against her had disappeared, but he built them up again so fast, she was left wondering if she had imagined it.

He was just as damaged on the inside as she was. He would always wonder if he was capable of feeling anything beyond some fleeting triumph in business. She could only hope he wasn't destined to remain as numb in his heart as she was. 'There's no one else, Tino,' she said quietly. 'There never can be anyone.'

'So, your life will always be empty.'

'It's better that way. It would be irresponsible of me to involve anyone in my life, when I have nothing to offer them.'

'You're wrong, Lisa.' Tino spoke from the heart as images of Stella and Arianna, as well as many others, crowded his mind. 'You have had an empty life, I understand that. But it can get better, I promise you.'

'You promise me, Tino? What do you promise me? That in time I can learn to care as much as you do?'

She used sarcasm like a shield, and he deserved her cynicism. 'I admit that I've still got a long way to go, but at least I have started the journey—' He stopped, self-conscious at showing such candour on a subject he was still building up faith in himself. 'And it's not that bad.'

Was this feeling currently tearing her apart Tino's idea of 'not that bad'? Lisa wondered, drawing a steadying breath. 'Then, all I can say is, you're very lucky, Tino…but I know that letting people in can never be for me.'

'But you were drinking a toast to your new life.'

'New pastimes, new occupations to run alongside Bond Steel, not a whole raft of personal involvements I know can only end in disaster.'

'A whole raft?'

For a moment she thought he was trying not to smile—and not in a nasty way, or a point-scoring way. 'You know what I mean.' She sounded edgy, and she was. She was determined he wouldn't turn this back into some sort of emotional ping-pong. She was going to stick to the facts whatever he threw at her.

'So, tell me about these changes.'

'I'm not even sure about them myself yet.' She couldn't see a hint of a smile on his face now, and was reassured enough to ask, 'Would you like that drink now?'

'Before I go?'

He was gently teasing her, Lisa realised, careful to remain unmoved. 'Yes. Champagne all right for you?' She glanced at the shelf where all her crystal glasses were lined up in rows.

'Lalique?' Tino murmured, but, in case she thought he was impressed, he added wryly, 'Are they dusty?'

'I doubt it.' Lisa smiled a little too now, but she still wasn't quite sure she was ready for his humour. 'Vera looks after me too well for anything in here to be dusty.' She knew what he was getting at. They both had so much, so many material things, but they had no one special to share any of it with.

'So, come on,' he pressed, 'I'm waiting to hear about these changes to your life—'

'Like I said, I'm not sure, Tino.'

'I think we'd better drink a general toast,' he suggested dryly.

Pouring the champagne, Lisa was careful not to touch his hand when she gave him the glass.'

'To us,' he said.

'To us,' Lisa echoed, staring at him over the rim of her glass. 'Won't you sit down?'

She pointed to the sofa where he assumed she had been making herself comfortable when he'd arrived. There was a cosy throw to wrap around her pyjamas flung over the back of it, and a pair of ridiculous fluffy slippers sticking out underneath. And now he saw that her feet were bare, and that her toenails looked like perfect pink shells…

Putting his glass down on the table, he looked at her… He could see she wanted to say something. 'Lisa?' he prompted. 'What is it?'

'About the flowers—'

When he had first arrived at the apartment, and she had tried to apologise, he had been ungracious. His head had been filled with memories of the hurt and anger he had felt when she'd walked into her room at Villa Aphrodite and made a mockery of his gift. But now it was different, now they were both calmer…and the least he owed her was a chance to explain. He held her gaze, willing her to go on.

'The flowers *were* special, Tino, very special, and so was the thought behind them. I can't believe I didn't realise they were your gift to me.'

The way she was looking at him now, with her eyes so wide and troubled, touched something deep inside him, and feelings welled up from some hidden place so that he wanted to go to her and hold her in his arms.

'I couldn't believe you would do something like that for me, that anyone would.'

She made a helpless gesture, as if she was hunting for the right words with the same lack of success he had run up against when he had first arrived. 'Won't you sit down with me?' he suggested gently.

She came to then, and stared at him with sharper focus. 'No—I'd better not. And, Tino, that toast we made—' She frowned as she looked at her glass. 'When I said, "to us", of course I meant "to us" independently.'

'Of course.' He kept his expression neutral. 'Us. Independently,' he added dryly.

This awkwardness between them was new. They could rage at each other, or deal analytically with each other across a boardroom table quite comfortably, but this tip-toeing around each other was like starting over, working through something very carefully to find out if it could be safe…

'I can't bear to be hurt, Tino.'

The frank confession made him doubly alert. She was looking at him, totally oblivious to the fact that she had her arms wrapped around her waist in a defensive gesture.

'I have to protect myself.'

'From me?'

She looked away.

'Lisa, please believe me… I do know what you're trying to say. Trust doesn't come in a rush, it grows slowly with time…and that's the same for everyone, not just you and me.'

She flinched at that. 'There is no you and me, Tino. There never can be. We're no good for each other. Surely you must know that. You need someone strong.'

'How do you know what I need?'

'I heard you cry out in the night, Tino. I may not know much about you, but that night proved to me that you're not the product of an ordinary childhood.'

'An ordinary childhood?' he repeated her words softly. 'Whatever that might be.'

'I don't pretend to know what happened to you, Tino. I only know what I see in front of me now, and what I heard that night when you cried out in terror like a little boy who was very frightened.'

He looked at her searchingly. 'No one has ever told me I do that before.'

'Maybe you've never done it before.'

'Maybe I've never felt safe enough to do it before.' He stopped. He'd gone too far and automatically pulled back. 'Truce?' Now it was his turn to feel awkward.

'Truce,' Lisa agreed softly, 'Don't worry,' she whispered, as if that was all he had on his mind, 'I won't tell anyone.'

'I never thought that you would.'

He reached out, and then stopped himself, clenching his hands to prevent himself from weakening. After another period of silence had elapsed and the tension between them had subsided, he tried again. 'You say we're no good for each other? I think you're wrong.'

'You would think that, but then you always believe you're right.'

He was relieved to see that as she made the comment it almost brought a smile to her lips.

Neither of them moved for a while, but then she surprised him, coming to sit down as he had hoped she would on the sofa at his side. For a moment he thought she had opened her heart to the possibility that there was another way than to live without love, but he was soon disillusioned. She had only come close to him to drive her point home…

Clenching both her fists, she pressed them into her chest so hard her knuckles turned white. 'There's nothing in here, Tino.'

He couldn't bear to see the look on her face. 'No!' Was that voice his? Without thinking, he dragged her to him.

'Please, Tino, let me go… I have nothing inside me… I've got nothing to give you.'

'No, Lisa, you're wrong. I can see inside you, and you're beautiful.'

And when she searched his face, and he saw the doubt fighting with her need to believe him, he shook his head and smiled tenderly at her. 'Don't you see, Lisa? We're the saving of each other…' And then he held her as if he would never let her go until she finally relaxed, and began to shudder uncontrollably in his arms.

'Do you really think so?'

Her voice was tiny like a child's and it made him want to cry for the first time he could remember…for both of them. 'I know it.'

Still sensing her doubt, he cupped her chin and brought her to face him again. 'I know it's true, because I love you, Lisa. I love you so much you've got no idea.' He kissed her then, and it was a beginning… It was as if they had never kissed before; it was a revelation to them both, like coming home.

CHAPTER THIRTEEN

LISA was still warm from the bath. How could he have forgotten how wonderful she felt in his arms when the need rose in them both like a white-hot flame?

'It was good, wasn't it?' she whispered when he finally stopped kissing her.

'*Is* good,' Tino corrected, still holding her, staring into her eyes. 'Better than good.'

How could she hold back her feelings when she didn't want to? How could she hold firm when her body, her heart, her mind, her soul called out to him, and when she only felt complete when she was with him? 'I love you, Tino.'

'Are you asking me, or telling me?'

They both laughed, and she buried her face against his chest. 'Do I still sound so uncertain?' She watched his lips tug up in a half-smile, 'I...love...you.'

He swept her up into his arms and carried her to the bedroom to seal the pledge they had made to each other. Lowering her down onto the bed, he dropped the towel he had been wearing round his waist, and slipped beneath the covers, drawing her into his arms. Stroking her hair, he dropped kisses on her eyes, on her cheek, on her brow...

'This is good,' he said tenderly. 'The best thing in the world is being in bed with you.'

'It's so much softer than a table,' she teased him. 'The worktable in a florist's shop,' she reminded him, 'the board-room table.'

'Yours, or mine?'

'Both, if I have my way.'

179

'Then it's to be hoped you do—I'm keen to make sure our lovemaking never becomes predictable.'

'No chance of that—' Lisa gasped as Tino moved down the bed, kissing every inch of her on the way. He flung back the covers so that the subdued light from the bedside lamp played across her naked body, turning it a deeper shade of peach.

'You're so beautiful,' he murmured, tracing the contours of her breasts and belly with the lightest touch to bring her pleasure. 'I want to taste you.'

Throwing her head back on the soft bank of pillows, Lisa moaned softly as he moved between her thighs, pressing her legs back with his warm palms until she was completely open for him, completely ready... She could refuse him nothing...not even her heart.

His dark hair was so glossy in the lamplight, so silky to her touch as she laced her fingers through the thick waves to urge him on... His tongue was every bit as skilful as his fingers, and there was no part of her he did not understand, or know how to play for the greatest pleasure. But as her excitement grew to fever pitch he drew back, smiling down at her, his eyes dark with passion, and his smile wolfish in the half-light.

'Don't keep me waiting—'

'Or?' he demanded.

'If you're naughty, I shall have to punish you.'

Arousal hit them at the same moment, and as their eyes locked Tino knew they were thinking the same thing. They had both suffered the consequences of violence, but they had worked through their fears together, and it had brought them closer than either of them had anticipated. They could push the boundaries because they loved each other, and because they could trust each other completely, and because, at last, they both knew without any doubt at all that they were safe.

'Better?' he asked Lisa later when she lay quiet in his arms.

'Can't speak...no strength.' Her body was floating on another dimension. She couldn't have called it back even had she wanted to.

'All the shadows gone?'

'Shadows?'

'We both have them,' Tino told her, shifting his head on the pillows to meet her gaze. 'You can't hide from someone who has spent his whole life blanking out the past—'

'That works both ways, Tino.'

'I know about the commune,' he said. 'I know about all the terrible things you saw while you were living there. I understand your reasons for running away, and for going back to live with your father. You were right to do that, Lisa. And in the end your mother did her best for you. No child should have been exposed to the dangers you were exposed to, and I believe she helped you to get out of there just in time.'

'Who told you all this?'

'Does it matter?'

It had to be Mike, Lisa realised. She hadn't confided the truth about her mother's extreme lifestyle to another living soul.

'Don't be angry with Mike,' Tino said as he read her mind. 'He only has your best interests at heart.'

'I'm not angry. It's just that I never talk about the past in case anyone thinks I'm looking for sympathy, or help. I know that no one can help me. I can only help myself.'

'If you thought of it as understanding, rather than sympathy, you might find other people out there just like you. You can share the road back with someone else, Lisa, someone who is also trying to break free from the past.'

'With you, Tino?'

'Why not? Just because your mother's life was chaotic

doesn't mean you have to order your own life with such an unforgiving hand.'

'I'm getting better.' She viewed their sated forms with a wry glance.

'You are better, because you know you can trust me, and you know that violence will never have any part to play in our relationship. Why shouldn't lovemaking be fun? Who's to say what's right or wrong between consenting adults, as long as no one else is hurt by their actions? What happens between us in the bedroom stays between us. And if you don't like something, you only have to tell me.'

'I like everything,' Lisa assured him, snuggling close, already feeling her body starting to yearn for his attention.

'Not yet,' Tino whispered, soothing her with long strokes down her back. 'First we talk.'

'First you talk.' Lisa raised herself on one arm to stare at him. 'You know so much about me, and I need to understand your nightmares. Tell me about the past, Tino.'

'I don't want to burden you.'

Putting one finger over his lips, she shook her head, silently encouraging him, prepared to wait for however long it took.

'Stella Panayotakis took care of me when I was a boy,' he said at last.

'Didn't your mother take care of you?'

'I never knew my mother—she didn't want anything to do with me.'

'Tino, I'm so sorry… I had no idea.'

'No one does. That's the joke. Tino Zagorakis, the Greek tycoon, doesn't even know if he is a Greek.'

'But your name?'

'I took it from the van that came to the orphanage each week.. "Zagorakis Cleaning Services". What a joke, eh?'

'The orphanage? Oh, Tino.' This was no joke, and Lisa fell silent the moment he started speaking again.

'Everything inside the orphanage was grey until the day that Stella Panayotakis came to work there. Stella taught me that life could be bigger than my life in the orphanage. She said my life could be exciting. She told me about the world outside the orphanage—a world that was raw, and vivid, and only waiting for me to take my part in it. She put dreams into my head, and promised they would all come true if only I believed... It was hard, Lisa, really hard and Stella Panayotakis made me believe.'

'And when you were successful you gave her an apartment building.'

'She told you that?'

'Stella is your greatest fan.'

'And now, I have more plans, bigger plans.'

Tino's enthusiasm was infectious. 'What are your plans, Tino? Please tell me about them.'

'Well...I am going to have more places like Stellamaris.'

'More islands?' Lisa drew up in amazement.

'I'm sorry, *pethi mou*, you do not know.'

'I don't know what?'

'When I bought Stellamaris, I named it for Stella, and then I used it as my base.'

'Your base? You mean for your business?'

'For my other business.'

'Stop talking in riddles,' Lisa warned, dropping a kiss on his chest.

'I bring young people to Stellamaris, and some older people too...to find themselves. The island is a sanctuary, a place to start again, and for some, a place to start. Many of the people on Stellamaris began their lives in orphanages. I make sure there is training there for everyone, and that Stella visits frequently. Stella was my inspiration, and now she is theirs.'

'Now I understand why you're so close to Arianna.'

'Stella was a single mother, and it was very hard for her

back then. Don't look so impressed, Lisa. I don't deserve any praise. I did nothing special…it was all Stella's doing. All I have ever done is give people the tools to help themselves. Their achievements are all their own.'

'And now?' Lisa looked at him intently. 'Tell me about your new plans?'

'They're not so much new, as an extension of my existing scheme. I have accumulated massive wealth, and now I want to use that money to help others as Stella helped me. I want to extend my programme right across Greece to begin with.'

'Nothing too ambitious, then,' Lisa teased him gently.

'Very ambitious,' Tino admitted, 'and because of that I will need someone at my side. I can't even start the work I want to do until I find that one special person—someone who shares my aims, my desires, my dreams…someone who knows what it feels like to be on the outside looking in. Can you be that person, Lisa?'

'Are you offering me a job?'

Tino tilted his head as he pretended to consider this. 'Can you think of anyone better qualified to take on this task than a successful businesswoman who has accepted that she can delegate some of her duties to other members of her team at Bond Steel, a woman who has suddenly discovered she has a heart, a woman who knows what it is to be an outcast, a woman of principle, a woman who is every bit as driven as I am, a woman who has recently declared she is looking for radical change in her life?'

Closing her eyes, Lisa took time over framing her answer. 'All this—' she touched his face gently in wonder '—and a new job in just one working week.'

'Exactly as we planned,' Tino pointed out. 'We make a great team.'

'And if I was looking for something more?'

'Something more?'

'More than just a job, more than simply joining your organisation to help you with this new project?' She tensed as Tino stretched beyond her to reach for his clothes. 'What are you doing?'

'Looking for something...'

Seeing the velvet case, Lisa exclaimed with concern. 'You were supposed to take those back.'

'Surely you didn't expect me to take them back to the shop after you'd worn them, did you?'

Remembering where she'd worn them, Lisa blushed. 'Perhaps not.'

'Oh, look, here's another one.' Falling back onto the pillows, Tino dragged her down with him. Now there were two velvet boxes. 'Which one? You choose.'

'You shouldn't be buying me presents.'

'Buying gifts for you is one impulse I will never allow you to control,' he informed her. 'Now, which one do you choose?'

'They say all the best things come in small packages.'

'Not always.'

'But maybe you are right this time,' Tino conceded. 'Why don't you open the small box and find out?'

Taking it from him, Lisa pressed the small gilt catch and gasped as the lid flew open. The emerald ring was a perfect match to the fabulous earrings. 'What's this? A down payment on my first month's wages?'

'You wish.'

'So, what am I to think?' she demanded wryly.

Taking her left hand, he tested the ring for size on her marriage finger. 'Thank goodness, it fits perfectly. Oh, and there's one more thing.'

'Yes?' Lisa could hardly tear her gaze away from the incredible jewel on her finger.

'When we're in bed,' Tino continued sternly, 'there'll be

no more talk of wages and business. In our private life there will be just you, me, and our love under discussion.'

'Our love…'

'We can hardly be married without it.'

'Married?'

'Is this going to be another one of your business contracts?' he teased.

'Not just another contract,' Lisa argued firmly. 'The most important contract of all.'

'So, will you shake on the deal?' He started to smile.

'I'll certainly show some reaction,' she promised huskily when he drew her close to kiss her again.

EPILOGUE

'No, NO, no...' Sprawled on the floor with her legs stuck out in front of her, Lisa waggled her finger.

'That won't work... You have to do it like this,' Tino informed her, sweeping their son onto his shoulders.

Now, instead of screaming with frustration, the determined two-year-old was screaming with laughter as Tino galloped with him around the room.

'Come on, let's gather up the pieces of your jigsaw,' Lisa suggested to the fairy princess at her side. Elena took her puzzles seriously, and hadn't welcomed her brother's interference, but the fact that she had insisted on wearing a tinsel headband and a pair of wings while she worked made Lisa think that Elena would grow up to have just the right mix of intellect and playfulness.

And who would have imagined that Tino would turn into such a wonderful family man? Lisa mused, pausing to watch him for a moment...or that she would have a wardrobe full of musty suits, and paint-spattered jeans?

And wasn't this better? Wasn't this wonderful? And wasn't the sight of their newest taverna going up to provide training for a whole new group of youngsters the most thrilling deal either of them had ever pulled off?

'You're looking very thoughtful,' Tino observed, hunkering down beside her. It took some skill to keep Lucas balanced on his shoulders when the toddler was intent on hanging upside down.

'I'm just blessing the fact that our paths crossed at all,' Lisa admitted wryly. 'That was some quirk of fate.'

'Quirk of fate?' Tino stared at her. 'Our meeting was no accident, Lisa…'

'What do you mean?'

Lowering his son to the ground as Elena held out her hand to Lucas to take him out to play, Tino explained, 'I read about you, then I saw your photograph…and the rest is history.'

'I suppose you were determined to bring me to heel? You were,' she accused him fondly. 'I can see it written all over your face…'

'Maybe,' Tino confessed, slanting her a smile.

That was the point…the whole point. They were so similar they could read each other like a book. But it had been more than the challenge that had brought him to the offices of Bond Steel that day… When he had first heard Lisa's story, something deep inside him had cried out to meet her. With a history such as they shared you needed more than one lifetime to try and explain yourself. With Lisa, he never had to try; she just knew.

He had always wondered, feared, that the past might have left some indelible scar on him, but, although from the earliest days Lisa had tested his control to the limits and beyond, she had helped him prove that he had left the past behind, and that none of the violence had travelled with him.

He only felt complete when she was with him, and now they had children too…a family, the one thing he had always dreamed about when he was a child in the orphanage. And even now, gazing at Lisa, and Elena, and Lucas, he could hardly believe the joy they gave him. The love of a woman was a wonderful thing, but the love of a family was the greatest gift of all.

THE RICH
MAN'S VIRGIN

by

Lindsay Armstrong

Lindsay Armstrong was born in South Africa but now lives in Australia with her New Zealand-born husband and their five children. They have lived in nearly every state of Australia and have tried their hand at some unusual – for them – occupations, such as farming and horse-training – all grist to the mill for a writer! Lindsay started writing romances when their youngest child began school and she was left feeling at a loose end. She is still doing it and loving it.

PROLOGUE

MAGGIE TRENT and Jack McKinnon conducted rather unreal conversations at times.

Why this should be so had something to do with the unreal nature of their relationship, Maggie felt. Nothing ever went according to plan in their lives. Their first meeting had been sheer coincidence, their second meeting sheer disaster, their third meeting should have had labels stuck all over it shouting, 'Spoilt, little rich girl determined to get her own way'—according, at first anyway, to Jack.

They'd parted after that extended meeting, not well, and determined never wittingly to come together again.

Yet just under a year later Maggie began one of her unreal conversations with Jack McKinnon on the subject of their two-month-old son who had started out life known as Trent/McKinnon—it had been written on his wrist band and on the label on his cot. They'd dispensed with the stroke after a week but stuck with the Trent McKinnon.

The gist of their conversation was this.

'This is a very proper baby,' Maggie said seriously one evening.

'I never thought he was a porcelain doll.'

'No. I mean, he's very well organized. He does everything by the book.'

Jack frowned. 'He's only eight weeks old. How can you say that?'

Maggie was attractively dressed in slim white trousers and a floral seersucker jacket trimmed with green. Her dark gold hair was tied back with a green scrunchie; her green eyes were clear and she was sitting beside a cot.

Trent McKinnon was asleep in the cot.

'I'll tell you. He adapted himself to a four-hourly schedule right from the start under extremely difficult circumstances. He burps beautifully and he mostly sleeps between feeds just as the book says he should. He has one wakeful period, after his two p.m. feed, where he'll accept conversation and he quite appreciates being carried around for a bit. He now sleeps through the eight hours from ten p.m. to six a.m.'

'Is there anything he doesn't do by the book?' Jack asked with a grin. 'He sounds almost too good to be true.'

Maggie considered. 'He hates having his hair washed. He gets extremely upset, but even that isn't going against the book exactly. They do warn that some babies hate it.'

'Screams blue murder?'

'Yes. Otherwise—' she shrugged '—there's nothing he doesn't do very correctly.'

'What are you worried about, then?'

Maggie stared down at her sleeping son with her heart in her eyes. 'I can't help thinking he would be horrified if he knew how—irregular—his situation was.'

She looked up and their gazes clashed.

'Born out of wedlock, you mean?' he said, and for a fleeting moment his mouth hardened. 'That was your choice, Maggie.'

She inclined her head. 'That was before—all sorts

of things happened,' she said quietly and ran her fingers along the arm of her chair. 'That was definitely before I came to appreciate the reality of having a baby and what a baby deserves.'

CHAPTER ONE

MAGGIE TRENT sold real estate.

None of her family or friends particularly appreciated her job, although her mother was supportive, until Mary Donaldson of Tasmania got engaged to Crown Prince Frederik of Denmark and it was revealed that she had worked in a real estate office.

From then on, everyone looked at Maggie Trent with renewed interest, even a little spark of 'the world could be your oyster too'!

In fact, the world could have been Maggie's oyster anyway, had she wanted it. She came from a very wealthy background. At twenty-three she was a golden blonde, attractive, always stylish and well groomed.

Nevertheless, she also had a well-developed commercial instinct and a flair for her job in the form of matching the right people to the right properties plus a very real 'eye' for the potential in houses that many missed.

This came from the Bachelor of Arts degree she'd done at university along with courses in architecture and draughting, as well as her natural interest in people and her ability to get along with them. She'd been born with great taste.

If she had a creed it was that nothing was unsaleable.

She was enjoying her life and her career far too much, especially with the property boom going the way it was, to contemplate marriage, although there was at least one man in her life who wished she would—not a prince of any designation, however.

But Maggie had two goals. One was to prove that she was a highly successful businesswoman in her own right. She had visions of opening her own agency one day. The other was to allow no man to make her feel inferior because she was a woman. Both these ambitions had been nurtured by a difficult relationship with her father, a powerful, wealthy, often arrogant man who believed she was wasting her time working at all and equated real-estate agents with used-car salesmen.

It was undoubtedly—she didn't try to hide it from herself—this mindset that saw her take such exception to Jack McKinnon, wealthy property developer, with such disastrous results—not that she'd ever intended to deprive him of his liberty!

She couldn't deny that was how it had turned out, though. Nor had the fact that she'd been deprived of *her* liberty at the same time seemed to hold much weight with him at all. In fact, he'd ascribed some really weird motives to it all that still annoyed her to think of…

Anyway, it all started one sunny Sunday afternoon.

She and Tim Mitchell were sipping coffee and listening to an excellent jazz band amongst a lively crowd on a marina boardwalk. Her relationship with Tim was fairly casual. They did a lot of things together, but Maggie always drew the line at getting further involved. Truth be told this was placing undue strain on Tim, but he did a good job of hiding it.

'Who's that?' Maggie asked idly. She was feeling relaxed and content. She'd sold a house that morning that was going to earn her a rather nice, fat commission.

Tim glanced over his shoulder at the new arrivals that had caught Maggie's attention and drew an excited breath.

'Jack McKinnon,' he said. 'You know—the property developer.'

Maggie stared at the man. She did know the name and the man, but only by reputation.

Jack McKinnon was a millionaire many times over and amongst other things he headed the company that was developing new housing estates in what Maggie thought of as 'her patch', the Gold Coast hinterland.

If she was honest, and she was, Maggie disapproved of the kind of housing estates Jack McKinnon developed. She saw it as tearing up of the rural land that had always been the Coast's buffer zone. The area where you could own a few acres, run a few horses, breed llamas or whatever took your fancy; the green zone that was a retreat for many from the high-rise and suburbia of the rest of the Coast.

Now, thanks to Jack McKinnon and others, part of that green zone was disappearing and thousands of cheek-by-jowl 'little boxes' were taking its place.

Unfortunately, the reality of it was that the Coast's population was burgeoning. Not only did it offer a good climate and great beaches, but its proximity to Brisbane, the state's capital, also made it desirable and future urban development was inevitable.

Doesn't mean to say I have to like the people involved in doing it and making a fortune out of it at the same time, she mused.

'Do you know him?' she asked Tim as Jack

McKinnon and his party, two women and another man, selected a table not far away and sat down.

'I went to school with him, but he's a few years older. Bumped into him a couple of times since. He's a Coast boy who really made good,' Tim said with pride.

Maggie opened her mouth to demolish the likes of Jack McKinnon, then decided to hold her peace. Tim was sweet and good company. At twenty-nine he was a dentist with his own practice. With his engaging ways and a passion for all things orthodontic, and the prices dentists charged these days, she had no doubt he would 'really make good' as well, although perhaps not on the scale of Jack McKinnon.

It was on the tip of her tongue to ask Tim what the man was like, but she realized suddenly that she couldn't fathom why she wanted to know, and she puzzled over that instead.

It came to her there was definitely an aura to him that she found a little surprising.

His dark fair hair streaked lighter by the sun fell in his eyes. He would be over six feet, she judged, slim but broad-shouldered and he looked lithe and light on his feet.

Unlike many of the 'white shoe' brigade, Gold Coast identities, particularly entrepreneurs, who had over the years earned the sobriquet because of their penchant for flashy dressing, Jack McKinnon was very casually dressed with not a gold chain in sight.

He wore jeans, brown deck shoes, a white T-shirt and a navy pullover slung over his shoulders.

There was also a pent-up dynamism about him that easily led you to imagine him flying a plane through the sound barrier, crewing a racing yacht, climbing

Mount Everest, hunting wild animals and testing himself to the limit—rather than developing housing estates.

As these thoughts chased through her mind, perhaps the power of her concentration on him seeped through to him because he turned abruptly and their gazes clashed.

A little flare of colour entered Maggie's cheeks and Jack McKinnon raised an ironic eyebrow. Even then she was unable to tear her gaze away. Somehow or other he had her trapped, she thought chaotically as more colour poured into her cheeks. Then he noticed Tim and instant recognition came to him.

That was how Tim and Maggie came to join Jack's party.

She tried to resist, but Tim's obvious delight made it difficult. Nor was there any real reason for her to feel uneasy amongst Jack McKinnon's party, at first.

Her slim black linen dress and high-heeled black patent sandals were the essence of chic. Her thick dark gold hair fell to her shoulders when loose, but was tied back with a velvet ribbon today. Her golden skin was smooth and luminous.

She was, in other words, as presentable as the other two women. Nor were they unfriendly, although they were both the essence of sophistication. One, a flashing brunette, was introduced as Lia Montalba, the other, Nordic fair, as Bridget Pearson. The second man, Paul Wheaton, was a lawyer who acted for the McKinnon Corporation, but who was paired with whom was hard to say.

The conversation was light-hearted. They discussed the music. The McKinnon party had spent the night out on Jack's boat cruising the Broadwater, and had some fishy tales to tell, mainly about the ones that got away.

The man himself—why did Maggie think of him thus? she wondered—had a deep, pleasant voice, a lurking grin and a wicked sense of humour.

All the same, Maggie did feel uneasy and it was all to do with Jack McKinnon, she divined. Not that he paid her much attention, so was she still stinging inwardly from that ironically raised eyebrow and her curious inability to tear her gaze from his?

Well, if he thought her scrutiny was the prelude to her making a pass at him, if that was why he was now virtually ignoring her, he was mistaken and she was perfectly content to be ignored.

Or was she?

It occurred to her that what he was doing was a deliberate insult and before much longer everyone was going to realize it, to her humiliation. Her blood began to boil. Who did he think he was?

Then he trained his grey gaze on her and said musingly, 'Maggie Trent. David Trent's daughter, by any chance?'

She hesitated. 'Yes,' she replied briefly.

'*The* David Trent?' Lia asked, her big dark eyes wide. 'Ultra-wealthy, from a long line of distinguished judges and politicians, grazier, racehorse owner, champion yachtsman?'

Maggie shrugged.

'Maggie doesn't like to trade on her father,' Tim murmured.

What an understatement, Maggie marvelled, considering how stormy their father/daughter relationship had sometimes been.

'Lucky you, Maggie,' Paul commented.

'Yes,' Jack McKinnon agreed. 'Do you actually do anything useful, Maggie? Not that one could blame you if you didn't.'

Even Tim, obviously a fan of Jack McKinnon, did a double take.

As for Maggie, she stared at Jack out of sparkling green eyes—green eyes sparkling with rage, that was.

'I knew there was one good reason not to like you,' she said huskily. 'I detest the little boxes you build and the way you destroy the landscape to do so. Now I have another reason. Wealthy, powerful men who are completely in love with themselves mean absolutely nothing to me, Mr McKinnon.'

She got up and walked away.

She had a rostered day off on Monday, and she spent the morning with her mother.

In contrast to her sometimes stormy relationship with her father, Maggie adored her mother.

In her middle forties, Belle Trent looked years younger. Her straight dark hair was streaked with grey, but it was so glossy and beautifully cut many younger women envied it. With her fine dark eyes and slim figure she was essentially elegant. She was also a busy person; she did a great deal of charity work.

Yet there were times when Maggie sensed a current of sadness in her mother, but it was an enigmatic kind of sadness Maggie couldn't really fathom. She knew it had to do with her father, that at times their marriage was strained, but for no real reason Maggie could put her finger on.

Belle never complained and there was never any suggestion that it might break up, although, with a certain cynicism, Maggie sometimes wondered whether neither her mother nor her father could face the Herculean task of sorting out a divorce settlement.

But that Monday morning as she had coffee with her mother at a chic Sanctuary Cove pavement café, Maggie had something else on her mind.

'Do you know anything about the McKinnon Corporation and Jack McKinnon, Mum?'

Belle stirred sugar into her latte. 'Uh—I believe he's a bit of a whizkid. He started with nothing, I heard. Somehow or other he persuaded a bank to finance his first development and he hasn't looked back since. He now not only develops the estate but he has a construction company that builds many of the houses. Of course housing estates are not the only string to his bow.'

'No?'

Belle shook her head. 'No,' she said. 'Once he made his first few millions he diversified into boat-building. McKinnon Catamarans have taken off. If you looked through this marina—' she waved a hand towards the forest of masts and all sorts of boats moored in the Sanctuary Cove marina just across the road from the shopping and restaurant precinct '—you'd probably find quite a few.'

'So, if he started with nothing, he must be—clever,' Maggie hazarded.

'I believe he's one of *those*.' Belle wrinkled her nose. 'You know, the kind of gifted person with a lot of foresight and a lot of drive who is always going to make good. I don't believe he's at all ostentatious about it, though.'

'Hmm…'

Belle raised an eyebrow. 'Do you know him?'

'I met him. Yesterday, as it happens. He was rather rude to me.'

Her mother blinked. 'Why?'

'I have no idea.' Maggie frowned. 'How come you know so much about him?'

'Your aunt Elena has decided to put him on her list of eligible bachelors,' Belle said ruefully.

They stared at each other, then started to laugh. Elena Chadwick was actually Belle's cousin. She'd never married yet she wrote a column in a weekly magazine dispensing advice on all sorts of marital problems. When anyone took issue with her lack of experience on the subject, she protested that it was her unbiased views that were invaluable. She was a great promoter of innovative methods for 'holding onto your man'.

She also kept and updated quarterly, to the delight of her readers, a ten most eligible bachelors' list; the other noteworthy thing about Elena Chadwick was her talent for unearthing all sorts of unusual facts about people.

'If I didn't dislike him so much,' Maggie said, still gurgling with laughter, 'I'd feel sorry for him with Elena in hot pursuit! On the other hand, I have no doubt that he can look after himself.'

'What's he like?'

Maggie considered. 'I don't know, but he could be the kind of man women ride off with into the sunset without giving it a great deal of thought. Some women.'

'Hmm…' Belle said, echoing her daughter's earlier *Hmm* of doubt and reservation, but accompanied by a searching little look that Maggie missed.

*   *   *

When she got home later, Maggie closed her front door and took her usual few deep breaths of sheer appreciation of her home.

It was a two-storeyed villa overlooking a lovely golf course on Hope Island. It had a small garden, a conservatory dining room overlooking a fountain and she'd inherited it from her paternal grandmother. She'd also inherited some of the lovely pieces that furnished and decorated it.

She'd been very fond of her father's mother. Everyone told her she took after Leila Trent, not only in looks but personality although, curiously, this was the one area where they'd failed to agree. Leila had always insisted that if Margaret Leila Trent took after anyone, it was her father, David Trent.

'But we never do anything but fight!' Maggie protested, more than once. 'Well, not always, but you know what I mean.'

'That's because, underneath, you're so much alike,' Leila insisted. 'Oh, you've got your mother's more gentle genes to balance it, darling, but essentially you're a Trent and, whatever else you might like to say about your father, that means you have a lot of drive and a lot of nerve. Your grandfather was much the same.'

Once, Maggie voiced the opinion that she should have been a boy—to gain her father's approval anyway.

Leila looked at her piercingly. 'Don't go down that road, Maggie. Your mother has and—' She stopped, then added slowly, 'You just be yourself.'

Leila would never elaborate on what she'd been about to say and six months ago she'd died peacefully in her sleep.

Maggie tossed her bag onto the settee and slipped off her shoes.

She'd managed to avoid Tim, although she'd spoken to him on the phone and accepted his apologies for what had happened. What she hadn't been able to accept was his complete bafflement over the incident.

'Jack's just—normally—not *like* that,' he said several times.

Oh, yes? she thought cynically, but she told Tim it wasn't his fault and said simply that she'd be in touch shortly.

'I hope that's not a 'don't call us, we'll call you' message, Maggie?'

Maggie said no, of course not, but now, as she padded out to water her garden in her bare feet, she frowned, because the fact was that since Sunday afternoon's incident she'd been curiously at odds with herself. She just couldn't put her finger on why this was so. Why her smooth, successful life she'd been enjoying so much was suddenly not so appealing to her any more.

It couldn't have anything to do with Jack McKinnon's insulting manner and words, surely?

After all, he'd completely misread her. He'd taken her for an idle little rich girl, a daddy's pet, so how on earth could that start her thinking along some strange lines?

Strange lines such as a sudden dissatisfaction to do with her relationship with Tim?

Not that you could call it much of a relationship, but there was the fact that Tim dearly wanted to make it into something more while she didn't, and she was suddenly feeling guilty about it.

It wasn't only that, though. To be tarred with the same brush as her father was extremely annoying. She might, according to her grandmother, have inherited some of her father's genes, but not, she devoutly hoped, his arrogance. She might have a fairly well-developed commercial instinct when it came to the property market, but a lot of people thought of her father as a ruthless businessman—she certainly wasn't ruthless.

As usual, her garden soothed her. She'd had no idea she possessed green fingers until she'd inherited her villa. In six months she'd transformed the small garden into a colourful showpiece. She grew roses and camellias, impatiens, petunias and daisies, yellow, pink and white. Her lawn was like green velvet and her herb garden provided basil, mint, coriander, rosemary, sage, parsley, thyme and oregano.

So she watered and pottered and pruned dead heads until both Tim Mitchell and Jack McKinnon faded from her mind, quite unaware that Jack 'the man' would raise his undeniably attractive head in the most unexpected way when she went back to work the following morning.

Maggie was the only agent not engaged with clients when an elderly couple walked into the office on Tuesday morning, so she took them under her wing and set about making her usual assessment of what kind of a property they wanted to buy. This could often be a tricky business, but with Sophie and Ernest Smith it proved to be more—it proved to be a marital war zone.

It transpired that they had sold their previous property, a house and eight acres, to a developer. Sophie had not been in favour of doing this at all and claimed she wasn't going to be happy anywhere else, anyway.

Ernest, with a lack of patience that indicated this battle had been fought many a time before, detailed to Maggie why he'd thought it was such a good idea at the time.

They were getting on and eight acres were quite a handful. Once developers got their eye on an area what option did you have but to sell out unless you relished the thought of being hemmed in by hundreds of houses? The price they'd been offered would assure a comfortable retirement...

'Yes,' Sophie Smith said grimly, 'but if you'd hung on as I suggested, we would have got a lot more for it!'

Ernest bristled. 'We weren't to know that, woman, and a bird in the hand is worth two in the bush!'

Maggie spent a few moments calming them down, then asked for more details. The Smiths were the first to be approached in their road by the developer, and the ones to sell out cheapest. Others in the road who had held out over a period of time had received better offers.

It was obvious to Maggie that, not only had Sophie really loved her property and not wanted to sell anyway, but that the higher prices some of her neighbours had attained were going to be a thorn in her flesh and a cause for discontent between her and her husband for the rest of their lives.

'Who was the developer?' she asked.

Ernest heaved a sigh. 'The McKinnon Corporation.'

As Maggie surveyed the two unhappy people before her once again her blood boiled directly on account of Jack McKinnon.

All the same, she might never have done anything about it had fate not intervened.

A few days later, she was doing a property assessment.

The owners had relocated to Melbourne over a year ago. They'd contacted her by phone with instructions to value the property with a view to putting it on the market and they'd posted her the keys.

The house, she discovered, showed every sign of not having been lived in for quite a time—it was distinctly unloved and it was a crying shame because it had obviously once been a beautiful home with loads of character. But the acreage was green and rolling, there were lovely trees on it and a delightful, secretive creek ran through it. A creek, she felt sure, you would find platypus playing in.

There was also a large brick shed. She left it to last to inspect and finally tore herself away from the creek to do so. The shed had two means of access: a set of double doors you could drive a vehicle through, but they were heavily barred and padlocked, and a stout wooden single door with a deadlock. She unlocked it and walked into the cavernous gloom of the building.

One corner of it had been converted into a rudimentary dwelling, she found, complete with kitchenette, bathroom and toilet. The kitchenette had a small two-burner stove. There were an old kettle and a couple of pots as well as some mismatched china and cutlery. The kitchen cupboard held some tinned food and dry goods, but there was little furniture, only a sagging settee and a Formica-topped table with four chairs. But there were, as she clicked a light switch then ran a tap, both electricity and water connected.

She made some notes and looked around again, but it was bare except for a large mound covered with tarpaulins in one corner. She was just about to investigate when the scamper of mice in the rafters caused her to grimace and decide against it.

That was when she heard a vehicle pull up outside. To her amazement, as she watched through the doorway, who should step out of the late-model Range Rover but Jack McKinnon?

She stared through the door wide-eyed, but there was no mistaking him as he stretched and looked around. He wore buff chinos and a dark green long-sleeved shirt with patch pockets, casually dressed again in other words, but still—how to put it?—a very compelling presence? Yes.

All the same— *Oh, no! No, you don't!* were her next sentiments. No way are you going to turn this little piece of heaven into a housing estate, Jack McKinnon.

She emerged from the shadows of the shed with an ominous expression on her face.

'Well, well,' he drawled as they came face to face, 'if it isn't little Miss Trent, green crusader and man-hater.'

He looked her up and down and decided, somewhat to his surprise, that if she were anyone but David Trent's daughter he would find her rather peachy despite her grim expression.

Peachy? he thought with an ironic twist of his lips. Where did that come from? You wouldn't exactly call—he dredged his mind for an example—Lia Montalba peachy. Svelte, stunning, sexy, sophisticated—yes, definitely that, but peachy? No. So why apply it to this girl? Did it indicate a succulent, fresh and rather innocent quality he detected in Maggie Trent alongside the expensive grooming and the stunning green eyes?

He shook his head, mainly to dislodge an image of her without her clothes—she was David Trent's daughter, after all—and reminded himself that she could certainly stand up for herself.

But that produced another inclination in him. As well as speculating on her figure, he discovered a desire to indulge in more verbal fencing with her.

Hell, Jack, he thought, isn't that a little immature? Not to mention a dead-end street with this particular girl?

In the meantime, Maggie discovered she was clutching her mobile phone as tightly as if she wished to crush it, so she put it, together with her notes, carefully on the roof of her car and planted her hands on her hips as she delivered her reply.

'At this moment, yes to all of those names, Mr McKinnon,' she said through her teeth. 'But since I'm here at the express instructions of the owner in my capacity as a real-estate agent, you *can't* be here legitimately so would you mind moving on?'

He smiled fleetingly, thought, Immature? Maybe, but what do they say? Men will be men! And he took his time about summing her up from head to toe again.

With a rural inspection to do, Maggie wore jeans, short boots and a pink blouse. Her hair was fish-plaited and she wore the minimum of make-up, only lip gloss, in fact. It was also her last assignment of the day so she'd gone home to change into something suitable for tramping round a paddock.

None of that hid the fact that she was long-legged, high-breasted and had a particularly lithe way of walking that was an invitation to imagine that supple, golden body in your arms, in your bed...

Nor, he noted, did his scrutiny of her breasts, hips and legs, her smooth, silky skin, indeed his systematic stripping of her, go unnoticed.

Once again, bright colour flooded her cheeks, but at the same time her eyes started to sparkle with rage.

He observed the wrathful turmoil he was exciting in her with another smile, this time dry.

'So that's what you do for a—shall we say hobby? But it so happens you're wrong, Miss Trent,' he said. 'I was also contacted by the owners. They want to know if this property has development potential.'

Maggie closed her eyes in sheer frustration. 'They didn't say a word about that to me!'

He shrugged. 'You're welcome to check back with them.'

She reached for her phone, but put it down on the roof of her car again as her emotions ran away with her. 'You can't—you wouldn't! It's so lovely. It would be a crying shame.'

'To destroy it and cover it with little boxes?' he suggested, and strolled into the shed.

Maggie followed him. 'Yes!'

'Listen.' he turned on his heel towards her and she nearly ran into him. 'A lot of you do-gooders amaze me.'

She backed away a step.

It was impossible not to be slightly intimidated by Jack McKinnon. He was tall, for one thing, and he moved with superb co-ordination. His grey gaze was boring right into her and the lines and angles of his face were set arrogantly beneath that dark fair hair. The arrogance was compounded by a beaky nose and a well-cut but hard mouth and—at such close quarters there was even more to contend with.

He was so essentially masculine it was impossible to be in his company without a sense of man versus woman coming into the equation.

That translated, she realized, to a competitive form of self-awareness that took her by surprise. An 'I can be just as judgmental of you, Jack McKinnon, because I can be just as alluring, sexy and damned attractive as—as Lia and Bridget are!'

She blinked as it shot through her mind. Could she? She doubted it. She had never mentally stripped a man the way he had stripped her and she was quite sure she couldn't render him as hot and bothered—and stirred up, she acknowledged honestly—as his lazy, sensual summing-up of her had. Not to mention—how dared he do that to her? Who did he think he was?

There was also, if all that weren't bad enough—and she wondered why she hadn't taken this into account before because even her mother had mentioned it!—the distinct impression that he was diabolically clever, as he proceeded to demonstrate.

'If you have real concerns about the environment and the impact of urban sprawl, take them to the city council. If you object to rural zonings being overturned do something positive about it,' he said contemptuously.

'Something?' she echoed unwisely.

'Yes. Campaign against it. Stand for council yourself. Use your ballot power to vote for a 'greener' council. It can be done. But don't rail against me in a virtually uneducated fashion, because I'm not breaking any laws at all.'

'What about moral and philosophical laws?' she challenged. 'What about enriching yourself at the expense of the environment and people like the Smiths?'

'I have no idea who the Smiths are but...' he paused and once again that grey gaze roamed over her, although this time clinically and coldly '...it's often the wealthy, the old money entrenched in their ivory towers and open green spaces, who lack concern and understanding for the less fortunate majority of the population.'

Maggie gasped. 'That's not true, of me anyway!'

'No?' He raised a sardonic eyebrow. 'You should try being one of that majority, Miss Trent. You should experiment with existing as a couple and raising a family on a single income because the kids are too small to leave, or child-care is too expensive—and see what it means to you to have your own roof over your head.'

'I—'

But he continued scathingly, 'You may think they're little boxes, but they're *affordable* and they're part of the great Australian dream, owning your own home. Come to that, it's a vast continent but inhospitable, so suburbia and the fact that we cling to the coast is another fact of life.'

He paused and eyed her. 'How much does your privileged background stop you from understanding some basic facts of life?' he asked her then. 'How many acres does your father own all green, untouched and lovely?'

That was when Maggie completely lost her temper. One innuendo, one insult too many, she raged inwardly, and looked around for some way to relieve the pressure of it all—she grabbed the door and banged it closed.

'I hope,' he said as the echoes of it slammed around the shed, 'this isn't what I think it is.'

'And I hope it demonstrates to you the force of my emotions about the likes of you,' she returned icily.

He looked around with a gathering frown and mentally castigated himself for playing verbal war games with this girl. 'Are your emotions savage enough to want to kidnap me?'

'Savage enough to make me want to scream and shout, throw things and slam things—' Maggie stopped abruptly. 'Kidnap you? What on earth are you talking about? The last thing—'

'One wonders if your antipathy is towards my housing estates or the kind of man you think I am?' His grey glance brushed over her insolently. 'So you have a key in your pocket?'

Maggie looked bewildered. 'What do you mean? A key? No. Why?'

He walked past her to the closed shed door and turned the handle. Nothing happened. 'This door is now deadlocked. From memory, you had a key in this lock but on the outside, didn't you?'

'Yes.' Maggie stopped and her lips parted as understanding of what she'd done started to seep through. 'Yes.' She cleared her throat. 'But there must be other ways out.'

'Show me,' he commanded. 'As far as I can see the only two windows have burglar bars fitted and both doors are locked now.'

'Oh, my…' Maggie breathed. 'I don't believe this! What about your keys? You must have had some.'

'No. I wasn't really interested in the house or the shed.'

'Well, well—phones,' she gabbled, and was hit by the memory of her mobile sitting on the roof of her car. She closed her eyes. 'Please tell me you've got your mobile phone on you?' she begged.

'I don't. I left it on its mounting in my car. This is all very affecting, Ms Trent,' he said with utter contempt, 'but whatever you *don't* like to call it, and for whatever reason you decided to deprive me of my liberty—' his gaze was cold enough to slice right through her '—you're going to pay for this.'

'Hang on, hang on.' Maggie took some deep breaths. 'It was an accident. Yes, OK, maybe I got a bit carried away, but I have every right to, on the Smiths' behalf if nothing else! There is no reason in the world, however,' she said emphatically, 'that would make me want to kidnap you!'

'The ubiquitous Smiths again,' he murmured, then said trenchantly, 'Lady, you were bestowing enough attention on me last Sunday to make the hairs on the back of my neck stand up.'

Maggie sucked in her cheeks in the effort she made not to blush. 'That was the power of my disapproval,' she offered stiffly.

'Oh, yeah?' He said it softly, but the two words contained a world of disbelief.

'Yes!' she insisted at the same time as a most treacherous little thought slipped into her mind— So why hadn't she been the same since?

But that spurred her on to say hotly. 'You can't

have it both ways, Mr McKinnon. Either I'm a man-hater or I'm not!'

He lifted an eyebrow. 'Perhaps I should qualify that—a hater of wealthy, powerful men completely in love with themselves.'

'Bingo! Now you've got it right.'

'I wonder,' he mused. 'There could be two sides to that coin, but anyway—' he looked briefly amused '—I don't agree that I'm in love with myself so you mightn't have to hate me totally, or the opposite,' he added softly.

Maggie stared at him. 'I have no idea what you're talking about!'

He rubbed his chin and narrowed his eyes.

'Look…' She hesitated as she tried to gather her thoughts, then she threw up her hands. 'If I'd *lured* you here then locked you in, that would be a different matter, but it's a supreme coincidence the two of us being here today!'

'You could be a quick thinker for all I know,' he countered. 'And there are women who take the most amazing liberties and—opportunities.'

She studied the harsh lines of his face. She thought of the pent-up dynamism she'd sensed in him. She had to acknowledge that he would be extremely attractive to most women and when you added his wealth to his looks and his aura, you had also to acknowledge there could be some women, gold-diggers, fortune-hunters, who would take what opportunities they could.

'You forget,' she said quietly, 'I probably have as much money in my own right as you do.'

He said, with a flash of irritation, as if he was suddenly heartily sick of her, 'I don't really give a damn for your motivation. I'd much rather you worked out how to get us out of here. I have a plane to catch in a couple of hours.'

Maggie looked around helplessly, then upwards. 'Maybe—maybe we can go through the roof?'

He swore comprehensively and pointed out just how high the roof was and that there was no ceiling. There was also no sign of so much as a set of steps, let alone a decent ladder, or…

Maggie finally stemmed the tide. She planted her hands on her hips again. 'You're a man, aren't you? Surely you can think of something?'

He folded his arms and looked sardonic. 'Even wealthy, powerful men have their uses? Isn't that a double standard?'

Maggie opened and closed her mouth a couple of times.

'Cat got your tongue, Miss Trent?' he drawled. 'Never mind, here's what I suggest. Since you got us into this—*you* get us out.'

CHAPTER TWO

'THAT'S...that's ridiculous,' Maggie stammered.

'Why?'

'I thought you had a plane to catch.'

'I get the feeling even my best efforts won't catch me that plane.'

She gazed around in serious alarm. 'That doesn't entitle you to twiddle your thumbs!'

He looked her over sardonically, but she was entirely unprepared for what he said next.

'Let's try and clear the decks here. If you're not trying to make some stupid statement about the kind of housing estates I develop, what are you after, Maggie Trent? My body?'

She went scarlet, instantly and—it felt—all over, and could have killed herself. 'In your dreams, mister,' she said through her teeth.

'Why so hot, then?' he taunted and ran his gaze up and down her. 'We might suit rather well. In bed.'

Her tongue seemed to tie itself in knots as all her mental sensors seemed to attune themselves to this proposition in the form of a picture in her mind's eye of just that—Jack McKinnon running his hands over her naked body.

What was particularly surprising about it was the fact that she didn't often fantasize about men. In fact she'd sometimes wondered if there was something wrong with her. The other surprise she got was the realization that this man had got under her skin from the very beginning in this very way, and succeeded in unsettling her even when she'd been telling herself she hoped never to lay eyes on him again.

Perhaps, but that didn't mean she had to like it, or him, she thought.

'Look—' she ignored his assessing gaze; she ignored her burning cheeks '—don't push me any further with this kind of—cheap rubbish!'

He smiled slightly as he took in the imperious tilt of her chin. 'Ever tried a real man, Maggie, as opposed to a good-mannered, docile boy like Tim Mitchell?'

Her lips parted.

'You might find your stance on men somewhat changed if you did,' he drawled, and went on before she could draw breath. 'And if you're not making a statement on housing estates, what's left?'

'You tell me,' she suggested dangerously.

This time he smiled quite charmingly, although it didn't take the sting out of what he said. 'A flighty, spoilt little rich bitch who hates not getting her own way?' he mused. 'A right chip off the old block,' he added with that lethal smile disappearing to be replaced by a cold, hard glance of contempt. Then he turned away.

'Hang on! What's that supposed to mean? Do you…do you know my father?' she demanded.

He turned back casually. 'Everyone knows about your father. His high-handed reputation precedes him by a country mile.'

Maggie bit her lip, but she soldiered on. 'I told you—well, no, Tim told you, but all the same—I don't trade on my father.'

'Your kind generally stick together in the long run,' he observed and shrugged his wide shoulders.

'What "kind", exactly, is that?' she queried with awful forbearance.

He looked at her indifferently. 'Old money, class, breeding—whatever you like to call it.'

'People who make those kinds of statements generally have none of those advantages—but wish they did,' she shot back.

He grinned. 'You're right about one thing, I have no breeding or class, but you're wrong about the other—I have no desire to acquire them. Well, now that we've thoroughly dissected each other, not to mention insulted each other, should we get down to brass tacks?'

'And what might they be?'

'How to get out of here. Is anyone expecting to see you this afternoon or this evening? Does anyone know you're here?'

Maggie pulled out a chair and sat down at the table at the same time as, with an effort, she withdrew her mind from the indignity of being tarred with the same brush as her father again or, if not that, being classed as a flighty little rich bitch.

That one really stung, she discovered. True, she could be hot-tempered, as she'd so disastrously demonstrated, but it had no connection with being spoilt or rich. How to make Jack McKinnon see it that way—she shot him a fiery little glance—was another matter. Then again, why should she even bother?

She frowned and addressed herself to his question. 'The office knew I was going to do a property valuation, but I wasn't planning to go back to work this afternoon so they won't miss me until tomorrow morning, oh, damn,' she said hollowly.

He raised an eyebrow at her.

'I've just remembered. I wasn't planning to go into the office at all tomorrow.'

'Why not?'

'I have a doctor's appointment in the morning and I was going to spend the afternoon—' She broke off and grimaced a shade embarrassedly.

'Let me guess,' he murmured. 'Getting your hair done, a facial, a manicure, a dress fitting, perhaps a little shopping in the afternoon?'

Maggie's cheeks started to burn because most of the things he'd suggested were on her agenda for tomorrow afternoon. But she ignored her hot cheeks and beamed him a scathing green glance.

'Listen,' she said tersely, 'yes, my hours can be elastic. On the other hand sometimes they're extremely long and I have a day off this week, two actually, because I'm working *all* next weekend. I do not have any more time off than anyone else in the office!'

He shrugged.

Prompting her to continue angrily, 'And if I'm the only woman you know who gets her hair cut now and then, has a manicure occasionally and shops from time to time, you must mix with some strange types, Mr McKinnon.'

He studied her hair and her nails. 'They look fine to me,' he said smoothly, but with an ironic little glint. 'Be that as it may, only your doctor and your beautician are likely to miss you tomorrow I take it?'

Maggie sat back with her expression a mixture of frustration and ire. 'Yes!'

'Anything serious with the doctor?'

'No.'

'So they're hardly likely to mount a search and rescue mission.'

'Hardly.'

'You live alone?'

'I live alone,' she agreed. 'How about you?'

'Yep.'

'What about this plane you're supposed to catch?'

He looked thoughtful. 'It could be a day or two before I'm missed. I'm—I was—on my way to a conference in Melbourne, but I planned to call in on my mother tomorrow in Sydney on the way.'

Maggie sat up. 'Surely she'll miss you?'

'She didn't know I was coming. It was to be a surprise.'

'That's asking for trouble!' Maggie said. 'You could have missed *her*.'

'Apart from complicating our situation?' He waited until she looked slightly embarrassed. Then he added, 'Not much chance of missing her as she's not fit enough to go out.'

This time Maggie looked mortified. 'I beg your pardon,' she said stiffly.

His lips twisted. 'As it happens I'm in agreement with your first sentiment.'

She looked startled. 'Why?'

'I'm sorry now I didn't let her know, but the reason I don't usually is because if I don't turn up exactly at the appointed time, she gets all anxious and unsettled.'

'Oh.' Maggie found she had to smile. 'My mother's a bit like that.'

They said nothing for a few moments, both locked

into their thoughts about their respective mothers, then he shrugged and strolled over to the pile of tarpaulins in the corner and started to pull them off.

Maggie confidently expected an old utility vehicle or tractor to be revealed, so she sucked in an incredulous breath when a shiny black vintage car in superb condition and a Harley Davidson motor bike, both worth a small fortune, were exposed.

'They didn't—the owners didn't say a word about these!'

'No? It does explain the security, however,' he said. 'This shed is like a fortress.'

Maggie frowned. 'It doesn't make sense. They haven't lived here for over a year, they told me. They don't have a caretaker. The house is a shambles but, well, who in their right minds would—sort of—abandon these?' She got up and walked over to the car and stroked the bonnet.

'You would have thought they'd put them up on blocks at least,' Jack said. He opened the car door and they both looked in.

The interior was as beautifully restored as the rest of it with plump, gleaming leather seats and the keys were dangling in the ignition. Jack slid into the driver's seat and switched it on. The motor purred to life.

He let it run for a few minutes, then switched it off and got out of the car. 'They must know they're here,' he said. 'Someone has to be starting this car regularly or the battery would be flat.'

'What did they say to you?' she asked. 'The owners.'

'I didn't speak to them, but…' he paused '…same as you; they gave my PA to understand that no one had lived here for over a year. They certainly didn't mention any vintage cars and bikes to her, but I wasn't planning to come into the shed so...' He stopped.

Maggie turned on her heel and ran across to the kitchen cupboard. 'These tins,' she said, pulling out a can of baked beans, 'don't look over a year old. Nor—' she reached for an open packet of cornflakes and peered inside '—would these have survived the mice I happen to know are here. But they're fine.'

She proffered the packet to him.

He didn't look inside. 'I believe you. Are you saying someone has taken over this shed?'

'It's quite possible! The nearest neighbours are miles away on a different road. The driveway in here is virtually concealed. You could come and go and no one would be any the wiser!'

'If it's true it's not much help to us unless they actually live here and come home every night.'

'Maybe they do!' Maggie said with a tinge of excitement.

He walked round the car and opened the boot. 'Well, that's something, in case they don't.'

'What?' She went to have a look.

'A tool kit.' He hefted a wooden box out of the boot, put it on the floor and opened it. 'Of sorts,' he added and lifted out an electric key saw. 'We may just be able to cut our way out of here somehow.'

Maggie heaved a huge sigh of relief. 'Oh, thank heavens!'

He glanced across at her. 'Hear, hear.'

'In time to catch your plane?'

'No. This is more a hobby saw; it's going to be a long, slow process.'

'Why don't you get straight to work?' she suggested. 'I'll make us a cup of tea.'

The look he tossed her was full of irony.

'I've never used one of those,' she said, 'but if you'd like to show me how, you could make the tea and I could do the sawing. Would you prefer that?' she queried innocently.

'No, I would not. We could be here for a year,' he returned shortly.

Maggie hid a smile.

'But what you could do is scout around for an extension cord. The nearest power point is too far from the door—' He stopped abruptly and looked frustrated.

'There's power!' she assured him. 'And water. I checked.'

He looked relieved this time, but in no better humour. 'OK. Start looking for a cord.'

Maggie resisted the temptation to salute and say, Yes, sir! And she toned down her triumph when she found an extension cord on top of the kitchen cupboard.

An hour later, his mood was even worse. There were no spare blades for the saw and the one in it was blunt.

'This thing wouldn't cut butter,' he said, having succeeded in cutting no more than a shallow, six-inch-long groove in the door. He threw it aside in disgust.

It was dark by now and the only light was from a single bulb suspended from the rafters. Its thin glow didn't reach the corners of the shed, and the mice, having decided they weren't under threat from the humans who had invaded their space, were on the move again.

Maggie had made tea an hour ago, then coffee a few minutes previously. She now stared down into the dark depths of her cup, and shivered. 'We're not going to get out of here tonight, are we?'

He came over to the table and pulled out a chair. 'No, Miss Trent, we are not. Not unless whoever is moonlighting in this shed comes home.'

'So you agree someone *is* doing that?'

'Was there power connected to the house?'

Maggie thought swiftly. 'No. That's strange, isn't it? On here but not up there.'

'Whoever they are, they may have found a way to tap into the grid illegally.' He suddenly slammed his fist onto the table in a gesture of frustration.

'I...' she looked at him fleetingly '...I do apologize.'

'So you bloody well should.'

He had wood shavings in his hair and he brushed them off his shirt. There were streaks of dust on his trousers.

'You don't have to swear.'

'Yes, I do,' he contradicted. He looked at his hands. They were filthy and several knuckles were grazed. 'Would you like to know what I'd be doing now if I wasn't incarcerated here? I'll tell you.'

He glanced at his watch. 'I'd just be arriving at my hotel in Sydney where I'd shout myself a sundowner and have a shower. Then I'd order a medium-rare pepper steak with Idaho potatoes, maybe some rock oysters to start with and a cheese platter to follow. I feel sure I'd wash it all down with...' he stared at her reflectively '…a couple of glasses of a decent red, then maybe some Blue Mountain coffee.'

Maggie flinched inwardly and couldn't think of a thing to say.

'How about you?' he queried.

She thought for a moment. 'Toasted cheese with a salad and an early night,' she said briefly.

He lifted an eyebrow. 'That sounds very bachelor girl.'

'I am a bachelor girl.'

'A very well-heeled one by the same token,' he murmured.

Maggie started to feel less embarrassed and guilty. 'Don't start on all that again,' she warned.

'Why shouldn't I? If you were an ordinary girl rather than ultra-privileged, and if you were without strong, unreasonable prejudices, I wouldn't be here.'

'Listen, mate, you offered the first insult!'

'Ah, yes, so I did.' He grinned reminiscently. 'I take nothing back.'

'Neither do I. But you,' she accused, 'went on doing it.'

He shrugged. 'You have to admit it was a rather bizarre situation to find myself in.'

Maggie frowned. 'What did you mean there being two sides to that coin? The one about me hating powerful, arrogant men or words to that effect?'

'Sometimes,' he said reflectively, 'girls are secretly attracted to power and arrogance in men even if they don't like to admit it.'

'I am not one of those, assuming they exist and are not a figment of your imagination,' Maggie stated.

He grinned. 'Very well, ma'am. And it doesn't

make you at all nervous to be locked in here with me in our current state of discord?'

Maggie hesitated. 'I know it must have looked rather strange, what I did,' she said slowly, 'and I suppose I can't blame you for wondering what on earth was going on. Therefore everything you said, even although I found it offensive—'

'All that cheap rubbish?' he interrupted gravely, although with an inward grin.

'Yes.' She eyed him briefly and sternly. 'Therefore everything you said was—understandable, perhaps, so—'

'I see.'

'Will you stop interrupting?' she commanded. 'This is hard enough as it is.'

'My lips are sealed,' he murmured.

She eyed him dangerously this time. 'Put plainly, I'd much rather you disliked me and were irritated by me than any other ideas you might have had, all the same!'

He laughed softly, then he watched her intently for a long moment. 'Are you really that naïve, Maggie Trent?'

'What's naïve about it? Well,' she hastened to say, 'perhaps I am, in a general sense. I did have a very sheltered—' She broke off and bit her lip.

'Upbringing?' he suggested.

'My father—' She stopped again. She might have her problems with her father—she did!—but broadcasting them to strangers was another matter.

'Saw to that, did he?' Jack McKinnon eyed her reflectively. 'I'm surprised he let you out of his sight.'

Maggie drew a deep breath, but discovered she couldn't let this go. 'The fact that I actually have a job and live on my own is testimony to a battle for independence that you might find quite surprising.'

He said nothing, but the way he stared at her led her to believe he might be reviewing all the facts he now had at his disposal, and changing his opinions somewhat. Good, she thought, and, with a toss of her head, stood up.

She would have died if she'd known that he was actually contemplating the—pleasure?—yes, of having her as his dinner companion at his mythical dinner in Sydney, then disposing of her clothes article by article in a way that drove her wild with desire even if she didn't like him particularly...

'You know,' she said blandly, 'it's just occurred to me that I could alleviate at least one of your discomforts.'

He looked supremely quizzical. 'You could?' And wondered what she'd say if he told her at least one of his discomforts sprang from the way he kept thinking how she'd look without her clothes...

She went over and rummaged in the kitchen cupboard. What she produced was half a bottle of Scotch. She gathered two glasses and a jug from below the sink. She rinsed them all out, filled the jug with water and placed everything on the table.

'It may be tinned food rather than steak, oysters and cheese but at least we can have a drink—we may even find it puts us in a better mood.'

He studied her offerings, then studied her expression. 'Miss Trent, you are a peach.' He reached for the bottle.

She was right.

After a Scotch and a meal of a heated-up Fray

Bentos steak pie and baked beans, Jack McKinnon
was rather more mellow.

'Tell me about the Smiths,' he said as she prepared
to wash the dishes.

Maggie looked rueful and did so as she found a
small bottle of dish detergent and squirted some green
liquid into the sink. 'The thing is—' she turned on a
tap '—is it ethical?'

'To offer people who hold out more money?' he
mused. 'There's no law against it.'

Maggie eyed the mound of bubbles building in the
sink. 'It's going to drive Sophie and Ernest mad for
the rest of their lives.' She switched off the tap.

'Don't you think the heart of this dilemma might
lie elsewhere?'

She turned to him. 'Elsewhere?'

'Such as...' he paused '...Ernest jumping at the
chance to get out of a property he was finding too
much for him—and even the original price was a very
fair one, believe me—while Sophie wanted to stay?
A marital lifestyle dilemma, in other words.'

Maggie started to wash the dishes in silence. 'Perhaps,' she said eventually.

'And did you know, Maggie, that I always exceed
the town planning regulations regarding open spaces,
sports fields and community centres like kindergar-
tens? They may appear to you like little boxes, the
houses I build, but they're always well provided with
those facilities. And while my houses may not be
mansions, they are not shonky.'

'I'll...I'll have to take your word for it, Jack.' She
rinsed the last dish, then turned to face him. 'On the
other hand, I could not but regret *this* property, for
example, being scraped bare and built on.'

He was sitting back looking relaxed, even amused, although she wasn't sure why.

'What?' she asked with a frown.

'I'm in agreement with you, that's all.'

She blinked. 'But you said—'

'I said I was contacted about it with a view to urban development. As you probably know that would mean applying for a re-zoning that I doubt I'd get, but that's not why I came to look at it personally.'

'It isn't?'

He shook his head. 'I'm interested in providing a buffer zone now.' He ruffled his hair. 'So I'm looking for the right properties to provide it. I'm also looking for one that I might live on. This could be it.'

Maggie stared at him with her mouth open and all sorts of expressions chasing through her eyes.

'I felt sure the irony of that would appeal to you,' he drawled. 'Why don't you sit down and have another drink with me before you explode?'

'I…you…this…I will,' Maggie said. 'Of all the…' She couldn't find the words and she dropped into a chair and accepted the glass he handed her.

'Double standards?' he suggested.

'Yes! Well…'

He laughed softly. 'But at the same time preserving the rural environment? That is a tricky one.'

'I was thinking about you joining the "ivory tower" club after all you said on the subject,' she returned arctically.

'Oh, I don't think there's any chance of that,' he drawled.

Maggie sipped some Scotch gratefully. It was getting cold. As she felt the warmth of it go down she watched him covertly.

He had his hands shoved in his pockets, he was sprawled back and he appeared to be lost in thought.

It suddenly struck Maggie with a peculiar little pang that Jack McKinnon was actually in a class of his own. Much as she would like to, she couldn't deny his ivory-tower-club theory, although she'd certainly fought her own battles against being drawn into the socialite/debutante kind of society he meant: the polo, the races, fashion shows, winter skiing/summer cruise followers.

She'd always longed for a broader canvas. She wanted to work; she wanted to travel, but a different circuit from the one her father and his friends travelled from one exclusive resort to another.

She wanted, she realized, to know people like this man and overcome his basic contempt for her kind. Yet, it struck her with some irony, only hours ago she'd been so angry with him, her thoughtless expression of it had reinforced everything he disliked about her 'kind'.

The mystery of it all, though, was why did it matter so much to her? There was a whole world of unusual, interesting people out there…

'So what do you suggest?'

She came out of her reverie at his question to find him watching her narrowly, as if he'd got the vibes that her preoccupation was to do with him, and she moved a little uncomfortably.

'Uh—what do you mean?'

He shot her a last lingering look, then got up and stretched. 'Where do we sleep, Miss Trent?'

'That's not a problem. I've already worked it out,' she told him as her mind moved like lightning. 'I'll use the back seat of the car. You can—' she gestured '—use the settee.'

He grimaced. 'Quick thinking, that.'

'You're too long for the car,' she pointed out reasonably.

'I'm too long for the settee and it looks filthy.' He crossed over and tested it, then looked down at it critically. 'On the other hand, if this is what I think it is,' he said slowly, 'I might not be so hardly done by after all.'

'What do you mean?'

He pulled off the cushion seats, pulled up a bar and the settee converted itself into a sofa bed. What was more, it was made up with fairly clean-looking sheets, a thin blanket and two flat pillows.

'Diagonally, I might just fit if I bend my knees.'

'Lucky you,' she said rather tartly.

He cocked his head at her. 'While you're left without a blanket or any covering—is that what you're suggesting?'

She shrugged.

'The penalty for such quick thinking,' he murmured, and laughed at her expression. 'Here's what we'll do. Did you happen to see a pair of scissors in the kitchen cupboards or drawers?'

Maggie went to check and came back with a rusty pair. 'Only these.'

'They'll do.'

'What are you going to do?'

'This. Not our property obviously, but desperate circumstances call for desperate measures and we can replace them.'

He made several cuts then, using both hands, he ripped the double blanket and two sheets in half. He handed her hers ceremonially along with one of the pillows. 'There you go. I may never belong to the ivory tower club, but I can be a gentleman of sorts.'

She knew from the wicked look in his grey eyes that the joke was on her, but not what the joke was. She suspected it could be more than the ivory tower club, but…?

'Don't worry about it, Maggie Trent,' he said softly, but with more humour apparent in his eyes. 'Go to bed.'

Maggie turned away slowly. Before she did go to bed, she removed her boots, released her hair and paid a visit to the bathroom. Then she climbed into the back seat of the car, only to climb out again.

'What?' He was seated on the sofa bed taking his shoes off.

'I think it would be a good idea to leave the light on.' She gestured widely. 'Might deter the mice from getting too friendly.'

'You're scared of mice?'

'Not *scared*,' she denied. 'I just don't like the idea of close contact with them. Do you?'

'Not particularly. OK. It can stay on.'

'Thank you.' She hesitated as she was struck by an amazing thought—that her arbitrary organization of the sleeping choices might have been a miscalculation. Or, put it this way, she would feel much safer and more comfortable if she were to share the sofa bed with him, purely platonically of course.

Her eyes widened as she combed her fingers through her hair and posed a question to herself— You're not serious?

'Maggie?'

'Uh—' some colour came to her cheeks '—nothing. It's nothing. Goodnight,' she said and could have shot herself for sounding uncertain.

'Sure?'

'Mmm...' She marched over to the car and got in again.

Jack McKinnon waited until she'd closed the door, wound down a window and disappeared from view. Then he lay back, pulled his half of the thin blanket up and examined his very mixed feelings on the subject of Maggie Trent.

Something of a firebrand, undoubtedly, he wouldn't be here otherwise—he grimaced. Plenty of hauteur, as well, a good dose of her father's genes, in other words, yet her personality was curiously appealing in a way her father's could never be, not to him anyway.

How so? he asked himself. She'd exhibited just about every failing you might expect from a spoilt little rich girl, even to ordering him to sleep on the sofa.

Perhaps it was the power of her emotions, then, he mused. Even if misguidedly, she was passionate about the environment. She felt deeply about the plight of the Smiths—he grimaced again. But there was something else...

Her *peachiness*? That damned word again... OK, then, she was lovely. About five feet four, he judged, her figure was trim, almost slight, but he got the feeling it might be delightful: delicately curved, velvety nipples, small, peachy hips—yes, the word did fit somewhere!—satiny skin and all that tawny hair, not to mention stunning eyes to set it off. But what was it that puzzled him about her—an aura of sensual unawareness?

Maybe, he thought, then amended the thought to—

sometimes… When he'd mentally stripped her she'd got all hot and bothered as well as angry. Now, though, being trapped in a shed with a strange man, virtually, who *had* mentally stripped her, appeared not to faze her. Why not?

Had a habit of command kicked in that didn't allow her even to contemplate things getting out of hand? Whatever, he concluded with an inward smile, it was rather intriguing and refreshing. Not that he'd do anything about it…

So why—he posed the question to himself—was he not more…absolutely furious about the current state of affairs? True, he'd been frustrated and irritable when trying to saw through the door, he'd been incredulous and angry when it had first happened, but…

He shrugged. All the same, he was going to have to come up with something tomorrow. He stared upwards. If he could figure out a way to get up to the roof, that might be his best shot after all.

Maggie arranged herself as best she could on the back seat of the car, only to discover that sleep suddenly seemed to be the furthest thing from her mind.

She was confused, she realized. Confused, tense and annoyed with herself. What an incredibly stupid thing to do! Would she ever grow out of these rash, hot-headed impulses that plagued her from time to time? When *would* they get out of this wretched shed?

Well, that explained the tension and the annoyance, she reasoned, but what was she confused about?

Jack McKinnon, it came to her. It seemed to be impossible to tear her thoughts away from him! Because she didn't understand him? Was that so sur-

prising? She barely knew him, but, going on what she
did know of him, his reactions *had* been rather surprising.

Yes, there was still that underlying contempt, there
had been open contempt, but he *could* have made
things much more uncomfortable for her. He could
have treated her far more severely and scathingly…
Had she misjudged him? Well, no, he had offered the
first insult. Then again, that had obviously been based
on her father's reputation.

All the same, she hadn't expected to end up liking
him…

She sighed exasperatedly and closed her eyes.

Jack woke up at three o'clock.

As he glanced at his watch he was amazed that he'd
slept so long; he didn't need much sleep. What also
amazed him was the sight of Maggie Trent asleep at
the table with her head pillowed on her arms.

He sat up abruptly and the rusty springs of the sofa
bed squeaked in protest.

Maggie started up, wide-eyed and alarmed.
'Who…what…?'

'Only me,' he said reassuringly. 'What's the matter?'

'I…just couldn't sleep. It was like being in a coffin,
no, a hearse,' she corrected herself. 'I felt seriously
claustrophobic.'

'You should have told me earlier!'

She eyed him, then smiled, a faint little smile of
pure self-mockery. 'I do sometimes find it hard to
admit I could be wrong about—things.'

He grimaced, then had to laugh. 'OK.' He got up.
'That admission earns you a spell on the bed.'

'Oh, you definitely wouldn't fit into the car, so—'

'Don't argue, Maggie,' he ordered. 'I have no intention of trying the car anyway.'

'But it's only three o'clock,' she pointed out. 'What will you do?'

'Seriously apply myself to getting us out of here. Come on, do as you're told.'

Maggie got up reluctantly, but she sank down onto the sofa bed with a sigh of relief. Then she frowned. 'Does that mean you haven't been serious about getting us out of here until now?'

He glanced at her. Her hair was spread across the pillow and even in the feeble light her eyes were discernibly green—he couldn't remember knowing anyone with those colour eyes, he thought, then remembered her father. Of course. His mouth hardened.

'Let's just say I don't like being thwarted.' He turned away.

'Did that annoy you,' she asked, 'me saying you weren't serious?'

He shrugged. 'It reminded me that I've been in this damn shed for long enough.'

'You've been—for the most part—you've been pretty good about it. I do appreciate that.'

'Yes, well, why don't you go to sleep?'

She didn't answer immediately, then, 'The more I think about it, the roof is the only way to go. I hate to say I told you so, but if we could get up there somehow, it is only an old tin roof and maybe we could prise one of the sheets open or apart or something. I'm actually quite good at climbing.'

He was stretching and he turned to her with his arms above his head.

Maggie took a strange little breath as the full impact of his beautiful physique hit her.

'Climbing?' he said.

'I used to do gymnastics, seriously, and I've done an abseiling course. I'm not afraid of heights and I have good balance.' She looked upwards. 'I wouldn't have any trouble balancing on those beams.'

He studied her thoughtfully, then stared around. 'If I got onto the roof of the car and you got onto my shoulders, you might just reach a beam.'

Maggie sat up. 'Yes!' She subsided. 'But what to use to attack the roof with?' she asked whimsically.

The toolbox he'd got the saw out of was lying on the floor next to the table. He bent over and pulled out a short chrome bar. 'Heaven alone knows what this is for, but it might do, although—' he grimaced '—whether you'd have the strength—'

She cast aside the blanket and got up. 'I could try!'

He hesitated a moment longer, then shrugged. 'We'll give it a go.'

Five minutes later they were both on the roof of the car.

'Just as well they built them solidly in those days,' he commented with a fleeting grin, and squinted upwards. 'OK, here's what we'll do.'

He had both halves of the blanket. 'I'm going to try and throw these over the beam. That should give you something to work with. Look—' he stripped off his shirt '—take this up with you. Once you get up there, if you do, you'll need as much protection from splinters as you can get and I'll also tie the bar into one sleeve. You sit down while I throw.'

This time she did say it—'Yes, sir!'—but good-

naturedly and even with something akin to excitement
in her voice.

He looked down at her. 'You're a strange girl,
Maggie Trent.'

'I know,' she agreed.

He opened his mouth as if to say more as they
gazed at each other, but changed his mind.

Maggie sat down cross-legged and tied his shirt
around her waist. It took him several attempts, but he
finally got both bits of blanket dangling over the
beam.

'Now for the tricky bit.' He knelt down. 'Climb
onto my shoulders. Don't worry, I won't drop you
and I won't fall myself—I also have good balance.'

'Are you a gymnast too?' Maggie asked.

'No, but I did some martial arts training in my mis-
guided youth.'

Maggie climbed onto his shoulders. 'Well, I'm
happy to know I wasn't completely wrong about you.'

'Oh?'

'I took you for a much more physical guy who'd
prefer to be climbing Mount Everest rather than building housing estates.'

'Really.' He grinned. 'That should provide an interesting discussion at another time. Are you comfortable, Miss Trent? If at any stage you would rather
not be doing this, for heaven's sake tell me. I won't
hold it against you and we can all be wrong at times.'

Maggie looked down at the top of his head and
placed her hands lightly upon it. 'Up you get—I was
going to say Samson, but your hair's not long enough.
I'm fine.'

'Here's hoping you don't have any Delilah tenden-

cies,' he commented wryly and brought his hands up
to wrap them around her waist. 'Here goes.'

He got to his feet slowly and steadily. At no time
did Maggie feel insecure and at all times she had to
appreciate his strength and co-ordination.

When he was upright, she carefully lifted her hands
until she was able to grasp the blankets.

'All right?' he queried, his breath rasping in his
throat.

'I've got them.' She tied the ends together and
wrapped her hands in them. 'If I could stand up, I
could reach the beam. It would be just above waist-
height and easier to vault onto. I'd also have the blanket as a sort of safety strap.'

'Are you very sure, Maggie?'

'Yep. Can you handle it, though?'

'No problem. Easy does it.'

Putting her weight on the blankets, Maggie levered
herself up onto her feet. 'I'm not hurting you, am I?'
she asked anxiously as she felt his hands close round
her ankles.

'What do you think I am?' he countered.

'Very strong. Well…' she swallowed '…here goes
again.' A moment later as he rocked beneath her but
stayed upright she was straddling the rafter.

'Well done, Maggie!'

She beamed down at him. 'Piece of cake. I did win
a state title, you know.'

'I believe you. So. If you can crawl along it towards the wall, where the roof is at its lowest you
could do a recce. Still got the bar?'

She untied his shirt from her waist and felt the
sleeve. 'Yes. Yuck, it is full of splinters and nails,
this beam, as well as cobwebs!'

'Be very careful.'

'Care is my middle name. Actually Leila is my middle name, after my grandmother—why am I babbling?' she asked at large as she started to crawl along the beam.

'Exhilaration? Stress? I don't mind. I don't have a middle name,' he said as he watched her inch her way forward.

'How come?' Maggie stopped moving and stared down at him.

He shrugged. 'I was adopted as a baby, although that may not have a thing to do with it.'

'You're joking!' she said incredulously. 'But you were talking about your mother!'

'She's my adoptive mother. Why am I babbling?' he asked humorously.

'Well, I'll be…' Maggie shook her head and started to inch forward again. 'Then you have done tremendously well for yourself! But it must have had some effect. Are you full of neuroses and so on?'

'Oh, definitely,' he said with a straight face, but a world of devilry in his eyes.

'I'm not sure I should believe that—ouch!'

'What?' he queried.

'A nail. I seem to have got my blouse hooked on it. Damn.' She struggled upright to the tune of tearing material as the front of her blouse ripped from the neckline to the waist.

'Take it off,' he suggested, 'and put my shirt on instead. The material might be tougher. Then use yours and a blanket to protect yourself.'

'Roger wilco!' She wrestled her blouse off, sitting easily enough on the beam with her feet hooked together beneath it. But just as she was about to put his

shirt on they both froze at a loud noise outside the
shed—a motor revving then being shut off followed
by a car door slamming.

'Maggie, come down,' Jack said softly but urgently.

'Of course. We're about to be rescued!'

'Perhaps. But if this shed has been hijacked and
there's something fishy going on, we may not be too
welcome and I can't look after you up there.'

'OK, OK, I'm coming,' she whispered and backed
along the beam until she was above him. 'Now!'

She slithered down the blankets and into his arms,
leaving his shirt and her blouse dangling on the beam.
At the same time the door was thrown open from the
outside, a powerful searchlight was shone in and a
string of expletives in a harsh male voice was uttered.

Maggie gasped and clutched Jack, completely dazzled by the light. He put his arms around her.

'Bloody hell!' the same harsh voice said. 'What is
this—some sort of kinky sex set-up?' And to
Maggie's utter disbelief the searchlight moved away
revealing, not one, but two men, and some flash bulbs
went off.

Jack growled in his throat, then he said into her
ear, 'One, two, let's get down, Maggie.'

'OK,' she whispered back, and on his call of two
they slithered down to the boot, then hit the floor
together. He held her in his arms only until she was
steady on her feet, then he strode forward to confront
the two men.

Things happened so quickly after that, she couldn't
believe her eyes. Both men backed away from him
until one of them, the man with the camera, tripped

and fell over a chair. He dropped the camera and Jack swooped onto it.

'I am sorry about this,' he said quite politely as he opened the back of it and exposed the film, 'but you wouldn't want to be responsible for some highly misleading pictures, now would you?'

The man got up nervously and dusted himself off. 'Not if you say so, mate,' he agreed.

'Good! Why don't you both sit down and tell me who you are? Sophie,' Jack added over his shoulder, 'you might be better off waiting in your car.'

It took a moment for Maggie to twig that he was talking to her, but as soon as she did she accepted the suggestion gratefully. It was still one of the hardest things she'd ever done—to achieve a dignified exit wearing only her socks, jeans and her bra. She did resist the temptation to run, however, until she was out of the shed, then she spurted to her car, climbed in with a sigh of sheer relief, and reached over into the back seat for the denim jacket she'd tossed there the day before.

It was fifteen minutes before Jack came out to her and he stopped on his way to retrieve his mobile phone and bag from his Range Rover and then to lock it.

He got into the passenger seat, glinted her a daredevil little smile and said, 'Home, James, I think.'

'What about your—?'

'Maggie, just go,' he commanded. 'I've done my level best to protect your fair name, let's not hang around.'

She switched the motor on and nosed the car forward. Two minutes later, she turned out of the concealed driveway onto the road and turned to him. 'I'm dying of curiosity! Who were they? What did you tell them? Do they still think we were…we were…?' She stopped and coloured painfully.

He was fishing around in his bag and he dragged a T-shirt out and shrugged into it with difficulty. 'Hang on,' he said as he began to punch numbers into his phone. 'What's your address?'

She told him.

It was someone called Maisie he rang—a Maisie who didn't object to being woken at four-thirty in the morning and given all sorts of instructions.

To wit, someone was to retrieve his Range Rover at the farm address, using his spare keys; someone was to pick him up at Maggie's address in about half an hour; a new flight to Melbourne was to be booked for him later in the day, no, he wouldn't be stopping in Sydney this time—what had happened to him?

'I was kidnapped by a girl, locked in a shed and— maybe I'll tell you the rest of it one day, Maisie, just be a love and sort all that out for me, pronto.'

He ended the call.

Maggie looked over at him. 'That's not funny!'

'No? I have to tell you it has been one of the funnier days of my life, Maggie Trent,' he said with his eyes glinting. His hair was standing up from his struggles with his T-shirt, and he ran his fingers through it.

She bit her lip and concentrated on her driving for a bit until he dropped his hand on her knee. 'All right. I apologize. Who were they? A private investigator and a journalist.'

Maggie's eyes widened. 'Oh, no!'

'As you say,' he agreed dryly, and told her the whole story.

The owners of the property had had a farm machinery hire business, now defunct. All the equipment had been stored in the shed, which explained why it was built like Fort Knox. They also had a wayward son, apparently, who'd stolen the vintage car and the bike on a whim and as a bit of a lark, and decided there was no better place to keep them under wraps than his parents' shed—he'd contrived to get copies of the keys made.

But he was also a garrulous young man when under the influence of liquor and drugs and the journalist, who wrote a motoring column and was a vintage-car freak himself, had got wind of the heist. He was also aware that the owner of the car and bike had hired a private investigator to look for them when the police had failed to trace them, so they'd decided to pool their resources.

'I see!' Maggie said at this point in the story.

'Yes,' Jack agreed. 'It all falls into place. How much more interesting to find Jack McKinnon and Margaret Leila Trent engaged in what could have looked like weird practices, though?'

She flinched. 'Do you think they believed our story? What did you tell them?' She pulled up at a traffic light on the Oxenford overpass.

'The truth, mostly. That the property was about to come onto the market and we were interested in it.'

'Perfectly true!'

'Yep.' He shot her an amused look. 'But I had to tamper with the truth a bit then. I told them the wind banged the shed door shut on us, locking us in.'

Maggie flinched again. 'That's a very small white lie,' she said, although uncertainly. 'Isn't it?'

'Almost miniature,' he agreed gravely. 'Uh—the light has changed, Maggie.'

She changed gear and moved forward a little jerkily. 'I know you're laughing at me,' she accused at the same time.

He did laugh outright then. 'Perhaps you should bear this incident in mind the next time you're moved to scream, shout and slam things,' he suggested and sobered suddenly. 'Because it wouldn't have been funny to be splashed across some newspaper because of who we are, *you* are particularly, and because it did look very strange.'

Maggie cruised to a stop at the next set of lights on the overpass. 'I never get these damn lights,' she said tautly, then sighed. 'You're right. I will.'

'Good girl. Anyway, I had to tell some more white lies. They think your name is Sophie Smith—'

'That was inspired,' she said gratefully and shivered suddenly.

He looked over at her and raised an eyebrow.

'I just thought of what my father would say if I got splashed across some newspaper in—those circumstances. He'd kill me! No, he wouldn't,' she corrected herself immediately, 'but he'd be furious!'

'He'd be more liable to want to kill me,' Jack said prosaically. 'However, although I suppose there always may be a question mark in their minds, those two have nothing to go on other than your car registration, and I don't think I gave them time to get it, in the dark.'

'It's not registered in my name. It's the firm's car,' she told him.

'Even better.'

'But—' she turned to him '—what about you? Do they know who you are?'

'They know and they're not likely to forget it.'

Maggie stared at him and shivered again. 'You can be very scary at times, you know.'

He shrugged. 'You've got a green light again, Maggie.'

She drove off. 'Not that I'm complaining,' she added. 'I'm very grateful to you for handling it all so well. Even my father would be grateful.'

'I wouldn't bet your bottom dollar on it.'

She drove in silence across Hope Island for a while, then as she turned into her street she said, 'What will we do now?'

He stirred. 'If I were you, Maggie, I'd go away for a while. Just in case they decide to snoop around a bit.'

'I can't just go away! I'm a working girl,' she objected, and pulled into her driveway.

Jack McKinnon looked through the window at her lovely villa and shrugged.

'Don't tell me we're back to all that nonsense!' she accused. 'What a spoilt little rich girl I am.'

His lips twisted as he transferred his gaze to her. 'Not entirely,' he said. 'Actually, I think you're one of a kind, Maggie Trent. On the other hand...' he paused and searched her eyes '...on the other hand you do bear some responsibility to your name and your family so it would be a good idea to take out some—' he gestured '—extra insurance. I'm sure that's what your father would advise and rightly so.'

He turned to look over the back of his seat as a car pulled up across the driveway. 'My lift has arrived.'

'Maisie?' she said.

'Not Maisie.'

'So…so that's it?' Her voice was slightly unsteady.

He grinned. 'A better outcome than it might have been, in more ways than one. You could still be balancing on a splintery beam trying to force open a tin roof.'

'Will you buy it? That property?'

'Don't know. Listen, you take care, Miss Trent.' He leaned forward and kissed her lightly, then he opened the door and slid out of the car, pulling his bag after him.

Maggie was still sitting exactly as he'd left her, with her fingers on her lips, when the other car drove off, taking Jack McKinnon out of her life.

Later in the day, a huge bouquet of flowers arrived for her with a simple message—'All's well that ends well, Jack.'

In the event, Maggie's mother was of exactly the same opinion as Jack McKinnon when she heard all about her daughter's ordeal. Not only did she insist that Maggie should go away for a while, taking a month's unpaid leave, but she also accompanied her for the first week.

CHAPTER THREE

THE ocean stretched forever beyond the arms of the bay. It was slate-blue and wrinkled. A layer of cloud rimmed the horizon, but the sun had risen above it and was pouring a path of tinsel light over the water. Long, lazy lines of swell were rolling in to crash onto the beach in a froth of sand patched white that looked like crazy paving until it slipped away.

To the south, the green, rock-fringed dome of Point Cartwright with its white observation tower stood guard over the mouth of the Mooloolah River.

To the north and much further away, the monolithic bulk of Mount Coolum stood out as well as Noosa Head, insubstantial in the distance. Closer to home Mudjimba Island lay in the bay like a beached whale complete with a tree or rock on its head to resemble a water spout. The whole area was known as the Sunshine Coast. It was an hour's drive north of Brisbane and it competed with the Gold Coast as a holiday destination.

Maggie withdrew her gaze from the distance and studied the beach. She was on the ninth floor of an apartment block in Mooloolaba, just across the road from it, a lovely beach, long and curved and protected from the dominant south-easterly trade winds. The road itself was lined with Norfolk pines, some as tall as the floor she was on.

There weren't many people on the beach although it was crisscrossed with footprints—the lull between

the serious early-morning walkers and the beach frol-
ickers.

It was an interesting spot, Mooloolaba. Its river was
home to a trawling fleet and wonderful fresh seafood
abounded. There were often huge container ships and
tankers anchored off Point Cartwright awaiting clear-
ance and pilots for their journey into Moreton Bay
and Brisbane, services that originated in Mooloolaba
together with an active Coastguard.

It was also a haven for many recreational mariners
on their voyages north or south. Mooloolaba was the
last stop before the Wide Bay bar, a treacherous wa-
terway between the mainland and Fraser Island, or the
first stop after it. Many a mariner had heaved a sigh
of relief to be safely inside the Mooloolah River after
a scary bar crossing and a sea-tossed trip south after
it. If you were sailing north, it was like a last frontier.

Is that what I'm facing? Maggie wondered suddenly. A last frontier...

She sat down at the small table and contemplated
her breakfast of fresh fruit and muesli, coffee and
croissants. She'd been in the luxury apartment for ten
days. It belonged to a friend of her mother's and had
no connection with the Trent name. Her mother had
spent the last week with her before having to go to
Sydney for a charity engagement she was unable to
break.

Her father, thankfully, was overseas on business
and she and her mother had agreed that he needn't
ever know about the episode in the shed.

She'd enjoyed the days with her mother—they'd
window-shopped, sunbathed, swum, walked, been to
the movies and read—but she was now bored and

ready to go back to work although she had two and half weeks of leave left, well…

She ate some muesli, then pushed the bowl away unfinished and poured her coffee. To be honest, she didn't know what she was ready for, but more of the same wasn't it and at the heart of the matter lay one man—Jack McKinnon.

She'd heard nothing more from him although she'd arranged to have her mail checked and all her phone calls rerouted to her mobile.

I wonder what he would think, she mused several times, if he knew how much I've changed my stance on him? If he knew I can't stop thinking about him, if he knew…come on, Maggie, be honest!…I seem to have fallen a little in love with him?

It was the strangest feeling, she reflected. While she'd been doing her 'trapeze act' she'd been a little nervous, but mostly fired with enthusiasm. She hadn't been aware of him as a man, only as a partner she could more than rely on. Now, the close contact with him invaded her dreams and made her go hot and cold in her waking hours when she thought about it.

Not only that, she might have felt annoyed by him at times—here she always paused and looked a bit guilty—but his company had *energized* her. It must have or why else would she be feeling as flat as a tack? Why else would she have this feeling she was at a last frontier in her life with nowhere she wanted to go?

Nor had her mother failed to notice her abstraction.

'Darling…' Belle regarded her seriously once '…did Jack McKinnon get you in just a little bit? Is that why you're so quiet sometimes?'

Maggie chose her words with care. 'If you have to get locked in a shed with a guy, he was all right.'

She got up abruptly, her coffee untasted. No good sitting around moping, she decided. Action was called for. She'd go for an invigorating swim.

The water was glorious. She swam out, caught a wave and surfed in expertly and she laughed at the sheer bliss of it as she lay on the sand with the water ebbing over her. That was when it came to her. If the mountain wouldn't come to her, she would go to it.

She packed her bags that morning and drove home.

Two days later, two very low-key days in case anyone was snooping about looking for her, she'd exhausted every avenue she could think of to get in touch with Jack McKinnon to no avail.

Either she was on a hit list of people to be kept away from him or he had the most zealous staff who kept *everyone* away from him. She couldn't even reach Maisie—no one seemed to have heard of a Maisie.

She'd even sat outside the headquarters of the McKinnon Corporation's head offices in her own car, not her firm's car, hiding behind dark glasses and a floppy linen hat, but she'd sighted neither the man himself nor his Range Rover.

She lay in bed that night, wide awake and with very mixed feelings as she listened to the mournful cries of the curlews on the golf course.

What had seemed so clear and simple to her in the surf at Mooloolaba was now assuming different pro-portions.

The polite spiels she got from a secretary saying

he was currently unavailable, but she'd be happy to take a message although she had no idea if, or when, Mr McKinnon would return it, were an embarrassment to her. Sitting outside his headquarters was the same—both were entirely out of character and she was finding it hard to live with the almost constant churning of her stomach and nervous tension involved.

Was she doing the right thing? It was all very well to tell herself that she didn't deserve to be brushed off like this, but if Jack McKinnon didn't want to be tracked down, should she respect his wishes?

Why, though? she asked herself passionately. Why was she such a *persona non grata* for him? Had she completely misread their, if nothing else, spirit of camaraderie in those last hours in the shed?

I guess, she thought forlornly, I really want an explanation from him, but that could be as embarrassing, if not to say as demoralizing, as what I'm going through now.

She turned over and punched her pillow, but still sleep didn't come. She got up and made herself a cup of tea. As she drank it and dawn started to rim the horizon it came to her that she would let it all drop. For one thing, she had no idea how to proceed now. For another, she wasn't feeling completely happy with herself.

She stared at the rim of light on the horizon and blinked away a sudden tear but when she went back to bed she slept until nine o'clock in the morning.

And it was a relief, although a sad one, the next morning, to have made the decision to stop her search.

Then her aunt Elena came to call, as she did fairly

regularly. Maggie invited her in and since it was that time of day asked her to stay to lunch—Elena was always good company.

She prepared open smoked salmon sandwiches drizzled with lemon juice and dusted with cracked pepper and she opened a bottle of chilled chardonnay to add to her lunch.

'How nice!' Elena approved.

'Let's sit outside,' Maggie suggested.

When they were comfortably installed on her terrace with a sail umbrella protecting them from the sun, they chatted about this and that until Elena said out of the blue, 'Your mother mentioned a while back that you'd met Jack McKinnon.'

Maggie went still and swallowed. 'What did she say?'

'That he was rather rude to you, so I'm thinking of taking him off my list of eligible bachelors.'

Maggie relaxed. Not that she had any qualms about Elena broadcasting the shed debacle, but she couldn't help feeling that the fewer people to know about it, the better. 'Oh, you don't have to do that on my behalf,' she said.

Elena settled herself more comfortably and sipped her wine. 'It's not only that, he's extremely elusive.'

Maggie eyed her humorously. 'That must be irritating for you.'

Elena grimaced. 'I've got *some* background on him. It's his love life that's the problem.'

Maggie hesitated, then she couldn't help herself. 'Background?'

Elena elucidated.

Jack McKinnon had been adopted as a baby by a loving but very average family. From an early age he'd exhibited above-average intelligence; he'd won scholarships to private schools and university, where he'd studied civil engineering and marine design.

Despite something of a mania for protecting his privacy, he appeared to be very normal considering his difficult start in life. He certainly wasn't ostentatious..no particularly fancy homes, no Lear Jets, et cetera.

'As for the women in his life—' Elena sighed '—he doesn't flaunt them and they don't talk once it's over.'

'What about...' Maggie thought briefly '...Lia Montalba and Bridget Pearson?'

'Both models, both Melbourne girls.' Elena frowned. 'I wouldn't class either of them as one of "his women". They were hired to advertise his catamarans. There's a big promotion coming out shortly, but both girls are back in Melbourne now.'

'Is there anyone at the moment?' Once again Maggie couldn't help herself.

'Not as far as I know. He does,' Elena said thoughtfully, 'have a hideaway. Maybe that's where he conducts his affairs.' She shrugged.

Maggie frowned. 'How do you know that?'

Elena tapped her nose. 'My sources are always classified, but he has a holiday home at Cape Gloucester—keep that to yourself please, Maggie! So, you reckon I should leave him on my list?'

'I...' Maggie paused as she tried to think straight. 'It doesn't matter one way or the other to me. Where...where is Cape Gloucester?'

'North Queensland. Up in the tropics near Bowen. I believe you have to drive through a cattle station to get to it, that's all I know.'

*   *   *

After Elena left, Maggie sat for a long time staring at the lengthening shadows on the golf course.

Was this fate? she wondered.

Everything she wanted to know including, perhaps, Jack's whereabouts, literally dropped into her lap?

Of course, she cautioned herself, he could also be in Sydney, New York or Kathmandu, but if he was at Cape Gloucester and she went up there, might that be the only way she would ever get the explanation she so badly wanted?

Working on the theory that what her mother didn't know about she couldn't worry about, Maggie left her a vague message and she packed her bags again and drove north. At least, she thought as she set off, she would be off the local scene, should a certain P.I. and journalist be looking for the mystery girl found in a shed in compromising circumstances with Jack McKinnon.

Or what might have looked like compromising circumstances, she reminded herself.

The Gloucester passage flowed between the mainland and Gloucester Island, a regal green island with several peaks. The passage, at the northern end of the Whitsunday Islands, was the gateway to Bowen and Edgecumbe Bay. It was a narrow strip of water and you could visualize the tide flowing swiftly through it. There were several sand banks and patches of reef guarded by markers.

It was remote and beautiful and, although you did have to drive through a cattle station to get to it, this was an improvement upon, until recent times, only being able to approach by sea.

There were two small beach resorts nestled into the tree-lined shores of the mainland, one overlooking Gloucester Island and Passage Islet, one overlooking Edgecumbe Bay. Maggie chose the one overlooking Gloucester Island; there was something about the island that intrigued her.

Her accommodation in a cabin was spacious and spotless and it was right on the beach. There was a coconut palm outside her veranda, there were casuarinas and poincianas, some laced with bougainvillea. Many of the trees had orchids growing from their bark; many of them were rather exotic natives like pandanus palms and Burdekin plums.

The coarse, dark crystals of the beach reminded Maggie of brown sugar, but the water lapping the beach was calm, crystal-clear and immensely inviting, especially at high tide. She spent an hour on her first evening sitting on the beach, watching fascinated as ripple after little silvery ripple raced along, tiny imitations of waves breaking on the beach.

Then she caught her breath in amazement as two strange ducks skimmed the water's edge—ducks that looked as if they were wearing leather yokes when in fact it was a strip of dark feathers on their creamy necks and chests. Burdekin Ducks, she was told, when she enquired.

There was only one other couple at the resort and she ate dinner with them before using a long drive as an excuse for an early night. In fact it was nervous tension making her yawn, she thought as she strolled back to her cabin. Had she done the right thing? Was he even here in his beach house tucked away amongst the trees beyond the resort? Why hadn't she gone to find out straight away?

'I'll be better in the morning,' she told herself. 'More composed. Less conscious of the fact that this is a man I'd pegged for the kind women rode off with into the sunset because they couldn't help themselves—and what's going to make me any different?'

She shook her head and went to bed.

The sun came up at six-fifteen. Maggie was walking along the beach at the time.

Gloucester Island was dark with its southern outline illuminated in gold; trees, beach and rocks were dark shapes pasted on a gold background as the sun hovered below the horizon. Then it emerged and light, landscape and seascape fell into place and fled away from her—and the tall figure walking along the beach towards her carrying a fishing rod was unmistakably Jack McKinnon.

Maggie took a great gulp of air into her lungs and forced herself to walk forward steadily, although he stopped abruptly.

When she was up to him she held out her hand. 'Dr Livingstone, I presume?'

He didn't reciprocate.

'OK, not funny—' Maggie dropped her hand '—but I nearly didn't find you, which brought to mind the Livingstone/Stanley connection, I guess. Are you not going to say anything?'

He took in her bare legs and feet, her white shorts, her candy-striped top and her pony-tail, and spoke at last. 'How did you find me?'

'That's classified. But if you were to offer me a cup of coffee, say, I'll tell you why I went to all the trouble I did.'

'Are you staying here?' He indicated the resort down the beach.

'Yep, although I've told no one why. Your secret is safe with me, Mr McKinnon.'

'Maggie,' he said roughly, then seemed to change tack. 'All right, since you've come this far the least I can do is a cup of coffee, I guess. Follow me.'

His house was only a five-minute walk away and from the beach you'd hardly know it was there. It was wooden, weathered to a silvery grey, two-storeyed, surrounded by trees and covered with creepers. A smart, fast-looking yacht under a tarpaulin was drawn up the beach on rails.

She followed him up the outside steps to the second storey and gasped at the view from his top veranda. Not only the Gloucester Passage lay before her, but also Edgecumbe Bay towards the mainland and Bowen, with its rim of mountains tinged with pink and soft blues as the sun got higher.

'You sure know how to pick a spot,' she said with genuine admiration. 'This is so beautiful.'

'It also used to be a lot further from the madding crowd before the road was opened,' he said.

'Including me?' She swung round to face him. 'What exactly is so maddening about me?' she asked tautly. 'Correct me if I'm wrong, but I thought a lot of our differences and misapprehensions about each other got sorted when we were trying to get out of the shed?'

He put the fishing line down and checked that the colourful lure with its three-pronged hook was tucked into a roundel on the rod out of harm's way. 'There are other differences you don't even know about, Maggie.'

He straightened and pushed his fingers through his hair. He wore khaki shorts and an old football Guernsey with the sleeves cut off above the elbows. He was brown, as if he'd spent quite a bit of time in the sun, and his hair was streaked lighter by it, and was longer, as if he'd forgotten to get it cut.

'If there are, why can't I know about them?' she countered. 'Believe me, I am not the spoilt little rich girl you mistake me for and I don't take kindly to being treated as such.'

His lips twisted and he folded his arms. 'So you don't think this exercise has labels stuck all over it shouting "Maggie Trent has to get her own way"?'

Her nostrils flared. 'No. If anything it shouts, "Maggie Trent deserves better".'

'Better,' he repeated.

'Yes, better. As in—why on earth can't we get to know each other better? For example, I wouldn't dream of judging you on your father.' She stopped and bit her lip, then soldiered on, 'You know what I mean!'

'Men,' he said slowly, 'and their grievances don't always work that way.'

'Then perhaps you should take more notice of women,' Maggie suggested tartly. 'Come to that, the whole world might be a better place if people did.'

A reluctant smile chased across his mouth and he seemed about to say something, but he merely shrugged and walked inside.

Maggie hesitated, then she shrugged herself, and followed him.

* * *

His house was simple and open plan, but there was nothing rough and ready about it.

The floors were gleaming polished wood through-out. There was a low double bed covered with a faux mink throw and several European pillows covered in dusky pink linen. One bedside table was stacked with books, the other bore a beautiful beaten-copper lamp.

Two corner leather couches sat about a vast wooden coffee-table bearing more books and some model ships, one in a bottle. A big cabinet housed a television, stereo and DVD player. Brown wooden and raffia blade fans were suspended from the ceiling and louvre blinds protected the windows.

The kitchen was all wood and chrome and state-of-the-art with black marble bench tops. There were several cane baskets with flourishing indoor plants dotted about and on the wall facing the front door there was a huge, lovely painting of two gaudy ele-phants in soft greens, matt gold and dusky pink.

'Yes!' Maggie stared at it enchanted. 'The perfect touch.'

'Thank you.' He pulled a plunger coffee-pot out of a cupboard and switched on the kettle.

She watched him assemble ground coffee, mugs, sugar crystals and milk. 'Where did you get it?'

'What?'

'The painting?'

He glanced over his shoulder. 'Thailand.'

Maggie pulled a stool out from the breakfast bar and perched herself on it. 'Is there anything I can say to make this easier?'

'You don't appear to be having much difficulty as it is.' He spooned coffee grounds into the plunger and poured boiling water over them.

Maggie inhaled luxuriously. 'Believe me, never having done this before, I'm a basket case inside,' she said, however.

He stopped what he was doing and regarded her expressionlessly. 'Done what?'

She laced her fingers together on the counter. 'Well, changed my stance on a man rather drastically to begin with. Not,' she assured him, 'that I had much to do with that. It just—happened. Unfortunately there's a whole lot of baggage I carry that makes it—'

'You're talking about locking me in a shed first of all, then cornering me here?' he suggested dryly.

A hot sensation behind her eyes alerted Maggie to the fact that it would be quite easy to burst into tears of frustration—to her absolute mortification should she allow it to happen. It was obviously going to be much harder than she'd anticipated to get through to Jack McKinnon.

'It's not that I'm only after your body, nor do I have any agenda to do with forcing you round to my way of thinking on housing estates,' she said quietly.

He smiled with so much irony, she flinched. 'That's just as well,' he commented, and poured a mug of coffee and pushed it towards her. 'Because while *your* body is perfectly delightful, and has even deprived me of my sleep on the odd occasion, I don't intend to do anything about it.'

Maggie's eyes nearly fell out on stalks. 'Say that again!'

He hooked a stool towards him with his foot and sat down on the other side of the counter from her. 'You heard.'

'I may have heard, but it doesn't make sense.'

'No?' He shrugged and sipped his coffee. 'I thought if I removed the thorn from your flesh of me not appearing to return your physical interest, you might feel better about things. You might even go away.'

Maggie stared at him as he put his mug down. Then she stood up on a rung of her stool and slapped his face.

His coffee-mug overturned as he moved abruptly and a brown puddle stretched between them. Then the mug rolled off the counter in slow motion and smashed on the floor. It was the only sound although the thwack of her palm connecting with his cheek-bone seemed to linger on the air.

There was something utterly terrifying in the way his narrowed grey gaze captured hers as she sank back onto the stool; it was still and menacing and full of unconcealed contempt. It was also as impossible to tear her gaze away as it had been the day they'd first laid eyes on each other, until he moved again and snaked out a hand to capture her wrist.

Maggie panicked then. She tore her wrist away and slipped off the stool all set to run away as fast as she could. Two things impeded her: she slipped on the wet floor and yelped in pain. By the time she'd righted herself and realized she'd got a sliver of china in her foot, he'd come round the breakfast bar, grabbed her by the waist and lifted her into his arms.

Forgetting everything but the awful insult she'd re-ceived, she launched into speech. 'Yes, yes, yes!' she said, her green eyes blazing. 'Yes, OK, it has been a thorn in my flesh! I went from hating and despising you to liking you and—and—feeling as flat as a tack because all I meant to you was a *bunch of flowers*, obviously, but there's a singular difference between what you're implying and the facts of the matter— what are you *doing*?'

He strode over to a leather couch and sat down with her in his lap. 'This.'

Maggie struggled to free herself, but he resisted with ease. 'Just keep still, Maggie,' he advised. 'You can't go anywhere with a splinter in your foot and I don't know if you make a habit of slapping men—'

'I don't!' she protested fiercely

'That explains it, then. You failed to realize it's just asking for some comeuppance.' He released her waist and put one arm around her shoulders.

'Come whatance…?' she said with a lot less certainty.

His lips twisted into a wry smile as he looked down into her eyes. 'This, Miss Trent—much pleasanter actually.' He bent his head and teased her lips apart.

It had occurred to Maggie that he was going to kiss her. What hadn't occurred to her was that through her rage and disappointment she could feel any spark of physical attraction, so her confusion was boundless on discovering herself pitched forward into a hot-house of sensual awareness; a sudden, wide open appreciation of Jack McKinnon, the feel of him, the taste of him, the sheer pleasure of him.

This can't be happening to me, she thought, but she was unable to resist the lovely sensations he was arousing in her as he kissed her lips, then her neck and throat, and it was all so warm and close and— most curiously—entirely appropriate.

So appropriate, she didn't protest when he slipped his hand beneath her top and cupped her breasts in their flimsy layer of silk and lace.

She even voiced her approval. 'Mmm…mmm.'

'Nice?' he murmured.

'Very.'

'How about this?' He circled her waist with his arm and started to kiss her deeply.

She clung to him and moved against him, loving the hard strength of his body against hers and becoming extremely aroused, so much so, she doubted her ability to withstand any kind of closure between them other than the final one between a man and a woman.

He was the one who brought them back to earth, slowly, until she was lying in his arms, her eyes dark, her mouth red, her hair gorgeously mussed and her breathing highly erratic.

She blinked several times, her eyes were very green and quite bewildered. 'Where did that come from?'

He smiled and kissed the tip of her nose. 'Powerful emotion often has its other side.'

'You mean being so angry with you made me—I don't know—vulnerable to that?'

'Perhaps.'

'How about you?'

'I—' he paused '—have wanted to do it before. Why don't you finish what you were saying?'

She shook her head. 'I've lost the thread—'

'No, you haven't,' he contradicted. 'You were all set to be extremely passionate about the "singular difference" between the facts and what I was imply-ing.'

He was so close she could see the fine laugh lines beside his mouth, a little nick in one of his eyebrows, she could smell soap on his skin and there was a patch of stubble on his jaw his razor had missed.

It came to her with a punch that she'd never looked so closely at a man before, never been interested enough to wonder, for example, how he'd cut his eyebrow and what it would be like to wake up in his arms…

'I…' She tried to collect her thoughts. '*You* seemed to be completely confident I'm one of those predatory girls who won't rest until she gets her man, *plus*—' she looked at him challengingly '—the hoary old spoilt-little-rich-bitch-who-has-to-get-her-own-way bit. That couldn't be further from the way it really is.'

'Which is?' He arched the split eyebrow at her.

'It's never happened to me before,' she said slowly. 'I've always had to fend men off. I've never before been…really, *really* interested. Oh, there've been a few flirtations and I've had some nice friends—Tim is one of them—but you could truthfully say I'm a bit of a novice who's been quite happy…' she sighed and shrugged '…doing my own thing, I guess.'

'Go on.'

'For some…' she paused '…mysterious reason that changed overnight when I was locked in the shed with you. Suddenly I was interested and no one,' she said with emphasis, 'seems to be able to give me one good reason why I shouldn't be, not even *you*, although you dropped me like a hot potato.'

'Maggie—'

'Look.' She laid her hand on his arm. 'Perhaps you are right about me. Perhaps I don't take no for an answer easily, but it's pretty important for me at least to be able to assess what this change means to me.'

He put his finger under her chin and tipped her face up to his.

'In other words…' she smiled fleetingly '…give me one good reason to say to myself, Maggie Trent, you came of age over the wrong man because there's absolutely nothing you can offer him—or there's someone else in his life—and I will go away.'

He stared into her eyes, fingered her chin lightly, then laid his head back with a sigh. 'Your father and I will never see eye to eye—'

'Forget about my father. It so happens I have the same problem with him. And I have taken quite some pains, believe me, to live my life the way I want to rather than the way he wants me to. Yes,' she added intensely, 'it may still be a pretty privileged life compared—perhaps—to how you grew up, if *that's* what you hold against me!'

He smiled slightly. 'No. There's not a lot I have against you, personally.'

'And there's no one else?' she asked seriously.

He watched her for a long moment, then shook his head.

'Well, then.' She gestured. 'Would it be such a bad idea if we got to know each other better?'

'Taking into consideration the fact that I have wanted to kiss you and you don't seem to mind being kissed by me?' he queried.

A glint of laughter shone in her eyes. 'I wasn't going to say that, although I suppose it is fairly pertinent, but there's a lot more to getting to know someone, isn't there?'

If I had any sense, Jack McKinnon mused as he studied the lovely crumpled length of her across his lap, I would end this now, for once and for all.

On the other hand, I did walk away from her and she was the one who wouldn't accept it. Does that absolve me? Not in her father's eyes, I have no doubt. Whichever way I travel with her, to the altar or simply an affair, David Trent is going to hate like hell me knowing his daughter in a biblical sense. But will it be revenge? Only if she falls in love and I don't…

What if I'm right and there's a genuine naivety—and all she's said so far bears that out—that would make it child's play to have her fall in love with me and want to marry me? Talk of revenge or poetic justice, if you like, and there's no doubt the bastard deserves it, but…

'Maggie…' he paused '…what if it doesn't lead towards wedding bells or a relationship, at least?'

She shrugged. 'I don't know—how can I? But the really important thing to me is to know that I didn't sit back and let something I judged special to me just pass me by.'

He grinned suddenly and bent his head to kiss her lightly. 'You're…I don't know, pretty special yourself, I guess.'

'So we could be friends, at least?'

'We could be friends, at least,' he agreed wryly. 'There is a proviso, however.'

'You're not the marrying kind?' she hazarded. She said it perfectly seriously, but there was a glint he was coming to know in her eyes.

'I—'

'I don't know if I am yet,' she interposed. 'Because—and not that this has anything to do with being rich, spoilt and privileged; I'm quite sure I would have been the same if I'd been born in a poorhouse—I can be very dictatorial, I'm told.'

'I wonder why I find that quite easy to believe?' he murmured.

'Some of my actions to date may have led you to suspect it?' she suggested with deep, suspicious gravity.

'One or two.' He circled the outline of her mouth with his finger. 'So how long did you plan to spend up here at the Cape?'

'I booked in for a week, but I have another week's leave up my sleeve. It seemed like a great place, especially for someone dodging journalists and P.I.s, even if you weren't here.'

He narrowed his eyes. 'How *did* you find out about this place?'

'I can't tell you that.' She hesitated. 'But don't worry, it won't go any further.'

He frowned.

'How long are you here for?' she queried.

'Same. Another week,' he said abstractedly.

'When did you arrive?'

'A couple of days ago.'

'Oh, good!' She sat up. 'That gives us plenty of time.'

He removed his arms and folded them across his chest. 'Are you planning to move in with me?'

She thought for a moment, then glinted him an impish glance. 'No. That *would* look as if all I was after was your body.'

'Perish the thought,' he murmured and drew her back into his arms.

'If you're going to kiss me again…' she began.

'I am. You have a problem there?'

'Not *per se*—'

'I'm glad to hear it,' he commented, and ran his fingers down her thigh.

'There is only the fact that—' She stopped and shivered as he stroked her neck and the soft skin just below the neck of her top. 'Uh—the fact that…'

'Go on,' he invited.

'Things could get out of hand rather easily.' She grimaced. 'For me, at least.'

'Then you'll have to rely on me to exert the will-power.'

She eyed him suspiciously. 'Are you laughing at me, Jack?'

'No. Yes,' he corrected himself.

'Am I so—laughable?'

He did kiss her, lightly, his grey eyes gleaming with amusement. 'No. You're unique, that's all.'

She lay back in his arms. 'That's one of the things I like about you.'

He raised an eyebrow.

'I feel safe with you,' she said.

He paused and lifted his head to stare into the distance.

Maggie waited but he didn't enlighten her about whatever he was seeing in his mind's eye. Then, with a strange little sound in his throat, he gathered her very close and kissed her deeply.

Once again it was a sublime experience for Maggie. She felt comforted and cradled but very alive at the same time, and supremely conscious of him, and she uttered a blissful sigh at the end of it that made him laugh.

'The next bit might not be quite as pleasant,' he said, still grinning.

'The next bit?'

'Mmm…' He moved her off his lap and sat her in the corner of the settee. 'Getting rid of the sliver of china in your foot.'

'Oh, that.' She waved a hand. 'I'd forgotten all about it.'

But although he was quick and decisive with his tweezers, she had to sniff back a tear or two as the sliver came out.

'I should have done that the other way around,' he said with a keen glance at her as he bathed her foot in a disinfectant solution.

She raised her eyebrows questioningly.

'Taken it out first and kissed you afterwards,' he elucidated as he peeled open a plaster.

She leant forward and cupped his cheek. 'Kiss me now, quick—and I'll be fine.'

But as his lips rested on hers briefly and they were cool and he smelt of disinfectant she had to resist an almost overwhelming urge to ask for more…

CHAPTER FOUR

THEY had five wonderful days.

They went sailing on his boat, *The Shiralee*, and fishing.

Maggie was in her element on a boat. One thing she did share with her father was a love of the sea and as she was growing up she'd crewed for him.

'I see you know what you're doing,' Jack said to her on their first sail.

'Aye, aye, skipper!' she responded as she turned the boat smartly into the wind so he could set the sails.

He climbed back into the cockpit and put his hands on her waist from behind as she stood at the wheel, and the jib ballooned out in the breeze. 'OK, cut the motor.'

The silence after the motor died was lovely, to be replaced by the equally lovely whoosh of wind in the sails and the rush of water against the hull.

Maggie leant back against him as they braced themselves against the tilt as *The Shiralee* heeled and sped along. 'She sails well,' she said.

He slid his arms around her. 'So she should, I designed her myself.'

Maggie smiled. 'No false modesty about you, Mr McKinnon.'

He turned her around in his arms. 'Not, at least, about boats. You're looking very trim, Miss Trent.'

Maggie glanced down at her short navy shorts and

blinding white T-shirt. She also wore a peaked navy cap with her hair pulled through at the back, and sunglasses. 'A suitably nautical presence for your boat, I hope?' she queried gravely.

'I would say so.' He removed her sunglasses.

Maggie raised her eyebrows.

'Your eyes are amazing. And it is a pleasure to see them not blazing or looking absolute daggers at me,' he said.

A gurgle of laughter rose in her throat. 'That feels like another lifetime ago.'

'On the contrary, it's only a day ago that you slapped my face.'

She coloured and he watched the tide of pink stain the smooth skin of her cheeks. All the same, she said, with an attempt at insouciance, 'Ah—just heat of the moment, I guess.'

'Isn't it always?' he murmured.

Maggie stilled. 'What are you trying to say, Jack?'

His gaze lingered on her face, then he grimaced. 'I'm not sure—'

'That I might be highly impulsive, if not to say irrationally so?'

'As a matter of fact—' he paused '—there is only one "highly" I'm conscious of at the moment in association with you and that's—kissable. How say you, Maggie?'

The growing frown in her eyes was replaced by something quite different. 'Actually, I love the sound of that!'

He laughed and started to kiss her thoroughly until the wind changed and the sails started to flap and they had to draw apart and concentrate on their sailing.

'Goodness, we did come close to those rocks!' Maggie called.

He was reeling in the jib. 'I suspected there was a touch of Delilah in you, now I'm wondering about a siren,' he called back.

Maggie watched him. He was precise and economical in his movements and his physique was breathtaking in khaki shorts and nothing else as he reached up to free a rope.

I knew it, she thought with a sense of satisfaction. There's definitely an action man in there.

There was also, she discovered, an inspired cook within the man.

He'd produced a divine chicken stir-fry served with saffron rice on their first evening together. He grilled fish to perfection. He had a marinade for steak that was to die for. A lot of the food he produced was seafood he'd caught himself—fish, crabs, oysters and painted lobsters.

They explored Bona Bay on Gloucester Island and Breakfast Bay. Once they sailed east through the passage and south to Double and Woodwark Bays and they fished off Edwin Rocks. Maggie caught a Spanish mackerel that day to her intense excitement.

'I've hooked a very large fish, Jack,' she told him as the trolling line she was manning sang out.

'You've probably hooked a rock,' he said prosaically.

'Don't be silly!' She was highly indignant. 'That's no rock! Will you please slow this boat down so I can reel him in?'

Fortunately they were motoring, not sailing, so he was able to stop and drop the anchor and Maggie was able to get the rod out of its holder and start winding in.

'Here, you better let me do it.' He came over to take the rod from her. 'I think it is a fish.'

'I told you so, but it's my fish. Stand aside!'

'Maggie—' he was laughing at her '—you'll never handle it.'

'Oh, yes, I will!'

She nearly didn't. She wound until her arms and shoulders were screaming in pain, and her face grew scarlet.

'Don't bust a gut,' he warned.

'It's nearly in,' she panted. 'Oh, there it is—glory be!' she enthused as the fish leapt out of the water. 'What a beauty!'

'Steady on, now.' He leant over the side of the boat with the gaff in his hands. 'OK! I've got it. Well done!'

Maggie collapsed in a heap and burst into tears.

Jack looked heavenwards, then secured the fish and bent down to scoop her into his arms. He sat down on the padded cockpit seat with her, holding her close. 'You're the most stubborn girl I know,' he said ruefully, 'but I do admire you. Don't cry.' He smoothed the tangle of her hair out of her eyes. 'You won!'

'I know.' She licked some tears from her upper lip and wiped her nose on the back of her hand. 'I just felt very sorry for it all of a sudden. It put up a great fight. I would have liked to let it go.'

'Too late now, but it won't be wasted. Is there any difference between buying fish to eat in a fish shop and catching it yourself?'

She considered. 'No. No, you're right. So you'll cook it?'

'I won't waste a scrap of it,' he promised. 'Even the carcass will be used for the crab pots and I'll reserve some for bouillabaisse.'

'You're a real hunter-gatherer—aren't you?'

'In certain circumstances,' he agreed.

'Good. I like that. Ouch.' She looked at her winding hand. 'This could be a bit sore for a couple of days.'

'I have two temporary solutions.' He picked up her hand and kissed the back of it, then her palm, and gave it back to her. 'The second solution is probably even more efficacious in the short term.'

'Oh, I don't know,' she began. But he sat her on the cushions and disappeared down below. Two minutes later he emerged with a bottle of champagne and two glasses.

He popped the cork ceremonially and poured the champagne. He handed her her glass and raised his to propose a toast. 'To a magnificent fighter!' he said, in the direction of the fish.

'Hear, hear!' Maggie agreed and dissolved, this time, into laughter.

He sat down and put his arm around her shoulders. 'I should have said—to two magnificent fighters.'

She laid her head on his shoulder, feeling more content than she could ever remember.

True to her word, she didn't move in with him, but apart from the hours she slept in her cabin at the resort, often restless hours, the rest of her time was all spent with him.

When they weren't walking, sailing, swimming or

fishing they puttered around his house, they read, they listened to music, they watched DVDs. Her current choice of reading material amused him.

'Don't laugh—I like Harry Potter! And the kids next door are fanatical fans so I have to keep up with the books and we always watch the movies together!'

'Did I say anything?'

'You looked—' She paused. She was snuggled into a corner of one of his settees wearing a long cotton shift, a charcoal background patterned with creamy frangipani flowers. 'You looked *askance*. But I read all sorts of books—crime, romance, adventure, although not science fiction generally.'

'Good.' He returned her gaze with a perfectly straight face.

'Is your taste in literature particularly highbrow?' she queried.

He held up his book cover.

'*Master and Commander*,' she read. 'Surprise, surprise!'

He grinned. 'I like sea stories.'

'That's an understatement. I'd say you have a passion for all things maritime!'

'I do have a couple of other passions,' he objected, and eyed the twisted grace of the way she was sitting with her feet tucked under her.

'Women in general or me in particular?' she asked gravely.

'That's a leading question.' His grey eyes glinted. 'Put it this way, I am enjoying getting to know you better.'

'Same here,' she said. 'I just have this *feeling* that women may come second in your life.'

He shrugged. 'A lot of my design work takes women very much into account,' he said.

'How so?'

'I'll show you.'

First of all he showed her the designs of his catamarans, then he showed her some of his house designs, and she was struck by certain similarities.

'There's absolutely no wasted space,' she said slowly as she studied the floorplan of two admittedly small, compact homes that even had nautical names, The Islander and Greenwich. 'It's all rather shipshape.'

He looked rueful. 'My main ambition was always to design boats.'

'But some of these space-saving ideas are really good. That, plus the fact that they are not shonky...' she paused, then glinted him a wicked little smile '...do take your houses out of the realm of little boxes.'

His lips twitched. 'Thanks, but they still don't fall into the category of your house.'

'For my sins I inherited my house from my grandmother. Where do you live when you're at home?'

'In an apartment at Runaway Bay.'

'A penthouse?' she suggested.

'No.' He grimaced. 'A sub-penthouse.'

'Could we be as bad as each other in the matter of our living arrangements, Mr McKinnon?' she said impishly. 'Incidentally, I don't have a marvellous hideaway on Cape Gloucester.'

'On the other hand, you're likely to inherit a cattle station and more very desirable Gold Coast property, amongst other things.'

Maggie blinked. 'How do you know all that?'

He paused. 'It's fairly common knowledge.'

'I suppose so.' But she frowned, then shrugged. 'I get the very strong feeling my father would dearly love to have a son to bequeath it all to rather than me. He's petrified I'm going to be taken for a ride by a man on the make or I'm going to fritter it all away somehow.'

Jack McKinnon gazed at her so intently, she said, with a comically alarmed expression, 'What have I done now?'

'Nothing.' He rolled up the house plan. As he did so he dislodged a book from the pile on the coffee-table and a photo fell out of it.

Maggie picked it up. 'Who is this?' she asked as she studied the fair, tall woman on board, by the look of it, *The Shiralee*.

'My sister Sylvia,' he said after what seemed to be an unusually long hesitation.

Maggie's eyes widened. 'Your real—'

'No. We're no relation. We were both adopted by the same family as babies. She's a couple of years older but we grew up together as brother and sister. She still lives with our adoptive mother in Sydney, who has motor-neuron disease now. Our adoptive father died a few years ago.'

'That must be why she looks sad,' Maggie commented. 'Lovely but sad. Has she never married?'

'No.' He picked up the ship in a bottle. 'Ever wondered how this is done?'

Maggie blinked at the rather abrupt change of subject, but she said, 'Yes! Don't tell me you did that?'

'I did. I'll show you.'

Cape Gloucester wasn't entirely reserved for relaxation, Maggie found over those days. He kept in touch with his office by phone and twice a day he spent some time on his laptop checking out all sorts of markets: stock, commodity, futures and the like. At these times he was oblivious to anything that went on around him.

He was also rather surprised, when she let fall an idle remark on the subject, to find that she knew her way around the stock market.

'I'm not just a pretty face, Mr McKinnon,' she assured him with mock gravity, then went on quite seriously to tell him about the portfolio of shares she was building on her own.

'So it's not only property you dabble—correct that—you're interested in?' he said.

She directed a cool little glance at him and told him exactly how much she'd earned in commission over the past twelve months. 'I do seem to have a flair for it,' she said with simple honesty.

'You do.' He frowned. 'You also seem to know your way around these rather well.' He gestured to the house and boat blueprints he'd shown her.

She told him about the courses she'd done at university.

'All of which,' he said, and smiled suddenly, 'leaves me with egg on my face, I guess.'

Maggie gazed at him, then she said, 'I told you it was a good idea to get to know me better.'

He laughed. 'You were right.'

She thought, after this conversation, that there was a subtle shift in their relationship, as if the playing field had been levelled a little between them, intellectually.

She caught him watching her thoughtfully sometimes, then he invited her to participate when he checked the stock market and some of their discussions on all sorts of things—life, politics, religion—became quite deep.

'Where did you learn to cook like this?' she asked once, halfway through an absolutely delicious seafood crêpe they were having for lunch.

'I grew up in a household where food was important.'

'Your adoptive family?' she queried.

'Yes.'

'Do you…have you…do you know anything about your own family?' she asked tentatively.

'No.' He helped himself to salad and held the salad servers poised above the bowl for a moment. 'I decided—' he lowered the servers gently '—to take the road they took.'

'Which was?' she queried, feeling a little chilled, but not sure why.

'If I wasn't good enough for them, the same applied in reverse.'

He said it quite casually, but she thought she detected a glint of steel in his eyes.

'But,' she heard herself object even although she had the feeling she was trampling on dangerous ground, 'there could have been any number of reasons…I mean, maybe your mother *had* to give you up, for example. I don't think it was as easy to be a single parent thirty-two years ago as it is now. I don't think it's easy *now*, come to that, but there is a lot more support and social security available.'

He sat back with his food untouched and something about him reminded her of the man she'd first met at a jazz concert on a marina boardwalk, very sure of himself, controlled and contained and—as he'd proved then—lethal.

'What would you know about it, Maggie?'

'I—well, nothing, I guess. Look, I'm sorry.' She took a sip of her wine in a bid to hide her discomfort, her discomfort on two fronts. The feeling she'd rushed in where angels feared to tread and her concern for him, she realized with a little rush of amazement. 'I shouldn't pry.' She half smiled. 'Or give gratuitous advice. But—'

'Listen—' he ruffled his hair and pulled his plate towards him '—it's all water under the bridge. It was water under the bridge when I was far too young to understand anything other than the presence of a loving family in my life even if they weren't my own. And that's all that counts really.'

The smile he cast her as he cut into his crêpe was completely serene, and she would have believed him if she hadn't seen that steely, scary glint in his eyes.

He was also quite a handyman, she discovered, and that he set himself an improvement project every time he visited Cape Gloucester.

His current project fitted in with one of Maggie's enthusiasms—gardening. His garden was quite wild and in need of taming, he said. There wasn't much more he could do for it since water was a problem. There was only tank water or extremely salty bore water.

But Maggie was more than happy to pitch in and help him prune and clear away the worst of the tangled overgrowth.

He had a book on the local flora and she also took it upon herself to identify as many of the shrubs as she could. To her delight, she found, amongst the native elms and Burdekin plums, some small trees she identified as *Guettarda Speciosa* that produced sweet-smelling night flowers.

'Listen to this,' she said to him one evening. They were relaxing on the veranda after a divine swim in the high-tide waters only a stone's throw away. The sun had set and he'd lit a candle in a glass and poured them each a gin and tonic in long frosted glasses garnished with slices of bush lemon harvested from a tree in his garden.

'"In India *Guettarda Speciosa* is used for perfume,"' she read from the book.

'How so?'

'Amazingly simply! You throw a muslin cloth over the bush at night so it comes into contact with the flowers. The dew dampens the cloth and it absorbs the perfume from the flowers, then it's wrung out of the muslin in the morning and bingo! You've captured the essence of the perfume.'

'Bingo,' he repeated and watched her idly. She wore a pink bikini beneath a gauzy sarong tied between her breasts. Her golden skin was glowing and her green eyes were sparkling with enthusiasm. 'Let's see if I can anticipate your next question—no, I don't have any muslin cloths.'

Maggie dissolved into laughter. 'How did you know?'

'You're that kind of girl. You like to get out and do things and, the more exotic they are, the better you like it. But despite the absence of muslin...' he leant over the veranda railing and plucked a creamy flower just starting to open '...you could wear a *Guettarda*

Speciosa in your hair.' He leant forward and handed her the flower.

Maggie smelt it. 'Lovely,' she pronounced. 'Thank you.' And she threaded the stem into the damp mass of her hair. 'They do also use it for garlands and hair ornaments in India.'

He smiled and sipped his drink.

'You've read this book, haven't you?' she accused. 'I wasn't telling you anything you didn't know!'

'No. But I've never had a girl to do the honours for before. You look very fetching,' he added.

She studied him. He was sprawled out in a canvas director's chair wearing only a pair of colourful board shorts, and his body was brown, sleek and strong. Coupled with how he was watching her, lazily yet in a curiously heavy-lidded way, the impact on her was one she was becoming very familiar with.

It was as if he could light a spark in her that caused her heart to race, her skin to break out in goose-bumps and a sensual flame to flicker within her just by looking at her. It was also a prelude, she knew, to an intimate moment between them.

Trying to fight it was useless, she'd discovered, although she didn't really understand why she would want to. He'd been as good as his word. He'd taken her to the brink several times, then brought her back, as if he knew she wasn't quite ready to cross that Rubicon. So it had been five days of loving every minute of his company and the things they did, five days of growing intimacy between them—and now this, she thought.

The sudden knowledge that the time was right?

She took a sip of her drink and saw that her hand

wasn't quite steady as it hit her. He hadn't moved at all. How, though, to transmit that knowledge to him?

'I know you think I'm impetuous,' she said huskily, 'and maybe I am, but not over this. I also take full responsibility for my actions. There won't ever be any recriminations.'

He stirred, but said nothing as his gaze played over her.

'Only if *you* want it, of course,' she added, and stumbled up suddenly in a fever of embarrassment— what if he had no idea what she was talking about?

'Maggie…' he got up swiftly and caught her in his arms '…*of course* I want it,' he said roughly, 'but—'

'Oh, thank heavens,' she breathed. 'I've never propositioned a man before—do you mind?' she asked anxiously.

A smile chased through his eyes, but it left them.. bleak? she wondered. Why would that be?

'It's just that some things can never be reversed.' He circled her mouth with his thumb as her lips parted.

'I know that,' she said. 'It doesn't seem to make the slightest difference to how I feel. And if you're trying to say you may not be a marrying man, I may do my darndest to change that, knowing me, but that's…in the future, and what will be will be. Just don't turn your back on me now; I couldn't bear it.'

He stared down into her eyes. They were glimmering with unshed tears like drowned emeralds, but her gaze was very direct and very honest. All the same he held back for some moments longer.

Moments where he thought back over the past days and how he'd had to rein in a growing desire for this

girl. Days during which he'd questioned his motives
time and again. Times when he'd told himself firmly
that she was just another girl, rather touchingly innocent at times, yes, then exceedingly determined at
others, but all the same, he could take her or leave
her...

He had to doubt that now, in the face of her.. what
was the word for it? Gallantry? Yes, and honesty. And
what his body most ardently desired. The truth of the
matter was, he reflected with a streak of self-directed
irony, he could no longer keep his hands off Maggie
Trent, or any longer deny himself the final satisfaction
of taking her.

'Turn my back on you,' he repeated and released
her to cup her face in his hands. 'I couldn't bear it
either.' He lowered his head and kissed her.

Maggie clung to him and kissed him back in a fever
of relief this time. Then he untied the knot of her
sarong and it floated away. Her bikini top suffered the
same fate shortly afterwards.

'The perfect gymnast's body,' he murmured as he
cupped her high, small breasts peaked with velvety
little nipples.

'Thank you.' She drew her hands down his chest
and trembled because it felt like a rock wall. Then he
was kissing her breasts and sliding his hands beneath
her bikini briefs to cup her hips and cradle them
against him.

Maggie shivered with delight and she stood on her
toes and slid her arms around his neck. 'You do the
most amazing things to me,' she said against the corner of his mouth.

He lifted her off her feet and she curled her legs
around him. 'If we're not careful this could be over

in a matter of seconds,' he replied with a wry little smile and walked inside with her, 'on account of what you do to me.' He nuzzled her neck, then lowered her to the bed.

He turned away and opened a drawer of the bedside table.

'If that's what I think it is,' she said softly, 'you don't need to worry. I'm on the pill—to correct a slight gynaecological problem I have but, according to my doctor, I'm protected against—as he put it—all eventualities.'

Jack looked down at her. 'Is that what you were going to the doctor for the day after we got locked in the shed?'

'Mmm… It's not serious, just a bit debilitating sometimes.'

He lay down beside her and said no more or, she thought dreamily, he let his hands and lips do the talking. He held her and caressed her until she became aware that areas of her body she'd never given much thought to before could become seriously erotic zones beneath his hands and mouth. The nape of her neck, the soft, supple flesh of the inside of her arms, the base of her throat and that pathway that led down to her breasts, her thighs…

She became aware that she could make him catch his breath by moulding herself to him and sliding one leg between his. She discovered that his touch on her nipples sent a thrilling, tantalizing message to the very core of her femininity.

She marvelled at his clean, strong lines and the feel of sleek, hard muscles, and she buried her face in his shoulder with a gasp as he parted her thighs and a rush of warmth and rapture claimed her.

'I just hope you're experiencing what I am,' she breathed as she started to move against him in a rhythm that seemed to come naturally to her. 'It's gorgeous.'

He laughed softly, then kissed her hard. 'To put it mildly, I'm about to die. Ready?'

'Yes, please!'

He claimed her and they rode the waves of their mutual desire to a peak of ecstasy.

They came down from the peak slowly. Their bodies were dewed with sweat and Maggie clung to him as if she were drowning and he was her rock.

'That was…that was…' she said hoarsely, but couldn't go on.

'You're right,' he agreed and kissed her eyelids. 'That was something else. No…' he pushed himself up on his elbow '…pain?'

Her lips trembled into a smile. 'Only the opposite, thanks to you.'

He considered. 'Well, maybe the gymnastics had something to do with it. It's very active.'

'No,' she said firmly, 'it was—*always you*, like the song.'

He grinned. 'OK, I won't argue with you. But if you have any plans to get up and go back to the resort tonight, forget 'em.'

'It was the furthest thing from my mind,' she said dreamily and snuggled up to him.

They slept for a while, then got up and showered, and he made a light supper.

They ate it on the veranda and watched the moon. Then he was struck by an idea. 'Muslin,' he said musingly and picked up her sarong still lying on the veranda floor. 'Anything like this?'

Maggie sat up alertly. 'That's voile and silk, but it's very fine, like muslin—it might just do the trick.'

He looked from the sarong in his hands to the *Guettarda Speciosa* just beyond the veranda railing with the perfume of its night flowers wafting over them in a light breeze. 'How do we anchor it?'

'Clothes pegs?' she suggested.

He nodded and disappeared inside to get them and between them they spread the sarong over the top of the tree.

'Morning will tell,' he commented as he applied the last peg.

'The morning after the night before,' she said with a humorous little glint in her eyes.

'There is that too,' he agreed. 'In the meantime—' he put his hands on her shoulders and drew her against him '—how about back to bed?'

'That sounds like a fine idea to me,' she whispered.

He tilted her chin and looked into her eyes. 'You know what's going to happen, though, don't you?'

She licked her lips. 'Another fine idea by me,' she said softly.

'But what you may not realize,' he temporized, 'is that I suddenly feel like a starving person deprived of a feast.'

She slid her hands around his waist and up his back and pressed her breasts against his chest. 'Who's depriving you of anything?'

He groaned and picked her up.

This time their lovemaking was swift and tempestuous, as if he had felt truly starved of her, but Maggie matched him every inch of the way as the barrier of never having done it before lay behind her and she could express her need of him with a new sureness of touch.

The bed was a tangled mess when they came down from the heights this time, but Maggie was laughing as she caught her breath. 'Wow! I see what you mean.'

He buried his head between her breasts. 'Sorry.'

'Don't be.' She ran her fingers through his hair. 'Let's just call it our epiphany.'

He looked up with something in his eyes she couldn't immediately translate. A tinge of surprise coupled with admiration, she realized suddenly, and it gave her a lovely sense of being on equal terms with him that carried her on to sleep serenely in his arms, once they'd reorganized the bed.

But the next morning it all caught up with Maggie in an embarrassing way.

All her life she'd suffered from a digestive system that took exception to too much excitement and too much rich food.

She woke up feeling pale and shaken and distinctly nauseous. Then she was as sick as a dog.

At first Jack was determined to drive her into the nearest doctor at Proserpine, but she explained between painful bouts of nausea and other complications what the problem was. 'On top of everything else I should have gone easy on the wonderful Mornay sauces and marinades,' she gasped.

He was sitting on the side of the bed watching her with concern. 'Are you sure? You may have picked up a gastric bug.'

'I'm quite sure! A bit of rest, just liquids and plain food for a while and I'll be fine.'

She saw some indecision chase through his eyes and she put her hand over his. 'Really. And I have a remedy I always carry but it's in my luggage back at the resort.'

He came to a decision. 'All right. Do you think you can talk on the phone long enough to tell the resort it's OK to release your vehicle and your luggage to me?'

'Yes.'

Several hours later, she was starting to feel better and Jack McKinnon couldn't have been a better nurse to add to all the other things she admired about him.

He'd made her as comfortable as he could with clean sheets on the bed and a clean nightgown from her luggage. He'd darkened the bedroom section. He'd made up an electrolyte drink for her to replace the minerals she might have lost, and some clear, plain chicken soup. He was as quiet as possible so she could sleep.

And by four o'clock in the afternoon Maggie felt quite human again.

He brought her a cup of black tea and sat on the bed while she drank it.

'I'm too excitable,' she said ruefully. 'That's what my mother puts it down to.'

He gazed at her. She was still pale, but her eyes were clear and she'd brushed her hair into two pony-tails tied with green bobbles.

She could have been about sixteen, he thought, a lovely, volatile child. Yet a brave one who'd matched his ardour in anything but a childlike way until she'd made herself sick.

'I may have been at fault,' he began.

'No. Well—' she smiled faintly '—you could be too good a cook.'

He grimaced. 'What about the rest of it?'

'The way we made love?' She breathed deeply. 'I could never regret a moment of that.'

'Neither could I, but—'

'You're wondering if this is going to happen every time you make love to me? It won't,' she assured him. 'These last few weeks have been—' she gestured '—quite turbulent for me. It was probably bound to happen sooner or later, but I'm feeling—' she chewed her lip '—much more tranquil now.'

He shook his head as if trying to sort through it all.

'But—lonely,' she added softly, 'in this vast bed all on my own.'

'Maggie—'

'If you could just put your arms around me, that would be the best thing that's happened to me today.'

He stared at her and she thought he was going to knock back her suggestion, then he changed his mind.

She sighed with sheer pleasure as he lay down beside her and gathered her close.

'How did the perfume go?' she asked drowsily.

'Your sarong smells lovely, but there was nothing to wring out of it—not enough dew.'

She chuckled. 'We may have to move to India.'

He stroked her hair.

But although they slept in the same bed that night, and although she drew strength and comfort from his arms and it was a magic experience on its own, that was all that happened until the next day when she could demonstrate she was as fit as a fiddle again.

The day after that, on what should have been their last day at Cape Gloucester but they'd made a mutual decision to stay on for a few days more, it all fell apart.

She had no intimation of the drama about to unfold when they swam very early that morning, naked and joyfully.

'This adds another dimension,' she told him as he lifted her aloft out of the sea. She put her hands on his shoulders with her arms straight and her hair dripped over his head. Her skin was covered with goose-bumps and her nipples peaked in the chill of it all.

'Know what?' He tasted each nipple in turn. 'If we hadn't just made love, guess what we'd be doing as soon as we got back? You taste salty,' he added.

She flipped backwards over his encircling arms and wound her legs around him. 'No idea at all!' she said as she floated on her back and her hair spread out on the water like seaweed. 'This water is so buoyant.'

'And you're particularly buoyant this morning, Miss Trent,' he teased. 'Not to mention full of cheek.'

She arched her body, then flipped upright, laughing down at him. 'I wonder why?' She sobered and stroked his broad shoulders. 'What is the masculine equivalent of a siren?'

'There isn't one.'

'There should be,' she told him. 'Anyway, you're it, Mr McKinnon. Enough to make any girl feel very buoyant, not to mention—wonderful!'

He stared into her eyes, as green as the sea at that

moment, with her eyelashes clumped together and beaded with moisture, and at the freshness of her skin. And he said with an odd little smile, as if there was something in the air she wasn't aware of, 'I haven't felt quite so wonderful myself for a while.'

She insisted on cooking breakfast, saying it was about time she earned her keep.

They'd showered together and she'd put on a short denim skirt with a green blouse that matched her eyes. Her hair was loose as it dried and she frequently looped it behind her ears as she cooked—grilled bacon and banana with chopped, fried tomato and onion and French toast.

'There,' she said proudly as she set it out on the veranda table. 'I may not be in your gourmet class, but I'm not useless in the kitchen either.'

'Did I say you were?' he drawled.

She pulled out a chair and wrinkled her nose at him. 'You've carefully avoided any mention of it, which led me to wonder if you'd simply assumed my privileged background had left me fit only to rely on someone else to provide my meals—what a mouthful, Maggie,' she accused herself with a gurgle of laughter.

He grinned. 'I did wonder.'

'Well, now you know. I'm actually quite domesticated.' She picked up her knife and fork, then paused and frowned. 'Was that a car in the driveway I heard?'

He cocked his head. 'I'm not expecting anyone.'

A moment later they heard a door bang, then footsteps crunching on the gravel path around the side of the house.

'Anyone home?' a voice called at the same time as a tall fair woman appeared at the bottom of the steps, then, 'Oh, Jack! I'm so glad I caught you. Maisie did say you'd decided to stay on for a couple more days, but one never quite knows with you!'

To Maggie's surprise, Jack McKinnon went quite still for a long moment, still and tense and as dangerously alert as a big jungle cat. Then he relaxed deliberately and stood up. 'Sylvia,' he said. 'This is a surprise.'

Maggie blinked and Sylvia, his adoptive sister, arrived on the veranda. She was as lovely as her photo and there was no trace of sadness about her as she greeted Jack, full of laughing explanations.

'I really needed a bit of time off—Mum and I were getting to the stage of wanting to shoot each other! So I flew up to Proserpine yesterday, hired a car and took off before dawn hoping to catch you and surprise you—oh!' Her gaze fell on Maggie. 'Oh, I'm so sorry. Maisie didn't say anything about...' She trailed off awkwardly.

'Don't be silly, Syl,' Jack said quietly. 'I'm always happy to see you. This is Maggie.'

Maggie got up and came round the table, holding out her hand. 'Maggie Trent, actually. How do you do?'

Sylvia's mouth fell open, as if she was completely floored, and she appeared not to notice Maggie's proffered hand. Instead, her gaze was riveted on Maggie's tawny hair and green eyes. Then she closed her mouth with a click. 'Not—Margaret Leila Trent?'

'Why, yes!' Maggie beamed at her. 'I don't know how you know that, but that's me.'

'Jack,' Sylvia said hollowly, and turned to him,

'don't tell me this is what I think it is. He'd…' she swallowed visibly '…he'd kill you if he knew…'

'Who?' Maggie said into the sudden deathly silence.

'Your father,' Sylvia whispered. Then she put a hand to her mouth and turned around to run down the steps.

'You stay here, Maggie,' Jack ordered. 'I'll be back as soon as I can.' He followed Sylvia.

CHAPTER FIVE

It was an hour before he came back, a tense, highly uncomfortable hour for Maggie.

She got rid of their uneaten breakfasts and tidied up, but there was a dreadful feeling of apprehension at the pit of her stomach and all her movements were jerky and unco-ordinated.

As far as she was aware he'd never met her father, so what could be involved? Then her mind fastened on something he'd said the day she'd found him here. Something about men and their grievances not being parted lightly.

She'd assumed when he'd said that, and something else she remembered about never seeing eye to eye with her father, that her father's arrogant, high-handed reputation and the ruthless businessman he could be, also by repute, were the things Jack McKinnon took exception to...

Then she remembered his reluctance—she put her hands to her suddenly hot cheeks—to have anything more to do with her after the shed incident. What had she precipitated?

When he came back she was sipping coffee, but sheer nerves made her rush into speech. 'What's going on? How is she? Where is she?'

There was a plunger pot on the veranda table and another mug. He poured coffee for himself in a completely unsmiling way that terrified Maggie all the more.

'She's booked into the resort for the time being. Maggie, believe me…' he pulled out a chair and sank into it '…I would rather—climb Mount Everest—than be the one to tell you this, but since you're here, and this has happened, I don't seem to have any choice.'

'No, you *don't*,' she agreed. 'You obviously *know* my father!'

'Not well,' he said rather grimly. 'Sylvia is the one who knows him, or knew him. They had an affair—' He stopped abruptly at the shocked little sound she made.

'It's common enough,' he said then.

'Well, yes.' She paused and laced her fingers together. 'And my parents haven't—it doesn't exactly seem to be a joyful marriage at times, but they are together so—' She broke off and looked at him with a painful query in her eyes.

'Your father desperately wanted a son and your mother couldn't have any more children.'

A bell rang in the recesses of Maggie's mind. Something her grandmother had said to her, then never explained. Something in response to *her* saying she should have been a boy. *Don't go down that road, Maggie. Your mother has and…* But Leila Trent had never completed the statement.

She blinked several times as she looked back down the years, and it all fell into place. The growing tension between her parents, her mother's anguish, carefully concealed so that her growing daughter would not be affected, but now it came back to Maggie in a hundred little ways… How could she have been so blind? she wondered.

She cleared her throat. 'Go on.'

'Your father met Sylvia about six years ago. They
fell in love—at least Sylvia assures me they did.
She…' he paused and looked out over the glittering
sea with his eyes hard and his mouth set '…fell for
him in a big way despite his being married.'

'Did…did he offer to leave my mother and marry
her?'

'He certainly led her to expect it. Then things
changed dramatically.' He turned back to her. 'Talking of gynaecological problems, Sylvia has had more
than her fair share of them and the net result is that
she's unable to have children. When your father discovered that, the terms of his proposition changed
somewhat. There was no more talk of marriage.'

Maggie went pale.

'I guess,' he said slowly, 'I need to fill you in on
a bit of background here. Possibly because we were
both adopted—there was never any secret made of
it—we had more common ground than many siblings
have, Sylvia and I. We looked out for each other as
we were growing up. There were times when we almost seemed to be on the same wavelength like twins.
So I knew exactly how Sylvia was going through the
mill with your father. And I knew she was too loving,
too special to be any man's mistress.'

'Did she agree with you?' Maggie asked.

He shrugged. 'Pertinent question. Did I rush in and
sort out her life as *I saw fit*?'

'Did you?'

'No. To give your father his due, he was infatuated.
Sylvia took the first steps to break it off herself, but
he wouldn't hear of it. She finally came to me and
begged for help. She said she doubted she would ever
love anyone quite like that again, but the sense of

inadequacy she felt—your mother may have had the same problem—over this inability to provide sons was crippling her and she had to get out.'

'You…you confronted him?' Maggie hazarded.

He smiled unamusedly. 'Yes.'

'How did you make him see sense?'

Jack stared at her. 'I threatened him with exposure to his wife and his, at the time, seventeen-year-old daughter. You may not realize this, Margaret Leila Trent, but your father, for all his sins and his thirst for a son, loves you dearly. He often talked to Sylvia about you with a great deal of pride.'

There were tears running down Maggie's cheeks. 'I didn't know,' she whispered. She stood up and walked to the veranda railing. 'It's all so sad!' She dashed her cheeks. 'My mother *still* loves him, I'm sure. Sylvia…?' She turned back with a question in her eyes.

'Sylvia went to hell and back.'

Maggie sniffed. 'And that's all you had to do to get him to stop seeing her?'

He folded his arms. 'Yes, but it didn't end there. We've been playing a game of tit for tat ever since.'

Her eyes widened. 'How so?'

'He tried to ruin me financially.' This time his smile was pure tiger. 'But two can play that game, as he's found to his cost several times.'

Maggie sank back into her chair and dropped her face into her hands. 'That's horrible.' She swallowed, then looked up. 'Of course. That explains the revenge element.'

He didn't deny it. He was silent for so long, Maggie found it difficult to breathe as she wondered what was coming.

'It crossed my mind,' he said and grimaced. 'More than once. That is why, Maggie,' he said slowly, 'I dropped you like a hot potato, or tried to.'

She bit her lip and coloured. 'You could have told me this a lot sooner.'

'It was hard enough to tell you now.' He gestured. 'But in the end revenge didn't come into it.' His lips twisted. 'You may be a right chip off the old block in some respects, but in others you're very sweet and lovely and refreshing and I...' he paused '...I just couldn't resist you even although I knew damn well I should.'

'I didn't give you much choice,' she said bravely. 'I...was just like the women who ride off into the sunset with you because they can't help themselves.'

He looked comically confused. 'What women?'

She waved a hand. 'Doesn't matter—'

'I've never ridden off into the sunset with a woman against her better judgement,' he protested. 'I've never "ridden" off with anyone.'

A spark of irritation lit Maggie's eyes. 'Will you leave it? It's just something I thought to myself once, in relation to you, that's all.'

A trickle of understanding came to his eyes. 'I see. Sorry, that was a bit dense.'

'Yes, it was. So, what are we going to do now?'

He finished his coffee and sat back, then, 'You may like to think the responsibility is yours, but it isn't, it's mine, and only I can redeem things. Go back to your family, Maggie, and forget me, otherwise you'll be torn to pieces,' he said very quietly.

'I...my father...' She couldn't go on and her throat worked.

'In a sense I'm as bad as he is,' he pointed out.

'He's also a man to whom sons may legitimately mean a lot, it is quite an empire and a very old name. Mid-life crises can happen to the best of married men and Sylvia is gorgeous. He—'

'Don't,' Maggie begged. 'Don't make any more excuses for him for *my* sake and if you don't mean them. Do you really think any better of him?'

He watched her impassively, then shook his head.

'The other thing is, only—' she pointed to sea where they'd swum '—a couple of hours ago we…we were…' Once again tears started to roll down her cheeks.

'You may never know how hard this is, Maggie,' he said abruptly, 'but one day you'll be grateful. Can you imagine having to tell your mother why your father hates me the way he does?'

That stopped Maggie in her tracks. 'Maybe she knew but decided to live with it?' she whispered.

He shook his head. 'From his reaction when I delivered my threat I could see that neither of you knew.'

Maggie made one last effort. 'What if Sylvia hadn't turned up or found out about me for, well, ages?'

He ran his hand through his hair and sighed. 'No doubt I'd have come to my senses before that.'

'Has this—has "us" meant anything to you at all, Jack?'

Her hands were lying helplessly on the table and he reached over to cover one of them with his own. 'Yes, it has, but I'm not the right man for you.'

'Why not? Apart from everything else.'

'You can't separate them, Maggie.' He hesitated, then shrugged. 'I just don't think I'd take well to domesticity.'

'A loner?'

He narrowed his eyes and looked past her. 'That's how I started out in this life. But—' he withdrew his gaze from the past and concentrated on her again '—for the *right* man,' he stressed, 'you're going to be a wonderful wife. A bit of a handful, prone to some excesses like locking people in sheds and—'

She pulled her hand away and stood up as his words acted like a catalyst. She wiped her face with her fingers, but although the tears subsided her heart felt as if it were breaking and all the fight drained out of her.

If he could even *think* of her with another man after what had passed between them, she had to believe that all he felt for her was a passing attraction.

Yes, maybe there was affection too, but not the conviction she held. The conviction that she'd fallen deeply in love with him. Not the pain at the prospect of being parted from him, nor the sheer agony of thinking of him with another woman...

No, she had to believe it hadn't happened for him as it had happened for her and—talk about being torn between him and her family—that would really tear her apart, going on with him under those circumstances.

And she remembered her original proposition—she would take full responsibility for her actions and there would be no recriminations. But how to act on those brave words? something within her cried.

She drew a trembling breath. 'What do they say? You live and learn.' She smiled, but she couldn't eradicate the bitterness from it. 'I'll go now,' she added simply.

He stood up and watched her like a hawk for a moment. 'Will you be all right?'

She cast him a look tinged with irony.

'Look, I know—'

'This will take a bit of getting over?' she suggested. 'Of course.' And she squared her shoulders and tilted her chin at him with further, this time patent irony. 'But I am a Trent, after all.'

'Maggie,' he said exasperatedly, 'I meant will you be all right physically? I long since stopped classing you with your father.'

'Perhaps you shouldn't have, Jack. Physically? Oh, you mean…? Well, I should be fine on both those fronts. I am on the pill and I've been careful about what I ate after the other day. No, I'll be fine.'

She stopped and stared at him. 'Provided I do this very quickly,' she said barely audibly and stood on her toes to kiss him briefly. 'You were…you were everything a girl could pray for. Take care.' She turned away and went inside. He moved, then stilled.

It took her all of five minutes to stuff her possessions into her bag and he carried it to her car.

She said goodbye unemotionally and he did the same. She even drove off with a wave. Two miles down the road she pulled up and was overcome by a storm of weeping and disbelief—how could it have ended like this?

To coin a phrase, she returned to the bosom of her family for a few days despite the new ambivalence of her feelings for her father, but some things had changed, she discovered.

Something in her mother's voice, when she rang her to say she was home, alerted her to it. A new lightness, a younger-sounding voice—I must be imagining it, Maggie thought—but when Belle suggested a family reunion on the cattle station, Maggie gave it some thought. The fact that her father was home had her in two minds, though.

Would she find herself unable to hide her hatred for his actions and the misery they'd caused her and Sylvia McKinnon? Was there any way she could heal the breach between David Trent and Jack McKinnon so there need not be this misery, for her, anyway? Come to that, could she hide her misery and despair from her mother?

In the end her curiosity got the better of her and she used the last few days of her leave to drive up to Kingaroy and the sprawling old wooden homestead, over a hundred years old but now extensively modernized, that had been the birthplace of the Trent dynasty.

She needn't have worried about hiding anything from her parents. By some miracle the breach had been healed. They were in love again and, despite observing the usual courtesies, there might have been only the two of them on the planet.

I don't believe this, Maggie thought. What has happened?

She watched them carefully, especially her father. The tawny hair was a little grey, he was close to fifty now, but even so he was attractive—it was not hard to see how he would have appealed to Sylvia six years ago despite a twenty-year age gap. And as always, when he set himself to be pleasant, he was more than that. He was vital, funny—entirely engaging, in fact, until you ran into the brick wall of the other side of his personality, the high-handed, arrogant side she had clashed with frequently down the years.

To her confusion, however, the weight of Jack's revelations didn't add a black hatred to her difficult feelings for her father.

Because she was so happy to see him making her mother happy again? she wondered.

Because a certain streak of common sense told her there were always two sides to a story such as— Sylvia had known her father was a married man and should have thought twice about breaking up any-one's marriage?

Because David Trent had conveyed enough admi-ration of her, his daughter, to someone else even al-though his thirst for a son had driven him to betraying her mother?

I don't know what to think, she acknowledged. I'm all at sea. What would happen if I told him about Jack and tried to smooth things between them? In this new mood he's in, maybe I could?

But something held her back. Would Jack McKinnon want her permanently in his life under any circumstances? She had strenuously to doubt it. As for her feelings for Jack, she just didn't know where she stood there at all.

Her mother did come down from her cloud nine briefly as Maggie was leaving.

'Darling, are you all right?' she asked anxiously as they were walking to the car. Maggie had taken leave of her father earlier. 'You still seem a little quiet.'

'I'm fine.' Maggie gestured to take in the wide blue sky and the vast dusty paddocks, and artfully changed the subject. 'I don't know how this happened.' She turned to Belle and put her arms around her. 'But I'm very happy for you, Mum. You're looking so beautiful.'

Belle trembled in her daughter's arms. 'You can tell?'

'See those steers in the paddock? They could tell,' Maggie said humorously but lovingly. She disengaged and got into her car. 'Take care of each other,' she added with a wave, and drove off.

She went back to work.

A month after her stay at Cape Gloucester, she went to see her doctor with an incredulous question.

'I thought you told me I was covered against all eventualities?'

'Sit down, Maggie,' he invited. 'What do you mean?'

'I'm pregnant! It's the only explanation I can think of, but I never once forgot to take my pills.'

The doctor digested this and said slowly, 'It was a low-dose pill. Sometimes they're not infallible, as I'm sure I told you—not that we were discussing them so much as a contraceptive at the time, but as a means of helping you with difficult periods. Have you had any cataclysmic upsets?'

Maggie closed her eyes and thought of explaining that she'd fallen in love overnight, she'd pursued her man relentlessly and given him little choice about taking her to bed—events that had gone around and around in her mind and pointed an accusing finger at her each and every time.

'Gastric upsets or the like?' the doctor added.

Her lashes flew up.

'I did mention how they could interfere with the pill,' he said gently.

Maggie put a hand to her mouth. 'I forgot all about that. I...I...was so carried away I didn't even think of it,' she admitted. 'Oh, what a fool I've been!'

'Tell me all about it,' he invited.

Half an hour later, still in a state of shock, she drove home.

The doctor's advice had been copious. Termination was her choice, but even the thought of it was horrific. If she didn't go ahead with that, the father of the child she was carrying deserved to know about it and no child should be completely deprived of its father even if circumstances prevented its parents from living together. And in that event, she should seek moral support from her family.

'If only you knew,' she murmured as she unlocked her front door. 'If only you knew! On the other hand, termination is out of the question, so...'

Three weeks later she was still grappling with her problems on her own when fate took a hand.

The property that had started it all was now officially on the market. It had been advertised and there'd been quite a bit of interest—none from the McKinnon organization or anyone bearing that name, however.

Maggie had been happy to be able to distance herself from it. As the agent who'd received the initial enquiries from the owners it should have been her 'baby'. In other words, even if another on their team sold it, she would still be entitled to some of the commission, but she'd waived that right when she'd taken four weeks' unexpected leave.

But there came a day when a woman rang in requesting an inspection and Maggie was the only one available to do it. Very conscious of the strain she'd put on the team with her unexpected leave, she temporized, then knew she should do it.

She arranged to meet the woman on the property at four in the afternoon and made a note of her name—a Ms Mary Kelly.

It wasn't as beautiful a day as the day she'd met Jack McKinnon on this little bit of heaven, Maggie thought as she pulled her car up behind a smart blue BMW. There were dark clouds chasing across the sky and a threat of rain, but it was still lovely.

She got out and went to meet Ms Kelly, a smartly groomed woman in her forties who also sparkled with intelligence and had a decisive air about her.

As they began their inspection Maggie said, 'Do you intend to live here, Mary?' They'd quickly got onto first-name terms.

'No. I'm doing this inspection on behalf of a— friend,' Mary replied. 'A second opinion is always helpful, isn't it?'

Maggie agreed, but realized suddenly that her usual 'selling persona' wasn't quite in place because she wasn't feeling very well. She struggled on, however. She dredged up several ideas she had for the house, she enthused about the creek, she was just about to suggest a tour of the shed when a violent bout of nausea overtook her and she had to run for a clump of trees where she proceeded to lose her lunch and afternoon tea.

Mary was most concerned and helpful. She dipped

her scarf in the creek, wrung it out and offered it to Maggie to wipe her face and hands.

'Thank you,' Maggie breathed and patted her face with the cool cloth gratefully.

'Something you ate?' Mary Kelly suggested.

'No.' Maggie shook her head, and for some reason, maybe because she'd told no one but her doctor, it all came tumbling out. 'I'm pregnant and this is, so I'm told, morning sickness in the afternoon.' She grimaced ruefully.

'You poor thing,' Mary said slowly and with a gathering frown.

'Oh, it hasn't been too bad! It just.. catches me unawares at times. There.' She rinsed the scarf thoroughly and handed it back. 'Thanks so much—unless you'd rather I kept it and sent it back to you properly laundered? Oh, by the way, no one at the office knows about it yet so—'

'I won't tell them,' Mary promised. 'Are you sure you're all right now?'

'Fine! Would you like to see the shed?'

'No, thank you, I think I've seen enough. Uh…' Mary hesitated as if she had her mind on other matters, then she said, 'Is there much interest in the property?'

'Quite a lot, I believe, although there've been no offers yet.'

'Do you think the owners have much up their sleeve—are prepared to negotiate, in other words?'

'Look, I'm not sure about that. I did have it originally, but Mike Davies is now the agent in charge, so to speak, only he wasn't available this afternoon. What say I get him to give you a call?'

'That would be fine, Maggie. Now you take care! How far along are you?'

'Roughly two months.' Maggie held out her hand. 'Nice to meet you, Mary.'

They parted and Maggie drove home slowly. Although she hadn't got to the shed, the whole exercise had woken all sorts of memories in her and reactivated all sorts of heartaches to fierce and hurtful from the dull pain they'd coagulated into.

She also knew she would have to make some kind of a decision very shortly. Follow her doctor's advice or go into hiding and cope with it all on her own?

In fact, there was only one lessening of the tension for her, and that was her growing curiosity about the baby. And the thought that it might fill the gap in her life Jack McKinnon had created.

She showered and changed into loose long cotton trousers and a long white shirt as the threat of rain earlier became a reality and thrummed on the roof in a series of heavy showers.

She made herself an early dinner, a snack really, of toasted cheese and a salad. She was just sitting down to eat it when her doorbell rang.

Her eyes widened in shock as she opened the door and Jack stood there.

'You!' she breathed and clutched her throat.

'Yes,' he agreed dryly. 'Let me in, Maggie. It's wet out here.'

'Of course.' She stood aside. 'But what are you doing here?'

'Come to see you,' he said briefly. 'Brrr… It's not only wet, there's a distinct tinge of winter in the air.'

'Come into the lounge. It's warm in there.'

He followed her through, then eyed her snack on the coffee-table next to the TV remote.

'I'm not very hungry,' she said defensively.

He looked around the lovely room, then his gaze came back to her and he looked her up and down comprehensively. 'How are you?' he asked abruptly.

She moved and pushed her hands behind her back because they were shaking. Nothing had changed about him, although he was more formally dressed than she'd ever seen him in a beautiful charcoal suit with a pale grey shirt and a bottle-green tie with anchors on it.

But his clothes didn't change him. They added a kind of 'high boardroom flyer' touch, but they didn't disguise the perfection of his physique. His streaky fair hair was shorter and tamed, but he still had a tan, and she could see him in her mind's eyes, aboard *The Shiralee* wearing only shorts…

She couldn't read his grey eyes at all—why had he come? Was it to say—*I made a mistake, Maggie. I can't live without you…?*

'Maggie?'

'I'm fine,' she said jerkily. 'Sit down. Would you like something?'

'No, thanks. Don't let your supper get cold.'

'Oh, that's all right.' She sat down and pushed the plate away.

He sat down opposite and studied her penetratingly. Then he said quietly, 'Any news?'

Foolishly, her mind went quite blank. What's he asking me? she wondered. How can there be any news? He was the one who sent me away… 'No,' she said bewilderedly.

His mouth hardened for some reason. 'I'd more or

less made up my mind to buy that property, you know.'

Maggie blinked. 'The one…?'

'The one with the shed that was hijacked to house a stolen vintage car and bike; the one you locked us into,' he said deliberately.

She blushed.

'But I decided to get a second opinion,' he went on, 'from someone whose judgement I value.'

'A second opinion,' Maggie repeated as the words struck a chord in her mind and it started to race.

'Yes,' he agreed. 'I think Maisie's name has cropped up between us before. She's my right-hand man. I rely on her extensively.'

Maggie blinked furiously. 'But there's no Maisie at the McKinnon Corporation, I checked,' she blurted out, then her cheeks burnt even more fierily. 'I mean—'

'That's because I'm the only one at the office who calls her Maisie. Her real name…' he paused and their gazes clashed '…is Mary Kelly.'

Maggie froze. 'She…she told you?' she breathed.

'Yes.'

'But that's not fair! I had no idea who she was. I would *never* have—' She stopped abruptly.

'Told her you were pregnant otherwise? How about telling me? I gather you hadn't planned to do that either.'

Maggie got up and paced around in deep agitation with the bottom line being—*So much for the I can't live without you, Maggie, bit.*

Then she turned to him incredulously. 'How would she know it was your baby?'

'She didn't. But she did know about what happened

in the shed because I alerted her to be on the lookout
for any unforeseen complications while I was away.
When she came back to me with her report this afternoon, she told me it was you who'd shown her
around—and the rest of it.'

Silence stretched between them until he added, 'I
was the one left to put two and two together—although Maisie is very adroit at reading between the
lines.'

Maggie sat down again suddenly. 'When I said
there was no news, I think I must have been still in
shock at seeing you again. My mind just went blank.'

'OK, reasonable enough. What about the two
months prior to tonight?'

Maggie rubbed her face, then she laced her fingers
and said urgently, 'I just haven't known what to do!'

'How did it happen?' he queried grimly. 'You
seemed so certain you were safe; you *told* me you
were on the pill.'

'I was,' she said hollowly and explained what must
have happened.

'Do your parents know?'

'No.'

He stared at her, taking in the faint shadows beneath her eyes and her slender figure beneath the long
white shirt and flimsy trousers. There was no sign of
any changes in her as yet—or, yes, there was, he
thought suddenly. There was a new air of vulnerability about her.

'There's only one thing to do,' he said. 'The sooner
you marry me, the better.'

CHAPTER SIX

MAGGIE reached towards her plate and took a carrot stick out of the salad, a purely reflex action as the impact of what Jack had said hit her.

Then she stared at him with the wand of carrot in one hand and her mouth open.

A glint of humour lit his eyes. 'A curious reaction. I can't read it at all.'

She closed her eyes. 'That's because I can't read my emotions at the moment at all.' Her lashes lifted. 'You're not serious?'

'Oh, yes, I am.'

'But, apart from all the complications you so carefully pointed out to me at Cape Gloucester, you don't particularly want to marry anyone, do you? Unless that was a sop to my sensibilities, but that's even worse because it means you particularly didn't want to marry me!'

'Eat the carrot or put it down, Maggie,' he suggested.

She stared at him, then threw it down on the plate because a moment or so ago she might have been shell-shocked and unable to get in touch with her emotions—that could have been true of her for the last two months, she realized—but she was no longer.

Jack McKinnon had hurt her almost unbearably, she now knew. Yes, a lot of it was her own fault, but that didn't alter her vulnerability to this man, and to let him marry her only because of their baby—was that asking for *more* hurt than she could bear?

'I got myself into this,' she said. 'I will handle it.'

This time it was a glint of anger that lit his eyes. 'Don't go all proud ''Trent'' on me, Maggie,' he warned. 'If you think that I, of all people, would allow you to wander off into the sunset with a child of mine, think again.'

Her eyes widened as she realized what he was saying, but there was more.

'If you think I would allow a child of mine to be swallowed up in the midst of *your* family—that is also simply not on the cards.'

She swallowed a couple of times. 'Look, I know that as an adoptee yourself you…you must feel pretty strongly about this, but I would never deny you access to your child—'

'And do you think you're strong enough to hold out against your father, Maggie, if he sees things differently? I don't. So we'll both be there for it, whether you like it or not.'

She stood up tensely. 'It's not a question of liking it or not! What I'm talking about is a shotgun marriage—'

'That is another possibility.' He lay back in his chair and steepled his fingers. 'You could find your father does come after me with a shotgun.'

'Nonsense!'

'I'm speaking metaphorically, but marriage, even to me, may be his preferred option for his only daughter rather than single motherhood.'

It came to Maggie in a blinding flash that perhaps even her sanity and therefore the welfare of her baby could be at risk if she allowed herself to become a pawn between these two powerful, arrogant men. Yes, two—I was right about you in the first place, Jack McKinnon! she said to him in her mind.

She put her hand on her flat stomach, thought of the life within her, and breathed deeply. Then she picked up the cordless phone on the coffee-table, and she dialled the Kingaroy homestead number, where she knew her parents were still holidaying.

She suffered a moment of anguish while the phone rang at the thought of their, particularly her mother's, new happiness, but how happy would either of them be if she ran away?

'Dad?' she said when her father answered. 'It's Maggie. Will you please just listen to me? I happened to meet and have an affair with a man you detest, Jack McKinnon. I know what all the bad blood is about, but I will *never* let Mum know. Unfortunately—'

She paused and listened for a while, then, 'Dad, please, if you love me at all, just listen. I was the one who did the chasing, not Jack. Unfortunately, and this was also my own fault entirely, I'm pregnant. Jack has decided I should marry him although our affair was—completely over before I realized I was pregnant. But while I'm immensely concerned about this baby's welfare, I don't think a loveless marriage is the solution—'

Once again she broke off and listened, then, 'No, Dad, I won't be doing that either. I appreciate your concern but this is the point I need to make you both understand—neither of you can make me do anything. In fact, if you continue this feud and—' she raised her eyes to Jack's '—either of you make my life unbearable, I'll go away where neither of you can find me.'

Her eyes didn't leave Jack's face while she listened again, then she looked away and said into the phone, 'I'm *sorry*, Dad, I know this must have come as a shock. Please break it gently to Mum. I love you both, but I meant every word I said.' She put the phone down.

Jack stirred at last. 'Was that slamming the shed door well and truly, Maggie?'

She shrugged. 'I've been living in a terrible vacuum since I found out. How to tell you? How to tell them? What to do? Until it suddenly came to me I'm no one's hostage and what I'll be doing is staying right here and continuing my job as long as I'm able, and letting this baby grow in peace. Yes, I was angry,' she conceded.

'Who's to say it would be a loveless marriage?' he queried.

'Jack—' she rubbed her face wearily '—you have given me absolutely no indication to the contrary—'

'Because I didn't burst in on you and sweep you into my arms?' he asked. 'Your father isn't the only one to get a shock today.'

She rubbed her knuckles on her chin. 'I know. I'm sorry.' She gestured helplessly.

'As a matter of fact, the thought of my own child has had a rather startling effect on me.'

'Me too,' she conceded. 'I mean, it could probably be quite an interesting child.' A ghost of a smile touched her lips.

'It would certainly give us a lot of common ground.'

His words hung in the air, but Maggie was too tired

and emotionally wrung out to continue the contest. She simply stared at him with deeper shadows etched beneath her eyes and her face very pale.

He frowned, then he got up and came round to her. He took her hand and drew her to her feet.

'You're extraordinarily brave and feisty, Maggie, but you don't have to bear this burden on your own. No,' he said as her lips parted, 'don't say anything now. But I do have your welfare, just as much as the baby's, very much at heart. Think that over, but, in the meantime, get a good night's sleep.'

His lips twisted, then he went on, 'It may have been equivalent to slamming the shed door, but you certainly cleared the air.' He kissed her gently. 'I'll see myself out. By the way, don't forget to eat. It's important now.'

Maggie inhaled deeply as he walked away from her, and closed her eyes. The brush of his lips on hers had taken her right back to Cape Gloucester and the times she'd spent in his arms and his bed.

'I really loved you, Jack McKinnon, but I don't believe you will ever really love me because if it hadn't been for—fate—you would never have come back to me,' she whispered. 'That is so sad.'

Despite the deep well of sadness she felt, after taking the phone off the hook, she went to bed and slept like a top, the first time for ages. This was just as well since her mother and father arrived on her doorstep early the next morning.

Over the next days Maggie continued resolutely along the course she'd set for herself.

She told Jack that she still couldn't see her way clear to marrying him because—apart from anything else and there was plenty of that!—if he hadn't seen himself as the right man for her before, a baby wasn't going to change things.

He took it with surprising equanimity, although she intercepted one tiger-like little glance from him that seemed to say, We'll see about that. But she didn't see it again and she decided she'd imagined it.

She told her parents that they had to accept the fact that she'd come of age in her own way and she'd made her own mistakes. She told them that Jack would always be a part of her life now because of their child and would they please, please make the best of it.

It was her mother who surprised her. To her intense relief none of the new closeness between her parents seemed to have been lost beneath the weight of her news. But while her father's face changed and hardened at every mention of Jack's name, Belle, if she felt any animosity towards the man responsible for this contretemps, didn't show it.

Then she took Maggie aside and said to her quietly, 'I know all about it now.'

Maggie stared at her. 'You mean…you mean…?'

'Sylvia McKinnon?' Belle nodded. 'Your father, well, we'd been at odds for some time before it happened. I felt inadequate and angry because I knew how much he longed for a son, he felt guilty and defensive and it coloured our whole relationship. I knew he was restless and unhappy six years ago and that there was probably another woman in his life although I didn't know—I didn't want to know who it was.'

Belle paused and Maggie spoke. 'You're making it

sound as if Dad—as if *you* were the one at fault; that's crazy!'

'Darling…' Belle smiled a little painfully '…I know that, but sometimes these urges are so powerful in men you can't fight them. The important thing is, your father finally fought it himself and he's come back to me. In many ways we're happier now than we've ever been.'

Maggie stared down at her hands a trifle forlornly.

'There is still,' Belle said, 'the problem of Jack McKinnon.'

'I know. Men don't part with their grievances towards each other lightly.'

'You're not wrong!' Belle looked humorous. 'Tell me about him? By the way, I may not get your father to do this yet, but I intend to meet him.'

Maggie hesitated, then she told her mother everything. 'Of course this is only between you, me and the gatepost,' she finished.

'Of course. So you fell in love but he didn't?'

Maggie got up and wandered over to the window. They were in her bedroom on the second floor and she looked down over her colourful garden. 'Yes,' she said at last. 'That's why I can't accept second-best from him.'

A week later her mother did meet Jack and, although it had to be inherently awkward and there was a certain reserve that Maggie detected in Belle, it went well. Jack was quiet but courteous.

He was the first to leave and Maggie found her mother staring at her—well, staring right through her, actually.

'What?' she queried.

'Nothing,' her mother replied absently.

'What did you think of him?' The question came out before Maggie could guard against it and she bit her lip.

'They could be two of a kind.'

Maggie's eyes widened. 'Jack and Dad? That's exactly what I thought in the beginning!'

'Yes, well…' Belle seemed to come to a decision, and she imparted some surprising news to Maggie. Her father had bid successfully on three cattle stations and for the next few months they would be spending most of their time on them in Central Queensland.

'That's quite a coup,' Maggie said dazedly.

Belle agreed. 'Will you come with us? We'd love to have you.'

'No. No… I'm fine here.' But would she be, she wondered, without her mother's moral support?

'Of course I'll come and see you frequently, darling,' Belle assured her, 'and I'll only ever be a phone call and a short flight away.'

It wasn't until months later that Maggie realized what a clever strategy of her mother's this was…

Three months went by and at last Maggie started to show some signs of her pregnancy.

They went surprisingly swiftly, those months. She made all the difficult explanations—much less difficult than the ones to her parents and Jack, but not easy either. It was one thing to announce you were pregnant and to produce a partner even if he wasn't a husband, quite another to have to explain you were doing it on your own.

Her boss was clearly concerned for her, but he did

agree it made no difference to her work and she could continue for as long as she wanted to.

'You have a real flair for it, Maggie,' he said to her. 'A born natural, you are.' Then he frowned and seemed about to say more, but he obviously changed his mind.

Tim Mitchell was the hardest of all to tell. He was horrified, he was mystified and he offered to marry her himself there and then.

She thanked him with real gratitude, but declined. And she gradually withdrew herself from the crowd they both moved in.

'You don't have to do that, Maggie,' Tim said reproachfully. 'You need friends at least!'

'Yes, but I'm a different person now. I guess I have different priorities. Tim…' she hesitated but knew she had to do it '…I'm a lost cause, but there's got to be the *right* girl for you out there and you should forget about me—like that, anyway.' She stopped rather painfully as her words raised echoes in her mind she'd rather forget. But after that, she always found an excuse not to see Tim.

The one person apart from her family she couldn't seem to withdraw from was Jack.

He came to see her frequently in those months, although he never repeated his offer of marriage. It puzzled her that he should do this—at least as frequently as he did. It made it harder for her because of all the memories it brought back, but every time she thought of refusing to see him, she also thought of her promise never to separate him from his child.

She knew that she *could* never do that and, not only because he simply wouldn't have it, but also because he'd let her glimpse the pain and trauma of being abandoned by your natural parents.

She told herself that it was going to be a fact of her life from now on, his platonic presence in it, and she might as well get used to it. And it was platonic. He didn't try to touch her; he didn't refer to Cape Gloucester.

It was as if the desire he'd once felt for her had been turned off at the main switch and that caused her a lot of soul-searching. Had it been *such* a light-hearted affair for him? Had he achieved his revenge with spectacular success? Was there another woman in his life now? Was he turned off by pregnancy?

Perhaps I should check that out with Aunt Elena, she thought once, with dry humour.

The same couldn't be said for her. Yes, she'd suffered a couple of months of numbness after leaving him. In contrast now she was visited acutely at times by cameos from their past, like the one when they'd dragged an inflatable mattress out onto the veranda under a full, golden moon...

'We could be anywhere,' she said dreamily as they lay side by side on a cool linen sheet and the dusky pink pillows from his bed. 'On a raft up the Nile.'

'What made you think of that?'

'Well, you can hear the water, it is a wooden floor. Gloucester Island could be a pyramid sailing past.' She turned on her front and propped her chin on her hands so she could watch him. 'Have you ever been up the Nile?'

'Yes, I have.' He had one arm bent behind his head and he cupped her shoulder with his free hand and slid his finger beneath the broad lacy strap of her sleepwear. 'Have you?'

'Mmm… With my parents when I was sixteen. I loved it. Sadly, however, the whole experience was so momentous, I made myself sick.'

A smile flickered across his lips. 'That could have been the Egyptian version of Delhi belly.'

She bent her knees and crossed her ankles in the air. 'I think Africa would suit you,' she told him reflectively, 'or would have in times gone past.'

'I do remind you of Dr Livingstone? How?' he queried amusedly.

'No. But maybe Denys Finch-Hatton. I've seen his grave in the Ngong Hills, you know.'

'Same trip?'

She nodded. 'And Karen Blixen's house. It's preserved in her memory. The Danish government gave it to the Kenyan government on independence. She's a bit of a hero of mine.'

He turned his head towards her. 'Are you trying to tell me I'm a disappointment to you because I'm no Denys Finch-Hatton?' he queried gravely.

She denied this seriously. 'Not at all.'

'You did say something about taking me for a more physical guy.'

Maggie curled her toes. 'I just got that impression—well, yes, it presented itself to me in the form of hunting wild animals, crewing racing yachts et cetera, but translated it seemed to me that you liked to test yourself to the limit.'

He was silent for an age, just stroking her shoulder, then, 'In lots of ways I do—and did. When I started out, using the bank's money, not mine, I took some huge gambles. I often had to strain every nerve just to keep my head above water.'

'Did you enjoy that?'

He grinned fleetingly. 'There were times when I was scared to death, but on the whole, I guess I did.'

'So I was right about you all along,' she said with deep satisfaction.

'Wise as well as beautiful…' He drew the strap of her top down. 'Striking as this outfit is, I've got the feeling it's going to get in my way.'

Maggie flipped over onto her back and sat upright. 'This outfit' was a camisole pyjama top in topaz silk edged with ivory lace and a matching pair of boxer shorts.

'That could be remedied.' She slipped the top off over her head.

He watched her as she sat straight-backed with her legs crossed, like a naked ivory statue in the moonlight, slim, beautifully curved, grave, young and gorgeous. Her hair was tied up loosely with wavy tendrils escaping down her neck.

He sat up abruptly. 'If we changed the location slightly, moved this raft east across the desert sands, say, I could be the Sheik of Araby and you could be a candidate for my harem.'

Maggie's lashes fluttered and she turned to him with an incredulous look, but a little pulse beating rather rapidly at the base of her throat.

'Jack! That's very—fanciful.'

He grimaced. 'Surprised you?'

'Uh—' she licked her lips '—yes.'

He shook his head wryly. 'I've surprised myself, but that's how you make me feel at this moment and you were the one who put us in another spot in the first place.'

She thought for a moment, then bowed her head. 'Do I qualify?'

'Oh, yes, fiery little one,' he drawled. 'You do.'

'Fiery?' She lifted her head.

He touched one nipple, then the other, then he trailed his fingers down her spine towards her bottom. 'Fiery, delicious, peachy—definitely peachy. I knew I was right about that even if I couldn't understand it at the time.'

'Right?' She looked confused. 'What do you mean?'

He laughed softly. 'Don't worry about it. Come here.'

She moved into his arms and not much later he made exquisite love to her in the moonlight, on their raft anchored in the sands of Araby.

Two things Jack touched on during his visits were rather surprising. His latest development project, a retirement village, and the property he'd bought.

'Not the one with a shed hijacked to hide some vintage vehicles, the one I locked us into?' she said, her eyes wide with surprise as she unconsciously repeated how he'd described it the last time it had been mentioned between them. 'I happen to know it's been sold to a company, Hanson Limited, or something like that.'

'It's one of my companies.'

It was a Sunday morning and he'd arrived just as she was starting a late breakfast. He wore a navy tracksuit and running shoes, his hair was windblown and he was glowing with vim and vigour.

'Good,' he added as he sat down at her breakfast table. 'I'm starving.'

'What have you been doing?' Maggie asked as she got out more plates and cutlery.

'A two-mile jog down Main Beach.'

'Then you might need something more substantial..like steak and eggs.' She looked at him humorously.

He scanned the table. There was yoghurt and fruit, rolls and jam and, striking a slightly discordant note, a steaming bowl of chicken noodle soup.

He eyed it. 'Going for oriental cuisine, Maggie?'

She shrugged. 'I just get this incredible craving for chicken noodle soup. It can happen to me at any time of the day or night.'

'Out of a packet?'

'Oh, no. I make it myself so I can keep the level of salt down and there are no preservatives. I'm taking very good care of your unborn baby, Jack.'

He laughed. 'I wasn't suggesting otherwise. Well, don't let it get cold, I'll look after myself.'

'There's some leg ham and a nice piece of Cheddar in the fridge.' Maggie lifted a spoonful of soup to her mouth and blew on it gently. 'Help yourself if you like.'

He raised a wry eyebrow. 'A continental breakfast? I will, thanks.'

'So you bought it after all,' she said when he'd assembled a much larger breakfast and was tucking into it.

'Mmm… I thought you might be interested. Maisie said you had some good ideas for the house.'

'I'm sure you could afford to pull it down and start again.'

'I know you may still cherish the opinion that I delight in destroying landscapes and pulling things down to put up new ones, but in this case I don't,' he said mildly. 'That house has a lot of character and potential.'

Maggie drank her soup, having had the wind somewhat taken out of her sails. Nor was it that that she had against Jack McKinnon any longer, she reminded herself. It was the fact that he could arrive uninvited at her breakfast table, make himself completely at home—well, she had suggested that, but all the same—and, treacherously, it reminded her of all the breakfasts they'd shared at Cape Gloucester.

One particularly came to mind…

'What will we do today?'

He eyed her seriously. They'd had an early morning swim and she wore her pink bikini with her sarong knotted between her breasts. They were drinking coffee at the breakfast bar.

'Nothing,' he said.

'Nothing?' She wrinkled her nose at him. 'How idle!'

'I didn't plan to be completely idle. Perhaps decadent would be a better word for it—starting now.' He put his mug down and carefully untied the knot between her breasts to release her sarong, then he reached round and undid her bikini top.

Maggie looked downwards, entranced and feeling her heart start to beat heavily at the sight of his lean brown hands on her breasts.

'It doesn't feel decadent to me,' she said softly and bit her lip as her nipples flowered and a wash of sensuousness ran through her body.

'Actually—' he looked up briefly '—I can't think of anything more lovely and fresh and entirely the opposite from decadent than you, Ms Trent.'

'So?' Maggie queried with difficulty.

'I was referring to the time of day, that's all. Eight o'clock in the morning is not renowned for its romantic properties. Moonlit evenings, starry, starry nights, dawn, perhaps?' He looked into her eyes and shook his head. 'However…'

She put her hands on his shoulders and rested her forehead against his. 'Eight o'clock in the morning feels very romantic to me.'

He lifted her off her stool to sit across his lap, and slid his hands beneath her bikini bottom to cup her hips. 'You are a siren, you know,' he said against the corner of her mouth.

'Not Delilah?'

'Her too… Come to bed.'

She came out of her reverie feeling hot and cold, aroused and with her senses clamouring for that touch on her body again as she remembered the slow, perfectly lovely way he'd made love to her despite it being eight o'clock in the morning.

I thought I had it all sorted out, she reflected bitterly. I was no one's hostage; I was this independent, mature—recently matured but all the same—person in charge of my own destiny. So why can't I forget Cape Gloucester and all the things he did to me?

'I did have some ideas,' she said abruptly, anything to banish those images from her mind. 'But they wouldn't—' she wrinkled her nose as she forced herself to concentrate '—come cheap.'

'Spoken like a true Trent,' he murmured, and

grinned at her expression. 'That's fine with me. If I'm going to do it I want to do it properly. Tell me your thoughts.'

She did. And she couldn't fight the quickening of interest she felt.

CHAPTER SEVEN

THE next time Jack came to see Maggie, as usual unannounced, he dumped a heap of blueprints on her coffee-table.

'What on earth…?' She stared at him.

'I'm planning a retirement village. I do not want it to resemble a bloody chicken coop, but it has to stay affordable. What do you think of these?'

She took her time as she paged through the designs. 'Ghastly,' she pronounced at last. 'They're so poky!'

'That's what I told the architect. He's withdrawn from the project. On the other hand, they are retirement homes, not vast mansions.'

Maggie pulled some cushions behind her back, which ached occasionally nowadays, and considered the matter. 'I think it would be a help if they were more open plan. Separate bedrooms, yes, but not separate boxy little kitchens, dining rooms and lounges, so you got a more spacious feel even if it isn't necessarily so.'

He waited alertly as she thought some more.

'And since they don't have gardens—'

'Retirees are generally longing to get away from being slaves to lawnmowers and the like,' he put in.

'Perhaps,' she conceded, 'but a decent veranda so they can grow some nice pot plants and herbs if they want to would be…would be a priority of mine.'

'There are going to be plenty of landscaped gardens,' he murmured. 'All taken care of for them.'

'It's not the same as suddenly being cut off from growing anything of your *own*,' she countered. 'In fact, if I were planning a retirement village, I'd set aside a section where those interested could have their own little plots to grow their own vegetables or whatever they liked.'

'You are a gardening fanatic, Maggie,' he pointed out and glanced at the riot of colour outside.

She shrugged. 'Those are my ideas!'

'OK. I'll come back to you on it.'

'Why me?' she asked.

'I think you might have a feel for these things which could be helpful to me, Ms Trent. I've never done a retirement village before. I've been more concerned with kids and families.'

'Oh.'

He looked amused. 'If you feel like doing some designing, some doodles even, I'd be very appreciative.'

Maggie blinked, but she allowed the matter to drop.

For some reason, she'd recently begun to feel as if she'd walked into a brick wall and nothing was of more than passing interest to her.

Or rather, one reason for it was loud and clear. Added to her memories, added to her growing desire to drop all her defences and say simply to Jack, Marry me, please, I need you and I can't do this on my own, was her growing curiosity about other women in his life. It haunted her. There were times when it made her hate him and be prickly and uncommunicative with him. It sapped her energy. It was entirely unreasonable, she tried to tell herself.

You wouldn't marry him when the offer was open. Perhaps the best thing for you *is* to hate him…

On the other hand, when she wasn't being cross and out of sorts with him, she had to admit that his presence in her life was a bit like a rock she was coming to rely on.

What a mess you are, Maggie, she thought frequently.

She was five and a half months pregnant when he called in one chilly evening after dinner time.

They talked about nothing very much for a while, then he fell silent as his grey gaze flickered over her. She wore a loose ivory wool sweater over dark green tartan stretch pants. The sleeves of the sweater were a fraction too long for her and sometimes she folded them back, but they always unrolled.

Was it that, he wondered, that gave her a waif-like air? The exposure of her fragile wrists? Her loose hair tucked behind her ears? Her cream flat shoes that reminded him of ballet shoes?

Or her secretive eyes?

Grave and secretive now, when they'd been like windows of her soul only a few months ago. Capable of teasing him, querying him or laughing at him in a swift green glance, expressing honest desire. Expressing joy or, of course, sparkling with anger. But that had been longer ago, the anger, and what crazy voice in him told him he'd prefer that to this secretiveness?

'How are you feeling?' he asked abruptly.

'Fine,' she replied automatically.

'No, tell me.' He'd come straight from a business dinner and hadn't discarded his jacket, although he'd loosened his tie.

Maggie pushed a cushion behind the small of her

back. 'Apart from a bit of backache I do feel fine. The morning—afternoon sickness has gone and I'm told this middle trimester, before you get too heavy and slow, is when you should really glow.' She grimaced.

'But you're not glowing, are you?' he said quietly.

She shrugged and stood up suddenly. 'According to my doctor every pregnancy can be different. Would you like a cup of tea? Or a drink? I'm dying for a cuppa.'

'Thanks, I'll have one too.'

She turned away, but not before he noted some differences in her figure. Her wrists might look fragile, but those high, firm little gymnast's breasts were ripening and her waist was no longer reed-slim...

When she brought the tea tray back, he studied it rather than her figure.

He knew she liked Earl Grey tea so he wasn't surprised at the subtle fragrance of citrus oil of Bergamot that rose above the lovely china cups as she poured boiling water into them.

He knew she drank hers black and sugarless, but she hadn't forgotten that he took milk. He knew she always deposited the tea bags into an antique silver dish decorated with griffins rampant.

'All the same, why is that, do you think?' he queried as he accepted his cup and took a shortbread biscuit from the salver she offered.

'Why is what?'

'Is it the strain of being a single mother? Is that why you're not glowing, since there aren't any other problems?' he said deliberately.

She sat down and tucked her legs up. 'You'd be the last person I'd confess that to—if it were true.'

'In case I repeated my offer of marriage? I'm not.'

She pushed her sleeves back and wrapped her hands around her cup. 'No, it wouldn't make any difference. It's still no one's fault but my own that I find myself a bit daunted at times, but especially not yours, that's why I wouldn't admit it to you.' She hesitated. 'It's probably only because it's such new territory and many a new mum might feel a bit daunted anyway.'

'Have you made any preparations for the baby?'

A glint of humour beamed his way. 'Jack, whenever my mother comes to visit me, which is frequently, we do nothing else. That's not quite true— we go to the movies, concerts and so on and every few weeks she insists I spend a weekend on the cattle stations with them. But this baby will have everything that opens and shuts; more clothes than any single baby could wear, many of them exquisitely hand stitched. She loves doing that kind of delicate sewing.'

'OK.' He finished his tea and thought for a bit. 'What about your other social life?'

She wrinkled her nose. 'What social life?'

'Well, girlfriends, then?'

Maggie sighed unexpectedly. 'One or two, but I think I may have been a bit—I don't know—I think I may have given off pretty strong vibes that I would rather be alone.'

'And Tim Mitchell?'

She flinched.

'Did he drop you like the proverbial hot potato?'

'Oh, no. He offered to marry me.'

'I hope you turned him down flat,' he said and was rewarded by a definitely hostile green glance.

'Tim would make a fine husband,' she said tersely.

'Come on, Maggie,' he drawled, knowing full well he was out to hurt and anger her further, as if he had the devil himself riding him, 'that would have been a recipe for disaster. At least you loved going to bed with me.'

'Don't say—'

'Another word? Why not? It's true. You certainly made love to me as if you loved every minute of it. You tracked me down where no outsider has ever been able to find me to do so, come to that,' he said lazily, then added, 'And all the while you had Tim Mitchell virtually sitting in your lap.'

Maggie gasped. 'That's...that's—'

But he broke in before she could go on. 'If you're contemplating a loveless marriage to anyone, Maggie, I fail to see what Tim Mitchell has over me. Then again, I did think that's what you were expressly holding out against.'

'I am. If you'd allowed me to finish you would have heard me say that Tim would make a fine husband for the right person who was not *me*.'

'Bravo,' he applauded. 'I'm all in favour of sticking to your guns. Did that ring a bell with you, though?'

'It gave me a distinct sense of *déjà vu*,' she replied through her teeth. 'Why are you being so—horrible?'

He shrugged. 'I thought you needed taking out of yourself a bit.' He ignored her incredulous expression. 'How's the job going?'

Maggie opened her mouth to dispose of this query summarily, but something stopped her. Did she need taking out of herself? Was she floundering in a slough of despond?

'I'm giving it up in a fortnight.' She sniffed suddenly. 'I seem to have lost my edge. It's become a bit of a chore rather than a pleasure. Besides which…' she looked down at herself ruefully '…I've got the feeling I'm about to burst out all over and driving around a lot and getting in and out of cars may not be too comfortable.'

He smiled, and it was almost as if he'd gone from tiger mode to gentle mode in the blink of an eye. 'You could be right. How about working from home? For me, I mean, or as an associate?'

Maggie stared at him.

'I adapted the retirement village to your ideas, but now I need an interior decorator.' He paused and looked around. 'You have some wonderful ideas and taste.'

Maggie stared at him with her lips parted this time.

'You seem to have pretty strong convictions about retirement homes,' he said into the silence with a tinge of irony.

'Are you furnishing them?' she queried.

'Not all of them. There are several levels of accommodation. The ones I will be furnishing are for single occupants, widows and widowers mostly, I guess. I'd like them to be—cheerful and comfortable. But even the ones I don't furnish will need colour schemes, carpets, curtains, kitchen and bathroom finishes, et cetera.'

'And…' she licked her lips '…you…you think I could do all that from home?'

'I don't see why not. Of course you can check out the site as often as you like, but Maisie could organize all the samples—fabrics, carpet, paint—to be sent here.'

She stared at him again, transfixed.

He waited for a moment, then added, 'I've also set aside some land that can be divided into plots for keen gardeners.'

Why that did it, she wasn't sure, but all of a sudden, although it was a huge project, it beckoned her in a way that lifted her spirits immediately.

She opened her mouth to say the first thing that popped into her mind—*What a pity you don't love me, Jack*—but at the last moment she amended it to, 'Why are you doing this?'

'I told you. Your welfare is important to me, as well as the kid's.'

She fell asleep with tears on her cheeks that night because that unbidden, out-of-context thought—*what a pity you don't love me, Jack*—had revealed to her that she still hungered for his love; perhaps she always would. Why it had popped into her mind, she wasn't sure. Because he'd taken her advice to heart on garden plots for retirees? That didn't make much sense. Or did it? Could they become quite a team in every respect but the one that mattered most and it broke her heart to think of it?

Her life changed, her outlook in most respects changed from then on, however. During the last few months of her pregnancy she became very busy and found it fulfilling. She did pop out in some directions, but she did also glow, at times, at last.

She also got closer to Jack and the McKinnon empire. She accepted an advisory position on his board, although she demurred at first on the grounds of the speculation it might produce along the lines of whose baby she was carrying.

'That's no one's business but our own, Maggie,' he said decidedly. 'Anyway, no one knows of our connection. I haven't told anyone.'

'Not even Maisie?'

'Not even Maisie, although she may suspect, but she's the soul of discretion. Have you told anyone?'

'Who the father is? No.'

They eyed each other until he said, 'Well, then? It could be the start of a new, more suitable career for you as a single mother.'

Maggie opened her mouth, but, much as she would have loved to refute this for reasons not at all clear to her, she couldn't deny it was something she should give thought to.

'You could be right,' she said eventually.

She got to know his sub-penthouse, which was where he did his business entertaining. It was elegant but restrained and she got the feeling that if he felt really at home anywhere, it was Cape Gloucester.

She experienced the dynamic businessman he was at firsthand and knew that she and her mother had been right: he could be as arrogant and ruthless as her father, but he did temper it so that all his employees were devoted to him and his partners in any ventures respected him highly.

Sylvia came to see her out of the blue one day.

'I got Jack's permission to do this,' she said as she stood on the doorstep.

Still blinking with surprise, Maggie said, 'You

didn't need his permission! Uh—come in. I didn't know you knew…'

'I didn't until a couple of days ago when I came up to tell him some news of my own. I do find,' Sylvia said wryly when they were settled in the lounge, 'that it's not a good idea to cross Jack these days. Actually, it never was, because even as a kid he had an infuriating habit of being right about most things.'

'I know the kind.' Maggie looked heavenwards.

'I suppose you do. You got sandwiched between two such men, didn't you?'

The reference to her father chilled Maggie a little and perhaps Sylvia sensed it because she went on in a sudden rush. 'I was as much to blame as your father was. I knew he was married. I should never have got involved.'

Maggie thawed, she couldn't help it, but she also said honestly, 'I wondered about that. Still, these things happen, I guess.'

'Something else has happened to me. I've fallen in love again when I thought it could never happen to me.'

'Not a married man?'

'Not a married man, but he will be married to me shortly.'

On an impulse Maggie got up and crossed over to Sylvia to hug her with some difficulty that caused them both to laugh.

'I'm so happy for you,' Maggie said, with a genuine feeling of warmth.

'Would there be—any possibility your mother and father have—have…?' Sylvia hesitated.

'Got together again?' Maggie supplied. 'Yes! They have and it's wonderful to see.'

Sylvia breathed deeply. 'That's an enormous relief. But has he forgiven you for Jack, and this?'

'This?' Maggie patted her stomach affectionately. 'He's putting a good face on it. I don't think they'll ever be friends, but somehow or other I made them see that they had to be civilized at least. Not that they've met yet.'

'Maggie, why won't you marry Jack?'

'Sylvia…' Maggie paused and searched Sylvia's blue eyes '…you could be the one person who knows how hard it is to pin the real Jack McKinnon down. I think there's a core in him that will always shy away…' she stopped to think carefully '…from any true attachment and it goes right back to being put up for adoption as a baby.'

Sylvia heaved a sigh. 'Even under a loving adoption arrangement, it can be like a thorn in your flesh or you can secretly hold the belief that your mother was this wonderful, wonderful person who is always tied to you by an invisible string. That's the path I opted for. Jack went the other way. You could be right but—'

'The thing is,' Maggie interrupted quietly, 'I'm an all-or-nothing kind of person.' She raised her eyebrows. 'In lots of respects I've come to see I might be a chip off the old block, after all.'

'He, Jack, I mean—'

Again Maggie interrupted. 'He's been wonderful in lots of ways.'

'He was wonderful to me when I—when your father—without Jack to pick up the pieces, I don't know where I'd be.'

'Yes, he is rather good at picking up the pieces, isn't he?' Maggie said slowly.

Sylvia looked awkward. 'I didn't mean you.'

Maggie grimaced and decided to change the subject completely. 'Tell me about your new man? And would you like to see the nursery?'

'Well, well, kiddo.' Maggie patted her stomach after Sylvia had left—she'd taken to talking to her baby ever since she'd come out of her slough of despond. 'That was your aunt. Come to think of it, that's yet another difficult situation resolved. Which only leaves us but, hey, between the two of us we can conquer anything!'

A couple of days later, she got an even greater surprise.

Jack held a dinner party to celebrate the retirement village foundations being dug.

Actually, it was Maisie who organized it all down to the caterers, the flowers and guest list.

Maggie received her invitation in the mail. Jack was overseas until the afternoon of the dinner, but she didn't RSVP until the last moment. She was in two minds.

Then she thought, What the heck? She was part of the team and although, at eight months, sitting for any length of time was uncomfortable, she felt absolutely fine.

She also went out of her way to look absolutely fine. She chose a long French navy dress in a silk georgette that, despite being a maternity dress, was the essence of chic. It was round-necked, sleeveless and spring-like in tune with the new season. The fine pintucking on the bodice was stitched with silver thread.

She got her hair and her nails done; her tawny hair was loose and lightly curled so that it looked gorgeously windswept as only an expert hairdresser could achieve.

Her shoes were a complete folly, she knew—high, strappy silver sandals she couldn't have resisted if she'd tried. She covered the few patches of pregnancy pigment on her cheeks with a glowing foundation and her lipstick matched her nail polish.

She stared at herself in her beautiful rosewood cheval-mirror and addressed her unborn child again...

'You couldn't say we were *hugely* pregnant, honey-child. I've been very careful dietary-wise and I've been pretty active. Incidentally, *you're* pretty active these days, a right little gymnast! But I am more, well, rounded, even in the less obvious areas, although it doesn't seem to look too bad. Not tonight anyway.'

She turned away from the mirror ruefully and swept her silver mesh purse off the bed.

Maisie was more positive about it when she met Maggie at the door of the sub-penthouse.

'Maggie,' she said affectionately—they'd become good friends, 'you look fantastic!'

'I second that.' Jack loomed up behind Maisie and Maggie took an unexpected little breath.

She hadn't seen him for a week, but it was more than that. He wore a dinner suit and the beautifully tailored black suit and white shirt highlighted his tall, strong lines and broad shoulders. It shot through her mind that she loved him however he looked.

Windblown and with blue shadows on his jaw,

wearing an old football jersey with the sleeves cut off
as he'd often been at Cape Gloucester—but this Jack
was electrifying.

She swallowed something in her throat. 'Thanks,
you two! You sure know how to make a very pregnant lady feel better.'

It was a buffet dinner for about twenty people and
because it was a calm, warm night there were tables
set out on the veranda high above Runaway Bay and
overlooking the Broadwater and the ocean beyond.

The food was inspired and fine wine flowed although Maggie didn't partake of the wine and she ate
sparingly. But the company was pleasant, she knew
everyone and she enjoyed herself.

All the same, she attempted to leave a little early.
She was making her explanations to Maisie when
Jack's hand closed round her wrist. 'Stay a bit
longer,' he said quietly. 'It won't be long before the
party breaks up. Then I can drive you home.'

'But I drove myself here,' she objected.

'Doesn't matter. You shouldn't be out and about
on your own at this time of night.'

'That's true,' Maisie agreed.

'I am a little tired, though,' Maggie said and stifled
a yawn.

'How about I settle you in the den where you can
put your feet up and bring you a cuppa?' Maisie offered.

'Oh, thank you!' Maggie said gratefully. 'My shoes
are killing me.'

Maggie had never seen the den and it brought a slight
smile to her lips. There was definitely a nautical fla-
vour to it.

There were gold-framed ships on the walls; there was a wonderful antique globe of the world and a polished brass sextant on the coffee-table. There were also deep, inviting buttoned leather armchairs…

'And this one,' said Maisie triumphantly as she pushed a lever on the side of the chair, 'is a recliner chair.'

'Just what I need!' Maggie slipped off her shoes and sank down into it gratefully.

'Tea's on the way!'

Maggie had her tea, then she stretched out in the chair, to find she couldn't keep her eyes open.

Half an hour later something woke her from the gentle slumber she'd fallen into. Her lashes lifted, and Jack was standing beside the chair looking down at her, Jack looking austere but divine with his streaky fair hair tamed tonight and that wonderful physique highlighted by his dinner suit.

Her lips parted as their gazes caught and held, then she struggled upright.

He held out his hand and helped her to her feet.

She opened her mouth to thank him, but the words died on her lips because he was studying her—in a way she knew well, a way that was anything but austere—from top to toe. The sleep-flushed curves of her face, the glorious disarray of her hair, her mouth and throat, her full, rich breasts beneath the fine navy georgette, the mound of his child…

His gaze was intent and heavy-lidded and the pressure of his fingers on hers grew.

He still wants me, Maggie thought chaotically as

her colour fluctuated and her breathing grew ragged. That's how he used to look at me before he made love to me, just like this… So that the power of his gaze was almost like having his hands on me.

Have I not been the only one to suffer from the unassuaged ache of being physically deprived of him? Not the only one plagued by so many memories of our lovemaking? she wondered wildly. But what does it mean? I was so sure that he'd stopped wanting me.

She was destined not to know what it meant. A phone rang softly on the desk.

He turned his head at last to look at it, a hard, irritable look, then as it rang on he shrugged and walked over to it.

'Maisie,' he growled down the line, 'what the hell—?' He stopped.

From then on he answered in monosyllables until he said, 'All right. Will you drive Maggie home?'

She looked a question at him as he put the phone down.

'Sylvia rang. Our mother is critically ill now and not likely to survive for more than a day or so.'

'I'm sorry,' she said quietly. 'Don't worry about me—but will you get a flight at this time of night?'

'No, and the earliest flights tomorrow are booked out so I'll drive. If I start off now, I'll get there early tomorrow morning, anyway. I'm sorry.'

'That's all right! Just—take care. On the road.'

'I will.' He picked up her hand. 'You take care too.'

The baby moved at that moment and she put her hand on her stomach with his over it.

He blinked as he felt the movement. 'How often does that happen?'

'Quite a lot nowadays.' A smile trembled on her lips. 'He or she loves doing cartwheels so we could have another gymnast on our hands.'

Maisie coughed discreetly from the doorway, and the moment was lost. 'Sylvia again,' she said apologetically.

For the next few days Maggie felt as if she were on cloud nine.

Don't equate wanting you with loving you and not being able to live without you, she warned herself, but it made no difference. The long months of unhappiness, of blaming herself for her situation, of feeling that she hadn't lived up to what he needed in a woman melted away behind her.

If he could still want her when she was eight months pregnant, maybe he always would? Had she been proud and foolish all that time?

But I didn't know, she thought dazedly. He hid it so well. Why?

This thought occurred to her as she was walking down a busy pavement in Southport on the way to her doctor. She didn't even notice the man who passed her, then turned round and came back to her.

Until he said, 'Hang on—don't I know you?'

Maggie blinked and stared at him uncomprehendingly.

'You weren't pregnant then and all you were wearing was a bra and jeans while you and Jack McKinnon were—supposedly, although I had my doubts—trying to get out of the roof of a shed.'

Maggie suffered a surge of sheer revulsion at the

hateful way the man's eyes gleamed, and recognition came to her. It was the journalist who'd been with the private detective when she and Jack had been locked in the shed.

When he put his hand on her arm to detain her, she wrenched it free. 'Go away,' she ordered and made a dash for her doctor's surgery only a few doors away.

She heaved a huge sigh of relief as she passed through the doors and no one followed her, although she supposed it was always possible he would hang around until she came out.

Maisie, she thought. I'll ring Maisie and ask her to pick me up. Maisie will know how to handle it.

She got out her mobile phone and did just that.

But the first question she asked Maisie was if she'd heard from Jack.

'I just got the call. Mrs McKinnon passed away this morning. I believe it was a blessed relief.'

'Oh, that's still so sad. Please pass on my deepest sympathy.' Maggie paused, then went on to explain her current situation.

'I'll come and get you,' Maisie said immediately. 'Just tell me where and stay put in your doctor's rooms.'

When Maggie ended the call, she looked around and discovered she was in the wrong corridor.

She turned back just as a little boy, looking gleefully over his shoulder at his mother who was in hot pursuit, raced towards her.

They collided.

The child fell over, but bounced up. Maggie, robbed of her usual agility, toppled over with one ankle twisted beneath her. She fell on her back and hit her head on the floor. She passed out like a light.

CHAPTER EIGHT

SHE swam up slowly out of a deep, dreamless sleep. She opened her eyes a couple of times, but it was too much of an effort to keep them open. The third time she did it, though, she moved her head slightly and something swam into her line of vision that caused her to keep them open—a crib.

She froze as jumbled, painful memories tumbled through her mind, some memories of labour and the enormous effort and concentration it had required, memories of all sorts of people attending to her and X-raying her, but no memories of a birth.

She clutched her stomach and found it flat but floppy rather than hard and round. She froze again and realized her deep sleep since then must have been sedative-assisted because someone had put her into a fresh nightgown and a crisply made bed in a strange room she'd never seen before. And someone had put a crib beside the bed.

She moved convulsively but found her lower limbs wouldn't move at all.. and Jack said quietly, 'Take it easy, Maggie.'

Her astonished gaze fell on him, sitting on a chair beside the crib. 'Jack!'

'Yes. How do you feel?'

'I have no idea.' She blinked rapidly. 'Is this—us?'

He looked briefly amused. 'A good way to put it. Uh—it says on the crib—Trent stroke McKinnon—

so I guess it must be.' He tilted the crib so Maggie could see into it.

There was a baby fast asleep in it.

'So it's all right? It's...*all right*?' she asked urgently.

'Fine. Quite perfect, in fact, so they tell me.'

Maggie fell back against the pillows with a gasp of relief. 'Girl or boy?'

'Boy. He's a little premature and he's spent a bit of time in a humidicrib but they reckon he's coping very well on his own.'

She studied the baby, not that she could see much more than the curve of a cheek, one tiny fist and a fuzz of brown hair. Then he moved and more of his features came into view—and Maggie held her breath. But with great seriousness, the infant Trent stroke McKinnon yawned, opened his hand, then slept on.

'He seems to be...very composed,' Maggie said in some confusion.

'Yeah.' Jack shoved a hand through his hair, then rubbed his unshaven jaw. 'A lot more composed than I feel.'

'How can that be so?' she queried seriously. 'After what he's been through?'

'You were the one who went through the worst.'

'I don't seem to remember a lot about it,' she confessed. 'Well, some parts of it, but it's all confused and fuzzy.'

'Just as well and not surprising—you had concussion on top of everything else.'

Jack paused, then reached for her hand. 'What happened was, you sprained your ankle when you fell, you have a bump on your head and they think you may have slipped a disc or done something to your back. Then you went into labour. Fortunately, Maisie arrived not long after it all happened and she was able to identify you and get your own doctor—they'd called out another doctor who has consulting rooms in the same building.'

'Why can't I move my legs?' she asked.

'You've had a couple of epidurals. The birth itself was quite straightforward so they chose not to intervene—seems this young man had decided not to muck around!' He smiled at her. 'But you were in a lot of pain from your back as well as your ankle so it was for your sake and it may take a while to wear off.'

She blinked dazedly. 'How long ago did this all happen?'

He looked at his watch. 'About eight hours ago. I got here just after he was born.' He smiled again and released her hand to stroke her hair for a moment. 'I've had my first cuddle.'

Maggie closed her eyes. 'Can I?' she said with absolute longing in her voice.

'Sure. Your parents are also here, incidentally. They went to have a cup of coffee.'

Maggie's lashes swept up. 'You—you and my father have met?'

He nodded. 'No fireworks, no hard words. We're all too concerned about you. And too taken with the baby.'

Maggie breathed very deeply. 'That's—I can't tell you how happy that makes me.'

He said nothing, just stroked her hair again.

'And my back?' she asked after a while.

'They're not sure. What with everything else going on—' he gestured ruefully '—they haven't been able to assess it properly. But they have taken X-rays. We're waiting on the results now. Your ankle just needs time.'

'Will you please give me my baby, Jack?' she begged. 'You see, I've been talking to it, to him,' she corrected herself, 'for weeks and weeks and I'm sure he can't understand why he hasn't heard my voice since he was born.'

'Of course.' He got up and picked Trent stroke McKinnon up gingerly. In the moment before he placed the bundle in Maggie's arms, he looked down at the child in a way that made Maggie catch her breath—with sheer pride and tenderness.

It shot through her mind that even if she never achieved a breakthrough to the real Jack McKinnon, this child would.

Then she accepted the bundle and her own attachment began. Her breasts tightened and she put a finger into her son's open palm and his tiny hand closed around it.

'Well, well, honey-child,' she breathed, 'we get to meet at last. How do you do? Oh, look,' she said to Jack, 'I think he's got your nose!'

Jack grimaced and felt his nose. 'If there's anyone he looks like,' he said ruefully, 'it's a Trent.'

They laughed together—and that was how her parents found them.

But when the injections wore off a couple of hours later, Maggie was once again in great pain, although at least the cause of it had been diagnosed. She'd broken a transverse process, a small bone running off the spine, in her lower back.

It would heal, she was told, of its own accord, but

many movements would be painful for her until it did so. All they could do was manage the pain for her until it became bearable, in about a week they estimated, but even then it would probably be quite a few weeks before she regained full mobility.

Unfortunately, they told her, all this would interfere with her ability to breast-feed her baby.

'No, it won't,' she said.

'Maggie,' her mother began.

'Mum, there has to be a way. Dad—' she turned her head to her father '—why don't you take Jack out for a drink while we work this out? He looks as if he could do with it.'

'Maggie,' David Trent warned, 'darling, it's not the end of the world if you can't breast-feed and it's just as important for the baby for you to recover well and quickly.'

'I will,' she promised, 'but I will also do this, *somehow.*'

It occurred to her a moment later that she never, ever thought she'd see what she saw then—her father and Jack exchange identical helpless glances.

Belle also saw it and she exchanged a laughing glance with Maggie before she shooed both men out. Then she sobered and turned back to her daughter. 'How?'

'I've read a lot about it and there's great support for breast-feeding mums. What we need is an expert, but I don't see why my milk can't be expressed for the next few days so I don't lose it, until I come off the painkillers—and I intend to do that as soon as possible.'

'But what about the baby?'

'We need to find someone with loads of milk who

wouldn't mind suckling him so he gets the hang of it, and they will have to feed him a supplement. Mum, please help me here,' Maggie said urgently, then looked exhausted. 'I want to do this!'

Belle eyed her daughter, then sighed. 'All right. All right.'

It was a traumatic and painful week for Maggie. Expressing breast milk might sound fine in theory, but in practice it could be excruciating. Transverse processes might be little bones, but they hurt like the devil when you broke them.

On the plus side, however, Bev Janson, who'd had her third baby the same day as Maggie's, had more milk than she knew what to do with and was grateful for the relief she gained from feeding another baby. Not only that, she and Maggie became firm friends.

And Trent stroke McKinnon throve through it all.

Then came the day when Maggie could sit up properly and she was given the go-ahead to feed her baby herself.

Her sense of triumph was huge. So was her joy.

'See?' she said to Jack. 'I knew there had to be a way.'

'Maggie…' He stopped, then shook his head at her. 'You're a bloody marvel. I don't think I've ever seen such guts.'

'The doctor said I could probably go home in three or four days.'

He hesitated. 'Have you had any thoughts about that?'

'No!' She grimaced. 'Too much on my mind.'

'We have.'

She eyed him. Apart from a couple of days when

he'd gone south for his mother's funeral, he'd spent time with her every day.

He'd taken the nursing staff by storm.

He'd brought her a DVD machine and lots of movies, including all the Harry Potter movies; he'd brought her books. He'd sent Bev a magnificent floral tribute and got friendly with her husband. On discovering the Jansons would dearly love to move into a bigger house than the one they were renting but couldn't afford to, he'd organized one at the same rent for them on one of his estates.

But he'd said nothing about marriage, although, when he was with her in her painful times, Maggie could have been forgiven for thinking he cared deeply about her.

Now, it was a Sunday, he wore jeans, deck shoes and a white polo T-shirt. He looked casual, big and…

Maggie paused in her summary of him. And what…?

'We have?' she repeated suspiciously. 'Who are we?'

'Your parents and I. We came to the conclusion it would be a good idea if you moved in with me.'

'Jack—'

'I have so much space and it's all on one level whereas your house is double-storeyed—'

'I know that!'

He half smiled. 'Then you'll agree that since you'll need a wheelchair for a while it makes sense not to have stairs to negotiate.'

She was silent as she stared at him fixedly.

'Your mother has offered to stay with us for as long as you need her,' he went on. 'There's also a gymnasium in the building and a swimming pool. Your doctors have recommended a programme of exercise under a physiotherapist's care to get your back and your ankle strong again.'

'I see,' she said at last.

'What do you see, Maggie?' he asked with his lips quirking.

'Something I never thought I would live to see,' she said. 'You and my parents ganging up on me.'

He opened his mouth to reply, but a nurse walked in with their baby in her arms. 'Feed time! Now listen up, you two.' She gave the baby to Maggie. 'We, the nursing staff, have decided it's about time this baby got a name. You can't go on calling him Trent stroke McKinnon for the rest of his life!'

'How about,' Jack suggested, 'Trent McKinnon?'

'Trent McKinnon,' Maggie said slowly. 'Do you approve, sweetheart?' she asked the baby.

Their child wrinkled his face and began to wave his fists, a prelude, Maggie was coming to know well, to a very vocal infant conniption. 'Call me what you like; just feed me!' Maggie said rapidly and started to unbutton her nightgown.

They all laughed.

'Yes, I like that,' she added, 'but he needs a middle name—can be very helpful in certain circumstances, kiddo! So, let's make it Trent Jack McKinnon.'

'Agreed.' Jack got up and kissed her briefly. 'I've got to go, but I'll be back this evening. Shall I set it all up?'

Maggie looked up from her baby with a tinge of confusion, then she nodded helplessly and turned her concentration back to Trent Jack McKinnon.

It all went according to plan.

Maggie grew stronger and used the motorized

wheelchair less and less, but it was still invaluable by the time Trent was two months old because it allowed her to do everything for him without placing the burden of his weight on her back and ankle.

One of the bedrooms in the sub-penthouse had been converted to his nursery cum her bedroom and, with his flair for good design, Jack had had all the surfaces, change table and so on, made to a height Maggie could cope with sitting down.

He'd also taken advantage of her mother's presence to catch up with business trips he'd put on hold while Maggie had been in hospital. So they hadn't seen a great deal of him—for which Maggie had been curiously grateful.

She tried desperately to analyze not only her feelings, but the whole situation as her strength returned, but all she could come up with was the fact that she only seemed to be able to take each day as it came with a sense of what will be will be.

Then her mother decided to go back to the cattle stations. She left the day Jack was due to return after a week in New Zealand.

For some reason, although Maggie was perfectly confident with Trent now, although she experienced no pain now and wasn't afraid to be left alone, the quiet, empty apartment acted as a catalyst for her.

She started to think of the future. She started to question Jack's feelings for her, and hers for him.

There had been no repeat of what had taken place in the den a few nights before Trent was born, but that wasn't so surprising in the circumstances, and she might have been partly responsible for it anyway. She had been preoccupied with her baby and getting herself fit again for him. Jack, apparently, had had a lot of work to catch up on. And her mother had been with them all the time.

Yet, lately, little things about him had started to catch her unawares.

She'd been talking to him over breakfast one morning when she'd found herself breaking off and watching the way he was drumming his fingers on the table. It was a habit she'd first noticed at Cape Gloucester and it suddenly reminded her of his fingers on her skin, exploring, tantalizing her until she was weak with desire…

She'd had to get up without finishing what she was saying on the pretext of hearing Trent.

He'd come back from one trip, but had only been able to spend half an hour with them before going off to a meeting. She'd unpacked his bag for him and she'd suddenly buried her face in one of his unlaundered shirts, feeling a little dizzy with longing for his tall, strong body on hers.

So not a lot has changed there, she thought, while she waited for Jack to come back from New Zealand. I still don't know where he stands, though, but I do know he's been wonderful in every other way.

She was sitting on her bed as she thought these thoughts, with Trent lying beside her obviously deeply interested in his teddy bear.

She leant over and tickled him under the chin. He made a trilling little sound, then grabbed her hand and started to nuzzle it.

'But in the end, honey-child,' she said to him, 'what it boils down to is this—if your mama thought only of herself in times gone by, that has to change. OK, I know! You're hungry.'

* * *

Jack got home just after Maggie had given Trent his six p.m. feed and was settling him.

She was still in the nursery when she heard him arrive and called out to him. 'In here, Jack!'

He came through a few minutes later looking rather tired. He wore khaki trousers and a round-necked T-shirt under a tweed sports jacket.

'A busy trip?' she queried.

'Yep.' He stretched. 'How's my son and heir?'

'He's fine. He was talking to his teddy bear today. Jack.' Maggie hesitated, then knew there was only one way to do what she had to do and that was to plunge right in. 'This is a very proper baby.'

Jack stared at his now-sleeping son for a long moment, then sat down on the end of her bed. 'I never thought he was a porcelain doll.'

'No. I mean, he's very well organized. He does everything by the book.'

Jack frowned. 'He's only eight weeks old. How can you say that?'

Maggie was still sitting in her wheelchair, attractively dressed in slim white trousers and a floral seersucker jacket trimmed with green. Her dark gold hair was tied back with a scrunchie; her green eyes were clear and free of pain.

'I'll tell you. He adapted himself to a four-hourly schedule right from the start under extremely difficult circumstances. He burps beautifully and he mostly sleeps between feeds just as the book says he should. He has one wakeful period, after his two p.m. feed, where he'll accept conversation and he quite appreciates being carried around for a bit. He now sleeps through the eight hours from ten p.m. to six a.m.'

'Is there anything he doesn't do by the book?' Jack asked with a grin. 'He sounds almost too good to be true.'

Maggie considered. 'He hates having his hair washed. He gets extremely upset, but even that isn't going against the book exactly. They do warn that some babies hate it.'

'Screams blue murder?'

'Yes. Otherwise—' she shrugged '—there's nothing he doesn't do very correctly.'

'What are you worried about, then?'

Maggie stared down at her sleeping son with her heart in her eyes. 'I can't help thinking he would be horrified if he knew how—irregular—his situation was.'

She looked up and their gazes clashed.

'Born out of wedlock, you mean?' he said, and for a fleeting moment his mouth hardened. 'That was your choice, Maggie.'

She inclined her head. 'That was before—all sorts of things happened,' she said quietly and ran her fingers along the arm of her wheelchair. 'That was definitely before I came to appreciate the reality of having a baby and what a baby deserves.'

Jack stared at her for a long moment, then he got up and started to push the wheelchair towards the door.

'I can walk or do this myself,' Maggie said.

'Stay put. I need a drink.'

She didn't protest any further and he wheeled her out onto the veranda, and left her to get their drinks. The sun had set, leaving a fiery pattern of cloud and sky to reflect in the calm waters below them.

He came back with a Scotch for himself and a tall

glass of lemon, lime and bitters for her with a sprig of mint in it.

Then he leant back against the railing and studied her. 'What are you suggesting, Maggie?'

She sipped her drink. 'Will you marry me, Jack?'

The silence lengthened between them until he stirred and said, 'Is that what you *really* want?'

What did I expect? she wondered. That he would leap at the idea? That he would declare his undying love for me?

She put her glass down on the veranda table and stumbled up out of her chair.

He caught her on the threshold to the lounge. 'Whoa! Why are you running away?'

'Because you haven't changed one bit,' she flashed at him. 'You never did understand me and you never will.'

He looked down into her anguished eyes, her scarlet face as she tried to pull away. 'Oh, yes, I do.'

'Then why say that, as if—as if it's just another of my mad, impetuous whims?'

'Blame your mother if you want to blame anyone for a desire on my part to be sure of your feelings,' he said harshly.

'My mother!' she gasped. 'What has she got to do with this?'

'A lot. She came to see me after we'd first met at your house.'

Maggie sagged in his arms with disbelief and confusion written large in her expression as she remembered her conversation with her mother about Jack and how she loved him... 'What did she tell you?' she whispered.

He led her towards a settee and they sat down side

by side. 'She told me that you could lead a horse to water but you couldn't make it drink.'

Maggie's mouth fell open.

He smiled briefly. 'She didn't use those words, but that was the gist of it. She told me there was no way I'd get you to marry me unless it was what you yourself had decided to do.'

'She...she really said that?'

He nodded. 'I told her that I had already received that impression and was prepared to bide my time. She then offered me some assistance. Under normal circumstances, she said she would never have dreamt of deserting you in any way, but it would provide *me* the opportunity to provide *you* with some moral support at least and who knew what might come of that?'

'I wondered about that,' Maggie confessed. 'Her going away like that. I put it down to, well, their reconciliation, Mum and Dad's, but I was a bit surprised. I put *that* down to selfishness on my part.'

He lay back and shoved his hands in his pockets. 'I also made a promise to your mother. She can be...' he smiled fleetingly '...a hard woman.'

'I wouldn't have thought that!' Maggie objected.

'Believe me, on the subject of her only daughter, she exhibited some—almost—tigress tendencies.'

Maggie blinked in sheer surprise. 'What did she say?'

'First of all she pointed out the error of my ways to me. To use someone like you as a tool for revenge against your father was diabolical.'

Maggie gulped a breath of astonished air. 'Did you tell her...did you tell her how I followed you and—?'

'No.' He put a hand over hers. 'And it made no

difference; she was *right*. With things the way they were between me and your father, with a girl like you, I was—inexcusable.'

'Was it only revenge?' she asked barely audibly.

He turned his head to her at last. 'Did it feel like it?'

'Not until you sent me away,' she whispered.

His hand tightened on hers until she made a small sound.

'Sorry.' He released her and sat up. 'She then explained that to turn up out of the blue and propose marriage because there was a baby on the way was the height of arrogance even if I still wanted you. And the promise she extracted was that I would stand by you in every other way until, if ever, you discovered I was the one *you* wanted.'

'Oh my,' Maggie breathed. 'Does that mean to say you did still want me? I thought so once, but that was just before Trent was born and it was only once…'

'Maggie—' he rubbed his jaw almost savagely '—I never stopped wanting you. I couldn't get you out of my mind even if I couldn't reconcile—I honestly didn't think I could bring the commitment to a marriage that was needed. There has always been a small part of me that—I don't know—was closed off to that particular traffic. The last nine months have changed all that,' he added.

She was silent, her lips parted, her eyes huge.

'You see,' he went on, 'yes, I cared about my adopted family and Sylvia will always be special to me, but no one has ever walked into my heart and taken it over the way you have.

'No one,' he said quietly, 'brings me the joy and pleasure just in their company you do. And that's one of the reasons I took what turned out to be an increasingly long, hard road these past months. Then there was what you did for Trent. I have never seen anyone battle such painful odds as you did for our son. So you not only have my whole-hearted love, but my utmost admiration, Maggie Trent.'

She wiped her eyes. 'If only you'd told me this sooner—'

He took her hand again, gently this time, but shook his head. 'If there was one thing that finally made me see how much I loved you, it was when your welfare became more important than mine.

'Maggie…' he paused '…sometimes, often, your first love turns out not to be what you think it is at the time. It can be powerful but fleeting, a crush maybe. Also, I had no way of knowing—you possibly had no way of knowing yourself—if you could ever forgive me, or—'

'If it hadn't all been a Maggie Trent, heat-of-the-moment whim?' she suggested gravely.

'I wasn't going to say that.'

'I couldn't blame you if you did.' She gestured.

'What I was going to say was,' he continued, 'there were so many complications it would have been perfectly natural for you to feel dreadfully confused. All I could hope for was that..time might be on my side. But if it's Trent that's made you come to this decision—'

She put her hand to his lips. 'Jack, I've had my own revelations. I'm a lot more like my father than I dreamt. I'm an all-or-nothing kind of person and that's why I thought it wouldn't work for me with you.'

She hesitated as he kissed her fingers. 'Yes, I

thought I was asking you to marry me for Trent's sake because I didn't know how you felt. But the truth is there's a plus side to the all-or-nothing person I am. I fell in love with you overnight. I will always love you—it may even be a bit of a trial to you at times, but that's me, and it was *always you*, for me.'

'A bit of a trial?' He pulled her into his arms and held her extremely hard as he buried his face in her hair. 'If you only knew how many times I've wanted to do this,' he said on an edge of desperation. 'If you knew how close I came to lowering my guard the night Sylvia rang.'

He lifted his head and looked into her eyes.

She placed a fingertip on the little scar on his eyebrow. 'If you knew what that did to me. Suddenly I was on cloud nine; nothing else mattered!'

'Then…' He hesitated. 'Your back?'

'It's fine, if I take care. Why don't you unplug the phone?'

'Good idea.'

But they didn't go straight to bed. They finished their drinks, he with his arm around her, and they talked.

He told her how he'd manufactured some of his business trips in the last few weeks because actually living in the same place with her had become more of a test of his endurance than he could bear.

She asked him how he felt about her mother now.

He rested his chin on the top of her head for a moment. 'What I said just now was a throwback to earlier times. I may have agreed with her, but there's a certain natural reluctance to think too blackly of oneself.'

She looked up in time to disturb a rueful expression in his eyes.

'I know the feeling,' she agreed.

He kissed her forehead. 'I've made my peace with your mother. To be honest, Trent has to take a lot of the credit for the new state of goodwill between the House of McKinnon and the House of Trent.'

'It's amazing what a baby can do.'

'Mmm… It's just as amazing what his mother has achieved.'

Maggie laid her head on his shoulder. 'I've missed this so much,' she whispered.

He put his other arm around her. 'Me too.'

They sat like that for an age, feeling warm and content, then it grew into more and he started to kiss her.

'The Nile? Or the sands of Araby?'

Maggie looked around Jack's bedroom. It was large, luxurious, but quite impersonal and they were lying on a vast bed, renewing their intimate acquaintance. 'Ah,' she said, 'this is going to take a bit of imagination.'

He looked up. 'I know what you mean. I bought it like this, this place, but it reminds me of a hotel. I haven't got around to changing anything but the den.'

'I could change it for you,' she offered.

'I've had a better idea, I'll tell you about it tomorrow. But talking of change—'

'I know.' She ran her fingers through his hair. 'I've changed a bit.'

He kissed the soft underside of her arm. 'You're still gorgeous. Actually—' he swept his hand down her body and returned it to her breasts '—apart from these, there's not much change at all.'

'All the swimming, gym work and physio has helped enormously,' she told him. 'But you've—lost a bit of weight.'

'I had the feeling I was fading away beneath all that longing for you, Maggie Trent.'

Maggie smiled and kissed the corner of his mouth. 'Well, now you've got me, what do you want to do with me, Jack McKinnon?'

He showed her. He visited all her most erotic spots with his usual care and attention until she was quivering and on fire, and her responses became just as intimate.

'This is going to be quite a ride,' he said with the breath rasping in his throat.

They were lying facing each other. She was in his arms with one of her legs riding high on his thigh.

'It always was,' she murmured.

He brought one hand up to cup her cheek and it was so exquisitely gentle a gesture and there was so much tenderness in his grey eyes, Maggie caught her breath and felt as if her heart could burst with love.

'Now?' he queried.

'Now,' she agreed. 'Yes, please.'

'I thought of a way to do this with the least strain on your back.'

'Oh?'

He rolled onto his back, taking her with him on top of him. 'Not only easy on your back, but you're in total control now, Maggie.'

'Jack,' she gasped as he entered her, 'I'm in no position to… You told me once you were about to die. I'm in the same situation!'

'Hold hard there for a moment, sweetheart,' he commanded, and clamped his hands on her hips. 'We might as well die together. How's that?' he asked as their rhythm co-ordinated.

'Well,' she conceded with a faint smile chasing across her lips, 'that's perfect.'

They said no more until they climaxed together, not only in physical unity but mentally transported as well.

'I love you, I love you, I love you,' she said huskily when she could talk again, with sheer sensual rapture still sweeping her body.

'Me too. I mean I love you, Maggie. When did you plan to marry me?'

She had to laugh, and slowly they came back to earth together. 'Uh—tomorrow?'

Of course it wasn't possible to arrange it that soon, but she got another lovely surprise the next day.

'I'd like to show you and Trent something,' he said the next morning after breakfast. 'We'll take his pram.'

'What is it?'

He studied her. She was feeding Trent and she looked voluptuous, languorous and completely serene. As if she had most satisfactorily been made love to recently, which, indeed, she had.

As have I, he reflected, and I will never let her go again.

'Wait and see.'

'There's a surprise in the air, honey-child,' she told Trent, and Jack grinned.

But her astonishment at his surprise was huge.

'Jack,' she said uncertainly as they stood in the

house on the property that had first brought them together, 'how did this happen?'

The house was no longer neglected. It wasn't furnished, but it had been renovated exactly as Maggie
had suggested. It was clean and sparkling and the
smell of new paint lingered on the air.

'You told me what you wanted,' he reminded her.

'Yes, but you never mentioned it again!'

'I wanted to do it as a surprise. I thought it might
be the perfect place for Trent to grow up.' He took
her hand and led her to a window. 'The garden has
been cleared and is all ready and waiting for you. I
thought you might even like to see if you could grow
some *Guettarda Speciosa* here and harvest their perfume.'

'Oh, Jack.' She stood on her toes and kissed him.
'Thank you, from the bottom of my heart.'

He held her close. 'Happy?'

'Yes, very happy. Almost happier than I can bear.'
They turned as Trent made a protesting sound from
his pram, as if he was taking exception to being ignored.

They linked hands and walked over to the pram.

'We're here, kiddo!' Jack said and they both bent
over the pram.

Trent wriggled ecstatically, then he smiled a blinding, toothless smile at them.

Maggie gasped. 'Did you see that—did you see *that*? Do you agree that was a smile and not wind?'

'Sure do. What's wrong with it?'

'He's only two months old! I didn't think it was
supposed to happen so early.'

'Maggie—' Jack tossed her a laughing look '—perhaps he's divined that we've got the message and are doing everything by the book now, so he can relax and please himself occasionally?'

THE BEDROOM ASSIGNMENT

by

Sophie Weston

Born in London, **Sophie Weston** is a traveller by nature who started writing when she was five. She wrote her first romance recovering from illness, thinking her travelling was over. She was wrong, but she enjoyed it so much that she has carried on. These days she lives in the heart of the city with two demanding cats and a cherry tree – and travels the world looking for settings for her stories.

CHAPTER ONE

'THERE'S more to relationships than sex, Zo,' announced her best friend with energy. 'You've got to be a bit more flexible.'

In the act of filling the kettle, Zoe Brown looked up and stared in disbelief. 'I beg your pardon?' she said. 'Where did that come from?'

Suze had rushed into the old-fashioned kitchen like a whirlwind, casting her briefcase to one side and her shopping bags to the other. She had not even sat down before she launched her bombshell. Now she perched on the settle against the wall with a small, complacent smile.

'I don't know what it is that Simon's done...' She paused expectantly.

Zoe cast her eyes to heaven. 'Is there anything you don't think is your business? What did you do? Stake out my house? Tap my phone?'

Suze grinned. But she was not to be deflected. 'Don't be coy. I don't have to spy on you to know what you're up to. We have no secrets.'

If only you knew, Suze.

Zoe found she had over-filled the kettle. She emptied some water out, and then switched the thing on before turning back to her friend.

'I knew something was wrong,' Suze announced loftily. Then added, with a slight diminution of ineffability, 'Besides, Simon called me.'

Well, that figured, thought Zoe. Suze had introduced her and Simon Frobisher in the first place. Simon was a member of Suze's Young Business Network. It was natural that he should confide in her when his fledgling romance with Zoe hit the buffers.

5

'Have you two had a row?'

'Not really,' said Zoe uncomfortably. 'We talked, but—'

Suze sighed theatrically. 'You talked!' she echoed. 'And another one bites the dust! I don't *believe* you.'

Zoe looked away. 'Is he very upset?' she said with compunction.

Suze pursed her lips. 'Confused is probably a better word,' she pronounced.

'I'm sorry about that.'

'It's understandable. He's a scarce commodity and he knows it. Single, straight, solvent. *And* a business that's going to make him a millionaire in the next five years. From his point of view, it's a seller's market.'

Zoe felt slightly better. 'You mean he isn't breaking his heart?'

In contrast to Zoe, who was barefoot in dusty cut-offs and a torn tee shirt, Suze was dressed in a business suit. But she kicked her legs against the settle like the five-year-old she had been when they'd first met at kindergarten.

'No, but he's scratching his head. He muttered something about sex…' Again Suze left an inviting pause.

'Did he?' Zoe's tone was discouraging.

'Aw, come on, Zo. Give.'

'Have a coffee,' said Zoe firmly.

She made instant coffee in two thick china mugs and padded across the kitchen with them. Suze took hers, but she frowned with irritation.

'I mean, you can't keep going through men like they grow on trees.' Her voice was full of righteous indignation. 'Quite apart from anything else, it's not fair to the rest of us.'

Zoe gave a hollow laugh. 'Is that right?'

Suze did not notice it was hollow. 'And it's beastly inconvenient. I never know who you're going to bring to a party.'

Zoe pushed back her untidy brown curls and hitched herself up onto the corner of the cluttered table. 'Well, if that's all you're worried about—'

'Or if you're going to bring anyone at all. And what he will be like if you do.'

'I'll make sure to send you the next one's resumé,' Zoe said dryly.

Suze Manoir grinned. 'Or you could just stick to the same man for more than a couple of dates,' she suggested. 'That would be a first.'

Oh, Lord, thought Zoe. Aloud she said, 'Yes, ma'am.'

'Oh, *you*,' said Suze, exasperated. 'Okay. I'll mind my own business. What do we need to do to get this house sorted?'

'Just about everything,' said Zoe wryly. 'Starting with re-wiring and moving on up.'

The kitchen of the Brown family house was big and untidy. Just at the moment about a third of it looked beautiful. A wild green arrangement of leafy summer branches and ferns hid the peeling paintwork round the fireplace and the stains on the old pine table. Zoe had set out dishes of roast beef, and the Thai chicken and vegetable salads that she had prepared yesterday, all covered in plastic wrap. She had even set little groups of solid candles, ready for lighting, on the fireplace and one corner of the table.

But that was the far end of the kitchen. The other two thirds, where they were sitting, looked like a shipwreck. A pretty shabby shipwreck at that, thought Zoe ruefully.

She and her sister had slapped a coat of paint on the walls at Christmas, just to make it look more cheerful. But the whole house had a patched and mended air. Whereas Suze had shown an interior decorator round her central London pad for a television lifestyle programme, and the Manoir house was immaculately presented.

Suze followed her eyes. 'Hey,' she said gently, showing that in this area, at least, she was right that they had no secrets. 'So it's a bit battered. Don't worry about it. That's why we're having the party here, after all.'

'Good point,' agreed Zoe. 'Okay, let's kick back and party.'

From the moment that they'd taken charge of their own

birthday celebrations, Suze and Zoe had given a joint party
at Zoe's house. They chose a day in the summer, when hopefully people would be able to go out into the garden, and
called it their Official Birthday. Suze said that the arrangement gave her more freedom than her parents' house and
more room than her own flat. But Zoe knew it was more
than that.

Suze knew that, ever since Zoe's father had left home,
money had been dreadfully tight—and, even worse, that
Zoe's mother had withdrawn into the cocoon of her own
world. The Official Birthday Party was Suze's way of helping out without admitting it.

'You're a good friend,' Zoe said with affection.

She went over to the big wipe-down board where the family left messages for each other. Today it had been wiped
clear—no phone messages for Artemis, her twenty-year-old
younger sister, currently out with boyfriend Ed, or notes
about washing seventeen-year-old Harry's rugby kit. Today
it was covered by one orderly list in Zoe's neat writing.
More than half the items had already been ticked off.

'You're so efficient,' said Suze with a sigh. She came up
and stood at Zoe's shoulder. 'You're really wasted here. You
ought to be running a government, not this mad house.'

Zoe flung up a hand.

'Oh, all right,' said Suze, as she always did. 'You know
your own business best. Got a job for next week?'

Zoe pulled a face. 'Just a couple of guided walks along
the Thames. I'll probably call the library department on
Monday morning, see if they've got anyone sick.'

'I wish you'd sign on with me again,' Suze said wistfully.
She ran her own very successful staff agency. 'People are
always asking for you.'

'Maybe after the summer,' said Zoe vaguely. She narrowed her eyes at the list. 'Put up fairy lights in the apple
tree. Glitter balls in the sitting room. Which do you want to
do?'

'Sounds like manual labour.' Suze looked at her elegantly

painted fingernails and shuddered. 'We'll do them together,' she decreed.

They went out into the garden first. Zoe brought the ladder out of the shed and slung it over her shoulder to carry it up to the orchard.

'High-ho, high-ho,' sang Suze, following behind with a coil of outdoor fairy lights.

Zoe grinned over her shoulder. 'I'm no dwarf.'

It was true. She was nearly as tall as her six-foot father, and certainly as striking, with her candid, wide-open brown eyes and mop of unruly chestnut curls.

'No, but you're certainly one of the workers of the world,' said Suze, watching as Zoe lodged the ladder against the tree trunk in a workmanlike manner. 'Now, if Simon were here he could do it. That's what men are for.'

Zoe pushed a dusty brown curl behind her ear and measured the angle of the ladder. She adjusted it.

'Well, Simon's not coming,' she said bracingly. 'Get used to it. And hang onto the ladder. You don't have to chip your nails. Just lean against it.'

She climbed nimbly up the ladder into the branches of the apple tree. The ladder wobbled. Suze collected herself and leaned against it, hard. It stopped wobbling.

Suze tilted her head to peer up at her friend. 'What do you mean, Simon's not coming?' she demanded, outraged. 'Tonight is going to be the North London party of the year. He can't chicken out.'

Zoe set herself astride a gnarled branch and looked down. She had done this many times before and she was dressed for it: thigh-hugging cycling shorts, elderly tee shirt that didn't matter if it got torn. She had added flexible surfing shoes before coming out of the house. They improved her grip on the gnarled branches of the apple tree. Her soft brown hair was coiled round in a rough bun and skewered into place so that it did not catch on a branch. She leaned forward cautiously, holding out a hand.

'Pass me up the lights. He didn't chicken out.'

Suze handed up a worn wooden wheel. A cable of fairy

lights was coiled round it like New Age barbed wire. The wheel was on a central pivot, and Zoe hooked the ends into the sling she had tied around her body for the purpose.

'Oh, don't tell me,' said Suze. 'When you returned him to store you told him he was off the guest list tonight.'

Zoe took a moment to replace a long hairpin more securely. Her wild curls never stayed in place, no matter how ruthlessly she restrained them.

'We both agreed we could do with a breathing space,' she said defensively.

'Oh, that's what it was, was it? Honestly, you're hopeless.'

Zoe clambered among leaves and twigs, uncoiling the lights. 'It seemed best,' she said in a muffled voice.

'Okay, I know you only want men on a short lease,' said Suze, unheeding. 'But you could at least have held onto Simon until after our party. That's only common sense.'

Zoe was startled into a grin. She paused and stuck her head through the leaves to look down at her friend. 'Suze Manoir, you're an exploiter of the defenceless,' she said reprovingly. 'I can't use Simon like that. It's not fair.'

Suze was unimpressed. 'Who needs to be fair? We've got three disco balls to set up.'

'We don't need a man to do that. I can put them up. No problem.'

But Zoe hesitated. She sat back, letting the leaves close around her. The afternoon sun, where it struck through the lush leaves, was sensuously hot on her skin. It was a beautiful day. It would be a perfect evening for a party.

But just now, in the hot stillness, there was no party. Just her and Suze. And Suze was her best friend. She had to tell someone the truth. It was beginning to suffocate her. If she couldn't tell Suze, who could she tell?

From her hiding place among the branches she began, 'Suze, there's something…'

But Suze did not hear. She was looking up, squinting against the sun, and laughing. 'You are so practical. You were born to be an entrepreneur.'

Zoe gave up. It was easier. You couldn't really bare your soul when one of you was sitting halfway up a tree and the other was on a pre-party high. She retreated among the foliage and carried on playing out the cable, placing the lights evenly along the very tips of branches.

And Suze did not even notice that Zoe had been on the point of sharing something. She was still contemplating the party.

'Of course you can put them up. Is there anything you can't do?'

Zoe parted the leaves again. They were greeny-gold and smelt wonderful, slightly damp and full of vegetable energy. She pushed them away from her face.

'Haven't found it yet.'

Suze shook her head. 'I can never think why I'm the one with the business career and you're still messing about temping.'

'Hair,' said Zoe calmly. 'Curly brown hair just doesn't go with a career. People don't take curls seriously. Whereas you've looked like a tycoon since you were four.'

Suze was a wide-shouldered blonde, with a habit of haughty impatience and legs to die for.

Now she sniffed. 'You could always get the hair straightened. Put in streaks, maybe.'

'I suppose so,' said Zoe, fixing lights fast.

'I'm serious Zo. It's two years since you left college. Don't you think you ought to stop messing about?'

'We're not all natural-born businesswomen,' said Zoe without rancour. 'I get by.'

'Sure, you get by. You earn your bread and you have a great life.' Suze struck the ladder with her fist to emphasise her point. 'But what about the future?'

Zoe looked down again at her, mildly surprised.

'Don't forget, I'm the one who still has a life,' she teased gently. 'When did you start to sound like your father?'

Suze gave a sharp sigh. 'I know. I know,' she said ruefully. 'Being a financial success is not all joy. Have you finished?'

'Yup. Now, if you can just stop shaking that ladder…'

'Sorry,' said Suze with a grin. 'Concentrate, Manoir. Concentrate.'

Zoe secured the last light and climbed rapidly, hand over hand, down through the branches. Clutching the trunk, she felt around for the top of the ladder with her foot. Suze reached up and directed it onto the top step.

'Thank you,' said Zoe. She slid to the ground and unhooked the wheel, with its residual cable. 'There we are. One tree dressed to welcome summer.'

'You're the business,' said Suze, admiring.

Zoe retrieved the ladder from her and retracted the extension. She clicked it back into place and hiked the ladder under her arm, turning back to the house.

'Who needs a man?' she said lightly.

Suze padded after her. 'Okay. Okay. You don't need a man to hang your party lights. What about the other stuff?'

And suddenly there it was again. Another ideal opening. *Go for it Zoe. Tell your best friend the truth.*

But she found herself prevaricating. 'What other stuff?'

Suze made a wide gesture, embracing the whole world of romance. 'Hanging together. Holidays. Giving each other breakfast in bed with the newspapers on Sunday morning.'

Zoe changed the ladder to her other side. It was quite unnecessary. The thing was not heavy. But it meant she didn't have to answer.

Not that it mattered. When Suze was into one of her 'Why You Ought to Live Like I Say' homilies, she was impossible to deflect anyway.

'I mean, with Simon you knew where you were. He's practical, too.' A thought struck her. 'And we were relying on him to pick up the booze, weren't we?'

'It's being delivered,' said Zoe hastily.

'I should have known you'd get it sorted.' Suze shook her head. 'What did he do, poor guy? Ask you to marry him?'

'Marry him? Of course not. I've only known him a couple of months.'

'Quite,' said Suze dryly. 'But men do seem to see you as settling down material. God knows why, with your record.'

The budding garden smelt of honey in the still afternoon sun. Zoe could not face spoiling it, after all. She would just have to wait for another opportunity.

She felt her coping mask twitch into place. The Zoe who could handle anything and make a joke of it, too. Privately she called it Performance Zoe.

'It's my cooking,' she said lightly. 'Ever since Gran taught me how to make bread and butter pudding I haven't been able to get men out of my hair.' She manoeuvred the ladder down a flight of four stone steps without difficulty and went to the battered garden shed. 'Can you open the door, please?'

Suze did. But, 'It's more than bread and butter pudding,' she said darkly.

Zoe disappeared inside. Various planks of the shed were rotting, and the tools were ancient, but it was painfully tidy. She hung the ladder on its allotted hook.

'I doubt it,' she said from the depths.

The house had been built on the side of a hill. As a result the garden was arranged into three wide terraces. The orchard was at the top, but this middle terrace was the largest, with a lawn and flowerbeds full of old cottage flowers. Bees buzzed among headily scented low-growing pinks. Suze flung herself down on the grass and stuffed her nose into a small grey plant with white flowers.

'Heaven,' she said dreamily. 'I suppose you do all the garden as well? No, don't answer that.'

Zoe emerged from the shed. 'What?'

Suze rolled over on her back, heedless of grass stains and creases on her expensive navy skirt. She looked up at her friend lazily. 'Come on, Zo. You know what a hot babe you are. Bread and butter pudding is just a bonus.'

Zoe sank down beside her and started plucking at the grass. 'Thank you.'

'It's true,' said Suze dispassionately. 'Men drool and

women weep. If you weren't my best friend I'd have put out a contract on you by now.'

Zoe picked a daisy out of the lawn and threw it at her. 'No, you wouldn't.'

'I might. If you got your claws into one of my men.'

There was something in Suze's voice that startled Zoe. She stopped pulling at grass stalks and looked at her friend, shocked. 'I would never do that.'

'You wouldn't have to,' said Suze dispassionately. 'It must be pheromones or something. All you have to do is turn up somewhere on your own and—wham!'

'Wham?' Even Performance Zoe blinked at that. 'Get real, Suze.'

Suze sat up and linked her arms round her knees. 'It's real enough. Men—some men, anyway—take one look at you and go weak at the knees.'

'Hey, I'm not that special. I'm not even beautiful.'

'I know you're not,' her friend said candidly. 'But there's something about you.'

'Pu-lease—' said Zoe. She tried to joke but she was unnerved all the same.

'There is,' Suze insisted. 'I've seen it, again and again.' She rested her chin on her clasped knees, thoughtful. 'At first I thought it was because you didn't *try* as hard as the rest of us. I mean, your clothes were okay, but you always looked as if you'd scrambled into them at the last moment before going out. I said that to David once.'

David was Suze's boyfriend before last. Zoe had wondered several times whether Suze was as completely over him as she claimed to be. Now her voice changed and Zoe was certain.

'And David said, "Yes, exactly." That soft, rumpled look gave a man the feeling that you'd only got out of bed a few minutes ago. And that it wouldn't take too much persuasion to get you back in again.'

Zoe sat bolt upright, forgetting all about Suze's possible broken heart. 'He didn't,' she said, True Zoe taking over momentarily and genuinely appalled.

'Yup.'

'But that's—so untrue.'

'But effective,' said Suze dryly.

Zoe's nails gouged into the grass. 'It's crazy. I—'

Suze stopped hugging her knees.

'Why did you really heave Simon?' she said quietly. 'The truth, now.'

And that was the trouble, thought Zoe, scrabbling at a dandelion with real venom. Oh, she could tell Suze the truth, all right. It would only take one sentence. *He wanted to go to bed with me and I bottled out.* Only Suze would not believe her. And Zoe had no one to blame for that but herself.

There was this big fable among their friends: Zoe Brown the *femme fatale*, and the men who never lasted. Only no one knew it was a fable. Not even Suze. And Suze thought she knew everything there was to know about Zoe Brown. She very nearly did, too. Just not—

They had always told each other their secrets, from the time their mothers had walked them to kindergarten together. Suze was still telling. It was only Zoe who held back. And Suze had no idea.

Of course Zoe did not lie. Well, not exactly. She had never stood up and actually told a falsehood about any of the men she had been out with. Only people made assumptions—the men themselves did nothing to deny them—and before she knew where she was the myth of Zoe the Butterfly Lover was born. Even her brother and sister thought she changed boyfriends so often because she got bored.

Whereas the truth—

Well, it could not go on. She had sworn it at New Year, looking in the mirror in Suze's bedroom, the only stone cold sober person in the house. She had laughed and kissed poor, bewildered Alastair at miserable midnight. The smile had been plastered on her face so hard that she'd felt it would crack.

That had been when she said to herself, No more. Everyone had been talking about their shiny new resolutions.

Well, that was hers. Tell Suze first. Then the rest of the world. The truth. Then she could wave goodbye to Performance Zoe for ever. And get on with the rest of her life.

Hello world, I'm a virgin.

Only she never seemed to find the opportunity. The trouble was that there was such a huge difference between what she was and what everyone—all her friends, even her brother and sister—thought she was. Even a nice man like David thought she could be persuaded to get back into bed—*back* into bed—without too much difficulty. And then, just today, here was her best friend telling her 'there's more to relationships than sex'.

Some of it was her own fault, Zoe knew. New Year was six months ago. There must have been chances to tell Suze. She had just run away from them. And, most damning of all, she had just unloaded her third escort of the year.

She said slowly, 'Okay. The truth it is. Simon's a great guy. It wasn't anything he did—'

Suze laughed wickedly. 'Okay. What was it that he *didn't* do?' And she leered with mock lasciviousness.

At once Zoe was wincing internally. But outside she was laughing back.

'Nothing to complain about. He made all the right moves. It wasn't him, honestly. It was me.'

'You don't have to tell me that. It's always you.' Suze pursed her lips. 'A complete split personality, that's what you are.'

'What?' said Zoe, arrested.

'If you ask me, you don't know what you want. You unload a swinger like Alastair because he doesn't want to play house with your barmy family. Then you hitch up with Simon who's so domestic he comes with a matching Labrador. And he can't keep you interested, either.'

Zoe shifted. 'It isn't quite like that.'

Suze was too intrigued by her own analysis to take any notice of Zoe's uncomfortable murmur.

'Don't you see a pattern? You only want what you haven't got at the moment.'

Zoe's heart sank. 'Suze, listen to me—' she began urgently.

But there was ring from the little telephone clipped to Suze's belt. She pressed a button and raised her eyebrows at the number displayed.

'Jay Christopher? What does he want?' She pressed another button and put the thing to her ear. 'Hi, Jay. What can I do for you?'

Zoe looked away across the garden. She could have kicked herself. Another ideal opportunity wasted. Again.

What is wrong with me? thought Zoe, despairing.

Meanwhile Suze had gone into crisp business mode. She even stood up to talk, prowling around the lawn as if she were patrolling her office. She snapped out questions like an interrogator, but most of the time she listened attentively.

'So that's more than a filing clerk,' she was saying when Zoe tuned in again. 'You need someone who can handle research. And work on their own initiative. And you want them by Monday. You don't ask much, do you?'

The telephone said something flattering.

Suze laughed, undeceived. 'And you know that nobody else would even think of trying. Okay, Jay, I'll do what I can. But I need the paperwork tonight and I'm not in the office. If you're serious about this, you'll have to drop it off here.' She spelled out Zoe's address.

The telephone said something else.

'Am I an online map service?' asked Suze sweetly. 'Look in the *A to Z*. The good news is it doesn't matter how late you get here. We're having a party.'

It was all the reminder that Zoe needed. She jumped to her feet. 'Time to get on,' she mouthed at Suze, and ran down the last set of steps to the patio and into the kitchen, command centre of Operation Party.

She began to attack the remaining two thirds of the big refectory table with energy.

Eventually Suze finished her phone call and followed. 'Interesting,' she said. She stood in the doorway, sucking her teeth. 'Er—Zo? About your jobs next week…'

'What?' said Zoe, scrubbing hard.

'I know you don't want to sign on with me permanently. But—what about a one-off? Two weeks, maybe four. A really stimulating job, too. Lots of initiative required, and you get to use your brain, too.'

Zoe knew her best friend well. Suze had not got to be a twenty-four-year-old phenomenon by focusing on the disadvantages of the employers who used her agency. 'What's wrong with it?'

'Nothing. Honest. It's a brilliant job.'

'Then why haven't you already got someone on your books who can do it?'

Suze sighed. 'I have. Well, a couple. But they've already got jobs for next week. And this is not a job that just anyone can do. They have to have that little bit extra.' She came and stood beside Zoe, nudging her companionably. 'Well, a lot extra, actually. You'd have been my first choice anyway.'

'You're wheedling,' said Zoe dispassionately. 'You always wheedle when there's something wrong. 'Fess up. What's the downside?'

'Well, it's in the West End,' admitted Suze.

'Uh-oh. You mean I'd have to leave the house before Harry goes to school.' She shook her head. 'No way. His exams are coming up.'

'If I can persuade them to let you arrive later? Say ten-thirty? That would mean you missed the rush hour on the tube as well.' Suze slipped an arm round her. 'Oh, come on, Zo. You know you need the money. And it'd be fun. We could have lunch together.'

Zoe hesitated. It was true; they needed the money. The plumbing had more leaks than she was able to keep up with, and a damp patch that she kept trying not to think about had appeared in the top bedroom ceiling. To have enough in her bank account to be able to call a plumber and hang the consequences sounded like heaven.

'If I could leave the house after I've seen Harry off…' she mused aloud.

'You're a sweetheart,' said Suze. She put on rubber gloves and took the scouring pad away from Zoe. 'I'll finish that.'

'I didn't say I would do it,' Zoe said hurriedly. 'I'll think about it. That's all.'

'You're a mate,' said Suze. 'That's all I ask. Thanks.'

Zoe did a rapid assessment of the contents of the fridge and shifted food around to make room for bottles of white wine.

Suze considered her thoughtfully. 'It is okay, me asking this guy tonight?'

Zoe was surprised. 'It's half your party. You ask anyone you want.'

'He's a client, but he's cool,' Suze assured her. 'In fact he's gorgeous.'

Zoe shrugged. 'Even if he isn't I can live with it. Lauren's bringing Boring Accountant Man, after all.'

They both groaned.

Suze said delicately, 'Speaking of cool—is your mum coming?'

The big house was theoretically the Brown family home. But Zoe's mother had lived a sort of semi-detached existence from her three children ever since her husband left. These days the house ran like a shared tenancy between four adults. And if anyone cooked family meals or did a major shop for the house it was Zoe, not Deborah Brown.

Zoe said without any delicacy at all, 'Not a chance. Any sign of a party and she heads for the hills.'

They were both silent, remembering. Philip Brown had walked out during Zoe's sixteenth birthday party. All the neighbours knew it. Suze's mother had been there with hot meals and a shoulder to lean on until Deborah had finally repelled her. Zoe and her siblings had been grateful for the hot meals, though. They'd stayed grateful until Zoe had taken charge and made sure that the house ran properly again.

'Shame.' Suze had gone through school envying Zoe her anti-authoritarian mother. She still had a lot of time for Deborah, though she thought the woman's withdrawal into her own world was hard on Zoe. 'She's still on Planet Potty, then?'

'Yes,' said Zoe briefly.

The doorbell rang. It was the drink for the party. Zoe and Suze helped carry in the cases. There was wine and bottled water and vodka and mixers and beer. And then four dozen wine glasses in their divided cardboard boxes.

'Sign here,' said the friendly delivery man. 'Glasses back clean by Monday. You pay for breakages. Have a good one!'

After that they were too busy for more confidences. Zoe did not know whether she was frustrated or relieved. Either way, it didn't matter.

'Help,' Zoe said as she and Suze formed themselves into a production line to unpack glasses. 'In less than three hours the house will be full of people expecting to be fed and entertained. So far only the garden is ready for them.'

But she and Suze worked well together. They were both practical and unflappable, and they had done this before. The food was set out, the drawing room disco was operational, and a bedroom full of the valuable and fragile was locked, with half an hour to spare.

Zoe showered and washed her hair quickly. She dried it fast, watching it spring into its corkscrew curls with resignation. 'Oh, well, there's nothing I can do about it. Curls are my curse.'

'Some curse.' Suze had extracted the tiniest possible slip of a dress from her briefcase. She climbed into it, then occupied Zoe's dressing table. She was peering in the mirror, outlining her eyelids carefully.

Zoe pinned her hair carelessly on top of her head and began to scrabble in her wardrobe.

'Why do I always forget how much effort it takes to organise a big party?' said Suze between clenched teeth.

'Because we're good at it.' Zoe debated between a white crop top and a black net shirt that was perfectly plain except that you could see through it. She opted for advice. 'Which do you think?'

Suze put her eye make up on hold for moment, swivelled round and considered gravely.

'Not white,' she decided. 'No tan yet.'

Zoe nodded, flung the white top back in the wardrobe and dug black satin underwear out of a drawer. Having decided, she dressed quickly, teaming the chiffon top with deep purple leather trousers, soft and clingy as gloves. Leaving Suze at the dressing table, she went into her *en suite* shower room and attacked the still damp curls with a comb. Soon they were falling into turbulent waves of gold and brown and chestnut, and even a hint of auburn.

She came out. 'What do you think?'

Suze had finished her eyes. She turned. 'Very Pre-Raphaelite,' she approved.

'Not as if I've just got out of bed?'

'Of course not.'

'So men aren't going to think I'm willing to jump right back if they ask nicely?'

Suze chuckled. 'Well, you know men. They live in hope.'

Zoe clutched her temples in mock despair.

'Never mind,' Suze consoled her. 'You can always dance with Boring Accountant Man. He doesn't back women into bed. Lauren told me he's holding out for a virgin.'

Her tone said it all, thought Zoe. He might just as well have been holding out for a tyrannosaurus rex as far as Suze was concerned.

'Really?' she said in a constrained voice.

'I don't know what Lauren sees in her weirdos. She must be on a mission to bring the twenty-first century to the un-enlightened.'

Zoe bent and fluffed up her hair unnecessarily. 'I suppose so.' She sounded depressed.

Suze put an arm round her shoulders and hugged her quickly.

'Don't worry,' she said cheerfully. 'I know you're the saviour of the world's party outcasts, but Boring Accountant

Man isn't going to be looking in your direction. Never seen anyone less virginal in my life.'

Zoe gave a hollow laugh. 'I'm glad about that.'

Suze chuckled. 'I don't believe there's a twenty-three-year-old virgin left in the northern hemisphere.'

Zoe winced. Only Suze did not see it, and the mask clicked into place, as it always did, without fail.

But bright, deceptive, *popular* Performance Zoe said naughtily, 'Definitely dead as a dodo.'

CHAPTER TWO

JAY CHRISTOPHER drove into the tree-lined street at half past midnight. The party house was not difficult to identify. Someone had tied balloons all along the iron railings and it blazed with lights.

He inserted the Jaguar into the tightest possible parking place with one smooth movement and switched off the engine. For a moment he sat there in the friendly dark, savouring the solitude. It had been a heavy week in every way.

'People!' he said aloud, with fierce self-mockery. 'Doncha just love them?'

He looked at the balloon-fringed house with reluctance bordering on dislike. But this was work, he reminded himself. He could deal with people when it was work.

He flicked open the slim briefcase on the passenger seat and found the big white envelope he was looking for. Then he flung the briefcase on the floor, out of sight of any potential car breaker. There was no point in bothering with a jacket. The night was too warm and he didn't think Suze Manoir's friends would welcome a fellow in a City suit. Anyway, he had already left his tie at Carla's.

At the thought of Carla his slim dark brows locked together. She had not contributed to the emotional horrors of this week. But he knew that she was not happy. It would have to end soon, Jay thought. It could not go on, not if he was making her unhappy. No matter how bravely she denied it.

He shook his head. It was so easy to know when women were getting in too deep. They stopped asking questions in case they couldn't deal with the answers.

Take tonight, for example. He had said, without thinking, that he was going to have to drive through a part of London he did not know. That he was going to a party. Carla could

23

so easily have asked, Whose party? Where? Could she come, too...? But she hadn't. Jay even knew why. In case he wouldn't take her. In case the party-giver was her successor.

So she had just sat opposite him in the restaurant and smiled and asked intelligent questions about his business and looked forward to seeing him on Sunday. And all the time there had been that terrible fear at the back of her eyes. And her voice had been calm and even. And she hadn't asked questions.

Yes, he was definitely going to have to end it. She was too nice a woman to do anything else. He could not let her start to hope that there might be any future for them. It would be completely false. He had made that plain when they started. Carla had said she understood that. But women had that habit of forgetting the rules when they fell in love.

Especially when they fell in love with men who did not understand love.

I might not understand love, thought Jay. But I've seen the harm it does. Oh, Carla, why can't you settle for honest sex and friendship?

But he knew she would not. His heart twisted with pity for her. Yet even as he winced at the thought of her distress he could not wait to get away. It suffocated him, all this terrible, exhausting emotion. It made him want to go out on the moors and run and run and run until he couldn't think, could barely breathe—and still keep on running.

Well, at least there would be no emotion at Suze Manoir's party. Jay laughed aloud at the thought. He got out of the car, stuffed the envelope under his arm and crossed the street.

It took him time to get into the house. Once in, though, it was relatively easy to find Suze. He tracked her down to a room with rotating disco lights and loud seventies music. She was dancing energetically to Abba, but as soon as he arrived she dropped her partner's hand and rushed across to him.

'Jay! You got here.'

'I even got in,' he said dryly. 'Who on earth have you got on the door? Murder Incorporated?'

'Oh that's Harry Brown and his friends. He's Zoe's brother.'

'Zoe?'

'She lives here. It's half her party.'

'Well, she certainly gives a great bouncer service,' he said. 'The guys out there have a technique that makes your average killer shark look like Miss Hospitality.'

'She's very efficient,' said Suze demurely. 'In fact—well, never mind. Have you got my contract?'

'Have you got my research assistant?' he countered.

'Maybe.'

She was looking naughty, he thought. Or it could be a trick of the whirling light.

He said, 'This isn't a game, Susan. I've got a major speech to give at the Communications Conference in Venice next month. And there isn't a single note or reference to build on.'

'Come and let me find you a drink,' Suze said soothingly. 'And you can tell me how you let it get away from you.'

'Something soft. I'm driving,' he said absently. 'It happened because I delegated, and the wretched girl hasn't done a thing.'

Suze opened the fridge. 'Juice or water?'

'Water, please.'

He wandered round the kitchen. The lighting was better than in the drawing room disco, but it was still clearly a room decked out for a party. There were candles and trailing greenery everywhere, and someone had sprayed 'Sixteen Again' on the mirror in gold paint.

'How old is your friend?' Jay asked, recoiling.

Suze poured water into a big wine glass for him.

'Twenty-three. But she says everyone should be sixteen at a party.'

'Original!'

Suze laughed and gave him the glass.

'She's not as daft as she sounds. She has her reasons.
Now, let me have a look at that contract.'

He gave her the envelope.

'It's a long shot, I know. If you can't help, then I'll call
the bigger agencies on Monday.'

Suze was running her eyes down the job description.
'Hmm? You know the other agencies aren't as creative as I
am.'

'No, but they have more people on their books.'

She looked up. 'You don't want more, Jay. You want the
right one. And I may just have her for you.'

He was intrigued. '*May just?* That doesn't sound like
you.'

Suze grinned. 'Well, she's thinking about it. I need you
to help me convince her.'

Jay sighed. 'And how do I do that?'

'Do I need to tell the great PR guru?' mocked Suze.
'Charm her. Challenge her.' She added kindly, 'You can do
it!'

There was a pregnant silence. 'The bigger agencies are so
much easier,' said Jay plaintively.

She laughed aloud. 'But not nearly so much fun. Now,
listen, we'll need to do a double act…'

Zoe had been going upstairs when she heard the altercation
at the front door. She had turned, intending to go and see if
she needed to intervene. Harry and his friends could sometimes take their bouncer duties a bit too seriously, she knew.

So she had been halfway down the stairs when she saw
him.

He was wearing dark trousers of some sort, and a wonderful shirt in sunset colours. Silk, she was sure. You would
not have got that purity of colour in any other material. Zoe
could not afford silk, but that did not stop her dreaming over
it in the shops. She knew the way the material moved on
the body, catching the light in a thousand different ways. As
the man had stood there, arguing with Harry and his suspicious mates, she'd been almost dazzled by that sheen, that

hint of gold, those little wasp stings of tangerine and apricot and purple among the principal colour.

What sort of man came to a suburban party in flame-coloured silk?

And then she'd looked at his face.

And stopped dead. Her heart had seemed to contract in her breast.

He hadn't been looking at her. He had not even seen her. If he had, he wouldn't have known her. But somehow—she knew him. She always had. Though she did not know his name.

She knew the face, though. The proud carriage of the head, like a Mogul Prince. The deep, deep eyes. The sculpted ascetic mouth, with its eloquent self-discipline and its alluring hint of passion suppressed. The energy. The fire. Banked now, certainly, but fire nonetheless. Oh, yes, she knew that face all right.

Zoe had retreated a step, backing round the corner into the shadows. She'd felt cold and very serious, as if she had just come face to face with her future.

Oh, wow! That's all I need.

It was ridiculous, of course. Nobody believed in love at first sight. It was an adolescent fantasy. A myth.

A myth like the twenty-three-year-old virgin? said a voice in her head ironically.

Well, all right, maybe it wasn't exactly a myth. Maybe it was pheromones. Maybe it was the party. They had a habit of lowering your inhibitions, parties! It was not important, anyway. It was not a feeling you could *rely* on.

It still gave you a hell of shock, thought Zoe ruefully. She felt as if she had walked into a wall.

Who on earth was he?

You don't want to know, said that voice in her head. There was a distinct warning note in it.

And it was right. Of course it was right. If she had to come face to face with the man she'd probably be as tongue-tied as a new teen with a pop idol whose poster she had had on her wall for years. That was about the level of substance to her feelings.

She did not want to have to deal with fantasies she should have outgrown ten years ago, Zoe told herself. She wanted to have a good time. That was what tonight was all about. Forget her money worries! Forget her non-existent career and her life on hold! Dance and have fun!

She would dance and have fun if it killed her, she resolved grimly.

So she had resumed her journey to her bathroom. And before she'd come downstairs again, she'd splashed water on her face so vigorously that she'd had to rebuild her make-up from scratch.

Suze took Jay back to the drawing room. Now that he'd had time to adjust, he saw it ran the depth of the house, from the street to the garden. At the far end the French windows were open to the night air. He moved towards them grate-fully, picking up the rhythm of the dance as he went. Beside him Suze gyrated, a lot less rhythmically.

'She'll be here somewhere. When last seen she was lis-tening to a man in a checked shirt talk about megabytes.'

Jay bent his head to her. 'Why?' he said simply.

'Zoe takes being a hostess seriously. She does ten minutes per no-hoper.'

Suze was twining herself round him sinuously as they walked. It would have been sexy if she hadn't been scanning the room all the time and talking nineteen to the dozen. Jay smiled at her with affection. God bless Susan, who didn't fancy the pants off him and wasn't going to break her heart over him.

'You're a star,' he said, taking her hand and dancing her powerfully through a little knot of wild arms and bouncing shoulders.

'Love it when you butter me up,' said Suze, unmoved by his touch.

They got to the windows.

'Maybe she's in the garden,' said Jay, with a longing look at the tall shadows of trees and laurel hedges.

'Maybe.' But Suze was not looking outside. He felt her jump under his hand. 'Ah, there she is.' She raised her arm above her head and waved vigorously. 'Zo! Over here!'

He looked into the shot darkness, with its shifting shadows of dancing bodies, and at first he saw nothing. Then the woman started to come towards them through the bopping crowd and he held his breath.

She was tall and graceful as a willow. As she got closer he saw she had a cloud of wild hair. He had no idea what colour. He could not tear his eyes away from her mouth. Her lips would have been voluptuous anyway, but she had painted them what looked like a dark purple. It was an aggressive colour, anyway. The whole image was aggressive. But he looked and looked, and saw vulnerability behind the image. More, there was a quivering sensitivity that their owner was trying hard to deny.

He found that he was not surprised she spent ten minutes with every no-hoper under her roof.

'Gorgeous,' he said, almost to himself.

Suze certainly didn't hear.

The woman's skin was milk-pale beneath an outrageously revealing black chiffon shirt. Under it, he could see a black bra in some shiny material. One thin strap was falling off her shoulder under the transparent sleeve. It was somehow more seductive than nakedness would have been. He felt as if he had been doused in ice water.

That graceful walk, that skin, that mouth…

Hell. Sixteen again, with a vengeance. Sixteen again, and hungry as a male animal for his conquest.

'Down boy,' said Jay grimly.

Suze had heard that, all right. 'What?' she said, startled.

'That is your candidate for my research assistant?' said Jay in disbelief.

'My friend Zoe. Yes. So?'

'Your friend?' This got worse and worse.

'Yes.' Suze faced him. 'And she really needs this job,

too, though she may not want to admit it. So go carefully, right? You could be the answer to the maiden's prayer.'

Jay groaned. 'Have you even heard of political correctness?' he said. He was racked by his baser instincts. The only possible solution was to laugh. 'Maiden's prayer, for heaven's sake!'

'I'm a traditionalist,' said Suze, unmoved. She reached out an arm and hauled her friend between them. 'Zoe, this is the man you've just got to meet.'

So what's wrong with this one?

Zoe suppressed a sigh and smiled resolutely at the tall man standing next to her friend. As far as she could tell in the disco lighting he looked all right. Heck, he looked as tall as her prince from the hallway. But he had to have some mega problem or Suze would never have called her over. The party had got to the stage where you didn't make introductions.

'Hi,' she yelled, trying to make herself hear above the dance beat and only half succeeding. She fluttered her fingers at him. 'Zoe Brown.'

He did not seem to realise that that meant she had not caught *his* name. He looked bored. Dark as the devil, sleek as a seal just out of the water, and *bored*.

No-hopers didn't usually look bored. They looked sulky or wary or too eager to please. And they couldn't believe their luck when a babe like Zoe stopped by.

The tall dark man did not seem to notice that she was a babe. In fact he did not take his eyes off Suze. He looked as if he'd been sandbagged.

'Hi.' It sounded strangled.

Suze smiled and turned her shoulder on him. 'Zoe, meet your fate.'

He looked startled.

Not nearly as startled as Zoe, though. As he bent his head she realised who he was. The deep, deep eyes. If they went somewhere where the light was normal that shirt would be flame-coloured. And silk. *Definitely* not a no-hoper.

And Suze said he was *her fate*?

'What?' she said, temporarily forgetting that they would not hear her. After all, she could not hear herself. She took hold of Suze's arm and shook it hard to get her attention. 'What—did—you—say?' she mouthed with great care. Her eyes burned with indignation.

Suze's naughty smile widened.

'Nine to five for the next four weeks,' she mouthed back.

'What?'

Suze sighed visibly. She looked up at the ceiling. The rotating light balls, hired for the party, were making a great success of turning the Edwardian mouldings into a starship re-entry burst. She shrugged and waved them both to the French windows, with great traffic policeman gestures.

There were no speakers in the garden, at least. Between the incessant beat and the noise of the party it was not exactly silent, but at least you could hear what people were saying. Not that most people came out here to talk. There were several couples, dancing or lying on the grass, heads close, not talking.

Out in the dark, where no one could see, Zoe flinched. Performance Zoe took her to task. *So what else is new?* No point in minding. That's what people do at parties.

She even did it herself sometimes. Only she just did it for the look of the thing. Then sidled out later, when she could. Not that anyone noticed her sidling out. If anyone were to suggest that popular Zoe Brown had never gone beyond a kiss in the dark, her friends would split their sides.

She did not want them splitting their sides tonight. Not in front of the Mogul Prince. Performance Zoe took control.

''Scuse me,' said Zoe, shimmying past a couple gazing fixedly into each other's eyes and shifting from foot to foot in a rhythm that was at least three tracks ago.

She made for the orchard terrace, pounding up the uneven York stone steps with the sure-footedness of long practice. The others followed.

Zoe turned, hands on her hips, ready for confrontation.

The smooth-as-a-seal man was already on to it, though.

He had obviously decided to stop being bored. Suze was beginning to look alarmed.

Suze's father was a judge. Nobody ever alarmed Suze.

The man said with dangerous quietness, 'Want to explain, Susan?'

Well, it sounded dangerous to Zoe. In fact the hair came up on the back of her neck at the deep drawl.

'Er...' said Suze, floundering.

She never floundered, either. She was as quick on her feet as Zoe. In fact Zoe had learned her 'Evasive Manoeuvres For When the Conversation Gets out of Hand' from Suze in the first place. And Zoe was the best.

'I've been conned, haven't I?' said the tall dark man in a level voice. 'I want a professional job. And you think you can unload one of your ditzy friends.' His eyes skimmed Zoe briefly. 'No offence.'

'Ditzy friend?' she gasped.

Suze sent her an exasperated look before returning to her main opponent. 'Chill out, Jay. I'm doing my best—'

'I need someone to *work*,' he said intensely. 'Not a filing clerk in a micro skirt.'

'Zoe can hack it.' Suze waved a hand. 'Zoe can do anything.'

The man swung round on Zoe and she swallowed hard. In the flickering light of the summer candles he looked about ten feet tall.

Ten feet tall and mad as a hornet was not the ideal prospective employer. *Thank you, Suze.*

She said furiously, 'I never agreed—'

He raised his eyebrows. 'Nor did I. A research assistant able to work on her own initiative?' he asked pleasantly, not taking his eyes off Zoe. 'I don't think so.'

Zoe stiffened. 'I beg—your—pardon?'

'I know what she can do,' snapped Suze. 'Zoe and I used to go to school together.'

His eyes were unreadable in the dark, but his whole stance said he didn't believe a word of it.

'Oh, yes? And when did St Bluestocking's start turning out unskilled filing clerks?'

Zoe flinched all over again.

Plenty of people thought she was wasting her university education by doing temporary jobs in a variety of offices. Only last week her father had taken her out to lunch and tried to probe, delicately, when she was going to get a real job. But no one had actually told her to her face that she was unskilled. Or implied that she was a thing of no worth because of it.

She forgot the passionate mouth and the mogul silk. She decided he was all ten feet tall hornet man. And she hated him.

She said clearly, 'I'm temping while I consider my options.'

It was true, too. Only—she had been considering her options for two years now and was no nearer finding a solution. She was not going to admit that to hornet man, though.

He looked her up and down. She could not see his face but she could *feel* the hard, swift appraisal. He took a couple of step towards her, lithe as a panther padding around its prey, assessing whether it was worth the effort of the chase or not.

Not that he could see much in the candlelit dark. Maybe her long, soft hair as it waved loosely about her shoulders in the night breeze. Or the glittery black see-through stuff of the shirt that left her shoulders visible and her slim midriff exposed. Enough to realise that she looked as cool as Suze, anyway.

And that, of course, was the trouble. She looked as cool and confident as any other girl here. More confident than most, maybe, especially when she was wearing these soft glove-leather trousers that hugged her slim hips and turned Suze green with envy.

She *looked* just fine. It was only inside that she knew she wasn't. Wasn't confident. Wasn't fine. Wasn't *normal*.

And wasn't going to admit to any of it. Well, not in front

of hornet man. She stuck her chin in the air and glared at him. And took a decision.

'You can stop looking me up and down as if I'm livestock. You get my time nine to five, starting Monday morning,' she told him crisply. 'And that's all your money buys you. Friday nights aren't in the package.'

Suze drew in an audible breath.

He was taken aback. His head went back as if she had driven a foil straight at his chest.

Then he said dryly, 'That sounds like St Bluestocking's, all right.'

Zoe was still angry. 'So apologise.'

Suze gave a soft whistle. But the man said slowly, 'For what?'

'For looking at me like that.'

'Aren't you being a bit over-sensitive?' He was amused.

Amused! Zoe decided she wanted blood.

'If I am, then you won't want me to work for you, will you?' she said with shining amiability.

'I never said—'

She shook her head. 'You know what over-sensitive people are like,' she told him earnestly. 'A real strain. Especially if management isn't geared up to cope. So disruptive in a small office. *Much* better if we just call it quits now.'

And just see if Suze can get you someone else by Monday morning, you jerk.

She thought he would backtrack fast. But he didn't. He looked at her for a long moment. In quite a different way this time.

Then he said, 'What makes you think that the office is small?'

Zoe gave a rather good start of surprise. 'Isn't it?' she asked, all artless confusion. 'I just thought if they let someone like you hire the staff they wouldn't be big enough to afford a proper human resources manager.'

Suze sucked on her teeth audibly.

But the man did not say anything for a moment. Then,

'I—see. Yes, I can follow your reasoning there.' His voice was tinged with unholy amusement.

For some reason Zoe suspected he had scored a point there, though she could not quite see what it was.

She said, 'I really don't think I should take the job if you're not sure about my temperament...'

He laughed aloud. 'I think you'll cope.'

'Oh, but I wouldn't want you to be uncomfortable—'

'Yes, you would,' he interrupted. 'And I don't blame you, either.'

That disconcerted her. 'Is that an apology?' she said suspiciously.

'I suppose it is.' He sounded surprised at himself. He swung round on Suze, a silent spectator for once. 'I apologise to both of you. I shouldn't leap to conclusions. Sorry, Susan.' He made her an odd, formal little bow, then looked at Zoe. 'And sorry Ms Bluestocking, too. I'll see you on Monday morning. No more snide remarks, Scout's honour.'

'Thank you,' said Zoe. She meant to sound dignified, but even to her own ears it came out just plain sulky.

Suze sent her a quick, worried look. Hornet man did not notice.

'That's settled, then,' he said cheerfully. 'So now I'll be on my way.'

Suze didn't like that. 'Going on to another party, Jay?'

He laughed. 'Weekend in the country. And I'm not going to get there until after three in the morning at this rate. I'm not going to be popular.'

'She'll wait up for you,' said Suze dryly.

But she did not say it very loudly, and Jay Whoever-he-was, running lightly down the steps and back among the partygoers, did not seem to hear.

Zoe let out a long, shaky breath and leaned against the trunk of the apple tree. Her legs felt as if they were made of cotton wool. Gently vibrating cotton wool.

'Tell me it's not true,' she begged. 'Tell me I haven't just signed up with Captain Blood!'

Suze was watching the slim dark figure find his sure-

footed way down the terraces and disappear into the house.
'Captain Blood?' she echoed absently.

'He looked me up and down as if I was in a corsair slave
market.'

Suze jumped and re-engaged attention. 'You watch too
many old movies. Jay Christopher is no pirate.'

'Then why does he prowl like one?'

Suze gave an incredulous laugh. 'He doesn't. You're just
saying that because you fancy him.'

Zoe jumped as if her friend had turned the garden hose
on her. 'You've got to be joking. Why would I fancy him?'

'Everyone does,' said Suze simply.

'Can't imagine why,' Zoe muttered.

'Get real, Zo. You saw the man. He's lethal.'

'He's rude and arrogant.'

'He can afford to be arrogant. You didn't seem to clock
it, but that was the man himself. Jay Christopher of Culp
and Christopher Public Relations.' There was a faint question mark in Suze's voice.

Zoe pushed her hair back. 'So?'

'The Big Cheese. The one the financial reporters write the
big profiles of.'

Zoe refused to be impressed. 'You know me. I don't read
the financial pages.'

'He hangs out in the sports section as well. To say nothing
of the gossip columns. Olympic medallist. One of the long-
distance races. You must remember him.'

But Zoe shook her head. 'You know me. No competitive
edge.'

Suze almost danced with frustration. 'You *must* remember. No one rated him. And then he just came from nowhere
and took the medal.'

A chord in Zoe's memory started to vibrate very gently.
She had a vague picture of an old television news bulletin—
a tall, proud figure with remote eyes, in spite of his heaving
chest and sweat soaked running gear.

Well, the eyes were right. Though that flame-coloured silk

suggested that he had not broken out into a sweat in long
while.

'Maybe I do remember,' she said.

'He set up his public relations agency with Theodora
Culp, the business journalist. Now it's one of the best in
London. Theodora's gone back into television, of course, so
Jay runs it single-handed.' Suze laughed. 'And you thought
he was a human resources manager.'

'I told him he was a *bad* human resources manager,' Zoe
reminded her. For some reason it felt like a small triumph.
Because she had been fighting back, she supposed, not melt-
ing into a warm puddle of sub-teen lust at his feet. She
would have died rather than admit it, but Suze was not the
only one who fancied Jay Christopher.

'He won't care. Jay's not mean. And he knows how good
he is.' Suze was thoughtful for a moment. 'They say one of
the big international advertising agencies is sniffing round
Culp and Christopher at the moment. If Jay sells out he'll
be making himself some serious money.'

But if Zoe was unwillingly attracted to the tall man with
the remote eyes, she did not give a hoot about serious
money. She did not have to say so. Her expression said it
all.

'You've got to admire him,' Suze urged. 'He did it all on
his own. His grandfather's a brigadier, and terribly well connected. But Jay wouldn't let him help out, even when the
business was just two men and a dog to begin with. Jay
would have every right to be insufferably pleased with himself. But he isn't.'

'No?' Zoe was sceptical.

'Well, not normally. You did seem to rub him up the
wrong way.'

Zoe bristled. 'It's mutual.'

'I could see that. Never seen a man wind you up so fast
in my life. And plenty have tried. You're always Miss I Can
Cope.'

If only you knew.

But she didn't say that. *Why* didn't she say that? She

wanted to get rid of this false image that her best friend had of her, didn't she? So why the heck did she flick back her hair, strike an attitude and go into the performance Suze expected?

'I still am. I got that man to apologise.' She even *sounded* complacent.

Megabyte Man would say I need a hard drive diagnostic.

'Yes. I suppose it's all right.' Suze sounded doubtful.

'It will be fine,' Performance Zoe said breezily. 'I've worked for some stinkers in my time. Now I've broken his resistance Mr Successful will be a piece of cake.'

Suze just looked at her.

Zoe's chin came up another ten degrees. 'So?' she challenged. 'You don't really think I can't handle him? Do you? *Me?*'

Suze put her head on one side. 'How long have we been friends?'

'Nineteen years,' said Zoe, literally.

'Then believe me. You really, really can't handle Jay Christopher.'

Performance Zoe snorted. She had a wide repertoire of dismissive noises.

'I know you. I know Jay Christopher.' Suze shook her head wisely. 'Take my advice. You don't want to go there.'

'And why not?'

'Don't forget—I know all your ex-boyfriends, Zo.'

Even Performance Zoe was silenced.

Suze shook off her unaccustomed seriousness. 'Come on. The night is young. We've got some serious partying to get in before dawn.'

She was not wrong. And Zoe was the life and soul of it. She danced with Megabyte Man, and Lauren's boring accountant, and Alastair, whom she had made miserable five months ago, and who now had a brilliant French girlfriend. She danced on her own. She draped her arms over the shoulders of her sister Artemis and Suze and did an untidy high-kicking routine.

As the sky began to lighten only the long-distance party animals were still there.

'Come on,' said Zoe, finding a fast song about a rodeo cowboy. 'Line-dance.'

They lined up and went into the rapid routine that they had worked out last Christmas. Amid raucous insults and much giggling, they managed to keep up for a bit. But in the end too many of them went right while the others went left. Finally Harry did a sideways jump into Suze and the whole line staggered. The music raced away from them. They ended up in heap on the floor, laughing.

'Great party,' said the stragglers, tumbling out into the grey morning.

By morning, though, there were only six people left in the shabby kitchen. Hermann, who was Suze's current favourite, sat on the corner of the scrubbed pine table, plucking at a guitar and singing softly. He was waiting for Suze to take him home to bed and everyone knew it.

Zoe's younger sister, Artemis, clutched her boyfriend sleepily round the waist as he systematically loaded empty bottles into a cardboard box. From time to time Ed put an absent hand behind his back and patted her hip encouragingly.

Suze and Zoe had bagged up all the food remains in three black sacks and were now loading the dishwasher with the last of the glasses.

This was after Suze had taken Harry on one side and briefed him tersely about his sister's imminent employment prospects.

'She really needs this job,' she ended fiercely.

Harry might be only seventeen but he was a realist. He nodded slowly.

'Yup. And not just for the money. She needs to do something for herself. And something to stop Mum thinking she only has to call and Zoe will be there. Okay, Suze. Leave it to me.'

Thereafter Harry wandered among the debris, theoretically

helping. In practice he was eating any food that he decided there was no room in the fridge for.

'You'll be sick,' said Zoe, matter-of-factly.

Harry grinned. 'I'm seventeen. My digestion is at peak performance.'

'It was our best party ever,' said Suze with satisfaction. 'Did you get to see Jay, Hermann? Hermann was at college with Jay,' she explained to Zoe. 'That's how I got a nibble at the Culp and Christopher account in the first place.'

'I saw him.' Suze's boyfriend executed a rippling final chord and put the guitar away. 'Nice of him to come.'

'Why shouldn't he?' demanded Suze, bridling.

Hermann was peaceful. 'He's running with the great and the good these days. Not a lot of time for simple socialising.'

Zoe sniffed. She was not surprised, somehow. The Mogul Prince had that look of a man who could hardly bring himself to bother with other people.

'Don't scare Zoe,' Suze warned. 'She's going to work for him on Monday.'

'I'm not scared. I was not intending to make friends with the man,' Zoe said crisply.

Artemis's Ed laughed. 'You can't scare Zoe. One flash of those big brown eyes and men just roll over with their paws in the air—don't they Zo?'

Artemis rubbed her cheek against Ed's bent back. 'Are you going to be long, lover? I'm wiped.'

Zoe was irritated. 'Like Suze was telling me earlier, there's more to human relationships than sex, Edward.'

There was burst of ribald laughter from the other five.

'That's a good one, coming from you, sis,' said Artemis fondly. 'The last of the *femmes fatales*.'

For once Performance Zoe did not flip into action automatically. Maybe because she was tired.

'Don't be ridiculous,' she snapped.

She seized a damp cloth and worked vigorously at the stains on the table where Ed's wine bottles had stood.

Artemis unwound herself from Ed's hips. 'Oh, come on, Zo. You know it's true. Your men hardly ever get beyond the fourth date. And I know that they call you and call you because I take the messages. So if it's not them getting bored, what is it? Picky, picky Princess Zoe, that's what.'

Zoe bit her lip. If they knew the truth they wouldn't laugh like this. On the other hand she had worked quite hard so that they *wouldn't* know the truth.

And Ed's next remark proved how right she had been to do so.

'Hey, don't worry, babe,' he said, straightening with the box of bottles in his arms. 'I think it's cool.' He flourished the box at Zoe in a sort of elephantine salute. 'My friend the heartbreaker. Ta-da.'

'Could solve your career problems,' suggested Suze. 'See if MI5 has an opening for Olga the Beautiful Spy.'

Zoe threw the cloth at her.

And everyone laughed. Just as they always did.

Zoe poured detergent, slammed the dishwasher shut, selected a program and switched it on. Everyone stood up with relief.

'Thanks for the help with the clearing up, guys. I love you tonight, but I'll really worship you tomorrow,' Zoe said. 'Hermann—take her home. She's out on her feet.'

'Little mother of all the world,' teased Suze.

But Suze was drooping, and everyone knew it. Hermann packed his guitar away in its case and put his arm round her.

'Lean on me, babe.'

Zoe looked away. Nobody noticed.

'All of three doors down the street,' scoffed Suze.

But she leaned into him gratefully and they wrapped their arms round each other. They were muzzy with sleep and low-grade lust. But they looked back to wave as they wandered off into the clear morning.

'Goodbye,' said Artemis and Ed, plodding off in the direction of his flat over the paper shop, leaning into each other and swinging their clasped hands. Artemis slept at Ed's at the weekends. Well, more like all the time now.

Harry wandered off to his room with a video and a paper plate of garlic bread.

Zoe decided she was too alert to go to bed. She made herself some hot chocolate. Hot chocolate was Zoe's long-term comfort drink. She had been brewing a lot of it lately.

She poured it into the heavy dragon-adorned mug her father had brought back from a trip. He had given it to her just before he'd told her he was moving out. It used to be a family joke: she got the things with dragons on them; Artemis had cats; Harry had crocodiles. No one had given Zoe anything with dragons on it since that day. She was glad.

She would have been quite glad if the dragon mug had been broken, but somehow it was too sturdy. Other mugs came into the house and got pushed off tables or dropped on the stone patio or trodden to dust when someone left them on the carpet after watching television. But solid old dragon just kept on going.

Seven years now. She had been sixteen then. That was why her parties always said, 'Sixteen Again'. At sixteen she had turned into—what was it Suze called her? Little mother of all the world. Yes, that was it. At sixteen Zoe had turned into the household's Responsible Adult. And she still was.

At least the thick dragons kept the drink warm. That was useful. The dawn had a chill to it.

Zoe went out onto the patio and sat down on the worn old bench. She held the mug under her chin, brooding.

Artemis was right when she said that Zoe never let a man take her out more than four times. Sometimes she did not let them take her out twice. They looked at her, saw her long legs and fashionably slim figure. They listened to her and heard a sharp tongue and a cool party girl with loads of friends. And nobody—*nobody*—saw that it was an act.

Responsible adult. Hot babe. Cool gal. The last virgin in the northern hemisphere.

'What a mess,' said Zoe wryly. She shivered, in spite of the hot drink between her hands.

Miss I Can Cope. That was what Suze had called her. She believed it, too. Zoe was not sure how. She knew that her family saw what they wanted to see. But how could her best friend be fooled?

Because you're good at the performance.

Well, good enough. Up to a point. One day soon someone was going to find her out. She felt the chill touch her again. Maybe she had met him now.

She had so nearly given herself away tonight, with the way she had stared at the Mogul Prince. He had seen it, too. She knew he had. He had looked at her so hard that she'd thought he was going to be able to draw her. And his face had told her absolutely nothing.

Had he seen through her act? Had he?

No, she told herself. Of course he hadn't. It had just been a trick of the disco ball lighting. And her own uneasy conscience, of course.

Heck, at one point it had even sounded as if he and Suze were play-acting. How was that for paranoia?

You've got to do something about that, she said to herself, as she had done so many times before. Stop performing. *Tell* someone.

But who? And how? And would they believe her, anyway?

The men in her life took their cue from her friends. And her friends knew that she was a sophisticated twenty-three-year-old with a cool life and a hot wardrobe. They even asked her advice about their love lives, for heaven's sake. And Suze was forever asking her to look out for any social incompetents who turned up at her parties. Because Zoe knew all there was to know about men and the dating game. Didn't she?

Not one of her friends would believe that twenty-year-old Artemis knew more about love than Zoe did. Heck, seventeen-year-old Harry probably knew more. And one day soon, if she did not tell them, she was going to trip up spectacularly over her half-lies and evasions.

Or she was going to get stuck in the performance. And she would be performing for the rest of her life. And *not one* soul would know her. Ever.

'Aaaargh,' she said aloud. And dashed the dragon mug on the weedy paved slabs.

It did not break.

CHAPTER THREE

JAY let himself out of the kitchen door, as he always did for his morning run. The old manor house felt asleep. He did some stretches, looking at the way the early-morning sun turned the Cotswold stone to the colour of warm butter. He smiled. His grandfather's house smiled back at him.

He stopped stretching and started off on the familiar route, his trainers picking up damp from the dew-wet grass.

Across the kitchen garden. Through the iron gate in the wall and into the woods. Along the grassy track that followed the stream back up the hill. It was easy, this first part of the course, a gentle slope and an even surface to run on. He found his pace and let his thoughts wander.

It had been an easy journey last night. The roads had been nearly empty. He had been in bed just after two. That was not so different from the hours he kept in London. Lethal if he were in serious training, of course. Only he wasn't. It was a long time since he had competed, except in the board-room.

A long time since I have had to try at anything.

Except he had had to try last night. Suze had been right. He had been surprised to find that the girl with the voluptuous mouth was so hostile to working for him.

No, he corrected himself, she was hostile to working for Culp and Christopher. She did not know *him*. At least, he hoped it was Culp and Christopher.

Anyway, he had followed Suze's advice. He had challenged her. And before she knew where she was, she was promising to turn up on Monday morning and make him eat his words. That had made him feel as if he had won a victory.

Careful, he told himself wryly. You don't want a resur-

44

gence of the old male animal. Not at work. Not after last time.

But the thought of Zoe Brown making him eat his words set his feet pounding faster all the same.

He had to make a conscious effort to slow down. On a three-hour-run you did not start off by sprinting. And Jay was a patient man. He was good at biding his time. Even better at self-control.

He remembered the way her satin bra strap had slipped under that damned transparent shirt and he had to remind himself fiercely that self-control was his strongest point.

And you don't pursue women who work for you either, he added.

But she's only temporary. After a week or two she won't be working for me. And by then she won't be hostile any more. I'll make certain of that.

He was back by nine-thirty. He changed rapidly and went into the breakfast room. His grandfather was there, eating grilled kidneys and fulminating over the newspaper.

'Good morning. Been for a run?'

'Yes.'

'What was your time?'

Jay's hair was still damp from the shower. He pushed his fingers through it. 'Not what it should be,' he said ruefully. 'I'm getting fat and lazy in London.'

His grandfather pursed his lips. 'No, you're not. But you're not enjoying yourself much, either. Are you?'

Jay was startled. 'Aren't I?'

His grandfather rattled the *Daily Telegraph* at him. 'It says here you're going to sell out to Karlsson.'

Jay poured himself juice. 'The word is merge, Gramps. They'd do the advertising. We'd do the PR. We'd share the research. There are lots of synergies.'

'Except they're a bunch of international sharks and you're an honourable man,' said his grandfather.

Jay shrugged. 'Can't stand in the way of progress,' he said lightly.

'You ought to compete again,' said his grandfather.

'You're not too old. Cross-country running is a mature man's sport.'

Jay's lips twitched. 'Thank you. I'm thirty-five, not ninety.'

'Better use of your time than making more and more money you don't need,' said his grandfather. 'It's time you—'

'—settled down,' said Jay, his mouth suddenly grim. 'So you've said before. Thank you for your advice.'

'I only—'

Jay put down his juice and leaned forward. 'No.'

'What?'

'No,' said Jay again, very quietly.

His grandfather had commanded men and negotiated with leaders, foreign and domestic, who had volatile temperaments and the means to enforce their will. He had never been silenced by anyone as he was by his grandson. He huffed a bit. But he did not say any more.

Before dinner that night, though, he said to his daughter-in-law, 'I—er—mentioned the future this morning.'

Bharati Christopher looked at him with calm eyes. She had iron-grey hair and her son's air of detachment.

'That will only drive him away.'

'But—'

'He will marry when he falls in love. Not before.' She added, very deliberately, 'He is like his father in that.'

Brigadier Christopher had thrown his son out long before Robert went on the hippy trail to India and met Bharati. But the old man never forgot that he had missed the first seven years of his grandson's life because he had stubbornly refused to admit that a cross-cultural union had ever taken place.

Now his eyes fell.

He harrumphed. 'I suppose Jay will go off to see that gardening trollop tomorrow.'

Her eyes lit with affectionate laughter. They had mended their fences a long time ago. 'Or tonight, if you start telling him how to run his life.'

But Brigadier Christopher had the last word.

'Not my Jay. He doesn't spend the night. Taught him that myself. Spend the whole night with a woman and she gets serious. Jay,' he said with satisfaction, 'knows how to keep his affairs under control.'

Zoe zipped through the rest of the clearing up in a couple of hours on Saturday morning. She liberated the family's few decent pieces of furniture from their locked sanctuary in her mother's room. By lunchtime the house was back to normal.

'When's Mother coming back?' said Harry, appearing heavy-eyed at two in the afternoon.

Zoe was stretched out on her stomach on the sunlit lawn, reading a novel. She squinted up at him.

'When Aunt Liz kicks her out, I guess.'

He flopped down beside her. 'I hope she stays away until the mocks are over,' he said, surprising her.

She sat up. 'Really?'

'She makes me jumpy.'

Zoe pulled a face. 'She only wants you to do well.

'When she remembers,' he said with brutal truth 'Then she tries to cram a year's worth of nagging into three days.'

Zoe gave a choke of laughter. 'Do you want me to change the locks?'

'No, but—don't persuade her to come back if she wants to stay with Aunt Liz,' he said in a rush.

'Harry—are you really worried about these exams?' she asked seriously.

'No.' He was matter-of-fact. 'I've done the work and I've got the brain. But everyone at school is going a bit mad. I need to stay focused and not get in a flap. And mother flaps me.'

She thought about that. 'You mean minimal fuss, right?'

'Yes.'

'So if I get a job which means I have to leave the house before you go off to school in the morning, that wouldn't bother you?'

He was surprised. ''Course not.'

'So what do you want to make these next few weeks least stressful?'

'Regular meals and no one crowding me,' said Harry promptly.

It was like being let off a major task. Zoe laughed and ruffled his hair.

'You've got it.'

And she would be at Culp and Christopher so early she would make the Mogul Prince's eyes spin in his head, she promised herself. This summer was going to be *fun*.

Jay Christopher snapped awake as he always did, instantly alert. He was alone in the mussed Sunday-afternoon bed. Surprised, he came up on one elbow, looking round.

The room was full of dusty sunshine, but the shadows were longer than he'd expected. The summer afternoon was hot and very still. There was not so much as a tweet from the birds in the tall trees outside, although all the windows were open to the air.

The woman was standing at the open French window. She had thrown a blue kimono over her nakedness. He had brought it back from Japan for her at Christmas. They had only just started seeing each other then. She had been delighted, dancing round the room, laughing.

She was not dancing now. She turned and stood there, watching him levelly.

Jay's heart sank. Here we go again, he thought. *Why are you like this? Are you commitment-phobic? What do I have to do to make you love me?*

He looked at his watch. It was the only thing he was wearing.

'Time I was on my way back.'

The woman's eyes flickered. He braced himself.

But all she did was pull the kimono round her and say quietly, 'Yes, of course.'

He drew a sigh of relief. He liked Carla. He never told her lies. He had been faithful ever since they'd got together.

And he was always honest about how little he was committed; how far he was from being able to commit.

She had always said that was enough. But lately it had not seemed enough any more. Some of their recent goodbyes had been positively scratchy. He had been here before. It was beginning to look as if it was time to move on.

Jay knew himself very well. He was not going to change. And Carla was too nice to hurt. The last couple of times he had left she had had that taut, holding-in look that he dreaded seeing on a woman's face. He knew it meant they were being brave, and he hated it.

But now she went and sat on the dressing stool and brushed her dark hair, chatting cheerfully through the bathroom door while he showered.

'Heavy week?'

'The usual.' Jay rootled through the bathroom cupboard for unscented shampoo. Ever since Carla had found that he did not like to use her lavender-scented stuff she had stocked up on an alternative. 'At least I've got rid of the troublemaker. New girl starts on Monday.'

He turned on the shower and got under it.

Carla knew about the troublemaker. She had even held hands with him fondly, all through an office party, hoping that it would discourage the girl's patent crush before any harm was done. It had not worked, but they had been friends then, united in their kindly conspiracy.

'Was it difficult?'

Jay soaped his hair viciously. 'She cried.'

'Poor Jay. That's bad.'

'You're laughing at me,' he said, pleased.

But her voice was odd. 'No. I'm laughing at me.'

He did not like the sound of that. He rinsed off his hair, the brief flare of hope dying. He stuck his head out of the bathroom door and she passed him his discarded underwear.

'Thanks.'

She carried on talking as he towelled off. 'Travelling?'

'Not too bad, for once. Brussels on Wednesday, but I'm

hoping I can get in and out in a day. Manchester, and then a couple of question marks.'

She laughed. 'It sounds so glamorous. But I've done it. I know it's all cramped planes and wasting time in dirty airports.'

'Wasting a lot less time since they invented laptops.'

'Do you ever want to stop?' she asked curiously.

Jay curbed a sigh. Here it comes, he thought. He could write the script.

Don't you ever get tired of your frenetic lifestyle? Wouldn't it be nice to stay in the same place for a while? We could put a home together. Share our lives.

He said quietly, 'No, I don't ever want to stop.'

He came out of the shower room in his underpants. Towelling the sleek dark hair, he looked at her.

He said gently, 'I'm a migratory animal, Carla. You always knew that.'

She looked away. 'Yes, but—'

He did not want her to hurt herself any more by making a case that he knew was hopeless. 'I've done the country house bit,' he said firmly, pulling on dark chinos. 'Along with the neighbours in for drinks at Christmas and the ten-year plan for the garden. I was brought up with it. That's how I know it isn't me.'

The country cottage, with its fruit trees and summer-silent birds, was hers. She was a gardener by training, a journalist and broadcaster by profession. But he was beginning to see that she was a home-maker by instinct. Only it would never be his home. He saw the moment when she accepted it.

'Yes, I see,' she said after a long pause. She stood up.

Jay braced himself. But she was only getting the fine silk shirt from where he had hung it on the wardrobe handle.

'Nice colour,' she said.

He knew she didn't mean it. Carla was a successful, professional woman. She liked her men in conservative suits. In Carla's world, real men wore crisp white shirts in town, earth colours in the country. She had never come to terms with Jay's taste for hot ochre and tangerine and emerald.

Today it was turquoise. His grandfather—his lost grand-father, soft-voiced and laughing in the endless dusty en-chantment of Jay's childhood—would have said that it was the colour of hopeful travel. Jay thought of it as that shade of the sea where it meets the sky: the horizon on a clear day with calm water. Carla would not have got on with his lost grandfather.

'I like it,' he said truthfully.

Carla shrugged, as she always did when they disagreed. For a moment he wondered if things would be better if they argued. But he knew, in his heart of hearts, that they wouldn't. He was a man born to be alone. He could not change that, no matter what Carla did.

She made a brave effort at a smile. 'Is the new girl nice? Or don't you know yet?'

Jay grinned. 'I know. She's a slick chick with her life under control. Gives great parties. Also I insulted her, and she hates my guts.'

'Good grief. Is that going to make for a good working relationship?'

He laughed aloud. 'Well, at least she's not going to fall in love with me,' he said with feeling. 'Couldn't take that again.'

He regretted it at once. Only, of course, once you've said it, you can't call it back. She looked stricken.

He had meant that he couldn't take another puppyish fil-ing clerk with her eyes following him all round the office and her passionate ill-spelled e-mails. But that was not what Carla had heard. And maybe that was not all he had meant, after all.

'Hell, I'm sorry.'

'Don't worry about it.'

He slipped his arms into the shirtsleeves and shook out the silk. For a moment the turquoise stuff billowed around his golden chest like a parachute settling. He glimpsed it over her shoulder in the mirror. The silk shimmered, like the cloak of one of the Mogul emperor's bodyguards that his grandfather had shown him in old paintings. Not his lost grandfather. The other one, the Brigadier, with his impeccable standards and his careful culture and the sherry on Boxing Day. Carla got on just fine with the Brigadier.

He buttoned the shirt briskly. Ran fingers through his still-damp hair. Looked at his watch again.

'I know,' she said dryly. 'You have to go or you'll run into the Sunday evening traffic.'

'You're an understanding woman,' he teased.

'Yes.' But she did not laugh.

She came down the rickety stairs with him, still in the kimono. She did not let it billow. She clutched it round her like a blanket in a storm. At the front door she put a hand on his arm as he went to slip the latch.

'Jay—'

He suppressed irritation. He had so nearly got out of the door without a fight! But he was a gentleman. Both grandfathers had seen to that, in their different ways. He turned to her courteously.

'Yes, my dear?'

She gave a faint smile. 'Thank you, Jay.'

'What?' He was bewildered.

'You have such lovely manners. But I'm not your dear. And it's time we both faced it.'

He searched her face. She was rather pale, but her eyes were steady. No pleas, no desperation. Jay had never respected her more.

'Is it?' he said gravely.

She swallowed, but then she nodded once, decisively. 'I made myself a promise. If you looked at your watch as soon as you woke up today I'd finish it. You did. So I am.'

He winced. 'I'm sorry.'

'Don't be. It's overdue.'

'I mean I'm sorry I hurt you,' Jay said painfully.

She shook her head. 'It's a shame. I could have loved you if— But you don't let anyone get close. Maybe you're right and you can't. Well, not me, anyway. Time I recognised that.'

He had nothing to say.

She bit her lip. 'I've met someone. It's nothing yet. But—it might be, in time. If you know what I mean.'

'Yes,' he said heavily. 'I know what you mean.'

Carla's chin came up. 'I don't want to cheat. Not on you. Not on him. Not on myself. So—I want to be free now. Free to look for a relationship that works for me.'

Jay drew a long breath. 'Can we be friends?'

'Maybe. I don't want to see you for a bit, though.'

He was surprised at how much it hurt. But he had no right to complain. Carla had never lied, either. This sort of rejection came with the way he ran his life. From the way he was.

'Very well.' He touched her face briefly. 'Call me when I can buy you a drink.'

She gave him a watery smile. 'Sure.'

On a burst of anger at himself he said, 'I wish—'

But she stopped him, soft fingers over his mouth. 'No, you don't. You know yourself very well, Jay Christopher. You don't have to tell white lies to comfort me.'

'No. I know I don't.' He kissed her quickly on the mouth. They had been making love just a couple of hours ago, but already it felt awkward, as if she were a stranger. 'I hope you find what you're looking for.'

She brushed back his hair. 'You, too. You'd be a prince—if anyone could ever get through.'

She closed the door before he reached the garden gate.

It was lonely journey back. He liked lonely.

He played sitar music. And Josquin des Pres. And Bach. Every girlfriend he had ever had hated them all. It was exhilarating, playing them again, not having to tread carefully any more.

But not as exhilarating as it had once been. He had hurt Carla. He had never meant to. He had tried not to. She had said she understood his limitations, accepted them. But in the end he had hurt her. It didn't feel good.

Was it always going to be like this?

You'd better give up nice women, he told himself bitterly. You can't change. And they can't cope.

But what was the alternative? One-night stands? He pulled a face.

His lost grandfather had said to him once, 'You must be careful. Very few men are made for solitude.'

But, as Carla had said, Jay Christopher knew himself very well. And he knew that he needed the right to walk away from a relationship—any relationship—the way he needed the right to breathe.

'Hello, solitude,' he said aloud. 'Welcome back.'

CHAPTER FOUR

DEBORAH BROWN came back on Sunday afternoon. She walked out into the garden, where Artemis and Ed were playing a deeply dishonest game of croquet and Zoe was swinging in a hammock, and it was as if the sun had gone in.

'What are you *doing*?' said Deborah, in a high, anxious, scolding voice. 'Harry should be studying. Zoe, you know how important it is. It's his whole life. How could you let all this noise—?'

Harry unfolded himself from the corner, where he was reading, and slipped indoors. Artemis put down her croquet mallet, stuck her chin in the air and announced that she was moving in with Ed completely. It had the effect Zoe would have predicted.

'You are punishing me,' said their mother tensely. 'This is because your father walked out on us.'

Artemis looked mutinous. Zoe flung herself out of the hammock and into the breach. As she always did.

'This is because Art's hormones are on full alert and Ed's cute,' she said patiently. 'Nothing personal.'

'Thanks, Zo,' said Ed, grinning.

Deborah Brown looked round distractedly. 'Where are my tablets?'

'Look, Ma,' said Artemis, stepping in between her and the pill packets in the house behind her, 'everyone lives with their boyfriend these days.'

Deborah seized the cue eagerly. 'Zoe doesn't.'

'Only because Zoe's got men coming out of her ears. She can't make up her mind,' said Artemis, quite convinced she was telling the truth.

55

Deborah didn't care. Ever since her husband had walked out she had had a pathological fear of change of any sort.

'I never interfere. You girls have your own flat up at the top of the house. Why can't things stay as they are?' Deborah's voice rose frantically.

'Because I want to grow up,' yelled Artemis, losing it.

So Zoe had to wade in and try to calm them both down. Artemis raged. Deborah gabbled maniacally, refusing to listen to anything either daughter said in case it sounded reasonable. It took the whole afternoon.

Then Artemis stamped out with a couple of cases and a sobered Ed beside her. Deborah took to her room and closed the curtains. And Zoe had time at last to finish her washing and get her clothes ready for the next day.

She was ironing a neat business shirt when Harry wandered in, back from wherever he had bolted to for sanctuary. She heard the front door and then he clattered down to the kitchen and stuck his head round the door.

'Bring out your dead. The place feels like a morgue. Where's Ma?'

'In her room.'

'Ah,' he said, understanding. 'A maternal moment?'

Zoe looked up and grinned. 'Horrible boy. Artemis has moved out. Ma's taken to her bed.'

Harry took the news with equanimity. 'Predictable.' He investigated the fridge. 'Is there anything to eat? I'm starving.'

'You can make yourself toast now, or I'll do scrambled eggs later.'

'I'm a growing boy. I can't live on scrambled eggs.'

Zoe sighed. 'Okay. Order in.' It was an extravagance, and money was tight. But her mother's housekeeping was erratic and Zoe's back-up food planning had gone awry this weekend.

Harry was gleeful. 'Great. Indian? Chinese? Italian?'

'Anything but pizza,' said Zoe, knowing that meant he would get crispy fried duck and plum sauce. 'And ask Ma if she wants some before you make the call.'

She finished ironing her shirt and hung it on a hanger before starting another one. Nothing of Harry's needed ironing, fortunately. As for Deborah, it was getting more and more difficult to get her to change her clothes at all. She would certainly not appreciate having her faded tee shirts pressed.

Zoe finished the ironing, folded the rest of the washing, threw away a pair of socks with holes in the toe and closed up the ironing board.

Harry came back from their mother's room, announced that Deborah was watching a video on her small television, and called in his order.

'One fried seaweed. One sesame prawn toast. Two egg fried rice. Crispy duck twice.'

Zoe bit back a smile.

He came off the phone and raised an eyebrow at the shirt on its hanger. 'Trying to impress?'

'Well, I was a bit rude to the new boss,' admitted Zoe. 'I'd like to—er—retrieve the position.' She twinkled. 'Actually, what I mean is I want to knock him cold. I've got a point to make.'

Harry sucked his teeth thoughtfully. 'Leave the top button undone,' he advised.

Zoe puffed. 'Thank you,' she said with irony.

'No, on second thoughts, make it two. These modern bosses take some impressing.'

'You'd know, of course, idle little toad.'

'I'm glad you brought that up. I've lined up a job for the summer.'

'Great,' said Zoe. 'What?'

But he only looked mysterious and refused to tell her. Zoe had effectively been substitute mother since Harry was ten. She knew enough not to push it.

Instead she got out plates and put them in the old-fashioned oven to warm.

'Harry—'

He was leafing through the television programmes. 'Yes?'

'Do you think everyone moves in with their boyfriend eventually?'

He looked alarmed. 'What has Naomi been saying?'

Naomi was his girlfriend.

'No, not you.' Zoe thought about it. 'Well, not yet anyway. I was thinking of, well, me.'

He laughed. 'The guy would have to work hard to get you to stick with him long enough to move in.'

'Yes,' agreed Zoe, depressed.

Harry thought about it. 'And Suze hasn't, has she? I mean Hermann's great, but she doesn't want to move to Germany, does she? She's still in that flat she wanted you to share?'

Zoe nodded, even more depressed. She had shared the flat with Suze for a few months after she came down from university. But first Artemis, then Harry had had their public exams, and Deborah had been locking herself away in her room and cooking family meals at midnight. There had been no choice, really.

'I don't think I'll be moving out again just yet,' she agreed brightly.

And added silently, *If ever.*

Monday morning was better. Zoe liked mornings anyway. Besides, she was always better when she had something to do.

And this morning what she had to do was show Jay Christopher that he had engaged a *treasure*. When she moved, as she would at the end of her contract, Jay Christopher was going to realise that he had made a big mistake by insulting her. A *big* mistake.

Zoe almost skipped into the cream and silver offices of Culp and Christopher. Jay Christopher, she thought, hugging herself, was in for the education of his life.

Though quite what she was going to do at Culp and Christopher nobody seemed to be sure. The Human Resources manager, a tall blonde, was manifestly not expecting her. She made a couple of investigative phone calls while trying to deliver a welcome spiel. It did not work very well.

'A degree in chemistry? Aren't you overqualified to temp?'

'Yes.'

What else did she expect her to say? thought Zoe, irritated. But the blonde was flustered by her brevity. She muttered a question into the telephone wedged under her ear and looked at the file in front of her.

'Er—yes. Well. So, do you think you're suited to the sort of work we do here?'

Zoe tried to be patient. 'That's why the Manoir Agency sent me.'

'Ah, but why did they choose you particularly?'

Zoe narrowed her eyes at her, losing patience. 'Just drew the short straw, I guess.'

Fortunately her answer fell on deaf ears. The telephone had obviously started broadcasting.

'Oh, it's Jay's doing, is it?' said the woman into the telephone. She made a note on her pad and then said, 'Right. I'll bring her along at ten.' She almost flung the phone down and turned back. 'Have you worked in public relations before, Zoe?'

'No,' Zoe admitted.

'Well, this is a very progressive company,' said the blonde, getting back on message with evident relief. 'We're committed to training. I'll make sure you go on one of the introductory talks that our chief gives. Jay Christopher,' she added unexpectedly, 'is just wicked.'

Zoe blinked. She thought of the man she had seen, tall as a tree and mad as a hornet. And up for a serious bit of re-education. She gulped. 'Wicked?'

Just what did that mean in a super-sophisticated office like Culp and Christopher? Zoe looked wildly out of the window and prayed for divine translation.

At home, with her twenty-year-old sister and seventeen-year-old brother, she knew what *wicked* meant. It was hip. It was far-out. It was wild. The ultimate compliment.

But that was in a house run for people who still spent their days in full-time classes and their nights dancing. The offices of Culp and Christopher Public Relations PLC were not like that. Culp and Christopher carried sophistication into a realm that made her eyeballs bubble.

The blonde, whose name she had been too nervous to catch, had already whisked her round so fast her toes had hardly touched the gleaming wooden floor. There were plenty of people milling about among the irregular geometric shapes that seemed to be desks. They were discussing their weekends, laughing, all friendly enough to the newcomer. But so far Zoe had understood less than half of the conversations she overheard. It was like travelling in foreign country. Who could guess what *wicked* meant in the realms of the super-cool?

The very grown-up super-cool, what was more. The blonde was wearing a dark grey trouser suit that was so well cut it seemed to flow into new shapes as she moved. It put Zoe's crisply ironed white shirt back where it belonged, on the bargain rack.

Oh, boy, am I out of my depth here.

And there was no way to disguise it. She gave up and asked, 'Wicked, like how?'

'You'll see,' said the blonde mysteriously.

That didn't help at all, of course.

'He's got a bad temper?' Zoe hazarded doubtfully.

She hoped that was what the blonde meant. Zoe knew about a lot about bad temper. She knew she could handle it, too. She wasn't sure how well she was going to handle the designer suits and the minimalist office.

The blonde grinned. 'Who knows?'

'What?'

'There was a movie we did some publicity for. *The Ice Volcano.* The girls started to call him that.'

Zoe blinked again. The man who wore flame silk shirts? *Ice?* This was worse than a foreign language. This was a foreign universe.

The blonde saw her confusion and laughed heartily. 'Jay

is very, very self-contained. When he's angry he goes all cold and quiet. Brings the hair up on the back of your neck. Ice. Only then he explodes…'

She leaned back, smiling reminiscently. It was obviously a great show.

'Does he explode often?' said Zoe warily.

'Hardly ever. But when he goes, he goes. Once seen, never forgotten.'

'Oh.'

The blonde got to her feet. 'Probably won't happen while you're here. Don't worry about it. Come on. I'll show you where the hot negotiating goes on.'

She did, pointing out various framed photographs of products and personalities on the walls as they went. The photographs were all high quality, and some were truly beautiful. But they meant nothing to Zoe. There seemed to be a lot of sportsmen in fields or beautiful women standing in front of film posters.

The blonde was dry. 'Jay is very big in the sports world. It might be a good idea if you mug up before you meet him.'

I've already met him. He looked at me as if I were a slave he wasn't very interested in buying.

'I suppose so,' she said carefully.

'We'll tell Poppy. If he isn't in yet, she can give you his publicity file and you can learn it by heart.' She zipped Zoe down a narrow corridor, indicating doors briskly as they passed. 'Ladies' rest room. Supplies cupboard—everything that you want is in there: stationery, disks, printer cartridges, privacy, gossip. The kitchen. Boardroom.'

'I'll remember,' said Zoe, trying to commit the layout to memory. She thought there was a fifty-fifty chance that she would succeed.

The blonde pushed open another door. This one was studded with silver saucepan lids and led into a botanical hot house. Climbing plants and fig trees grew right up to the glass roof and the roof was *high*.

Instantly Zoe forgot the location of the stationery cupboard and the boardroom.

'Are there spiders in there?' she said involuntarily.

Her guide looked surprised. 'Never thought about it.'

'I bet there are. Hundreds of them. I *hate* spiders.'

'Don't worry, you won't be working in here. This is restricted territory. Jay's PA lives here. You don't get in without a visa.' She waved the note Suze had given Zoe to bring. 'Ah, here she is.'

For a moment Zoe wondered wildly if she were actually talking about a ten foot Swiss cheese plant. But then another tall blonde appeared from behind it. She was carrying a tiny trowel, with a gold handle, and had a pile of smart maroon laminated brochures stuffed precariously under her arm. She looked distracted.

'Hello, Isabel,' she said to Blonde Mark I, scattering brochures.

Ho. So they don't like each other. Zoe was good at interpreting tones of voice. She bent and gathered up the fallen brochures.

'Hi, Poppy,' said Blonde Mark I coldly. 'This is the girl from the agency I called you about. Zoe Brown. I've done the paperwork, but you'll know where Jay wants her to work.'

It was sweet enough. But so was poison, thought Zoe. Dislike was clearly mutual.

She sighed. She hated office wars. It was tough enough being a temp anyway, without having to work out departmental battle lines.

She said hastily, 'They said something about a research project? But I can file and do word processing as well.'

The blonde called Poppy looked taken aback. Isabel smiled maliciously.

'Your call,' she said. 'I don't know a thing about it. Suze at the temp agency said Jay rang through to her himself.'

'Then we'll ask Jay.'

Isabel went into exaggerated surprise. 'He in yet?'

'Er—no.'

Isabel grinned. 'Been to stay with the gardener bird, has he?'

Poppy narrowed perfectly made-up eyes at her adversary. *The Battle of the Blondes,* thought Zoe. She moved carefully out of range.

'I'm not discussing Jay's private life with you, Isabel Percy, so you can stop fishing. If you don't know what to do with her, you can leave Zoe here with me. I'm sure you've got plenty of work to do.'

Isabel recognised defeat. She shrugged and turned to Zoe.

'Sorry about that. If you need to talk, you know where I am. Human Resources, second floor.'

'Thank you,' said Zoe in a neutral voice. Rule One, when joining a new office, was be polite to everyone.

'Jay will tell you everything you need to know,' said Poppy quickly.

'It's still kind of you,' Zoe told Isabel. 'I appreciate it.' Rule Two was don't take sides.

Isabel raised a hand in farewell. 'Good luck. Don't get eaten by the spiders. See you around.'

She went.

The hard look went out of Poopy's face. She went back to faintly worried, which Zoe suspected was her habitual expression.

'Suze didn't say anything else about where you'd be working?' Poppy asked. 'Like research into what, for instance?'

Zoe shook her head. 'But I could start with Mr Christopher,' she said, mindful of Isabel Percy's advice. 'I obviously ought to know more about him and this agency than I do.'

'Of course.' Poppy looked relieved. She dived round a curtain of leaves so fat they looked as if they ate people. Had eaten several recently, in fact. Zoe followed, taking care not to brush against the plant in case it had teeth.

Behind it there was an oasis of relative normality.

'Wow,' said Zoe, forgetting Rule Three, never comment

adversely on the working environment, 'a real desk. Drawers and a leg at each corner and everything.'

Poppy was rummaging through a pile of papers that leaned like the Tower of Pisa, but at that she looked up and grinned.

'Don't let the trendiness in the main office fool you. Culp and Christopher is as good as it gets. The trick desks are just for fun. Ah, here it is.'

She fished out a battered A4 folder. Zoe put the brochures she had harvested down on the desk and accepted it.

'Now, where are you going to sit? Probably not the boardroom; you never know who's going to use it. Um—what about Jay's waiting area?'

Zoe nodded obediently and settled into carved oak chair that looked at least four centuries out of step with the rest of the decor. She resisted the temptation to put her feet on a carved chest of similar design that served as a coffee table.

The folder proved to contain what looked like the draft material for a profile of Culp and Christopher Public Relations. Zoe looked at their client list with interest—she had worked for at least three of the large public companies who figured on it. But what was really intriguing was the staff—former newsmen, sports stars, politicians, even a token aristocrat.

Above all the stuff about Jay Christopher, Olympic medallist, adviser on track and field sports to a series of government bodies and all round public relations guru, made compelling reading. Hermann had said he was running with the great and the good, Zoe thought. Now she saw what he meant.

'Coffee?'

She looked up and found that Blonde Mark II was standing beside her, waving a glass jug. It steamed.

'Thank you,' said Zoe, surprised. Jay Christopher's PA ought to be too senior to get coffee for an incoming temp.

Her hostess fished a tall thin mug out from a disguised cupboard in the coffee table chest.

'Jay drinks the stuff by the tanker load. If you get desperate there's always coffee brewing in here.' She poured dark fragrant liquid into the futuristic crockery. 'He's passionate about it. If you give him half a chance he'll give you a history of coffee-drinking from the year dot.'

Privately Zoe doubted that the great man would give his new temp thirty seconds of his valuable time. Her father was a busy and ambitious man. On the whole it was a type she was not keen on.

'Milk? Sugar?'

Zoe shook her head.

Poppy did not disguise her relief. 'Good. Jay takes it black, no sugar. There are packets around here somewhere, but I can't always find them.' She poured some for herself and perched on the edge of the chest. 'Find anything interesting in there?'

'Well, now I know what a public relations company does, I think. And what a big cheese Jay Christopher is.'

'Well, that's an improvement,' said a cool dark voice from the doorway.

Zoe rocketed to her feet, spraying coffee widely. Poppy was unmoved. She got up more slowly and kept her cup horizontal.

'Hi, Jay. This is—'

'We've met,' he said crisply.

This morning he was wearing a soft dark suit even more beautifully cut than Isabel Percy's. The shirt underneath was imperial purple.

More silk, thought Zoe, eyeing it with mixed feelings. On the one hand she always wanted to touch silk, let it run through her fingers. On the other, she really, really did not want to touch Jay Christopher.

He was still tall, dark and handsome. Sexy as hell. And mad as a hornet?

He strode through the foliage to a door so discreet it was nearly invisible. 'Bring in the life-giving, Poppy, my love. And we'll see what Zoe has to offer Culp and Christopher. Other than her assessment of my place on the cheese index.'

Face rigid, Zoe followed.

He flung a small document case across the room so that it landed neatly on a glass coffee table and turned to her.

He was exactly as she had remembered, Zoe thought. In the light of day she could see that his skin was an even golden ochre and his eyes a strange greeny-hazel. But for the rest he was exactly what her nightmares had told her: too tall, too sleekly dark, too handsome. He even had a haughty nose and beautifully kept hands, which she had passed over on her last inventory of his assets. Well, face it, she had not got further than that controlled and passionate mouth.

She looked anywhere but at his mouth. 'If you remember, working here was not my idea,' she said with spirit.

She saw him put the irritation away from him like a jacket he'd taken off. He was no longer mad as a hornet. He was charming. Determinedly charming.

She watched the beguiling smile which put an indentation in one cheek and thought, *Your performance is nearly as good as mine.* The smile was—almost—irresistible. Zoe regarded him with total suspicion.

'Right. Now, what can you offer us?'

She outlined her office skills stiffly. All the more stiffly as he didn't seem to be listening very hard.

His smile grew. 'You really don't like me very much, do you?' he said.

Zoe breathed hard. 'Do I have to like you?'

He beamed. 'You'll do.'

Great. More and more like the slave market.

'Gee, thanks,' she said with heavy irony.

He ignored that. He slung himself down behind a light glass and chrome table and switched on a computer that he'd magicked out of a hidden wall cupboard. At once he was flicking away absently. He seemed to have no more than half an eye on the messages that flashed up on the screen and then disappeared.

'Not at all. Take a load off. Sit.'

It was not a gracious invitation but she was quite glad to comply. Her head was beginning to spin slightly.

'Thank you.'

He carried on scrolling through his messages on the screen. 'So. They showed you round? What do you think of the place?'

Zoe was taken aback. 'I don't know anything about public relations.'

'Neither do most of our customers. And they come through here all the time. I'm curious as to what they make of us. So, tell me, what were your first impressions?'

'Schizophrenia,' she said honestly.

He stopped flicking for a moment. 'What?' He sounded genuinely intrigued.

'Well, the decor—' She waved her hand. 'You don't seem to be able to make up your mind whether you want to be a set for a sci-fi film or the waiting room of Louis Quatorze.'

'Really?' He looked at her curiously. He did not seem offended. 'No one's ever said that before.'

'Maybe nobody has dared to.'

'You're a real original, aren't you?' He said it with the air of a connoisseur, as if she ought to be flattered by his approval.

She was not flattered. Suddenly, blessedly, she was hopping mad.

'Am I? Is that supposed to be compliment?'

Jay shrugged. 'I don't pay compliments. Especially not to women who work for me.'

'That must make for a happy work place,' said Zoe, bristling.

For a moment he looked startled. Then he smiled again, with a lot less conscious charm, she thought.

'Makes it peaceful, at least,' he said ruefully. 'Almost the only house rule we have. Don't screw the company. You can make private phone calls. I don't care what time you get in or leave, as long as you do your own work. But if you start a steaming affair with a colleague you get your cards and leave at the end of the week.'

Zoe was so angry she could have danced with temper if she had not been wearing her best clothes and trying to be dignified. 'What about an affair that's only slightly simmering?' she asked sweetly.

His eyes narrowed. 'A barrack room lawyer, are you? Fine. The definition is: any relationship that causes sheep's eyes across the computer.'

'And how do you define sheep's—?'

Suddenly he tired of the game. 'Anything other people notice,' he snapped.

'Oh, well, that's all right,' she said unwarily. 'I'm good at keeping things secret.'

When he was angry his eyes went a flat, brownish green, she thought. He looked at her for an unnerving, silent minute.

'Are you deliberately trying to provoke me into sacking you on your first day here?' he said at last softly.

She stood her ground. She had paid attention when Suze talked, after all.

'You can't afford to sack me. You won't get anyone else in the time and you've run out of good will in the agencies,' Zoe pointed out.

It was a stand-off. They glared at each other until the door opened and Poppy came in with a tray. She took in the atmosphere in one glance, put down the coffee, and backed out fast.

But it broke the tension.

'Come to think of it, how do you manage to get through staff so fast?' asked Zoe, bland as cream. 'Do they collapse on the treadmill?'

'They fall in love with me,' said Jay, even blander.

She gasped, gagged, and collapsed into a coughing fit.

His eyes lost that green angry look. He looked satisfied, damn him.

But he still had good manners. 'Would you like some water?'

She shook her head, eyes streaming. He passed her a neatly laundered handkerchief.

'That's the other house rule,' he said, pouring coffee while she mopped her eyes and got her breath back painfully. 'Never mind the end of the week. If you fall in love with me you leave at once. On the hour. Clear?'

He gave her the coffee cup. Zoe took it with a hand that was only just not trembling with rage.

I ironed my best shirt so this comedian could patronise me, she thought in fury.

She said aloud, 'No need to worry about that. I'm the original Hard-Hearted Hannah.'

He was pouring his own coffee, but at that he stopped and looked round. One eyebrow flicked up in amusement. 'No man gets to the fifth date with me,' she told him, smiling so hard her teeth hurt. 'Ask Suze. I don't fall in love.'

He pursed his lips in a silent whistle. It was disbelief incarnate. It was the last straw.

'I'm too easily bored.'

'Bored?' He did not sound pleased.

'Yes.' Zoe sipped her coffee. She was shaking with indignation but he would never have guessed it. Performing Zoe was in control again, and she was *good*. 'I agree with you. Office affairs are messy. And never worth it.'

His eyebrows flew up.

So he didn't like that, did he? Good! She could have hugged herself with glee.

She gave him her best hot babe smile, all eyes and intensity.

'So chill out, dude. You'd never be a candidate.'

CHAPTER FIVE

So HE'D never be a candidate, wouldn't he? Ms Hip Chick was making a big mistake if she thought he'd ever *want* to be a candidate.

But even as the words formed in Jay's furious brain he was finding other words pushing them out of the way. And not just words.

Hell!

Wrong time. Wrong place. Wrong woman. Oh, boy, was she the wrong woman, with her curls that she couldn't keep under control and that spit-in-your-eye-as-soon-as-look-at-you manner.

He said it all to himself as he stared into her taunting brown eyes. Didn't make any difference. He still had to wrestle his libido back into its cave.

Down boy!

'Zoe Brown—' he began darkly.

She put a hand on her hip and tilted her head at him defiantly.

Hell and double hell.

Precision and self-control at all times, Jay reminded himself. That was what made success. Whether it was long-distance running or business, the same principle applied. You focused on one goal—*one*—and you tuned out all distractions. Zoe Brown was going to be harder to tune out than most, but he would do it. Oh, yes, he would do it.

If he could still run when he could no longer feel his legs and there was nothing but will driving him on, he could neutralise the impact of a voluptuous mouth and a bad attitude. Maybe he could even turn it to his advantage, now he came to think of it. After all, she really, *really* didn't like him. And most of her predecessors had liked him too much.

So he smiled blandly, straight into her hot eyes.

'That's a good start. Carry on hating me. That is definitely your unique selling point.'

'What?'

'It will compensate in full for your inexperience. Even for a certain amount of inefficiency.'

'I am not,' said Zoe between her teeth, 'inefficient.'

'No?' He was deliberately sceptical. Suze had told her to challenge the girl. She'd said that was the only way to knock the self-doubt out of her. Well, this was going to be the challenge of her life.

'If you'll just tell me what you want me to do, I'll even show you,' she told him, with a fierce smile.

He raised his eyebrows. 'Then come with me.'

She steamed beside him down to the open plan office so angry she could barely speak.

'Abby,' he said to a tall woman with soft dark hair and gentle eyes. 'Zoe is joining us. Point her in the direction of a computer, would you?'

'Sure, Jay.'

And to Zoe, 'I'm giving a keynote speech at a conference in Venice. Public Relations in a Changing World. I scribbled out some notes and left a list of things I wanted checked and updated. It's all on file.'

He seized a notepad off Abby's desk and scribbled down some words. He tore the page off and handed it to Zoe.

'There you are. That will get you into the file. Talk to me at the end of the day about how long it's going to take.'

He left.

Abby smiled at Zoe. 'I saw you earlier, didn't I? Welcome again.'

'Thank you.'

'That sounds like the stuff Banana was doing. Interesting. Well, look, take the desk under the window for now, and we'll get you logged on.'

The Venice file was enormous. More a rag-bag than a decent way of organising information, Zoe thought. She was pleased. This was what she was good at. She lost herself in

archived magazine articles and forgot challenging Jay
Christopher. Well, nearly.

She still knew who they meant when a voice above her
head said, 'I hear the Volcano has gone up again.'

She looked up.

Abby was standing by her desk with a tall, fierce-looking
woman in an eye-hurting magenta leather catsuit.

'Molly di Paretti,' said the woman, holding out a hand.

At least she wasn't another battling blonde, thought Zoe.
She stood up and shook hands.

Molly di Paretti smiled and the ferocity disappeared.
'Abby and I are off to hit Patisserie Pauline. Coming?'

Well, Jay had said he didn't care what time she got in or
left as long as she did her work. Presumably he did not care
about expeditions in search of coffee, either.

'Great,' she said.

She saved her work and logged off without sitting down
again. They went.

Patisserie Pauline turned out to be a small half-shop, with
a bar along one wall and half a dozen marble-topped tables
in its depths. It was full of the smell of coffee and warm
pastry.

'Bliss,' said Molly.

'You're a carbohydrate junkie,' said Abby amused.

'Guilty.'

Zoe looked at the magenta catsuit and shook her head.
'With a figure like that?'

'I know,' said Abby. 'Life's not fair.'

'Look, I was heavy once. Then I lost it and learned to
prioritise. One of Pauline's brioches is worth giving up fish
and chips for.' Molly flicked an imperious finger at a round
woman behind the counter. 'The usual, Pauline. Plus one for
the new member.'

She led the way to the back of the shop, where people
were already seated at all the tables but one. It had a little
reserved notice in the middle. Molly flicked it off and put it
on the counter behind her. She sat down. Zoe was not en-

tirely sure that the table had been reserved for them, though. Molly had the look of a rule-breaker. Zoe was envious.

'Now,' said Molly, purple elbows on the table, leaning forward. 'Tell. What has he done with the body?'

Zoe recoiled, 'Body?'

Abby intervened. 'Molly's distorted sense of humour,' she explained. 'She means your predecessor. Banana Lessiter.'

Zoe began to feel as if she had broken through into another dimension. 'Banana?'

'Barbara Lessiter. She called herself Banana.' Molly was impatient. 'What's he done with her? She was still alive and lusting after him all over the office last Wednesday.'

'I *see*.' Zoe was suddenly enlightened. 'That must be why he warned me against falling in love with him.'

'He didn't!' The others stared at each other, between shock and amusement.

'Yes, he did. It's a dismissal matter, apparently. That must be what happened to—er—Banana.'

'You've got to be right,' agreed Molly. She whistled. 'Wow. She really must have got him running scared.'

Zoe choked. 'Scared? Jay Christopher? That's a joke, right?'

Molly shook her head. 'You have no idea. The man is—'

'A good boss and an all-round decent guy,' interrupted Abby reprovingly.

Molly was unrepentant. 'Oh, sure. But he never lets a woman get too close, either. Come on, Abby, admit it. He cares more about his art collection than he does about his girlfriends.'

'I don't know any of his girlfriends.'

'Well, you wouldn't, would you? He just told Zoe. It's the quickest way to get your cards.'

Zoe said slowly, 'He said there was a no dating policy for the whole office. Not just him. Is that true?'

Molly pulled a face.

But Abby said, 'Yes, there is. And I agree with it.'

'Emotions will be left in the umbrella stand,' muttered Molly.

Abby ignored her. 'It takes the pressure off. You can break up with your boyfriend and not have to make a choice between seeing him at the next desk every morning or leaving your job. Which,' she added tartly, 'if you went through men as fast as Molly used to, is a definite plus.'

Molly grinned.

Zoe winced inwardly. There were plenty of people ready to say that *she* went through men quite as fast as Molly could.

'Is that what Banana did?'

'Don't know what she did,' said Molly. 'Though, knowing her, it probably involved taking her clothes off. I mean we all let our hormones ride us sometimes, but Banana's galloped.'

Zoe winced again. And hid it, as she always did.

Here we go again. Another bunch of nice women who are going to rub my nose in it every time I turn round. Am I really the last virgin in captivity?

'Still, she wasn't subtle, but I gather she was effective. Until Jay, of course.'

'Poor Banana,' said gentle Abby.

Molly snorted. 'It's amazing he put up with her this long. She's been all over him since the Christmas party.'

Abby looked horrified suddenly. 'Oh, no! The party!'

'What?'

But their coffee arrived, along with a basket of mouth-watering pastries. By the time they had chosen, and tasted, and pronounced, Abby was easily able to change the subject. And she was desperate to do just that, Zoe saw. She wondered why. Molly and Abby seemed such friends!

Still, people were not necessarily all that they seemed. Self-effacing Abby turned out to be the woman the popular press called Fab Ab. She was married to an international tennis star turned businessman. Even Zoe, not a reader of the gossip columns, had heard of her. Maybe friendship was different in celebrity circles, thought Zoe, going quiet.

She did not have long to nurse her doubts. Abby cornered her in the luxurious ladies' restroom less than an hour later.

'Molly's getting married next month. Jay wants C&C to give her a surprise party. I just remembered it when we were having coffee. Trouble is—Banana was supposed to organise it.'

'Ah,' said Zoe, relieved that she had not misjudged Abby after all.

'If Jay's sacked her, I'll have to find out how far she's got and run with it.'

'Do you want me to have a trawl through her desk and see if she's left any notes?' Zoe offered. 'I've inherited her other files, after all.'

'Would you? That would be such a help. Molly's bound to get suspicious if she sees me rummaging through Banana's desk.'

'Sure thing. No problem.

Zoe took the desk drawers apart. There were notes. They showed that Banana had done precisely nothing except get a budget out of Jay Christopher and ring round a few restaurants. It was a generous budget, Zoe saw. You might not be allowed to fall in love with him, but he was lavish when he celebrated your falling in love with someone else. But there was still nowhere booked to hold the party.

'Help!' squeaked Abby, when she told her.

'Do you want me to do it?'

Abby was doubtful. 'You've only just got here.'

'I can handle it,' said Zoe with conviction. 'It will be a nice change from sorting and filing.'

'Then thank you,' said Abby with real gratitude. 'I'll give you the address list.'

Jay wandered through the open plan office around four. There was a comfortable buzz of activity. When he walked in, it neither revved up nor fell to ostentatious concentration. Jay noticed that with approval.

'Well?' he said, pausing by Tom Skellern's desk.

Tom was on the telephone to a City editor on behalf of a new client fighting off a takeover. He raised his thumb to Jay and continued with the conversation.

Jay turned to the next desk. 'Molly?'

'If you're asking about Zoe Brown, she'll be okay,' said Molly crisply. 'Abby will look after her. She's a nurturer.'

He pursed his lips. 'You think Zoe Brown needs looking after? I'd have said that she was more than capable of taking care of herself.'

'Now we've found her a computer and somewhere to sit, she probably is,' Molly said dryly. 'It would have helped if we'd known she was coming.'

'But we're supposed to be good at handling the unexpected, Molly. That's what public relations is all about,' he told her blandly.

'Ho, yus?' said Molly, roused. 'Well, you really got the gold medal for the way you handled Banana, didn't you?'

Zoe had just come back into the office. Jay caught sight of her. There was no doubt about it. The woman would be trouble on wheels if he gave her half a chance. But she moved like a dancer. He liked that. Pure aesthetic appreciation, he assured himself.

'What?' he said absently.

'Banana Lessiter? Remember? She used to work here until she clearly did something unexpected. We were asking ourselves where you had buried the body. Weren't we, Zoe?'

Arriving, Zoe stopped dead, startled. Jay gave her a wide, charming smile.

'Barbara has moved on to follow a new interesting career opportunity,' he said fluently. He was still smiling at Zoe. 'How does your first day feel?'

'Fine,' she said warily. She did not trust men who smiled straight into your eyes. Especially when that smile could charm birds off the trees and they knew it. And when they had told you that hating them was your unique selling point. Did Jay want to test exactly how immune she was to him? 'So far I'm doing just fine.'

Oh, yes, she would certainly do fine, thought Jay. He was giving her the full wattage and all she did was stand beside her desk and narrow her eyes at him. At a comparable stage in her employment Barbara Lessiter had started leaving cru-

cial buttons on her shirt undone. And Barbara Lessiter was
not alone. Zoe Brown was definitely a find.

So why did he feel annoyed? Even outraged? He did not
want her to melt when he looked at her, after all.

He pulled himself together. 'Have you looked at the file?
Do you know what you're doing yet?'

Abby had guided Zoe through more than the ladies' rest
room and her predecessor's files. In the last two hours Zoe
had read every speech Jay had made to the industry this last
year. He seemed to make a lot of speeches.

'"Advertising stimulates the appetite. Public relations fo-
cuses a spotlight",' Zoe chanted.

Jay raised his eyebrows. 'Quoting me already?'

'Seems like a good idea,' said Zoe with composure.

He grinned. 'They've been telling you I'm a despot.'

Molly raised her eyes to the ceiling eloquently.

'Don't worry, Moll. I can take it,' he told her comfortably.
And, to Zoe, 'I prefer to think of myself as an oligarch. An
enlightened oligarch, of course. What I say goes. But what
I say is reasonable.' He looked round at the others. 'Right?'

There was a chorus of ironic agreement. Jay's grin widened.

'And to prove how enlightened I am, you can ask Banana
Lessiter to the next office party,' he said generously. 'And
I won't say a word.'

But he said several words when Tom Skellern cornered him
in his office a week later.

'I'm in love,' he announced exuberantly.

Jay grinned. Tom was an old fashioned chivalrous knight
under his dark glasses and designer suiting. 'Congratula-
tions.'

'With Zoe Brown. The new girl.'

Jay stopped grinning. He did not like that at all.

He said warningly. 'Tom, you know the rule. Just because
you're up for a directorship—'

'That's why I'm in love,' said Tom impatiently. 'I've been
doing the Hyder-Schelling tests on her. And she's perfect.'

'Why on earth have you been doing recruitment tests on Zoe Brown? We've already recruited her.'

'Yes, but just to do your dogsbodying for Venice.' Tom sat on the corner of his desk, suddenly serious. 'If we're going into this merger, we've got to boost our in-house research and response capacity. Otherwise Karlsson will swamp us. I've been roughing out a profile—and Zoe Brown fits it to a tee.'

Jay's eyes narrowed. 'Does she know you've been doing psychological tests on her?'

Tom was hurt. 'Of course. And not just her. All the girls. They thought it was fun.'

Jay was still not happy. He sighed, and said with palpable reluctance, 'Okay. Show me what you've got.' He held out his hand for the sheets.

Tom stabbed a finger at the top one.

'Look. Look at that score. She's total woman. She nurtures. She plans. She budgets. She takes her time to react. She thinks logic is not wholly reliable. She daydreams. She reads romance. Hell, she even knows how to cook—look…''to make a bread and butter pudding, butter slices of bread on both sides, whisk two whole eggs and a yolk in a pint of full cream milk—'''

'Give it here,' said Jay, whipping it out of his hand. 'You've been doing it again, haven't you? Slipping the Tom Skellern Ideal Wife Test in with the multiple choice questions.'

Tom laughed. 'It's important that they show initiative. Any monkey can tick multiple choice.'

'Tom—'

'Look, we agreed that we needed a really female female, didn't we? Especially if we're going to take this merger thing seriously. All those kooks in Karlsson are high on ambition and the need to prove they can drink more beer than we can. That's not the market.'

'It's a big segment of the market.'

'But not *all*. Don't the nurturers and the dreamers get a vote any more?'

'And you think Zoe Brown is a nurturer and a dreamer?' Jay said slowly.

'I know she is. The Hyder-Schelling tests cannot lie. Besides,' he added wickedly, 'she brightens the place up. Have you seen the red boob tube yet?'

Jay threw the sheets down. 'I'm not employing a woman because you want to go to bed with her bread and butter pudding. And that's final.'

Zoe saw a lot of Jay. Every time he came back into the office, from Brussels, or Manchester, or even a trip just down the road to Westminster, he summoned her into his office.

'Poppy and Isabel will put you top of their hit list,' teased Molly. 'The Battle of the Blondes escalates.'

For once Zoe did not laugh, though normally she enjoyed Molly's cynicism as much as anyone. And she was responsible for dubbing the inter-office rivalry the Battle of the Blondes, after all.

'It's nothing personal. It's just because I'm working on this speech, of course,' she told them seriously at Patisserie Pauline. 'It's only ten days away now. He's in a flap about it.'

'A flap? Jay?' Molly shook her head. 'I don't think so.'

But Abby shook her head. 'He's probably feeling guilty. It's a big honour to be asked. He should have done it months ago. Banana really let him down there.'

Zoe was intrigued by the woman about whom she had heard so much.

'What was she like?' she asked.

Abby shrugged. 'Used to be Molly's assistant. Did the music business, mainly. Wasn't here long. I didn't know her well.' She thought about it. 'Very hip. Very temperamental.'

'What do you think, Moll?'

'I think she should have kept her hormones in her handbag,' said Molly crisply.

Yet the girl who turned up at the private room in the Pacific Grill Rooms for Molly's surprise party didn't look temperamental. She didn't look like a case of galloping hormones, either. She wore designer rags that left some surprising bits naked to the air, and she was as tottery as a young antelope on her massive heels.

Zoe could not help herself. 'That's the man-eater?' she said, astonished.

'That's the one,' said Abby. 'Wouldn't think it to look at her, would you?'

The antelope had eyelashes that would have made Bambi sick with envy. She cornered Jay and used them to great effect.

'Oh, I don't know,' said Zoe.

Jay got the antelope a drink, made his excuses and walked away. Banana was the only woman in the world Zoe had ever seen pout prettily. Mind you, that could have been the wide innocent blue eyes that went with it.

Innocent. Huh! I bet she knows more than I do about just about everything.

The antelope stopped pouting and looked round for company.

'Hi,' she said, descending on Abby and Zoe. 'What a horrible boss you have.' She sounded envious. 'Still, at least he forgave me enough to let me come.'

She was also the only woman Zoe had ever known to drink a margarita and chatter breathlessly at the same time. How did she do that?

'What did you do to him, Banana?' asked Abby. She was no gossip, but she was as intrigued as everyone else.

The antelope was not offended. She shrugged. 'Waited till everyone had gone home. Went into his office with a bottle of champagne and some cushions.'

She finished her cocktail and replaced the empty glass with a full one from a passing waiter. She did not stop talking. She did not even look at the tray. Just identified the slim glass stem by touch alone.

Experience, thought Zoe in unwilling admiration. *Drinks, men—she can handle the lot.*

'Hey, you only live once,' Banana went on. 'That's what I told him.'

Abby shook her head, mock astonished. 'How did he manage to hold out?'

'You tell me,' said Banana, unaware of mockery. 'I think he must be afraid of his emotions. Or women.'

Abby choked. Even Zoe, who had only a few weeks' acquaintance with Jay Christopher to judge by, boggled a bit.

Banana noticed that she was being teased at last. 'Well?' she challenged them. *'Well?'*

Abby flung up her hands. 'Pass. I'd have said that Jay was pretty enthusiastic about women. But maybe he's over-compensating.'

'Now you're being ridiculous,' Banana said loftily.

The party was getting noisy. The band was setting up. Banana reached for her third margarita, gave them both a vague smile, and limboed off in the direction of Tom Skellern.

Abby looked after her with amazement. 'What is she like? Cushions and champagne! I'm surprised Jay didn't have a seizure laughing at her.'

'Er—yes.'

'You wouldn't think she was a kid on her first date. Someone should tell her that grown-up men like to do their own hunting.'

Zoe tensed. *Here we go again,* she thought. *Performance Zoe, you're on stage again.*

'And not get their prey too soon,' she said lightly.

They exchanged world-weary looks and Abby laughed. Another one successfully convinced, thought Zoe, wondering why she bothered.

Yet it was so easy. That was the interesting thing about really sophisticated people. They had their own rules. If you were used to living a lie anyway, you picked up what new people expected *fast.* There was not a single person at the Culp and Christopher party who would have noticed that there was any difference between Zoe Brown and themselves.

Except Zoe Brown.

She danced and circulated and laughed at the in-jokes tirelessly. She was pleased with her performance.

Jay even congratulated her. 'You,' he told her, doing that full spotlight smile thing again, 'are one of my better discoveries. Come and dance with me, Discovery.'

He took her onto the floor for an energetic bop. He did not touch her—much. But he made her feel as if she was dancing with an expert. And that she was an expert, too.

When the music modified into a slow dance he returned her to a stool at the bar and summoned the overworked barman. By sheer force of personality, as far as Zoe could tell.

'That's a good trick,' she said dryly.

His eyes glinted. 'Isn't it? He knows a good customer when he sees one. What are you drinking?'

'Fizzy water,' said Zoe firmly.

She was intending to stay with Suze in her Kensington pad tonight. That meant going home on the night bus. She had stopped swigging alcohol an hour ago. The bus was fine, but you needed your wits about you, given the way it swayed as it whipped through the traffic-free streets. She had slept through the stop outside Suze's elegant street several times before she'd learned that. These days she paced her party drinking carefully.

He did not try and talk her out of it. He gave the order, asking for a glass of red wine for himself, she saw.

'Abby tells me you put this party together on your own,' he told her. 'Good work.'

Zoe accepted the compliment without excitement. 'I have a younger brother and sister. I can do parties.'

And how true that was! Well, other people's parties anyway.

He did not pick up that there was anything wrong. He said enthusiastically, 'You certainly can. And Molly didn't suspect a thing.'

On the dance floor Molly di Paretti was slow-dancing

dreamily with the man she was going to marry. She looked as if she belonged in his arms, and they both knew it.

'She looks happy, doesn't she?' Zoe hadn't meant to sound wistful. Hadn't known she even felt wistful until she heard some note in her voice that shouldn't have been there. Not if she was having this great time that she was telling herself she was.

Jay must have heard it, too. He cocked his head.

'Don't go broody on me, Discovery,' he said in mock alarm.

Zoe pulled herself together. 'Broody? Me? Nonsense. I'm a party girl.'

He laughed, clearly convinced. And delighted about it.

His next words told her why. 'Yes, Suze told me your men don't last long. Never felt the urge to pair-bond?'

Zoe did not allow herself to wince. She said carefully, 'I just like to keep my options open.'

'You're a girl after my own heart.'

'So I hear,' she said acidly.

He might have turned down Barbara Lessiter. He might outlaw inter-office relationships. But everyone knew that he was a serial flirt. Even if the battling blondes hadn't been willing to pour out all the gossip Zoe would have worked it out from his press cuttings.

Every time he gave a speech he got his photograph in the paper. In every photograph, as far as she could see, he was escorting a different woman. All beautiful, all elegant. And all different.

According to Isabel of Human Resources, he had just dumped the latest girlfriend, too. Apparently she was a television gardening expert who was unusually gorgeous and had been getting stacks of fan mail ever since she'd walked into a hosepipe spray by mistake.

Poppy, bristling with secretarial discretion, had said that she did not know anything about that, implying the reverse.

Isabel had ignored her. 'She asked him for a commitment and he walked. She's absolutely broken-hearted,' she'd told the ladies' rest room.

Poppy had sniffed. 'Probably just had her head turned by the publicity. They never lived together, you know.'

Then she'd looked annoyed with herself for having betrayed so much.

'No, he never lets a woman get that close,' Isabel had agreed, restraining her triumph, but only just. 'Doesn't even stay the whole night, they say.'

Silence had fallen. They'd all shivered. The sheer aridity of it had chilled them all. Poppy and Isabel had exchanged half-ashamed glances, their rivalry momentarily overtaken.

Every woman there was thinking the same thing, thought Zoe. Every single one of them was thinking, There but for the grace of God go I.

So now she looked at Jay with unflattering steadiness.

'Hey,' he said mock alarmed. 'I'm no Bluebeard. I just don't make promises I can't keep.'

Zoe recognised that. She nodded. 'Nor do I,' she said fairly.

'There you are, then. We're the same, you and I.'

She bit back self-mocking laughter. *If only he knew!* 'I doubt it.'

'Oh, but we are. And the world envies us. It's the twenty-first century metropolitan dream.'

'Life as one long party?' she said sceptically.

He said coolly, 'Recreational sex and no responsibilities. That's what everyone wants really. The pair-bonders—' he nodded at Molly, now rubbing her cheek against her George's shoulder '—are the oddballs.'

Zoe looked across at them almost angrily. 'Is it being an oddball to be honest about your feelings?'

Jay studied her curiously. 'I don't tell lies about feelings. I—'

She snapped her attention back to him. She was shaking with an odd sort of grieving anger. 'Set the rules?' she supplied sweetly. 'No sex in the office. No commitments outside it. You're the sort of man who thinks that if he doesn't stay the night he's made the terms of the contract clear.'

His eyebrows twitched together.

'You've been listening to gossip,' he said, perfectly pleasantly. But suddenly he wasn't laughing any more.

Zoe could have kicked herself. But she was not a liar. Well, not about that sort of thing. And she was not a coward, either. She lifted her chin.

'Is gossip wrong, then?'

There was a pause. The party noises screeched on all around them. But Zoe had the distinct impression Jay was not hearing them. His high cheek-boned face looked suddenly pinched, as if he were cold. Or in pain.

'No,' he said at last, curtly.

She spread her hands. *Case proved*, they said, as clearly as words.

That was when Banana Lessiter staggered out of the gyrating crowd and made an unsteady beeline for Jay.

'Oh, Lord,' said Jay under his breath.

'I don't know what you're worried about,' Zoe said maliciously. 'I don't think she's into pair-bonding in a big way. She doesn't even work for you any more.'

'That's what worries me,' said Jay. He looked harassed. But the acid-bitten look had gone. 'Sorry, but you're on your own in this one. I've fought her off twice so far this evening. This is where the true gentleman takes evasive action.'

Smooth as an eel, he slid among the dancers. By the time Banana got to the bar he was not even visible in the crowd.

'Where's he gone?' she demanded, slurring a little.

'Evasive manoeuvres,' said Zoe truthfully.

'But I wan' him to dance with me.'

'I think he sort of guessed that.'

The girl looked at her, uncomprehending. 'Dance,' she said, and smacked her fist on the bar. 'Dance. Dance. Dance.' With every thump of her fist she swayed a little bit further from the vertical.

'I rather doubt it,' said Zoe. 'Why don't you sit down and have a coffee?' She waved at the barman, who was deep in conversation and not looking. 'And a glass of water. Several glasses.'

Banana seemed to think well of the idea. She began to

hoist herself onto one of the tall bar stools. And then just
seemed to give up midway. For half a second it looked as
if she might make it, getting half a buttock onto the seat.
But then gravity and two spaghetti legs took over. She put
her hand to head and folded up as neatly as a concertina.

Zoe was off her bar stool before she knew it. She pulled
Banana clear of the fallen bar stool and turned her on her
side. She had another go at attracting the attention of the
barman. But, crouching on the floor, she had even less success.

To her surprise, Jay arrived, speeding out of the crowd as
if he was on rollerskates.

'What's wrong? Has she taken something?' He felt her
forehead. 'Clammy.'

Zoe had seen this before. She had seen Harry through
more than one encounter with serious alcohol while her
mother watched old videos in her room.

'Too much to drink, I guess. She was swigging back mar-
garitas earlier.'

'Damn. She told me it was the first time she had had them.
I should have realised and stopped her.'

Across the prone body, Zoe raised her eyebrows. 'Do you
think you could have? Banana seemed pretty determined to
get her own way to me.'

He had that cold look back. 'Yes, I could.' He sounded
angry. More with himself than anyone else, she thought.
'Too late to think about that now, though. What she needs
is water. Then hospital, I suppose. Just in case she really
has drunk enough to make this alcohol poisoning.' He had
more success with the barman. 'Hey, Derek. Chuck us over
a jug of water.'

The barman did.

Jay propped the girl up while Zoe dribbled water between
her lips. Remembering Harry, flopping and incapable at fifteen, she massaged the girl's throat to make her swallow.
Eventually her eyelids began to flutter and she moaned.

The barman was hanging over them by then, along with
several of the other guests.

Jay took charge. 'Nothing to worry about, guys. Party on. I'll see she gets home safe.' And then, when they had gone back to the dancing, he said quietly, 'Call us a cab, will you, Derek? Zoe, can you help me with her?'

'Sure.'

It was gone three when they got her into the Accident and Emergency Department of a big London teaching hospital. The waiting room was almost empty. A weary-eyed triage nurse assessed Banana's state and whipped her straight into a cubicle. Unpleasant noises ensued.

Jay grimaced. 'Looks like we got here just in time.'

'At least if she's sick they won't have to pump her stomach,' said Zoe practically.

That surprised a choke of laughter out of him. 'Tell me, do you always look on the bright side?'

'No point in doing anything else.'

The receptionist at the glass-walled desk beckoned them over. 'Just a few details…'

Between them they did not know much. But then Zoe had the idea of looking through the girl's sequined evening purse. It contained her small pocket diary and gave her home address and assorted details, including her blood group and the fact that she had no allergies.

'Pity she didn't remind herself that alcohol was poison at the same time,' said Zoe acidly.

'Oh, I don't know.' He was maddeningly tolerant. 'She's just young and inexperienced.'

'Huh!' That caught her on the raw. She said unwarily, 'Still, I suppose it's better than being old and inexperienced.'

'This will teach her a valuable lesson—'

Another nurse was coming towards them.

'Can you tell me something about her? And this party tonight? When did she last eat? Is she likely to have taken recreational drugs?'

Jay shook his head. 'Not at any party of mine.'

'But maybe someone brought something that you didn't know about—'

'These guys work for me. They wouldn't risk it.'

Looking at the set of his mouth, Zoe found she believed him.

So did the nurse, evidently. 'Well, it could just be too much to drink. I'll tell the doctor.' She disappeared.

Zoe suddenly began to feel immensely tired. As if he sensed it, Jay put an arm around her and steered her towards a bench against a wall. He pushed her gently onto it and stood back, looking down at her with concern.

'Like a coffee?'

She smiled palely. 'Out of a machine? No, thank you.'

'Snob,' he said peacefully. 'Does it matter if it's wet and warm?'

'I'm not cold.'

And she was not. The harsh hospital lighting made everything seem dreamlike. She was neither hot nor cold, nor awake nor asleep, but floating somewhere in the suspended animation of near exhaustion.

'You're wiped, aren't you?'

She closed her eyes. 'I've been up since five. How long before that means I've been awake for twenty-four hours?'

He was startled. '*Five?* Why on earth—?'

'My brother has finished his exams. He's got himself a summer job. Guiding field trips for schoolchildren. He'd never have got himself out of the house if I hadn't. Afterwards I couldn't go back to sleep. So I did some housework.'

'And then you ran around preparing my Venice paper all day. And ran the party all night. Topping it off with a crisis.' He sounded remorseful. 'Poor old Discovery. You really are a tower of strength, aren't you?'

Zoe pulled a face. 'You really know how to flatter a girl.'

He shook his head. 'No flattery. I told you. I tell the truth.'

And quite suddenly it was all too much for her. All the deceit and the games and the feeling of everything getting away from her. She just didn't want it any more. She was so *tired* of it.

She said baldly, 'Well, I don't.'

He went very still.

'I've not been telling the truth so long that when I try I can't do it.'

Zoe tipped her head back against the wall. The harsh light made her eyelids ache. She stared at the ceiling almost dreamily. She felt as if she were in free fall, as if all the conventions and pleasant, safe habits of every day had fallen away. All the rules, too.

She said in a flat voice, 'Don't run away with the idea that you know one single thing about me. You don't.'

Jay sat down on the bench beside her, carefully not touching her. But she could feel him watching.

'Want to tell me about it?' he said quietly.

And quite suddenly she did. Well, she wanted to tell *someone*.

There was no reason in the world why she should tell Jay, of course. She didn't know him. What she did know she didn't like. He was serial flirt with a tough break-up technique and no conscience. Or that was what they said. It seemed to be true. He was the last person in the world she would have expected to confide in.

But the small hours, the nearly empty waiting area, and those fierce lights seemed to have got her spaced out quite as much as any recreational drug would have done.

He was also her boss and the owner of Culp and Christopher. Which meant he paid her salary. You didn't tell things you wouldn't tell—hadn't told—your best friend to a man like that, did you?

Of course you didn't. It was crazy.

Knowing it was crazy, Zoe watched a fly walk across the ceiling towards one of the panels of white light and said idly, 'You remember those oddballs we were talking about earlier?'

'Lovebirds and pair-bonders?' he said in a still voice. 'Are you telling me you're secretly married, Discovery?'

A little laugh shook her.

'No. Odder than that. Sorry, Jay, you've got a *real* weirdo on your hands this time. I'm a virgin.'

CHAPTER SIX

JAY stared at her. She did not look at him. Her eyes were fixed dreamily on the ceiling. She looked tired to death. But she did not look as if she was drunk. Or lying.

He said cautiously, 'Is this a wind-up?' Of course she could have gone mad. 'You're telling me you're—er—untouched by human hand?'

Zoe's tired eyes lit with a rueful smile. 'Yup. That's about the size of it.'

Jay saw the smile with relief. Well, at least she wasn't completely barking yet. He thought about what she had said for several moments.

At last he said, 'Why?'

She avoided his eyes. It did not take much to work out that she was embarrassed. Covering it well, but embarrassed all the same.

Another argument for her sanity, judged Jay. He thought fast. Undoubted sanity made her claim all the more odd.

She was gorgeous. She was funny. She was sensible. She *could* not be a virgin. Not in metropolitan London in the twenty-first century.

She saw his disbelief. Her eyes slid away from his. 'I suppose I just—never got round to it.'

'Ah.' Curiouser and curiouser. 'But actually I meant—why tell *me*?'

She flushed faintly. 'Oh. Sorry. That.' She considered. 'You said, *Want to tell me about it?* People don't usually say that to me,' she said simply.

Jay stared. 'What?'

'I don't have crises. My friends and family have lots. So I'm the one who listens.'

He nodded slowly. 'Makes sense.'

It didn't. It had to be a lot more complicated than that. But now was not the time to point it out. Not if he wanted her to carry on confiding.

Jay was astonished at how much he wanted her to confide in him.

She gave a rueful laugh. 'You're kind, aren't you?' She sounded surprised.

'Is that so unbelievable?' said Jay, wounded. Then, hurriedly, as she opened her mouth, 'Don't answer that.'

She smiled, more easily this time. 'Well, you have to admit, you did warn me against—er—intimacy. You said it was a sacking offence.'

'I didn't mean you weren't allowed to tell me things.'

'Didn't you?' Her eyes were shadowed. 'But that's the start of intimacy, isn't it? Telling someone something private. Something—special. Something you don't want to tell the world.'

Was that she what she had done? Told him something she didn't want to tell the world?

Yes, he thought. Suddenly he felt ten feet tall.

Aloud, he said, 'When I warned you off, I'm afraid I was thinking of something a bit more basic. It included sending me overheated e-mails and trying to get my clothes off.'

'Oh!'

He smiled at her, straight into her eyes, the way he always did to women who moved him. 'As long as you keep your hands to yourself, you can tell me anything you want to.'

But she wasn't noticing the penetrating smile. She was too busy picking over her own part in the conversation.

She shook her head ruefully. 'It doesn't begin to make sense. Why on earth would I start unloading on a man who pays my salary? It's not only unprofessional, it's a quick and easy way to talk myself out of a job.'

He realised, suddenly, that he had not been thinking of her as an employee for hours. Even before she had dropped her confiding bombshell. Certainly he would never have said, *Want to tell me about it?* to Barbara Lessiter. Or anyone else in the office, probably.

It started another idea running. Not a welcome one.

'Do you *want* to talk yourself out of a job?'

'Oh.' Zoe looked astonished. 'No, of course not. I like what I do. I like helping Abby and Molly and Tom. I like doing your research. I was even wondering if there might be a chance of a permanent job—' She broke off, flushing deeper. 'No, I didn't mean that. Hell, I'm being stupid to-night.'

She jumped up and walked about the overlit room for a bit.

She was making a valiant attempt to curb it but she looked really upset. He saw that she was biting her lip and she was frowning.

Jay did not say anything. But he was relieved that she did not want to leave him. Hugely relieved. He was not quite sure why. It seemed out of all proportion.

Though Zoe Brown was good at her job, no question. One of the best they'd ever had, in fact. But even so—when had he last cared enough about whether someone joined the firm to hold his breath in case they turned him down?

He did not like the implications of that. He put it out of his mind. Now was the time to address himself to immediate problems, he thought. That was what he was good at: problem-solving. He brought his cellphone out of his pocket and went into practical mode.

Eventually Zoe stopped pacing and came and stood in front of him. She looked oddly young and brave, in her tired party gear.

'I'm sorry. This is the last time and place to start hustling for a job. I apologise,' she said formally.

He was not going to let her see his relief. Of course he wasn't. Especially as he was not sure where it came from. He didn't share things he didn't understand.

Instead he gave her one of his best knock-'em-dead smiles. Not the one for women who moved him. The one for women he wanted—needed—to charm.

'I agree. We'll talk about the job in the office.'

He meant, *And now we'll talk about you and your ex-*

traordinary announcement. Only she took it as a rebuke. She hardly seemed to notice the high-voltage charm. Instead, she looked away.

'Okay,' she said in a constrained voice.

Then the nurse came back with the doctor. And it was too late to explain that he hated the idea of her leaving.

They were intending to keep Ms Lessiter in for observation for twenty-four hours, they said. They thought it was just the drink, but they weren't quite sure what was going on. And as they could find her a bed—for once—they would run some more tests in the morning.

Jay nodded. 'And after that? Will she need to be looked after?'

The doctor grinned. 'My guess is that she'll have the mother and father of a hangover and the ward staff will give her hell. Apart from that she should be fine. This is just a precaution.'

Jay nodded. 'Keep me posted.' He fished out one of his business cards. 'If there's anything wrong I will get in touch with her family. But they don't live in London. And I don't see much point in letting them know their daughter has been partying too hard, do you? Not if that's all it is.'

The nurse took the business card.

'So you're not—er—her partner?'

'Former employer,' said Jay briefly. 'And—before you ask—I'm not doing cold compresses and warm drinks for Banana Lessiter. It wouldn't be safe. If she needs nursing I'll pay for it. But that's where my responsibility stops.'

The nurse looked rather shocked, but the doctor laughed. 'It shouldn't come to that. But call tomorrow and she can tell you herself.'

Jay hesitated. 'Can we see her?'

'If you like. She's making sense of a sort.'

She was making enough sense to rear up from her hospital trolley and fling herself onto Jay's breast.

'Take me home. I wanna take your clothes off...'

Zoe blenched, and even the tolerant doctor looked taken

aback. Only Jay was unmoved. He detached the girl's indecently busy hands without fuss.

'We've been through this before,' he said calmly. 'Thanks, but no thanks.'

'But I wanna—'

'Got it,' said Jay. 'You want. I don't. No room for negotiation on this one. Sorry and all that.'

The doctor looked at him with admiration bordering on awe. 'She does this often?'

Jay stepped back and checked the fastenings of his clothes. 'Couple of times. She hasn't been tanked out of her head before,' he added fair-mindedly. 'But she wasn't listening to reason, either. The only thing is to say no and keep on saying it as you back out of the door.'

They exchanged a look of total masculine comprehension.

'I'll bear it in mind,' said the doctor. He sounded as if he meant it.

Banana let out a wail like a thwarted six-year-old. The nurse urged her down again, repressing a smile.

'Relax. A porter will be taking you up to the ward in a few minutes.'

Jay looked at Zoe. 'Well, that seems to let us off the hook. Coming?'

She said goodbye to Banana, who ignored her, and followed him out of the hospital.

'I'll have to find the bus stop for—'

'I'll take you home, of course,' he said, shocked.

'And how are you going to do that?' she said dryly.

He stepped out of the brightly lit entrance. In the darkness an engine switched on. From the shadows a car detached itself and slid up to the kerb in front of them. Zoe stared at it, half-astonished, half-annoyed.

'Don't tell me. You're a magician.'

Jay shook his head. 'Just a guy with a cellphone and a friendly limo service,' he told her solemnly.

'A friendly limo service that follows you around after dark?'

He laughed aloud at that. 'No. They already knew I'd

need a car some time tonight. I just called them when you were pacing around back there.'

'Oh.'

He opened the door behind the chauffeur for her. 'Where am I taking you?'

She gave him the address.

It was not what he was expecting. Annoyed with this further failure on the part of his office administration, he raised his eyebrows. 'I thought you lived in North London?'

He saw that she was surprised. 'I do. But when I know I'm going to be out really late I beg a bed for the night from a friend. No taxi driver in the known world wants to go to Muswell Hill after midnight.'

'Ah.'

He closed the door behind her and gave the address to the driver. Then went round the car and got in beside her. It was a big car. He had room to stretch out his long legs. There was also plenty of room on the back seat. And if Zoe did not exactly huddle in the corner—well, she made sure that there were several cubic feet of air space between their bodies.

Jay did not like that.

'Relax,' he said acidly. 'I'm not going to sack you just because our shoulders happen to touch.'

She tensed. He could feel it. But not because she was cowed.

'That's a relief,' she retorted. 'Is it all right if I have it in writing?'

Jay smiled to himself in the dark. That was his Zoe, coming out fighting.

'On your desk Monday morning,' he assured her.

He stretched comfortably, letting his arm extend along the back of her seat. She sent him a sideways look. He caught the turn of her head. 'I'm counting on it,' she said coolly.

And she turned in the seat so that she was almost facing him and his fingers did not reach her shoulder.

Oh, yes, she was fighting her corner, all right. Jay watched her as they flashed through intermittent light from the darkened streets.

'So who's the friend?' he said lazily.

He felt her jump. He saw the bright glint of eyes before her lashes veiled them.

'Oh—Suze.'

'Ah, Susan. Of course.' It was stupid to be relieved that the friend's flat she went back to did not belong to man. It had nothing to do with him who she dated, after all. But he was relieved. He couldn't deny it.

'She's my oldest friend. She brought you to our party,' she reminded him.

'I remember. She must be quite a bit older than you.'

Zoe sighed. 'I'm twenty-three. Suze is twenty-four.'

'Ah, but Susan was born forty. A sophisticated forty.' He added thoughtfully, 'Which makes her about five years younger than my friend Hermann. Otherwise I'd be worried by the age difference.'

Zoe chuckled involuntarily. 'I know what you mean.'

He looked at her curiously. He wished he could make out her expression. 'I wouldn't have thought you had much in common.'

'You'd be wrong. We went to school together. We've seen each other through a lot.'

'Ah.'

He badly wanted to say, *Does she know you're a virgin, too?* But he couldn't. Not with Petros sitting in front.

'In fact, I shared the flat with her for a few months after college. But then—' She stopped. 'Well, stuff happened.'

He was intrigued. But Petros stopped him pursuing that one, too. Next time, Jay thought savagely, he was going to bring his own car.

Zoe leaned forward. 'Just here, on the left. Leave me on the corner, if you like. It's only a step.'

'I always see my dates indoors,' said Jay firmly.

'But I'm not—' She stopped, gave a quick look at the back of Petros's head, and subsided. 'Thank you,' she muttered.

Did she not want to sully his reputation for being irresistible? Jay was touched—and rather annoyed. He had been to a lot of parties with women like Susan Manoir. He knew what the men there were like. He did not want Zoe Brown to think of him as just another high-gloss stud, he found.

The chauffeur parked at the end of the street. Jay leaned forward and touched his shoulder.

'Wait. I may be a few minutes.'

'Sure thing.'

Jay walked Zoe to a solid redbrick Edwardian block. She brought out a key, turned to him with her hand out.

'Thank you for seeing me home.'

He ignored the hand. Instead he took the key from her. 'Inside the door.'

She raised her eyebrows. 'I'm not going to be mugged by a mad overnight cleaning lady. That sort of thing doesn't happen in apartment blocks with carpeted corridors.'

'It won't if you're not on your own,' he agreed. He unlocked the door and waved her in ahead of him. 'Go on.'

She hesitated a moment. Then shrugged. 'You have an over-developed sense of responsibility.'

'So Susan gives you a key,' he said as they got into the old brass-studded elevator.

'She keeps wanting me to move back in.'

He could ask now. 'Why did you move out in the first place? You obviously still get on well. Didn't like her boyfriends?'

Zoe looked startled. 'Of course not.'

'Well, then?'

The elevator arrived at Suze's floor. The ceiling lights were dimmed discreetly. They walked down thick-piled carpet. It was all very expensive and absolutely silent. They stopped at the door.

'Well?' persisted Jay.

Zoe rubbed her eyes tiredly. There was something about him that was implacable, somehow. She gave a deep sigh, stopped rubbing her eyes, and gave up her attempt at family discretion.

'There was trouble at home. My young brother was run-ning wild. My mother needed reinforcements.'

She unlocked the door. It led straight into the main room. It was in total darkness, the furniture just ghostly shapes. From the kitchen there was the quiet hum of a fridge de-frosting itself. Apart from that the place was silent.

Jay did not wait to be invited in. He pushed the door closed behind him and hunted down a table-lamp without much difficulty.

'Is Susan in?' he asked softly, switching it on.

'Don't expect so.'

Zoe slid off her strappy sandals and padded over the pol-ished wooden floor into the internal corridor. She was back inside a minute.

'No. Her bedroom door's open and there's no one there. She's either still clubbing or she's gone off to meet Hermann somewhere. They were talking about Paris.'

'Good,' said Jay. He stopped whispering. 'You can give me a coffee and tell me the rest of this saga.'

Zoe was genuinely taken aback. 'You can't drink coffee at this hour.'

Jay grinned. 'Watch me.'

She shrugged. 'Fine, if that's what you want. But you'll never sleep.'

Jay's eyes gleamed. 'You don't know me well enough to say that.'

Something flickered in Zoe's stomach at the careless in-timacy of that. It implied that she might—that she *could*—

She did not want to think about that. She flung up her hands. 'Okay. Okay. Your choice! Your nightmares! Just don't blame me.'

'I won't.'

She went into the small kitchen area and filled the kettle. Jay followed her, and sat down on one of the pine chairs at the table. He watched her rummage deep in the cupboard under the microwave until she found a small cafetière.

'You do know this place well, don't you?' he said thoughtfully.

Zoe straightened, reaching into the fridge for a packet of ground coffee. 'I live in hopes I'll move back one day,' she said unwarily.

'When you're no longer needed as reinforcement?'

'Yes.'

He nodded slowly. 'Your father is dead? Abroad? In prison?'

Zoe put down the foil pack so suddenly that coffee skittered across the pristine work surface like fingerprint powder. *'Prison?'*

'He's the natural reinforcement,' he pointed out. 'Not you. If he's not around, there has to be a really good reason.'

She gave a harsh choke of laughter. 'There is. She's called Saffron. Nearer my age than Mum's, with a heart like a calculator.'

Jay digested this in silence.

She shook her head. 'Damn. Why did I say that?'

Jay looked at her flushed face as she shovelled the spilt coffee into the cafetière with jerky movements. She seemed really furious with herself.

He said gently, 'Because you needed to, at a guess.'

Zoe put down coffee and cafetière, and stood back. She was looking at the mess on the work surface with something like horror. As he watched she put up both hands and pushed her hair back, pulling so tight he could see the pale skin stretching over he temples. Her hands were shaking.

'I don't know what's got into me tonight,' she said in a suffocated voice. 'I never say things like that. Mum always wants me to slag off Saffron and I won't.' She whipped round, hands on the work-top behind her, and glared at him. 'Did you put something in my drink?'

Jay raised his eyebrows. 'Oh, sure,' he said dryly. 'I always carry truth serum with me.'

At that, she smiled reluctantly. 'Sorry. Stupid of me. Just that tonight—'

'Yes,' he said softly. 'Tonight has been strange.'

If she had been sitting opposite him at the kitchen table he would have taken her hand then. But she wasn't. She was

three feet away, staring at him as if she could not imagine
how she had let him in here.

'Weird. I'd never have thought of having coffee with you
after midnight in a million years.'

'Gee, thanks, Zoe. You're just great for the ego.'

She brushed aside his wounded ego without apology.
'Well, not like this, I mean.'

The thought flittered across his brain that he had never
before sat across a kitchen table at four in the morning with
a woman who worked for him. Still less asked her to tell
him her life story. He dismissed it.

'So, what else do you need to get off your chest?' he said
lightly. 'Lives at home. Doesn't want to. Dreams of getting
away...'

'It's not like that—' she began. But then the kettle boiled
and she had to concentrate on making the coffee.

Jay sniffed the rich air appreciatively. 'Kaldi, you're my
man.'

Zoe looked up, confused. 'What?'

'Kaldi. Ethiopian shepherd. Supposed to have discovered
coffee.'

'You mean it wasn't Sir Walter Raleigh?'

'Hey, English pirates didn't discover all the recreational
drugs of choice,' he said, reaching for the cafetière.

Zoe searched a cupboard, failed to find mugs, and opened
the dishwasher. She hooked out a couple of elegant black
and gold mugs, sniffed them, decided they were clean, but
ran them under the hot tap just to be certain.

'High housekeeping skills,' murmured Jay, entertained.

Zoe was practical. 'No, but I know Suze. I don't want to
add salmonella to this evening's new experiences.'

She banged the mugs down on the table between them.
He pressed the filter down through the coffee sludge. Zoe
was turning back to the fridge, but for some reason she
stopped, mesmerised. He was doing it very, very slowly.
With relish, even. Her colour rose inexplicably.

'You look as if you've done that before.'

He gave her his wicked up-and-under look. 'My speciality.'

She swallowed. 'Yes. Well. Er—milk?'

He declined. Flustered, she spent a great deal longer than was necessary poking around in the fridge for juice. By the time she came up for air he had set a chair for her opposite him.

'So talk!' he commanded, taking the juice away from her.

She sank onto the chair, watching him pour first her juice then his coffee.

'That poor man outside in the car—'

'Believe me, he won't be complaining. The longer I stay out, the more he earns. At triple time,' Jay told her, amused. *'Talk.'*

She huffed a bit. 'I don't think I can,' she said candidly. 'I don't know how I came to tell you anything in the first place.

'So you said. I guess it's just timing. Look on me as your friendly neighbourhood busybody, if it helps. Pretend we're leaning on the back fence.'

She looked at him. He was devastatingly attractive, with his smooth dark hair faintly tumbled and those spectacular cheekbones.

Zoe's lips twitched. 'Oh, yes, I can just see the hairnet.'

'Hold that thought,' he said, unoffended. He drank some coffee. 'So run it past me again. You're twenty-three. Yet you still live at home. You look like a dream. Your friends all think you're a raver. You ought to be a raver. And yet you're a virgin.'

She stiffened. But his tone was so utterly dispassionate that all her defensiveness fell away from her. She bit her lip.

'Yes.'

'And,' said Jay shrewdly, 'you're not happy about it.'

Zoe winced.

His voice softened. 'Want to tell me why?'

'Well, like you said—everybody thinks I'm a raver.'

His brows twitched together. 'Don't understand.'

Zoe struggled to explain. 'I have friends. Good friends.

They think they know everything there is to know about me. And I've got this big secret—' She spread her hands eloquently. 'It's like I'm cheating. All the time.'

He shook his head, still bewildered. 'Cheating how?'

'Living a lie,' she said impatiently. 'And I've been doing it for *years*.'

'Ah. I think I begin to see.'

He swirled the coffee in his mug.

'Let's look at this another way. What was it that turned you off men? Something traumatic?'

Zoe sighed. 'There you go. That's why I've never told anyone. Nothing turned me off men,' she said impatiently. 'I'm not off men. Some of my best friends are men.'

'Well, then—'

'If I told Suze now, she'd think I'd suffered some big tragedy. Been beaten up or something. It's not true. No man's ever hurt me. No one's ever let me down. I just— never got round to sex.'

'Never got round to it?' Jay found he was speechless.

Defensiveness crept back. 'I was busy.'

'But what about all those men you know? Quite apart from your own hormones, what about the other side of the equation? They can't all have been busy, too?'

'Ah.' Zoe looked faintly uncomfortable. 'Well, you see, they all thought I'd got someone else.'

He shook his head. 'I can't get my head round this. How did they think you had someone else? How come you didn't have someone else?'

She shrugged. 'Our old friend timing, I suppose. My parents started to break up just as I was doing my first public exams. Then, when I was at university, I came home a lot because my brother and sister were still at school and—' She bit her lip. 'My mother went onto an alternative clock, making breakfast at midnight, that sort of thing. Someone had to keep the household fed and laundered.'

'Reinforcements,' he said, enlightened.

She flushed. 'If you like. Anyway, the boys at university all thought I had a boyfriend at home. And the boys at home—when I saw them—thought I had a boyfriend at college. So did my sister. And I always had plenty of friends who were men, sort of in the general crowd. So nobody noticed the difference.'

His eyebrows hit his hairline. 'But what about you?'

She looked surprised. 'I told you. I was busy.'

'Very few adolescent girls are so busy they fail to notice that they fancy the pants off the man of their dreams,' he said dryly.

She flushed deeper. 'Maybe I'm just cold hearted.'

'Do you think so?' he said ironically. 'Then what's all this about?'

He leaned forward and touched a gentle forefinger to the corner of her eye. It came away with a teardrop on the tip.

Zoe was horrified. She blinked rapidly.

'That just because I'm tired,' she said defiantly.

'And wound as tight as a spring about to break,' he agreed amiably.

She leaped up. 'No, I'm not. I'm nowhere near breaking point,' she said fiercely. 'Nowhere near. Do you hear me?'

He titled his chair back and looked at her ironically. 'Sure. That's why you're shouting, is it? So I can hear you?'

Zoe stopped dead, as if he had shot her.

She looked at his lounging body. Suddenly all the implications of the scene rose up and hit her in the face. This was a man who was so sexy his female staff e-mailed him love letters. They were alone in the flat while the stars glittered outside. She was young and attractive and unattached. What was more, she—in his phrase—fancied the pants off him.

And they were on opposite sides of the kitchen table while she shouted and he glared.

Suze would have been in his arms by now. It was too much! Any minute now she *was* going to cry, Zoe thought. She stumbled over to the counter and tore off a great wad of kitchen paper. She blew her nose loudly.

Jay got to his feet.

'Hey,' he said, touched. 'It's no big deal.'

'I'm *tired*,' said Zoe again loudly. She blew her nose harder.

He skirted the table and put an arm round her. She resisted for a moment. But he was strong and, heck, half of her wanted to feel what it was like to be in his arms anyway. She let him pull her against his body. It felt like a rock.

Or, no, like sun-warmed earth, solid and fertile. She buried her face in his shoulder for a moment. It did not feel natural—she stood awkwardly, all elbows and knees, and her feet were in the wrong place. But he did not seem to notice. And he smelled like heaven.

Only a moment, she promised herself. She rubbed her face against the linen jacket a little, savouring the scent of sandalwood with a deep underlying note of healthy male skin. She hoped the movement was unobtrusive. *Pathetic, or what?*

And if she was going to be that pathetic, she might as well go the whole hog.

'Okay,' she said into his jacket. 'So what do I do?'

Jay smiled. She could feel him smile, even with her face against his shoulders. Did he smile with his collarbone, for heaven's sake? How much did she not know about men's bodies that she had never realised?

'Back fence gossips don't give advice,' he said smugly.

He put his other arm round her. Purely for comfort, of course, thought Zoe. And she had been held lots of times. Kissed lots of times. Only somehow she had never felt so naked in a man's arms before. Crazy, when she was still dressed from head to toe. *But he knows more about me than anyone else in the world,* she thought.

It was a sobering thought. It brought her upright. Though it felt like death to leave that unemotional embrace.

She grabbed some more kitchen paper and blotted her eye make-up carefully.

'Sorry. That was stupid.' She sniffed. Then said in a stronger tone, 'You're not just a busybody. You're not my therapist.'

He frowned quickly. 'Heaven forfend.'

'So tell me like a friend.'

Jay was surprised. He hesitated for a moment. Then shrugged.

'Fine. If you want the truth, as a friend, I think you're making a fuss about nothing.'

Zoe took some time to assimilate that.

'So why doesn't it feel like nothing?'

'That's what interests me, too,' he said. She could feel him watching her. 'What does it feel like?'

'A bloody great mountain range with me on the wrong side of it,' she said explosively.

Jay's eyes narrowed. 'The unknown is always intimidating.'

'You don't understand,' said Zoe exasperated. 'It's not just that I haven't done it. It's that all my friends think I have.'

'So do it,' he said, bored.

'How?' she almost screamed.

'Tell one of all those men that there's a vacancy,' he advised. His eyes glittered like some particularly satanic polished stone. 'Does it really matter who?'

It did, but Zoe did not know why. Or how to explain it. Or how to defend her sentimentality from this super-sophisticate's derision. He probably saw this as a strictly practical problem. He would have no patience with her quivering vulnerability.

Get a grip, Zoe.

She muttered, 'Probably not, if it's happened thousands of time before. But first time—if you don't know your way around at my age, it's sort of embarrassing. I'm not a freak, and I'm not a victim of nameless tragedy.' She thought about it. 'Well, actually, yes, I am a freak, I suppose. But I'm not anti-sex. Just anti-embarrassment.'

There was a silence. Suddenly Zoe realised that the middle of the night was *cold*.

'If you really want my advice,' said Jay in a level voice, 'and strictly as a disinterested bystander, I'd say find a stranger, do it once, and forget about it.'

She swallowed. 'That's easier said than done.'

'Oh, I don't know.' The hard voice sounded almost like an insult. As if he meant it to be an insult. 'What you need is something disposable. A lover to go.'

It hurt. Zoe did not know why, but it made her feel like a piece of trash. Boring trash, at that. Tears threatened again, shockingly. She bit down hard on her lower lip. She was not going to cry in front of Jay Christopher.

'Thank you for your advice,' she said coolly. 'I'll give it some serious thought. And now you really mustn't keep that poor driver waiting any more.'

She held out her hand again, firmly. This time he was not going to ignore it and talk his way into her confidence again.

But it seemed that this time he did not want to ignore it. He took her hand. Crushingly. Shook it twice, hard.

And then—

And then, he jerked her off balance and back into his hard arms. This time she had no time to think about elbows or feet or anything else. This time she had to concentrate on breathing.

It was a hard kiss. Not the sort of kiss you gave a girl who had just told you her most shameful secrets. Not a kiss you gave a girl you had made feel naked in your arms. Not a kind or gentle kiss at all.

'How can you?' choked Zoe, cut to the heart.

She hauled away from him, dashing her hand across her mouth as if she wanted to wipe away the memory of his touch. 'Why did you do that?' she said in despair.

He glittered down at her, his jaw rigid.

'Don't think you'll have a problem,' he drawled. He brushed his thumb across her lower lip, where it still throbbed. 'You can stop worrying about being cold. Not a chance.'

Zoe stood as if turned to stone. Jay waited a second or two, then gave a soft laugh.

He walked out before she could think of one single thing to say.

CHAPTER SEVEN

NEXT morning Jay went for a run. A long run on the Heath. He was furious with himself.

Why *had* he done that? Zoe was a member of his staff. Okay temporary. But that did not make any difference. He had his standards. Hell, he had sacked Barbara Lessiter for breaching them. And then, alone in the small hours with a woman he had known was tired to the point of exhaustion, he'd done exactly the same thing.

No, what he had done was worse. She had trusted him. And he'd betrayed that trust.

His feet pounded rhythmically on the rough grass. Later the sun would bake it dry, but at this hour of the morning he sent up little silver sparklers of dew with each footfall. Normally he would enjoy it. There were stages of his long-distance runs which were pure purgatory. But this piece of Heath, high and relatively flat, with the distant towers of the City shimmering in the dawn light, was balm to body and spirit. Usually.

Not this morning. He kept seeing Zoe scrubbing her hand across her mouth as if his kiss had contaminated her. And he lost focus.

A stitch knifed into him. Jay was used to running with pain. You just made your pace even, breathed regularly, and ran through it. In the end it went away. Not this morning.

He kept hearing himself say, 'What you need is…a lover to go.' He did not recognise the hard voice as his own. Yet he knew he had said it.

The pain intensified, as if someone was turning a stiletto in his side. He tried to breathe through it. It was no good. He stumbled. Nearly fell. Slowed to an uneven lurch.

107

Jay was enough of an expert to know that this was going to get him nowhere. He stopped dead, a hand to his side.

What was he going to do? Somehow he had to put it right. He wanted—no, he *needed*—to wipe out that look of betrayal. Zoe had such an expressive face, God help him.

He breathed with care until the pain subsided. Then he straightened slowly.

What was he thinking? What did it matter how expressive her face was? She was an employee. A temporary employee, sure. But still she worked for him. She could be as expressive as she liked. *It had nothing to do with him.*

And yet—he had not liked it when she'd first come to work for him and she had told him he'd never be a candidate. He went hot, remembering. No, he had not liked that at all. He had told himself it was all for the best. But he had called her in to his office every chance he had. Some of his excuses had been so thin he'd half expected her to challenge them, too.

Face it, Jay. You broke your own rules with Zoe Brown. And you did it long before she spilled out her secrets.

He was shaken. He did some stretches, carefully. Then he walked back to his house, frowning. He did not even try to break into a jog.

Okay, so he'd broken his own rules. Well, he would pay his own price. He would keep out of the office as much as possible. Certainly he would keep away from Zoe. When her contract was up—well, then he could think again. But until then he would just give her some space.

It cost him restless days and sleepless nights. He snapped at everyone. He jumped every time his mobile phone rang. He got a mountain of work done. And he bit the head off anyone who asked him what was wrong.

He scanned his e-mail hourly for messages from her. But when they came they were only about the Venice speech.

On Friday morning he gave up and went in to the office. He told himself it was to pick up the material he would need for the seminar. But he knew perfectly well that Poppy could have had the stuff biked round to his Hampstead house if he'd wanted. He didn't. He wanted the chance—just the chance—of seeing Zoe.

And his gamble paid off. Almost as soon as he was in the building, he saw her coming down the silver staircase with Abby and Molly di Paretti. The other two smiled broadly but Zoe would not meet his eyes. In fact she dodged round Molly and disappeared, while the Fab Ab buttonholed him.

'You've got a new wall ornament,' she said.

Jay was looking after Zoe's retreating figure. 'What?'

'The London Youth Clubs have sent you a presentation baseball bat,' said Abby. 'Along with an invitation to run in their All-Time Greats event in September.'

Jay wanted to follow Zoe so badly that it hurt. 'Why are you telling me this?'

Abby looked surprised. 'The Youth Club is my account. You gave it to me. I think it would be great if you did the run.'

'You know I don't compete any more,' he snarled. He took a step towards the door, in the direction that the girls had taken.

Abby took hold of his arm and made him face her. 'And I need to talk to you about the PR for *Lemon Sherbet Three*. The film company is having a row with the UK distributors.'

Jay gave up. 'We'll have a round up meeting at midday,' he said, resigned. 'Tell me then.'

She nodded. 'Boardroom. Noon. Got it.'

She sped away. As she got to the door he called, 'Ab—'

She turned warily. 'Yes?'

'Sorry I snapped.'

She gave him a kind smile. 'Don't worry about it. We all have off days.'

But when she got to Patisserie Patricia her smile had died.

'If you ask me, the Volcano is going to blow,' she said, sinking down behind a tall glass of iced coffee. 'Is that why you didn't want to talk to him, Zoe?'

Zoe seized the excuse thankfully. 'He's been getting mad at me. This Venice talk.'

'But you've done such a good job on getting all the ma-

terial together,' said Abby, indignant. 'You really saved his
bacon. It's not like Jay to ignore that. Is it, Molly? He's
always really nice if you do a good piece of work.'

Molly said slowly, 'I've never seen him like this.'

'Too right,' said Abby with feeling. 'I thought I wasn't
going to hold him off for you, Zoe. There was one point he
looked like he was going to pick me up and put me out of
the way.'

Zoe did not meet their eyes. 'The Venice talk must be
getting to him.'

'Garbage,' said Molly. 'He gives talks all the time.'

'Yes, but I don't think he's even started on it yet,' Zoe
said earnestly. 'And he's supposed to deliver it on Monday.'

'That would do it for me,' agreed Abby.

Molly said nothing. But she narrowed her eyes in a way
that made Zoe feel guilty. She did it again when later a
summons came from Jay's blonde PA.

'He wants to talk to you, Zoe,' Molly said, putting the
phone down. 'Better get up there now.'

Zoe went white.

Molly picked up the pile of cuttings and prints-offs in her
pending tray and slapped them into her arms. 'He probably
wants you to do a first draft of his speech,' she said with
emphasis. 'God knows, you've done everything else.'

Everything else? Zoe stared at her in wild suspicion. Were
her feelings for Jay Christopher written all over her face, for
heaven's sake?

'Keep your head down and don't say more than you have
to,' Molly advised, oblivious. 'Good luck.'

The advice was unnecessary. As soon as Zoe came face
to face with Jay across his impressive desk she was absolutely tongue-tied.

Where was Performance Zoe when you needed her? she
thought in despair.

Jay seemed to be preoccupied. He waved her into a seat
and concentrated on the papers in front of him for what felt
like hours. It was intimidating. It occurred to her that it was
meant to be intimidating, and her sense of justice reasserted

itself. After all, she was not the one who had laid hands on him first.

Zoe glared at the top of his head and began to feel a bit better.

She said acidly, 'Am I going to sit here all day, or would you like me to come back when you've finished the cross-word puzzle?'

Jay looked up at that, though he did not meet her eyes. He said abruptly, 'I owe you an apology.'

Zoe stared. 'What?'

'The last time we met I kissed you. I knew you didn't want it and I kissed you anyway. I had no right to do that. I'm sorry.'

It was what she had been saying to herself all week. *He had no right!* And now that he'd come right out and apol-ogised she felt—well, cheated.

'Guys don't normally apologise for kissing me.'

'I'm not a guy; I'm your employer. It was—inappropri-ate.'

'You know, you can sound so stuffy sometimes.'

He smiled faintly. 'Stuffy, maybe. It's still the truth. You work for me. That puts you off-limits. I shouldn't have for-gotten that.'

Zoe found her anger had evaporated. It was rather a lonely feeling. She had been talking to that anger all week.

She said sadly, 'I suppose I was inappropriate, too. Telling you all that about—'

'It didn't help,' agreed Jay. 'Turned up the volume on intimacy, I suppose you could say.'

She shook her head. 'It may have felt like that to you. To me, it was like spilling everything out to one of those late-night phone-in programmes on the radio.'

'A faceless voice in the dark? Gee, thanks.'

'Well, not faceless, maybe. But remote. And—'

'No come-back,' said Jay slowly. 'I'm strictly disposable in your life, aren't I?'

Did he sound hurt? Zoe could not believe it. Yet somehow

she felt ashamed. As if she had stamped on his feelings in pursuit of her own need to unload. She bit her lip.

'I think it was more that we had no history,' she said honestly.

He looked at her for a long moment. The heavy-lidded eyes were quite inscrutable. Then he leaned back in his chair.

'Explain,' he invited.

'You see, all my friends know me very well. If they find out I've been keeping this huge secret they will either not believe me or feel cheated. Maybe even both.'

'A stranger is safe because you have nothing to lose?' he said on a note of discovery.

'I suppose so.' She sounded subdued, even to her own ears. She rallied, trying to make a joke out of it. 'I guess I wanted you to turn into a psychiatrist and tell me what to do.'

He stared at her for a long minute, unblinking. 'I didn't think psychiatrists were supposed to give advice.'

'So what do they do?'

'Listen, I gather. Ask the right questions, hopefully.'

For some reason Zoe was outraged. She snorted. 'Money for old rope,' she muttered.

His mouth tilted suddenly. 'That sounds a bit harsh.'

Zoe waved that aside. Suddenly she was urgent. 'Okay. Forget the radio psychiatrist. What would you have said to me if I'd told you that as a friend?'

He raised his eyebrows. 'You mean, imagine we have a history?'

'Yes.'

He pondered. She saw him reach a conclusion. He hesitated for a moment. Then shrugged.

'Fine. I told you that night, if you remember. I gave you the full benefit of my considered advice then. You didn't,' he added with point, 'seem to appreciate it.'

She flushed. 'You said I was making a fuss about nothing.'

He had also said, *'Find a stranger, do it once and forget about it.'* But she wasn't going to think about that just now.

'I might have been harsh,' Jay allowed. He surveyed her watchfully. 'I think you have to ask yourself why you are making such a fuss. There's nothing to be ashamed of, after all. We all start out virgins.'

Zoe gave a startled little spurt of laughter, as if he had said something genuinely shocking.

'I never thought of that.'

'Well, hang on to it,' he advised.

'Yes, but—'

'And it doesn't matter what your friends think.'

'It matters what I think, though. And I think I'm a fraud.'

She had never said it so baldly, not even to herself. She fell silent, feeling sick.

Jay's expression told her nothing. He studied her as if she were an interesting specimen page for a long minute.

Then he said, 'Maybe you didn't go to bed with anyone because you weren't in love.'

'In love?' She snorted with derision. 'Now you're really thinking I'm nuts.'

'It is just conceivable.'

'No, it isn't.'

His eyes glinted. 'Many people think being in love is indispensable.'

Was he laughing at her? Zoe's chin came up and she glared at him, eye to eye.

'That didn't stop any of my friends,' she said deliberately. 'Did it stop you?'

His expression did not change. But somehow she knew that she had struck home. She could feel his withdrawal, though physically he did not move a muscle. The elegant body still lounged there as casually as if they were old, old friends who bared their souls to each other all the time.

'No,' he said at last. His lips barely moved. His voice was light, level. 'No, lack of love didn't stop me. Maybe it should have.'

Zoe looked ironic. 'Don't do as I do, do as I say? Thanks for the insight.'

He looked irritated. 'Look, this is no big deal. It's a just a physical thing you go through. Like—like the pain barrier when you're running. It's not the reason you do it, but it happens. You get through it.'

'Wow, sounds irresistible. Come to bed with me and I'll get through it.'

Jay grinned. But he said, 'I think you're looking at this the wrong way. For some men it would be a great compliment.'

'Yeah. The sad sickos who see virginity as a trophy. Like I'm going to do a deal with one of them.'

'We're not all like that. There are men for whom it would be—' he struggled to put his feeling into words '—a great sign of trust. Respect. Even love.'

Zoe looked at him oddly. 'Oh, yeah? Respect, huh? Do your girlfriends respect you?'

He stiffened. 'I hope so.'

'And how many of them have been virgins?'

'None, as far as I know.' He thought about it, and added involuntarily, 'God, I hope not. No, I'm sure not. I've never been—' He stopped.

'A sad sicko who sees it as a trophy?' supplied Zoe, half-weary, half-triumphant. 'See what I mean? Catch Twenty-two.'

He got up and began to move restlessly round the room. 'I don't believe it. There has to be a solution.'

'If there was, don't you think I'd have found it?' flashed Zoe. 'I've been pretending like this for five years. Ever since I was the last eighteen-year-old virgin in Muswell Hill. Short of a miracle, I'm stuck like this for life.'

He looked at her—the crop top, the slim thighs, the clear skin and clearer eyes—and said from the heart, 'That's ludicrous.'

'Yeah? You think so? Well, let me tell you it isn't. It's like the old Marx Brothers thing. I don't want to be a member of any club that would accept me. Any guy who is into deflowering virgins is someone I want to avoid like the plague.'

Jay said impatiently, 'So don't tell him.'

'Oh, great. That's a real sign of trust.'

He was getting annoyed. 'So there's no easy answer. How like life. There's going to be a tough answer somewhere, though. Go look for it.'

Zoe said with spurious affability, 'Do you know you do that all the time?'

'Do what?'

'Patronise me. We get into an argument and you're soon losing it. So you patronise me. The next time you do it I'll take that baseball bat off your wall and brain you with it. I swear I will.'

'You could always try sounder arguments,' he said lightly.

But Zoe had gone beyond the possibility of laughter. She jumped to her feet glaring.

'There you go again. Don't you dare patronise me ever again, you—you—you *spin doctor*.'

Jay blinked. 'Is that mean to be an insult?'

'Too right.'

He turned on her, his eyes glittering dangerously. 'Then let me tell you, I am very good at what I do.'

'Sure. Probably the best there is,' said Zoe viciously. 'Doesn't mean it's worth doing.'

He stopped pacing as if she had thrust a fist straight into his heart. 'At least I'm doing something,' he said very quietly. 'Not whingeing that life shouldn't be as it is.'

Her eyes widened in shock.

'Yes, you can hand it out, can't you?' said Jay, still in that same deadly quiet voice. 'You're allowed no holds barred, a pretty young thing like you. Doesn't matter who you hurt. God, I'm so tired of noisy women who don't give a stuff about anything except their own petty neuroses.'

Zoe was very pale. 'I'm sorry you think it's petty. I suppose in comparison with publicising *Lemon Sherbet Three* it must lack a certain global significance.'

Jay winced. 'I didn't mean that.'

She ignored him, going to the door a little blindly. 'But, as I keep trying to tell you—it's not a neurosis. It's a question of ethics.'

He snorted. 'Ethics, schmethics. It's a practical problem, pure and simple. All you need is a bit of courage to sort it out.'

She turned and met his eyes.

'Okay. Here's a solution. You know all there is to know about sex and you're not into trophies. You do it.'

They stared at each other. Equally appalled at what she had said. Equally silent.

Zoe was the first to break eye contact. Her smile was twisted.

'See? That's not just a practical problem. Is it?'

And she walked out.

Jay did not want to go to the reception. It would be full of media types, networking. Besides, he did not have time. He was off to Venice tomorrow, and he had not begun to think of what to tell the international public relations consultants who were coming from five continents to hear his great thoughts. He was desperate for some time to himself.

But his host was thinking of commissioning a television programme about youth athletics, and Jay was chair of the committee that was lobbying hard. Maybe tonight would clinch it. So he briefed himself on the latest figures on training facilities, inner-city population and youth crime, climbed into a formal dinner jacket—and went.

He did not manage to catch sight of Zoe Brown on his way out of the building. He supposed she had already left for the weekend. He wondered how she spent her free time. And with whom.

His hands clenched at the thought. Damn, that was not sensible. He could not afford to think things like that, not while she still worked for him.

He stamped into the reception looking like a conquering emperor in a seriously bad temper. And the moment he walked in the first person he saw was Carla.

She was looking very beautiful. He would have to talk to her, Jay knew. He curbed his temper ruthlessly. It was more difficult than he would have believed possible.

She was wearing cream silk, very plain, with the watery aquamarines he had given her in her ears and at her throat. Bless her heart, she smiled with unaffected pleasure when she caught sight of him in the doorway. The frustrated temper eased a little. When she made her way over to him he even managed a decent smile.

'Hi, Carla. You're looking very glam.'

'Thank you, Jay. How are you?'

'Fine. You?'

'Better every day,' she told him gaily.

He looked at her searchingly. 'Is that true?'

Her eyebrows flew up. 'What's happened to you, then?'

Jay was confused. 'What?'

'You don't ask uncomfortable questions like that.'

'What do you mean?'

'Well, for one thing it's not polite. For another, you don't want to know the answers.'

He blinked.

Carla smiled, putting an exquisitely manicured hand on his arm. 'Jay, we were an item for six months. In all that time I told you a lot of comfortable platitudes. You never questioned them once. So what's with the tell-me-the-truth game?'

He said slowly, 'I hurt you a lot, didn't I?'

Carla shook her head, smiling steadily. 'You're a fun date and a terrific lay. And you never make promises you can't keep. I had my six months of fantasy. My friends envy me.'

Jay was shaken. He said to the look in her eyes, 'I never realised—'

'I did,' said Carla, suddenly curt. 'My risk. My choice. And it was worth it. Don't you dare be sorry for me.'

The party seethed around them. He said in a rapid undervoice, 'Can I give you dinner after this? Can we talk?'

'No.'

He was taken aback.

She looked past his shoulder, the smile firmly in place. 'I've moved on, Jay. From the sound of it, you're doing the same thing.'

'What?'

'Going back is no solution. We may not be too happy at the moment. But we'll come through that.'

Someone was coming over, going to join them. She took her hand off his arm. The smile she gave him was wide and friendly. And if her eyes were a bit too bright, well, no one but Jay would have noticed. Jay, after all, had looked into her eyes, up close, a thousand times.

He felt like a heel. The worst heel in the world. *This woman slept in my arms and I didn't take care of her.*

Carla shook her head at the look in his eyes. 'The past is great compost, Jay. Leave it to do its work.'

She turned to the new arrival, delighted, made introductions, and then drifted away. He did not see her again.

He had not intended to drink, so he had taken his own car. He sat in it, the top down, savouring the night air, trying to wrestle his thoughts into coherence.

He could not. All he could think of was what he had done to Carla. And, almost worse somehow, how Zoe had looked when she'd walked away from him today.

Is there no end to the damage I do?

He made up his mind.

The roads were nearly empty at this time of night. He had a brief flicker of unease about turning up on her doorstep unannounced. But he did not have a phone number for her. He had never had to call her. He would just have to take a chance that she was in—and willing to open the door to him.

Zoe was doing the week's ironing. She liked ironing normally. She used it to work out her problems. It was mindless and soothing. Besides, everything ended up looking wonderful and smelling better.

But tonight, for some reason, it wasn't working. She burned a tee shirt she needn't have tried to iron. And then the catch on the ironing board didn't engage properly and when she pressed on a particularly dense bit of quilted jacket the board collapsed. She saved the iron and kicked the jacket clear. But she ended up sitting on the floor with a nasty burn on her arm, where she had not quite fielded the iron fast enough.

She felt very cold and shaky. She recognised it. Shock.

'Or another petty feminine neurosis,' she said aloud bitterly.

She had been trying to whip up indignation against Jay all evening. It was surprisingly difficult. The sneaking suspicion that he was right kept flitting across the back of her mind. Well, a bit right. Maybe.

She leaned sideways and pulled out the plug of the iron. Then she set it carefully on its end, in the corner. Her hands were shaking. Shock, definitely. Low-grade but still shock.

'Hot sweet tea,' she said aloud. 'Run cold water on the burn.'

She wished her mother would come down and help her. Deborah must have heard the crash of the falling ironing board, surely?

But she knew it was hopeless. If Deborah heard the crash she would just assume it was nothing to do with her and carry on watching her movie.

Face it, Zoe, you get yourself up or you stay sitting on the carpet for ever.

Zoe stood up carefully. Her arm throbbed and her legs were weak as water. But she was not hurt.

'I can do this,' she said, hanging on to the kitchen table.

It seemed like one of Jay's five-thousand-metre runs to get to the cold tap.

That was when the doorbell rang.

'Damn,' said Zoe with real feeling.

She considered not answering. It was past eleven, after all.

But anyone who rang the doorbell at past eleven was serious. Maybe Harry had decided he couldn't hack leading eleven-year-olds through salt flats, after all. Maybe he had dived for home and lost his key again. Clinging to the furniture, she made her way through the house and opened the front door.

And stared, open-mouthed.

It was Jay Christopher. Jay Christopher in a dinner jacket. His mouth was pinched as if he were in pain. But his jaw was determined.

'I'll do it,' he said.

Zoe put a hand against the doorframe to steady herself. Her legs still felt as if they were made of lint and her head was beginning to swim. Her burned arm throbbed, too. She had not the slightest idea what he was talking about.

'Sorry?'

'I've been thinking about it and I've decided. I'll—' Jay broke off suddenly. He leaned forward, his eyes growing intent. 'What's wrong?'

'N-nothing.'

'Yes, there is. You're shivering.'

She was, too. Although the summer night was almost as warm as the day.

He said sharply, 'What has happened?'

'It's nothing. I knocked over the ironing board, that's all. I burnt myself. Nobody heard—'

Zoe was in tears, mortifyingly. Neurosis, indeed! She turned away, trying to hide it from him.

But Jay pushed into the house and put his hands on her shoulders, turning her back. His sleeve brushed the burn on her arm and she yelped. At once he held her away from him, eyes narrowing as he saw the mark.

Shivering even harder, she said, 'It's not serious. I just need to run it under cold water.'

'Then let's do that,' said Jay calmly. He kicked the door closed without even looking at it. 'Kitchen is this way, right?'

She leaned as heavily against him as if she were a convalescent. He got her into the kitchen, took a chair to the sink and made her sit down. Then he held her arm under the cool stream of water.

'Feel faint?'

She smiled wanly. 'A bit.'

'Keep your head down. It will pass. I'll just check on the iron.'

She did what he said. It seemed easier. Besides, she was grateful. It was a long time since anyone had taken care of her. It was worth putting up with a bit of bossing.

He came back. 'The iron's cold. You did all the right things. Good girl.'

He put a cool hand to her forehead. It felt almost professional. Certainly quite without feeling. So Zoe was horrified to find that she wanted to lean against him and say, Hold me.

She cleared her throat. 'Thank you,' she said huskily.

Jay was wearing his hidden laughter look. His eyes glinted down at her.

'For what? Calling you a good girl? I thought you'd take a baseball bat to me if I patronised you again.'

She gave a watery chuckle. 'Thank you for not saying one word about neurotic women and their petty crises.'

'A burn is hardly neurotic.' He leaned over her shoulder to look at it. She felt the warmth of his body under the dark jacket, the strength...

Her mind flipped sideways. Try, it said.

What?

What have you got to lose? it said.

What do you mean?

Lean against him and see what he does. You know you want to.

I can't—

He's right. You're a coward.

Jay looked down at her. 'Hey, you're shaking again,' he said in concern. He slipped off his jacket and put it round her. 'That will have to do for the moment. I'm making you some tea. Then you can tell me where I find a blanket to put round you.'

Zoe moistened her lips. She was deeply, darkly ashamed of her secret thoughts.

'So much fuss for a little burn,' she said with constraint.

'I'll be fine. Just give me a minute. Though tea would be nice.'

Tea would get him away from her, over to the other side of the kitchen to make it. And maybe she would start to think clearly again.

Maybe she would have, if it had not been for that jacket. She rubbed her cheek against its comforting warmth. And smelled soap and the sea and some woody aromatic, not pine or sandalwood, but something like both, only more elusive. And a lot more exotic. Whatever it was, it was a clean, clear smell; sharp as a knife and utterly like Jay. Her senses swam.

I want him.

She jumped as if she had just impaled herself on a blackberry thorn.

I've wanted him since I first saw him. Since I told him everything there was to know about me. Since he kissed me.

'Do you take sugar?' said Jay, oblivious.

Zoe tried to speak. It was not easy. 'No,' she croaked on her third attempt.

'Well, I'm putting some in. It's supposed to be good for shock.'

How come it's taken me this long to realise? What sort of freak am I?

And her thoughts began to spiral faster and faster, out of control.

Jay came back with the tea. He had put it in the horrible dragon mug. 'Here. This will make you feel better.'

Zoe looked up at him dumbly. Her mind was still in free fall.

He smiled down at her, his face so gentle that she almost did not recognise him. He took both her hands and clasped them round the mug. Her fingers twitched but she took the mug. In fact she clutched it like a lifeline.

'Are you alone in the house?' he asked.

Zoe shook her head. 'My mother's in her room. She—er—can't have heard.'

He looked at the devastated ironing board. It had lost half its mechanism and brought down the clothes horse in its collapse. It was self-evident that it must have sounded like a falling tree in the confined space. Jay raised his eyebrows. But he refrained from comment.

'Just as well I arrived when I did, then.'

Even in the face of his courteous disbelief she still wanted him. Her hands were clammy with it.

Zoe swallowed. 'Yes.'

She had never felt like this before. Never felt a need to touch a man so fierce it seemed a physical impossibility not to give in to it. She clutched the mug so hard that her knuckles went white. She tried to collect her thoughts.

'What was it that you came for?' she said distractedly.

'Ah.'

Something in his voice—or not in his voice, in his eyes, in the way he was looking at her, though she had her head bent and could not even see him out of the corner of her eye, but she knew he was looking at her—*something* told her that this was not easy for him. Important, yes. Very important. But not easy. In fact, hard as hell.

She looked up, surprised. 'Yes?'

He cleared his throat. 'I've been thinking about your—er—solution. To the problem you think you have.'

She frowned, bewildered.

The wonderful golden skin did not flush, but his eyes slid away from hers.

'You were right. I was being glib. You have got more than a practical problem.'

'*Oh!*' Zoe's skin, however, flushed instantly and unmistakably.

'And you were right about something else. I'm not into trophies. But I do have all the relevant qualifications.' His voice was level.

'What?'

'I have it on the best authority,' said Jay in a hard voice, 'that I am a fun date and a terrific lay.'

It was somehow terrible. He looked as if someone had cut his heart out, thought Zoe. Whoever she was, the woman

who'd told him that had devastated him. Suddenly Zoe
wanted to take him in her arms and tell him it was a lie.

But she had no right. And besides—maybe it wasn't a lie.
She huddled his embracing jacket round her and couldn't
think of one single thing to say.

It did not matter. Jay was laying out his argument like a
presentation to a client, all common sense and shining reason.

'You don't want to lie. You don't want to be a trophy.
You need a man to help you through the transition. I can do
that.'

'Oh,' said Zoe. She felt as if she were in a falling elevator.
No solid ground anywhere and a distinct rushing sound in
her ears.

'In fact I'm probably uniquely qualified to do that,' said
Jay, bitterness seeping out. 'Mr No Commitment.'

'I—see.'

He leaned against a cupboard and looked all the way
across the kitchen at her. Zoe shivered. His expression was
brooding.

'No claims. No promises. No history. I'm the dream
ticket, aren't I?'

Oh, you are! You are!

'I-er—I hadn't really thought about it,' said Zoe.

She was not certain if that was true. Certainly when she'd
flung her challenge at him she had never thought for a moment that he would pick it up. Okay, this evening she had
been shivering with desire just to touch him. But she was
hurt and in shock. Surely anyone could be allowed a little
fantasy at moments like that?

Except—where did it come from, that sensitivity to his
touch, his voice, his glance, even the scents of his damned
clothes?

Jay's voice gentled. 'Think about it now.'

She did. It brought an image of his hands on her, so clear
that she broke out in a sweat. The elevator reversed polarity
and took off like a rocket.

She said in a gasping voice, 'You really wouldn't mind?'

He laughed. 'You sound like a polite child. There's no need to be grateful. It's no hardship. You must know that you're gorgeous.'

He paused expectantly. Zoe did not say anything. Her head was so light she felt that she was curving round Mars with a comet tail of fire blazing after her.

'You know me. I'm not a good man. There are women I have hurt. But I can do this thing.' And, as she still said nothing, he added, 'Only if it will help, of course.'

Zoe, her ears ringing, was heading out of the solar system by now. She managed to gasp, 'Oh, it will. It will. I accept.'

That was when her numbed fingers lost their grip. The hated dragon mug crashed onto the tiled floor and broke into a thousand pieces. The shards scattered, powdering the floor and her discarded footwear. A great jagged piece with teeth lodged in her tumbled left shoe.

And Zoe, who loathed the dragons and all they represented, broke into inconsolable tears.

CHAPTER EIGHT

JAY was surprisingly competent with her tears. After a brief moment of pure, masculine horror, he picked her off the chair and crunched through the broken pottery to the French window. Hesitating only a moment with the handle, he shouldered his way out onto the night-time patio. There he dropped her onto the old wooden bench.

'Put my jacket on properly, or you'll get cold.'

Zoe sniffed.

He gave an exasperated sigh and whipped a pristine handkerchief out of his trouser pocket, stuffing it into her right hand. Then he took her left hand and inserted it into the left sleeve of the jacket and pushed.

Zoe blew her nose.

Gosh, I'm being pathetic, she castigated herself. But it felt wonderful to be so close to him, having him care for her. She let herself flop about like an awkward kindergarten pupil as he hauled. It gave her the chance to lean against him. Even—briefly—bury her nose in his crisp shirt-front. Heart-stopping!

Pull yourself together. You're not four years old.

Well, she had not been behaving in a very grown-up way since he'd arrived. But the way she felt in his arms was certainly not child-like. Time to take a hold on life again!

Zoe straightened, reluctant to leave his arms, knowing that she had to. 'It's all right. I've got it.'

At once, he stepped back.

Zoe tried not to feel bereft. She dealt with the other sleeve herself. The jacket was much too big, yet it felt as if she belonged in it. The lining slipped along her bare arms like a secret kiss. The way the lining moved against her skin, it had to be silk. Soft as a kiss but warm as a blanket, she

thought, savouring the sensation. She gave a small, voluptuous shiver.

Jay said in a worried voice, 'You shouldn't be that cold.
It's a warm night.'

'No—it's—I'm fine,' she said hurriedly. 'Thank you.'

He still looked down at her, frowning. 'Maybe that burn
is worse than it looks. How does it feel now?'

She had almost forgotten the burn. She shook her head.
'Fine, honestly. The cold water has taken all the heat out of
it.'

He was still doubtful. But he said, 'Stay there,' and went
back into the house.

He came back with her shoes. He had clearly shaken all
the shards of pottery out and, by the look of it, run them
under the tap for good measure. They were certainly shiny,
and slightly damp, inside and out, as well. He also had a
worn piece of tartan cloth over his arm.

'All I could find,' he said briefly, offering it to her.

Zoe was pulling on her shoes. She looked up, shaking her
head, laughing. 'It's the cat's blanket. Cyrus won't take it
very kindly if I pinch it.'

'But—'

She straightened. 'Don't worry. I'm all right now. Truly.
And I've got a kitchen floor to clean up. That will get the
blood moving.'

'I'll get you some more tea first,' Jay said decisively.
'Then we'll see,'

He was as quick and efficient at that as he was at everything else. He brought it out to her and sat on the old chair
opposite as she sipped. He leaned forward, looking at her
keenly in the moonlight.

Zoe said uncomfortably, 'You're doing all the right
things.'

He gave a ghost of laugh. 'Am I?'

She was flustered. 'I mean the treatment for superficial
burns, shock—everything. Very professional.'

He sat back, shrugging. 'I've run training weekends for
kids. I thought it was a good idea to learn basic first aid.'

She was glad that he did not seem to be studying her under a microscope any more. 'I would have thought that was just strained muscles and stuff. I mean running isn't exactly a high-risk sport. Is it?'

She saw the flash of white teeth as he grinned in the darkness.

'You have no idea what eleven-year-olds can do to themselves if they put their mind to it. If you ever get yourself stuck down a pot hole, I could probably get you out of that, too.'

'A pot hole?' gasped Zoe.

He smiled reminiscently. 'A little anarchist called Brian. Good runner, too. Just never got the idea of doing what he was told.'

Zoe made a discovery.

'You liked him.'

'I suppose I did.' He sounded surprised. 'He kept going off on his own all the time. I could identify with that.'

'You?' She was sceptical.

'Oh, yes. There's a lot more to me than a spin doctor who lights a trail to land third-rate movies, you know.'

She flushed in the dark. 'Sorry about that.'

'No need. I had it coming.'

'Even so—it wasn't fair. I didn't know you well enough to say a thing like that.'

He gave a soft laugh. 'No?'

She was oddly shocked. 'Of course not. A couple of conversations and a lot of gossip don't add up to knowing someone.'

'So why do I feel that you've known me since the first moment you looked through me?' Jay asked quietly.

'*What?*'

'Why do you think I was upset when you tweaked me about *Lemon Sherbet Three*?'

'I didn't know you were,' said Zoe, shaken.

'Oh, I was. And not because I expect the staff to sign up to my Napoleon image, either. I was upset because I thought—she could be right.'

'But—'

'You see clearly, Zoe Brown. I was worried that you were seeing through my protective colouring. And seeing how thin it was.'

She stared at him blankly.

'No!'

She saw one eyebrow lift. 'No? So what did you think of me?'

She shifted uncomfortably. 'I just thought you were—very busy.'

His expression was wry. 'You thought a lot more than that.'

He did not throw, *'You could never be a candidate,'* in her face, but he was tempted. Only it was not very chivalrous, when she was so shaken. And he was supposed to be here as her knight in shining armour.

He said, 'It's okay. You don't have to answer that.'

Zoe shook her head. 'No, it's a fair enough question. If you really want to know—I was surprised that you were so good at your job.'

Jay stared. It was the last thing he'd expected.

Zoe said thoughtfully, 'After all, you're hardly a people person, are you? I've watched you. Sometimes you look as if you've overdosed on humanity and are just desperate to get away from all of us.'

Jay went very still. 'You do know me, don't you?' he said, almost inaudibly.

Zoe was pursuing her own line of thought. 'You do what you have to. But people have to stand in line. Nobody gets more than their ration out of you.'

His head went back as if she had struck him. There was a turbulent silence.

He said at last ruefully, 'Ouch. You know how to hit where it hurts, don't you?'

Zoe was confused. 'I didn't mean—I was only saying what I felt. You asked,' she ended with a touch of indignation.

'I did. I did indeed. I can see I shall have to think before I ask in future.'

Zoe peered at him in the darkness. He sounded amused. But he also sounded as if it were a bit of an effort.

'Sorry,' she said, conscience-stricken.

Jay stuffed his hands in the pockets of his formal black trousers and looked up at the fingerprint moon.

'Probably good for me,' he said dispassionately. 'I've suspected for some time that people walk round me a bit too carefully. Never get to be the boss, Zoe. It changes things.'

He sounded half-sad, half-angry. Not angry with her, though, she thought. She hoped. She could not bear it if her thoughtless words had really hurt him.

He drew a long breath. Then said in quite a different tone, 'Now—to practicalities.'

At once Zoe stopped palpitating over his possible feelings and bounced right back into the present. She sat bolt upright.

'What—now?' she said, in stark horror.

Jay laughed aloud. 'Get real. We have a journey to go on first.'

She liked that 'we'. She relaxed. 'Thank heaven,' she said unwarily.

He stuffed his hands deeper in his pockets. 'And the first thing we need is neutral territory,' he said, as calmly as if he were discussing a PR campaign. 'You'd better come with me to Venice.'

Zoe spluttered.

'What have you got against Venice?' he said patiently.

'Nothing. I mean, I've never been. But I haven't got a ticket. And it's so *soon*.'

'I'll get you a ticket.' Jay was calm. 'And the sooner the better.'

'Oh,' said Zoe hollowly.

He took his hands out of his pockets and came over to her. Zoe tensed in the darkness. But he just buffed her cheek lightly.

'Believe me.' His voice was kind. 'Once you've made up

your mind to do something you don't want to, the best thing is to get it over with.'

'Oh,' she said again in quite a different voice.

She felt cold suddenly. It had nothing to do with the summer night air. She huddled his jacket round her, and the scents of his skin assaulted her like a reproach.

'This is very kind of you,' she said with constraint.

He did not answer that. He was thinking. 'I'll send a car to pick you up tomorrow. About eleven. Bring a business suit for Monday, and some walking shoes so we can do the ritual sightseeing.'

Her heart fluttered madly. *I don't believe I'm doing this.*

'All right,' she said aloud.

He touched her cheek again. 'You'll be back Monday night. Then you can get on with the rest of your life.'

She swallowed. Monday night! After two days in uncharted territory, who could guess where she would be going by then?

Get a grip, Zoe. Get a grip.

She stood up. 'That will be great,' she said distractedly, as if he had just offered her a job, or a ride to the station on a wet morning. 'I'd better tell my mother. And clear up the mess in the kitchen. Um—your jacket.'

She struggled out of it and handed it across. He hooked a finger into the tab at the collar and swung it over his shoulder.

As they went into the house he put a brotherly arm round her. Zoe was sure it was meant to be brotherly. But it made her quiver from her breastbone to her toes. She moved away from him and speeded up.

'Goodnight,' she said, opening the front door with indecent haste. 'I'll see you tomorrow.'

Jay was not dismissed so easily. He leaned one arm against the lintel and looked down at her very seriously.

'Only if you want to. Never forget, this is your idea. Any time you want to back out, you just say so.'

She wanted him to kiss her so much she almost pulled him into her arms. Almost. What stopped her was the thought that the kiss would probably be kind and brotherly. She did not think she could bear that.

'I'll keep that in mind,' she promised brightly. 'Goodnight.'

She had the door closed on him before he was down the path to the gate.

One good thing about being in a flat panic about a man was that it put everything else into a new perspective, thought Zoe. Last week she would have prepared her mother so carefully, filled the fridge with food, alerted the neighbours. Now she just went into Deborah's room, as soon as he had gone, and laid her cards on the table.

'I'm going to Venice tomorrow,' she said baldly. 'I'll be back Monday. You're on your own for the weekend, Mother.'

Deborah was lying on her bed, staring unseeingly at American football on the television.

She said, 'But you can't.'

'Yes, I can. People do it all the time.'

'You can't leave me here alone.' Deborah's voice rose in alarm.

Zoe looked at her with some sympathy. She was not so far off alarm herself, for all that Jay had said she could back out at any time. And she did not quite know what it was she was afraid of, either. But she did know that she had to face it.

'Sorry, Mother. This is something I've got to do,' she said quietly.

She was ready in the hall a good ten minutes before the limousine was due to collect her. She had packed and re-packed her overnight case, to say nothing of trying on every outfit in her wardrobe. She had settled on slim navy trousers and a soft linen jacket she had shamelessly hijacked from her sister's wardrobe. She'd twirled her hair on top of her head. Inserted big hoop earrings. Dug out some gold espadrilles from the back of her wardrobe.

She looked at herself in the hall mirror. Sophisticated, she thought. Careless, even. The full casual traveller who hopped countries at less than twelve hours' notice.

Or—her sense of humour reasserted itself—she would look like that if it were not for the convulsive way she was clutching her passport. Or the way her legs trembled every time she thought of Jay.

A big black car slid smoothly to a halt outside the gate. Zoe let the curtain fall and smoothed her jacket. She felt sick.

The doorbell rang.

For a moment she almost did not answer it. The stairs were behind her. She could turn and bolt back up them.

Only—then what? Like Jay said, now she had made up her mind, the sooner she got it over with, the better. Except that it had all got a lot more complicated than she had ever imagined. Now that it included Jay, would she ever get it over with?

There was only one way to find out. Zoe's chin lifted.

'Forward into the future,' she muttered. 'Goodbye, Mother,' she called out.

There was no reply. She was not really surprised. She was mildly sorry—but she had more important things to think about just at the moment.

She opened the front door.

'I'm ready,' she said quietly. And not just to the uni-formed driver.

Jay, she found, travelled business class. And he worked while he did it. He was friendly enough, but as soon as they were belted into their seats he had his papers out, making notes on the work she had given him.

'I'm going to break the back of this on the flight,' he told her. 'Then we can concentrate on showing you Venice when we get there.'

'Thank you,' said Zoe.

She was monumentally calm. So calm she even impressed herself. She certainly convinced Jay that last night's emotionalism had been dispelled. She could almost hear his sigh of relief, though he was much too civilised to say anything.

Zoe was mildly surprised at herself. This did not feel like Performance Zoe. After all, she had nothing to hide from Jay. He knew all there was to know about her. Yet nothing felt quite real.

Oh, well, no doubt it would sort itself out.

She stayed calm all through the flight, though she refused the meal and even a glass of champagne.

'Very wise,' said Jay with a faint smile.

'What?'

'Turning down the fizz. Champagne should be drunk on a terrace at sunset, to the sound of music. It loses its magic at thirty-eight thousand feet with your nose up against some-one else's seat.'

Zoe laughed. 'That's because you're too tall. My nose isn't anywhere near anyone else.' She stretched, laughing, and wriggled her freshly painted toenails. 'Look at that. I've never travelled anything but economy class in my life. This is a treat all on its own.'

He did not laugh. 'Sometimes I remember how very young you are.'

She gave him a naughty look. 'Not that young. Just poor.'

Jay was ironic. 'Poverty is relative.'

She was instantly contrite. 'Of course. I should have said *relatively* poor. When my father left we still had a roof over our heads and an education in progress. The roof just crum-bled a bit, that's all.'

He looked at her curiously. 'Was life difficult after he went?'

Zoe shifted her shoulders. 'We got through,' she said eva-sively.

He hesitated, as if he wanted to pursue the subject further. But then the screen on his laptop went dark and he was recalled to the work in hand. He went back to his draft speech.

Zoe was relieved. Perhaps he didn't know quite *all* her secrets, she thought wryly. Probably just as well if it stayed like that. After all, she was not likely to see him again once she left Culp and Christopher, was she?

After that her pleasure on the luxurious flight dimmed, for some reason. She stopped staring out into the brilliant sky and even dozed fitfully.

It was the sort of sleep where you had dreams.

She was sitting in a boat. It was a tall, silent boat, coming up fast on a fortress in the dark. She was terrified and cold and alone. She thought, *I can't do this.*

Then suddenly she wasn't in the boat any more. She was inside the fortress and running, running, running... And someone moved out of the shadows. She stopped dead, trying not to breathe. But it was hopeless. Her breathing sounded like an avalanche. A shadow detached itself from the darkness, moved towards her. She thought, *My enemy?* And then the shadow fell over her, engulfing her and—and—and—

And she woke up.

Jay took his hand off her shoulder and sat back. 'Seat belt,' he said briefly. But he gave her an odd look.

It was only a dream, Zoe told herself. Only a dream.

But she was glad that he did not try to touch her on the way from the airport to the hotel.

And when they got to the hotel she forgot fears and dreams alike in sheer amazement.

'It's a palace,' she said, awed.

Jay was signing them in. A double room. Of course. Zoe stood and stared at the cherubic trumpeters on the marvellously painted ceiling and tried to pretend that she did this all the time.

The bellboy loaded their cases onto a six-foot brass birdcage and summoned them to follow him. The elevator was discreetly hidden behind panelled doors decorated with pastel nymphs and knowing satyrs. Zoe avoided the satyrs' eyes. Jay seemed unaware.

'It probably was a palace originally,' he said indifferently. 'A merchant's palace anyway. In Venice rank strictly fol-

lowed profit on the high seas. They weren't big on idle aris-
tocrats.'

Zoe was impressed. 'I never did history,' she confessed.
'I was always more of a scientist. My degree is in chemistry.'

He gave a choke of laughter.

'What?' she said, suspecting mockery.

'And this is the woman who rebuked me for not being a
people person!'

She chuckled wickedly. 'Ah, but I learn about people
from life, not books.'

He shook his head. 'Well, this weekend you're going to
learn about Venice if it kills me.'

And then they got to their floor and she found he had
booked not just a double room but a whole suite. She was
embarrassed by this extravagance, and said so disjointedly
as soon as the bellboy had left, well tipped.

Jay shrugged. 'I promised you no pressure.'

It silenced her utterly.

He was disposing his things with the automatic efficiency
of a man who had worked in a lot of hotel rooms. He put
his laptop on a small baroque desk, plugged it in, adjusted
the lighting to suit. Then he hung up his suit and a spare
pair of trousers and took his sponge bag into the bathroom.

It all took about three minutes. He had finished before
Zoe managed to rouse herself from her stunned stillness. She
had sat down on an antique wooden chair and was staring
fixedly at a lavish bowl of fruit in the middle of a rather less
antique coffee table.

Jay came out of the bedroom and looked at her shrewdly.

'Get your walking shoes on,' he said briskly. 'We'll do a
circuit, so you know where to find things. Shake away the
aeroplane blues.'

Zoe licked her lips. 'Yes. I mean, what a good idea. Thank
you.'

She gave herself several mental shakes and did as he said.

It was obvious that he knew Venice well. He took her to
the Grand Canal first. But when he saw that she found the

press of people almost overwhelming in the hot sunshine, he whisked her over a couple of little bridges, through a tiny square and into a herring-bone-paved side street.

To their left, the water lapped gently against stones that were green with age and watery moss. To their right, the decorated façade of a three-storeyed merchant's house cast a warm ochre shade. A cat dozed beside a marble fountain. A shutter banged back. A small boy ran out of a house and was chased back inside. And all the while the water lifted and murmured like an animal padding beside them.

'It's amazing,' said Zoe, awed.

Jay gave a long sigh of pleasure. He looked round. 'Yes. There's nowhere in the world like Venice.'

On the other side of the little canal a striped awning rolled down to shield the street from the evening sun. As if by magic, it seemed, a cake shop was appearing as the building seemed to wake out of its lazy afternoon doze. A woman came out and pushed back wooden shutters decorated with two china masks and a single elegant high-heeled shoe, to reveal a window of mouthwatering pastries. It was beautiful and strange and somehow menacing.

'How can they make a cake shop look like a carnival assignation?' said Zoe, pointing it out.

'Style. And deception. The twin principles that Venice lives by,' said Jay. He sounded pleased. 'Always has. Let me show you.'

He took her through dark little streets, across tiny canals that looked like people's private driveways and down main thoroughfares. The water was cool and mysterious beside their feet, like a lazy, watchful snake, Zoe thought. While the buildings were warm as toast to the touch. The colours were like every painting of Venice she had ever seen: buildings in cherry and terracotta and straw and the exact shade of crisp pastry. The landscape was studded with grey stone bridges and fountains and statues, like diamonds on a rich fabric. And through it all the sinewy, silent water.

At last they came back to the Grand Canal again. By that time Zoe's head was spinning.

'I'm lost. I thought the Grand Canal was back there.' She waved a hand behind them.

Jay looked even more pleased. 'It is. We're on the great loop of a meander. Now we cross the Accademia Bridge here, and we'll go and see the Big Attraction.'

The Piazza San Marco was full of people again. But Zoe did not care. She sank onto a rattan chair in one of the outdoor cafés and sighed with exquisite satisfaction.

'I never knew—' she said in wonder.

'You can see just as much in books, of course. Or television. But you don't sense it,' agreed Jay. He summoned a waiter with his usual ease and ordered English tea. 'Later we'll have Bellinis. I always like to leave cocktails until after dark when I'm here.'

Zoe did not quibble with that. 'You seem to know Venice very well.'

He smiled. It was one of his real smiles, not the up-and-under sexy stuff that she saw him use on clients or difficult women. It felt as if he had let his guard down and was letting her see him. More than see him. Warm her hands at the flame of his intelligence.

'Venice was the first city that reconciled me to Europe.'

'What?' She was genuinely startled.

He stretched his long legs out in front of him, screwing up his eyes. She thought he watched the tourists as if they were a mildly interesting form of wildlife.

'I'm only half-European, you know. The later flowering half. I was born in India. Kerala. That's where my mother comes from. We lived there with my grandfather until I was seven.'

Zoe was surprised. She had heard about his grandfather. 'The Brigadier?'

The passionate mouth curved. He was laughing at himself. She thought he was no longer strictly policing himself, curbing his instincts, banking down his passions. There was an alluring suggestion that he had loosed control. Oh, for the moment he was just lazily content. But potentially—Well, she could not guess. She had never seen him look like this. So relaxed. So alert. So accessible.

It made her want to touch him. More than touch. Curve against his body and stroke his skin and turn his mouth towards her and—

Careful, Zoe!

He said lazily, 'Not the Brigadier. My mother's father. He was a wholly different kettle of fish.'

She thought, He liked that grandfather a lot. Maybe even loved him. She had never thought of sexy, sophisticated Jay Christopher as loving anyone before. It was intriguing.

'What was he like?'

His face softened. 'The ideal grandfather. He knew brilliant games. He told stories. He taught me to swim—and how to recognise fish and birds and plants. He was a scholar and a philosopher. But most of all he was kind.'

Yes, he definitely loved him.

'Why did he bring you up?'

'Oh, the usual. My father was a hippy drop-out on the Maharishi trail when he met my mother. He persuaded her to leave college and go on the road with him. She got pregnant. He didn't tell his family—he said they were British snobs and he never wanted to see them again. My Indian grandfather took them both in and they married. So I was born in this wonderful house on the beach. I used to fall asleep every night to the sound of the surf. Sometimes when I close my eyes I can still hear it.'

There was a world of loss in the deep voice. Zoe leaned forward.

'When did you leave?'

'When I was seven. I told you.'

Their tea came. She drank, watching him watch the crowd.

'What happened? Did your father decide to go back to England after all?'

'No. My father was long gone by then. Later we heard he'd died of pneumonia somewhere. We were never quite sure when, exactly. But as soon as my English grandfather

found out he came looking for me. They sent him my father's papers. That was how he found out that he had a
grandson.' His voice changed, flattened. 'So he came and
took us back to England.'

Zoe said slowly, 'And you hated it.'

Jay shrugged impatiently. 'It was okay once we got to the
country. At least that was green and there were trees.
London was bad. All that concrete. I was used to colours
and spices and heat. Even the rains are warm in Kerala. At
least on the coast, where we lived. In London everything
was the colour of old chewing gum. And it smelled like wet
Mackintosh.'

'Horrible!'

'To a seven-year-old, it was pretty much hell, yes.' He
drank his tea, his eyes shadowed.

'But you went back?'

'My English grandfather wouldn't allow it. So, no, not
until I was eighteen. And then later, of course, when I started
to earn money and could afford it. But it wasn't the same.'

Zoe's heart turned over, he sounded so bleak. 'Why?'

'Me. The place was the same. Full of books and open to
the sea breezes. But I'd changed.'

'Well, of course. You'd grown up.'

'It was more than that. I'd started winning races, you see.
I was eighteen and I liked the buzz. And the attention.'

'Understandable.'

'Ah, but my lost grandfather told me to be careful of that.
''You can like winning so much you lose sight of what it is
you're doing to win,'' he said. But I didn't take any notice.'

She said bracingly, 'At eighteen boys don't take any notice of anyone. It's in the job description.'

His eyes lit with sudden laughter. He came out of his
reverie, turning to her. 'And how do you know that?'

'My brother Harry. He tuned me out some time around
fifteen.'

'Tuned *you* out? You brought him up?'

'It's been a kind of communal effort,' said Zoe ruefully.
'Mother's spaced out. Father's off pretending he's hunk of

the month. We sort of brought each other up. Only I was the eldest so I did the shopping.'

Jay's eyes were warm on her. 'Then I think it's time someone spoiled you to death.'

She looked around the square and grinned from ear to ear. 'Somebody is.'

He took her hand. She thought he was going to squeeze it. Another of those brotherly caresses which she ought to be getting used to.

But he didn't. Instead he raised it to his lips. It was not a real kiss, just a brush of his lips, his breath on her knuckles. It was not sexy. It was not playful. In fact it felt oddly formal, like a declaration of some sort. It felt was as if he was honouring her in some way, like a courtier paying respect to a queen he had suddenly decided was worth it.

And it was not brotherly.

Yes! thought Zoe.

CHAPTER NINE

WHEN they had finished tea, Jay gave her a rapid and informed tour, dodging tourists.

'Venetian art was looted from everywhere in the known world,' he said, pointing at the Basilica in a friendly way. 'Carvings, columns and capitals courtesy of Genoa and Constantinople. Constantinople, of course, had already pinched a lot from China.'

And, when they got to the Doge's Palace, 'The four figures in porphyry were probably acquired after the sack of Acre. The ownership of property is provisional and strictly temporary.'

'I suppose it is,' said Zoe, entertained.

'Bridge of Sighs,' he said waving his hand at the dark little prison tunnel over the small canal. 'Once you crossed that, you stopped caring about property, I guess.'

She shivered. 'It's not all joy, is it, Venice?'

'What is? It has *energy*.' He paused. 'And that gives me an idea. I think I know how to close my speech, now. Zoe, you're a genius.'

And he rushed her back to the hotel at top speed.

In the suite he flung himself at the laptop computer immediately. Zoe wandered around a while, self-conscious again. But he was so absorbed in what he was doing that it was impossible to remain embarrassed.

She decided to bath and wash the dust out her hair.

'Fine,' said Jay absently, his fingers flying, his eyes on the screen.

So much for the evil seducer, pouncing on her the moment she got her clothes off, thought Zoe with irony. Not very flattering. But somehow—right.

She sang in the bath.

142

When she padded out, wrapped in the hotel's fluffy white robe with her hair in a towel, Jay was standing in the long open windows looking out at the street below. She went to stand beside him.

'Look at that,' he said softly.

The building opposite was arched and columned fantastically. The roofline had a carved frieze that looked as if it had been done with curling tongs. It was built of biscuit-coloured stone, with heavily carved wooden doors of treacle-brown. Zoe knew the colours because she had seen them earlier. But the sunset turned them to pure gold.

'Oh,' she said on long breath of wonder.

He put his arm round her and they stood looking—at the golden evening, the busy pavement, the gondoliers in their long dark gondolas. And the water, darker than anything else, unimaginably dark below the surface of brazen ripples that were conferred by the dying sun.

'See,' he said. 'Energy. Mystery. Everything. God, I love this place.'

'I can see.'

He jumped then, and looked down at her.

'Feeling okay?' he asked, his eyes searching.

Zoe knew he was not talking about her health, or the effects of sightseeing, or even the seductively lazy bath. He was checking to see that she did not want to back out yet. She felt totally cared for.

'Feeling wonderful,' she told him honestly.

Jay gave her the widest grin she had ever seen.

'Great,' he said with enthusiasm. 'Then here we go for Venice by night.'

She wore soft silky trousers and a gold strappy top that looked a lot more expensive than it was. She gave up on her hair, which just turned into a waterfall of fox-brown curls as a result.

'No jewellery?' said Jay, emerging from the bedroom in one of his spectacular silk shirts.

'Forgot it—sorry. I don't have much, and wear less. Does it matter?'

'On the contrary,' he said with a maddeningly mysterious smile.

She decided not to challenge him. Tonight the shirt was peacock-green. It made him look like an emperor. You challenged emperors at your peril.

She told him so, and he laughed.

'Tonight we're on the same side,' he said. 'No challenge necessary.' They strolled through the streets hand in hand. Like friends. Like lovers.

The gold of the miraculous sunset slowly died away, as if someone had pulled a cloth of gold out towards the sea. That left the lights that were set by people. Windows and streetlamps and little lanterns on the prows of the gondolas.

'They look slightly dangerous,' said Zoe, as a gondola swept up to some steps and some laughing passengers climbed out.

He was surprised. 'Do you think so? They're perfectly safe. The gondoliers are incredibly expert. It runs in the family, you know.'

'Not dangerous like that. I suppose I mean sinister. As if they're full of clever men plotting.'

He hugged her, laughing.

'I shall have to bring you here during carnival. The masks can be very beautiful, but they are unsettling.'

Zoe loved him hugging her. She rubbed her cheek against the peacock silk shoulder. She felt proud and mischievous at the same time.

His arm tightened. 'Venice has made sinister an art form. You know they used to have a Signori di Notte? It was specially set up to keep the peace at night.' His voice dropped thrillingly. 'The time of assassins, thieves and spies.'

Zoe wrinkled her nose at the assassins. 'And lovers,' she pointed out.

His arm was suddenly a steel bar.

'And lovers,' he agreed in a still voice.

That was when the trembling started. A slow, sweet, deep trembling that she had never felt before.

And suddenly she thought—Could he be right? Could it be that she had never wanted to make love to anyone because she had never been in love? It was not the fashionable answer. Not even the rational one, in some way. And yet she felt in her bones that no one before had been possible. And Jay was more than possible. He was the only one.

Nonsense, she told herself. It was the night and Venice and all the hocus pocus of gondolas and streets that weren't streets, but treacherous, shifting, mysterious water. This was fantasy, pure and simple.

But his arm round her wasn't fantasy. Nor was the account of his childhood. She was sure that nobody else in Culp and Christopher knew about that.

And nor was the look in his eyes.

She had seen Jay's up-and-under, sex-is-a-state-of-mind look. She had had the benefit of the sexy stare straight into her eyes. She had seen him challenging and she had seen him shameless. In all the weeks she had known him she had never seen him look at anyone like this.

Steady. Slightly questioning. Sure, and yet—not sure.

She thought—*I'm the one to make him sure. The next move is mine.*

She waited for the alarm to hit her. After all, only last night in her mother's room she had been all but falling apart with panic. It did not come. It felt right that the next move was hers. And when the time was right she would make it.

Jay took her to a candlelit restaurant. The tables were covered in heavy damask and an array of crystal, and the conversation was the low hum of people who took their food seriously. He was obviously known there, too.

The waiter led them to a secluded table, murmuring confidentially.

Jay nodded. 'Two Bellinis to start with, Carlo.'

Jay held the deeply red cushioned chair for her. The table was by a floor-to-ceiling window, open to the shifting murmurous night.

'Fit for lovers?' he murmured in her ear.

Zoe bit back a naughty smile.

'Very appropriate,' she assured him gravely.

His eyes were warm hazel and very close as he smiled down at her. It was like a kiss.

'I'm relieved.'

He sat in his own seat and took her hand proprietorially. Just as if that was what he always did.

Zoe's heart fluttered. She was not alarmed—but this was new. And new took dealing with.

Still, she could deal with it. She could deal with anything. She swallowed and summoned up all her hot babe repartee.

'Do you do a lot of this sort of thing?' she asked chattily.

Jay's smile did not change. 'No. You're my first,' he told her.

And watched with pleasure as she choked.

Two drinks arrived. They were the colour of sunrise and they hissed.

'Our Bellinis,' said Jay. 'Local invention. Champagne and peach juice. And probably a secret ingredient, though no Venetian barman will tell.'

He toasted her silently. They clinked glasses and drank.

Zoe considered. 'A bit sweet. Touch of the alcopop.'

It was Jay's turn to choke. 'Don't tell them that,' he begged. 'It would be like insulting the flag.'

Zoe twinkled at him. 'Oh, all right then. You're no fun, though.'

'Just trying to watch out for you,' he said peacefully. 'But if you think it would be exciting to get us thrown out, go right ahead.'

She laughed aloud. 'No, no. You're the expert. I'll do what you tell me.'

He took her hand to his lips again. 'That's quite a responsibility. I'll try not to let you down.'

The inner trembling increased. It shook through her. Like an earthquake getting ready to break. Like a drowsing lion flexing its muscles.

Jay looked at her all the time.

Zoe did not notice what they ate. She knew the waiter and Jay discussed the food briefly and the wine at length.

She remembered fish so fresh that it tasted of the sea, wine that slid over her palate like distilled flowers. But then even the water tasted as if it had just bubbled up from some fresh spring.

What's happening to me? Getting carried away by the taste of water, for heaven's sake?

But it wasn't the water. It wasn't even the marvellous wine. Or the luxury. Or the glamour that was Venice. Or the starry night. Not even the warm wind on her bare arms as they left, though it made her shiver voluptuously.

'Cold? Or do you want to walk?' asked Jay softly.

Zoe swallowed hard. The time was right.

'I'm not cold,' she said deliberately. 'And I don't want to walk.'

He went very still. 'Home, then,' he said.

And summoned a gondola.

In the suite Zoe thought he would lead her straight through to the bedroom. He did not. Instead he switched on a couple of the table-lamps and drew her towards the couch. She sat obediently, but nerves made her clumsy. A couple of the luxuriously fat cushions plumped onto the floor.

Jay sat down beside her and took her hands.

'You're shaking,' he said gently. 'Don't shake, my love.'

'I-I don't seem to be able to stop,' Zoe said candidly. She tried to lock her jaw. It did not work. 'S-silly, isn't it?'

'No,' he said in a caressing voice. He pushed her hair gently off her face. 'No, it's not silly at all. It's just unnecessary. We won't do anything you don't want. I promise.'

'Th-thank you,' she said politely.

He gave a shaken little laugh. 'And you don't believe a word of it.'

Zoe gulped. 'Yes, I do.'

He turned her to face him. 'Really?'

She moistened her lips and saw his eyes darken.

'R-really,' she said uncertainly.

Did they darken because of her? Was it possible? A super-sophisticate like Jay Christopher?

Yet he did not feel like a super-sophisticate, sitting here beside her. So close. So reassuringly strong. So alarmingly hot. He felt like—the only man in the world she wanted to make love to her.

She suddenly realised why she had ducked out of the arms of all the Johns and Alastairs and Simons. She had liked them. She had enjoyed their company. At least twice she had desperately wanted it to work. But, in the still, quiet core of her, she had known she did not—quite—trust them. It had just not been *right*. And now it was.

She trusted Jay. Totally.

She tried to tell him and could not find the words. So she reached for him instead.

Jay took her in his arms with care. The memory of that earlier kiss was not a good one. It did not exactly haunt him. But he could not forget how she had looked as she scrubbed his touch off her mouth.

In spite of that she had trusted him with her secret, though. Now she was trusting him to make the experience a good one.

That was a tough one. All through dinner she had sat beside him trembling. She thought he did not know. But he was too alert to her every move not to feel it.

Hell, be honest, Jay. You want her so much you can hardly see straight. Every time she breathes in your blood surges. Of course you knew she was trembling. You even wanted her to tremble harder—only because of what you were doing to her, not because of her own apprehension.

Well, forget what he wanted. He had a task to do here. And that was to get her so fogged up with lust and curiosity that she forgot how terrified she was. Who knew better than he how to do just that?

He began to kiss her gently, teasingly. First her hand— yes, he had seen the way she reacted to that. Her bare shoulders. Her throat. The scent of her skin made his head swim.

But he clamped down hard on his own reactions. This was for her, he told himself. This was for *her*.

He slid the thin strap down her bare, warm arm. He remembered how the bra strap had slipped under the sheer provocation of that black chiffon shirt the first time he saw her. His body quickened at the too explicit memory. In spite of himself, his hands grew urgent.

Zoe gave a small moan. At once he loosened his hold.

But she turned on him, her own hands suddenly demanding, and kissed him fiercely.

Jay shut his eyes. Careful, he told himself. Careful!

But he did not tell Zoe. More cushions hit the floor as she writhed against him.

'Please,' she said in a panting under-voice. 'Please.'

She jumped up, kicking her espadrilles away, and, taking him by the hand, half ran to the bedroom.

Jay knew it was going too fast. He tried to slow her down. But it seemed as if she was caught up in some feverish drive of her own and couldn't hear him. She let him take her clothes off but not as slowly as he wanted. And she tore off his own.

'Zoe—'

But she pulled him down onto the bed with her, her soft hair all tangled and her eyes as wide as a fox in a trap. He could not bear to think of his Zoe trapped.

'Stop this,' Jay said with authority.

She froze.

He unclenched her frantic fingers from his neck.

'This,' he said, 'should be a lot more fun. Now, will you stop trying to do the driving and trust me?'

She bit her lip. But he saw the fierce, trapped look die out of her eyes and breathed a private sigh of relief.

'Better,' he said. 'Now, concentrate. Make notes, if you like. We need to find out what you like.'

He was thorough. He had plenty of experience to build on. But he was hungrier to satisfy her than he had been for anything since his very first race. Since the last time he hadn't been sure he could win, Jay acknowledged wryly.

'This?' he said, working his way up from her toes. 'This? How about this?'

150 THE BEDROOM ASSIGNMENT

He was rewarded. At first she was surprised. Polite, but surprised. Then intrigued. Then—he knew exactly when, because her breathing changed and her limbs seemed to unfold somehow as her muscles relaxed instinctively—the first unselfconscious quiver of response ran through her.

It was going to be all right, thought Jay. He should have been exultant. But suddenly all he felt was a chill. Almost grief.

He could not understand it. It was going to be all right, after all. Zoe was going to come with him on this. Venice, the night, the wine—they had all done their stuff. Good old Venice. He tried to be grateful.

But there was a little pain round his heart, like a rose splinter that he had picked up a long, long time ago and not noticed until now.

Venice had got Zoe so far. And now it was up to him to get her the rest of the way. It was what he was good at, after all. He had walked away from so many women into his healing solitude. And, however sad they had been, however lonely, they had never said that he was not an attentive lover.

Remember that, Jay. That's why you're qualified to do this thing for her.

He kissed the soft flesh just inside her elbow. Then, overwhelmed, buried his face against her for a moment.

'You smell so good,' he said, shaken.

He lifted his head and she met his eyes for a long, long moment. Her own widened. The room was full of silence and shadows. For a moment it felt impossible to tell where he left off and she began.

Zoe said his name on a wondering note.

Jay's heart seemed to contract in his breast.

Don't get carried away. There's only one thing you can do for this woman. So make damn sure you do it right.

He used all his skill to arouse her. His blood pounded but he stayed slow, deliberate. He knew exactly how to inflame her senses, one by one, with exquisite precision. And he did it. Her anxieties, her self consciousness, did not stand a chance. *She* did not stand a chance. This was Jay Christopher, bent on the seduction of his life.

He felt her every response, the little tiny ripples and the big, building need that swept all inhibitions out of its path. It seemed as if her senses uncurled at his touch, like a flower turning towards sunlight. It moved Jay more than he would have believed possible. He kissed her lingeringly.

Zoe clung. He knew from the way she writhed in his arms that she could not wait much longer.

Then he let her do what she wanted.

She urged him inside her. He hesitated only a moment. But he was not superhuman and she was breathless with an imperative need that he recognised even if she didn't.

It was a mistake. A terrible mistake. He knew it at once and froze, shocked.

Zoe cried out. 'No. Leave me alone. I can't bear it.'

He nearly did. But then he thought how much it had cost her to get here. How much she had trusted him to get her through this.

An inner voice jeered. *You're supposed to be the expert, Jay. Can't you do it after all?*

He paused, agonised. Hardly believing what he was doing, he held himself very still. But he did not withdraw.

He said with difficulty, 'Zoe, my love, we need to get this over.'

Jay realised too late that he had called her 'my love'. What was he thinking of? Love was never part of their bargain. He could have bitten his tongue out. But it was impossible to recall it.

He did not notice that he said 'we'. But Zoe did. She stopped thinking about her straining flesh and stared up at him, amazed.

Zoe, my love! She could not believe it. She had asked him for practical help. Was she being given the moon without asking? Without even suspecting it was available?

She touched her palm to his warm shoulder in wonder. He felt as if he were on fire.

He still did not move. But he said urgently, 'Darling, if you make me stop now, we've got it all to do again.'

We! Again! She swallowed shakily.

He was supporting himself on his elbows, but he touched his fingers to her face. It was as fleeting as the thistledown that blew past her cheek in the summer garden at home. Gone before she had time to turn her head into the caress. Zoe felt cheated.

But Jay was saying soberly, 'I know I can't stop it hurting. But I can get you through it quickly.' He smiled down at her, straight into her eyes. 'It's what I promised, after all.'

She nearly did not recognise him, his eyes were so blazing with tenderness.

'Think,' he said softly. 'Just once and you don't have to dread it ever again.'

That smile made her head spin. It also made her feel brave. She thought, *Smile at me like that and I don't have to dread anything.*

She nearly said so. But she was shy. Crazily shy, in the circumstances. And not sure that it was what he wanted to hear. And suddenly bodies seemed the best communicators after all.

She ran her palms over his shoulders, savouring the warmth and strength and sheer otherness of him.

'Oh, well,' she said, doing her best to keep it light. 'In for a penny, in for a pound, I suppose. Go—' She broke off, gasping.

He had delivered one clean, swift thrust and pain tore through her like a typhoon.

From a long way away, she heard him say, 'Oh, *love.*'

Eventually the nuclear cloud blew away and she opened her eyes. She was lying on the big gilded bed in a room full of antiques and the man who made her head spin was lying propped on one golden arm, watching her.

'Zoe?'

'Present,' she said, trying to make a joke of it. Her voice cracked.

His mouth tightened. 'That was unforgivable. I should never have—'

But she stopped him by putting her fingers over his mouth. It was amazing how good it felt to have the right to do that, to touch his lips.

'Don't. It's over. Like you said.' Her voice got stronger. 'About time, too.'

His jaw was so tight it must hurt. 'I'm sorry. You were unlucky,' he said curtly.

Zoe brushed her lips against his naked shoulder quickly. She was not quite so sure she had the right to do that, and didn't want to risk rejection.

'*We* were unlucky,' she corrected.

She fell back among the pillows, eyes closed. She was not shy, she told herself rebelliously. It would be ridiculous to be shy after making love to the man. Well, sort of making love to him. And she was a twenty-first century independent woman, after all. She just did not feel up to meeting his eyes quite yet, that was all.

He brushed the hair off her face softly. 'You're a kind girl.' He sounded very far away.

Suddenly she wanted to say *I love you*. But she was absolutely sure that she did not have the right to do that. Well, she thought, brave behind her closed eyelids, not yet.

And suddenly she thought— He booked a suite. He may not even want to spend the night in my bed. They say he never stays the night, don't they? Her eyes flew open in horror and she sat up.

'What is it?' said Jay, concerned. 'Are you hurt? Do you want something? Water?'

'No—but the couch—the sitting room.' She was incoherent in her alarm at encroaching on him.

Jay's face was rigid. He did not touch her.

But he said quietly, 'No. Sleep with me.'

She searched his face. Were they wrong about his rule against spending the night with his lover? Or was tonight something that broke his rules?

She thought of that blaze of tenderness she had surprised

on his face. That had not looked like a man who was keeping his own rules of detachment, either. And he had called her *Zoe, my love*.

The first time she saw him—the very first time, in his sunset silk shirt—she had thought, This is love at first sight! And laughed at herself. Well, she was way beyond laughter now. She shook her head, dazed.

He misinterpreted the gesture.

He said almost inaudibly, 'Sleep in my arms. Let me do that for you, at least. For both of us.'

And suddenly Zoe saw how hurt he was. How angry with himself. For a moment her body had felt as if it was splitting apart, but it was not Jay's fault. He had used all his skill and all his knowledge and it had not been enough. He was raw with self-disgust and she had brought him to it. It was up to her to put it right.

She said, 'Hold me, Jay.'

His arms closed round her. He carried their locked bodies back among the pillows very carefully.

Her eyes closed tight at once. But she was not asleep, he knew. He did not challenge her. And eventually her breathing slowed, became regular, and he knew she had fallen asleep at last.

But Jay lay there, with her sleeping head against his shoulder, and stared open-eyed into the darkness.

CHAPTER TEN

ZOE woke to the sound of bells. She stretched languorously, not opening her eyes. *I feel different,* she thought drowsily.

Different and peaceful and somehow proud. And surprised. As if she had won a war that she had been fighting for too long.

I thought I was going to get deeper and deeper into lies for the rest of my life. And now it's all behind me.

But much, much more important—what was in front of her? The future suddenly looked a lot less predictable. It was exciting.

I slept in the arms of Jay Christopher, who never spends the night. And who called me his love. This is a very surprising day.

Zoe gave a long, long sigh of pure satisfaction. The bells pealed out joyously, celebrating life and victory and morning. A wide schoolgirl grin started behind her eyelids.

'Too right,' she told the bells, eyes still closed, savouring the triumph that was her life.

She opened her eyes and sat up, stretching her arms exuberantly above her head.

'Today is the first day of the rest of my life. Look out world!'

And it was so easy.

Thanks to Jay. She would never have screwed her courage to the sticking point if he hadn't held her to it. She owed him, big time. She had to tell him. She turned—

That was when she realised that she was alone in the bed.

For a moment she was taken aback. The words had been on the tip of her tongue, all ready to bubble out. But his pillow looked as if it had been pounded to pieces during the night and there was no sign of Jay at all.

'Oh,' said Zoe, her mood temporarily flattened.

But then she thought, He's probably an early riser. Maybe he's gone out jogging. Or he couldn't sleep through the bells.

The schoolgirl grin broke out again.

She got up, pulling the hotel's bathrobe over her nakedness, and padded out to the sitting room.

The floor-to-ceiling windows were flung wide to the brilliant morning. And Jay was standing at one of them, looking out over the canal. No shirt, but he was wearing dark trousers. His hair was rumpled and his feet were bare. Zoe's heart lurched.

I slept in that man's arms last night. I want him.

He had his hands in his pockets and he was frowning. Lost in his thoughts, he certainly did not hear her.

She padded across to him and slipped both hands round his arm. He jumped, stiffening. Zoe was too happy to worry about it.

'Listen to them,' she said, rubbing her face companionably against his shoulder. 'Triumph in a few notes.'

He did not return the caress. But, after the tiniest pause, he said in an amused voice, 'The bells? They're supposed to be calling the faithful to prayer, you know.'

'Nah. It's Venice showing off. I'm the best, you suckers.'

She waved her arms above her head, taunting the rest of the world.

Released, he moved away from her. 'You're very chirpy.'

Zoe was in tearing spirits and saw no reason to hide it. 'I'm wonderful.'

Some of the constraint fell away from him. 'Glad to hear it. Do you want coffee?'

She stretched again, beaming. Below, the gilded water gleamed. Sunbeams struck diamond rainbows off the columns and colonnades of the square palace opposite. The morning air felt sharp and warm at the same time.

'I want everything,' she said with relish.

He laughed.

'I want to do everything. I want to see everything. I want

to *fly*.' She flung her arms wide, embracing Venice, life and the universe.

'Start with coffee,' Jay advised.

She realised that there was a tray on the coffee table. He poured her a cup and brought it over to her.

'Not as hot as it was, sorry.'

She took it, her exuberance dimming a little. 'Have you been up long?'

'A while,' he said uncommunicatively.

She remembered—*he doesn't stay the night*. It was only a tiny pinprick in the fabric of her delight, but it was there all the same.

She said ruefully, 'Ouch. My fault, I suppose? Did I snore?'

Jay looked startled. Then he shook his head, smiling. 'No. You were very well behaved.' He raised his coffee cup to her. 'A positive pleasure to sleep with.'

Zoe twinkled back at him. 'That's a relief.'

He looked at her searchingly. 'You really are all right this morning?'

The grin broke out again. She could not stop it.

'I'm bloody marvellous.'

'You're not just—saying that?'

'Oh, come on. Would I?'

'Yes,' he said unexpectedly.

Zoe stared. 'What? Why?'

His eyes were greeny-hazel and oddly remote.

'Because you're kind and you're brave and you tell people what they want to hear,' he answered literally. 'I want to hear that I didn't hurt you last night. So, hey presto, my wish is granted. This morning, for one day only, the Zoe Brown all-singing, all-dancing extravaganza.'

She pulled the robe tighter round her. Suddenly the crisp morning seemed chilly.

'You're crazy.'

'No, I'm not,' said Jay intensely. 'I'm a man with a bad conscience trying to get the truth out of a world-class actress.'

Zoe winced. But she said with spirit, 'And to think you had the gall to call *me* neurotic! I think you can't have had enough sleep. I must have snored after all, and you're just lying about it to be kind.'

Their eyes met in a duel that she did not wholly understand.

She dropped the sarcasm. 'Look at me, Jay,' she said quietly. 'If I were any more pleased with myself I'd burst.'

There was a pause. For a moment his eyes flickered, as if he were confused. Then he shrugged and turned away. 'That's all right, then.'

They talked about Venice. And the day's itinerary. And breakfast. And her crazy family. She even made a joke about Deborah's midnight pot roast. They laughed and they were friends.

But it dimmed the day a bit.

Zoe had an energising shower, then climbed into slim pale trousers and a crop top. Her mirrored image looked back at her, wide eyed and—excited.

Excited?

'The start of the rest of my life,' she murmured. 'And his.'

She went back into the bedroom, brushing her curls vigorously. Jay was standing by the bed. He turned—and for a moment she hardly recognised him. His face was a rigid mask but his eyes looked agonised.

'What is it?' she said involuntarily, going to him.

'So little blood for so much pain.'

She realised he had been looking at the stained sheet. Her heart turned over. She took his hand. It felt inert in hers. As if he did not want her to touch him. Zoe began to feel alarmed.

'That's nothing,' she said. 'There'd be more blood from a grazed knee.'

'I hurt you.'

Zoe's voice rose. 'Okay, so I made a fuss. But this is *nothing*. The burn hurt more than that.'

Jay detached himself. 'But *I* didn't burn you.'

And the day dimmed a little more.

They both made an effort, though. Zoe resumed brushing her hair. Jay shook off his constraint, raised an eyebrow at the way her curls clung to the brush and said, 'I've never seen hair sizzle before.'

'Curls,' said Zoe, refusing to acknowledge the constraint between them. 'The bane of my life. No serious person has curls. I'll probably have to shave my head before I can embark on a serious career.'

'Don't you dare,' said Jay.

She hoped he would touch her hair then. He didn't. But at least he watched with apparent fascination as she twined it into a pony tail and clipped it round with a bright turquoise elasticated fastening with a daisy button it.

'You look about twelve,' he commented.

Zoe narrowed her eyes at him. 'I've got a degree in chemistry and on-the-job experience of all necessary life skills from plumbing to party-giving. I am not twelve.'

The constraint eased a bit more.

'Sorry,' said Jay, amused.

He opened the door of the suite for her.

'Okay, I happen to have been a little slow in launching my great career,' Zoe allowed. 'I have been taking stock of my available options.'

'I'm sure there are hundreds,' he said politely.

And a whole new dimension of them since last night. She bit back a grin. 'Just watch me.'

He touched her hair then, ruffling it as if she were the twelve-year-old he'd mentioned. 'You're a tonic, Discovery.'

They went down in the cherub-festooned elevator.

Breakfast was served with maximum pomp in the restaurant.

'You can't possibly need that many plates and glasses to eat a croissant,' said Zoe, torn between amazement and contempt.

'This is an international hotel,' Jay told her, entertained. 'You can have everything from hominy grits to ham and cheese. To say nothing of that pickled fish that the Scandinavians eat. You need a variety of fighting irons to deal with a menu like that.'

'There is no way I'm eating pickled fish for breakfast,' announced Zoe, horrified.

'Relax. It's not obligatory.'

And nor was the restaurant, apparently. He led her through it to an open air terrace. The tables there had bright gingham cloths instead of stiff white damask, and a marked diminution in the crockery and glassware.

'You get your own orange juice and buns from that table under the awning,' Jay told her. 'They come and take orders for whatever else you want. Coffee, tea, eggs, mixed grill.'

She wrinkled her nose at him. 'And I suppose you come here regularly, too. What on earth do you do for kicks? You've done everything in the world before,' she complained.

At once he went very still. 'Not everything.'

At once Zoe recalled his stillness this morning, when she'd found him frowning out at the canal. And later, contemplating her physical hurt.

She could have kicked herself. *Damn! Why can't I learn to keep my mouth shut? Now he's thinking about last night again.*

He obviously *hated* everything about last night. The day dimmed a lot more.

But then she squared her shoulders. Oh, well, there was nothing she could do about it. Except get back to neutral subjects as fast as she could—and try to avoid putting her foot in it again.

She said lightly, 'Well, enough to give me some considered vocational advice. What do you think I should do as a career?'

He relaxed visibly. 'What do you want to do?'

'If I knew that, I'd be doing it.'

'Okay, let's look at it another way. What did you like about university?'

'Friends. The course. Independence,' said Zoe promptly.

The waiter arrived and they ordered.

When he left, Jay said, 'Your course. What did you like about that?'

She chuckled. 'Oh, chemistry is wonderful. So elegant. Everything fits, if you know what I mean. The boys used to like it because they were licensed to blow things up. But I just loved the ideas. I used to draw patterns of chemical structures. And I'd work on an experiment for weeks if I had to, until I got it right.'

He smiled, ticking off on his fingers. 'Okay. No violence. Plenty of order. Plus patience. And persistence. Sounds good.'

She pulled a face. 'Not very marketable. I mean, I'd have quite liked to go into food chemistry, but you need a second degree and I wasn't good enough for that.'

'Don't put yourself down,' he said. 'There is a very strong movement to offer you a full-time job at Culp and Christopher.'

Zoe was genuinely astonished. 'You're joking.'

His mouth tilted with wry self-mockery. 'On the contrary. I'm fighting it off with all my might.'

'Oh.' She did not like that. But her curiosity was too great for her. 'Why?'

His look was ironic. 'You're seriously asking me why I don't want you working for me?'

She winced. 'No,' she said hastily, 'I think I'll pass on that. Tell me why the fans—my few fans,' she added acidly, 'want to take me on in the first place. What have I got that would be any use to you—er—Culp and Christopher?'

He hesitated.

'See?' She tried not to let her disappointment show. She did it well. So Performance Zoe was not quite dead yet, then. 'Nothing. It would be just another job making the tea and running around after everyone else.'

'It wouldn't.'

She was disbelieving. 'Really? So—hypothetically—what can you seriously see me doing at Culp and Christopher?'

Jay's eyes danced. 'Actually, you're not going to like this.'

Zoe's eyes narrowed. 'I don't like making the tea, but it doesn't kill me. Come on. Tell the truth and shame the devil.'

'Well, I—that is they—the others—Tom and his cohorts—want you because you're ordinary.'

He was right. She did not like it. She narrowed her eyes at him in a glare.

'See? I told you you wouldn't like it.'

'Ordinary—how?'

'Well, we've got a bunch of specialists at the moment.' Jay gave her that sudden blazing smile that kept even the most cynical employee on his side when times got rough.

She mistrusted it deeply, even under normal circumstances. Here, this morning, she thought, *He's hiding something.*

He went on, 'Actually, they're all oddballs. Though we don't say it, of course. Molly is nearly as weird as the rockers she hangs with. Or she was until she found herself a regular guy. And the Fab Ab, of course. Our token upper class bird and Interpreter to the Seriously Rich. Lady Abigail, no less. Does good work, too, in spite of the handle. Then there's Sam—she knows movies, and quotes the screenplay of everything Harrison Ford's ever done. But there isn't one regular soap-watching, romance-reading, family-running woman in the whole bunch.'

Zoe sat very still. *What is he hiding?*

The smile intensified until she thought she would burn up in it.

'I don't call you Discovery for nothing. That's why.'

Zoe nodded slowly. *What doesn't he want me to see?*

She said aloud, 'I'm not ordinary. I woke to bells, the sun is shining and I'm in love.'

His blazing smile flickered, seemed to freeze for moment.

She gave a soft laugh. A soft, false laugh. Oh, Performance Zoe was back with a vengeance. So much for hello to the rest of her life!

'Relax, Jay. With Venice, I was going to say. I've fallen in love with Venice.'

'Of course you have,' he agreed.

Their coffee arrived, and with it eggs and a great bowl of fresh fruit.

Zoe picked up her knife and fork and attacked her scrambled eggs with gusto.

'Gotta keep my strength up. Gotta lotta sights to see.'

It was a lifeline, the sightseeing. As soon as they finished breakfast Jay bought her a guidebook and they retraced the steps of yesterday's walk. Only this time they went inside the palaces, the museums, the galleries. Jay offered to buy her an instant camera but she refused.

'I want to drink it in. Hold it in my memory. I can't do that if I'm peering through a little hole taking pictures all the time,' she said crisply. Adding conscientiously, 'But thank you.'

He nodded. 'You're a real original, aren't you?'

She sent him a swift look. 'Not so ordinary, after all?'

Jay sighed. 'I knew I should never have told you that.'

She had got her exuberance back. Okay, some of it was performance. But some of it was the sheer energy of last night.

Zoe danced along beside a weathered stone wall. 'I forgive you.'

'Thank you,' he said gravely.

She knew she was being teased. She turned round and skipped backwards in front of him, looking wicked.

'Who wants to be a rotten old spin doctor anyway?'

The thin handsome face lit with laughter. 'Oh, quite. You sound like my Indian grandfather.'

She raised her eyebrows. 'Sounds like a good guy.'

'Yes.' His face softened wonderfully when he talked about his Indian grandfather, she saw. 'That's more or less what he said the last time I saw him.' His eyes were very green. He looked away. 'He did not like what I'd become. He'd like it even less now.'

Zoe stopped dead. Big stuff coming, she thought.

She said carefully, 'Do you? Dislike what you've become, I mean?'

He hesitated. 'Maybe.'

She sucked her teeth. After a pause, she said, 'Know why?'

He came back from whatever dark place he had been visiting. 'I do, and it's all too easy for me.' He hesitated, as if he was struggling for words. 'When I was running I had to train every day, in a structured way. No quick fixes. No spin, if you like. I was as good as I deserved to be. Oh, sometimes I got a little lucky. But I couldn't *talk* my performance up. If it was sub-standard, it was sub-standard. I couldn't argue with the results.'

She digested this. 'Yes—but life is not as simple as a race, is it?

Jay looked at her, arrested. 'What do you mean?'

'Well, when you do one of your public relations campaigns you're telling people about values. Not just about who won. About how you measure the winning.' She stopped. 'I don't now what I'm talking about. Sorry.'

Jay said slowly, 'For a woman who is suspicious of spin doctoring you are making a lot of sense.'

But Zoe was embarrassed. She started walking again, energetically, to hide the fact. 'How did you get into PR anyway?'

Jay's face lit with spontaneous amusement. 'Self-defence.'

Zoe goggled. 'What?'

'It was after I won my first big medal. A couple of journalists made a complete prat of me. Entirely my own fault. So I thought—I'll look into this. Next time I won I got the story I wanted into the press—and athletics got the boost it should have done first time around. So then I thought—there's a job here. I've been passing on what I learned then ever since.'

'I see,' said Zoe slowly. She thought about the research she had done for his speech tomorrow. 'But it's more than that, isn't it? I mean, it's about more than celebrities planting stories?'

'Yes.'

'So tell me about that.'

But he flung up a hand. 'It's my day off. You want to hear the Jay Christopher Philosophy of Public Relations, you listen to my speech tomorrow.'

She was surprised. She had not been at all sure that he was going to let her go to the conference. She'd half expected him to hide the fact that she was with him. It broke all his professional rules, after all.

'You want me to come? Really?'

'Couldn't do it without you,' he said lightly.

She didn't believe him. But it warmed her almost as much as if she did.

Instead she tossed her head so that her pony tail swung and said carelessly, 'Then you got it.' She thought about it. 'I'll even give you my totally ordinary thoughts on your analysis,' she added wickedly.

Jay stayed calm under this provocation. 'I look forward to it.'

Zoe looked at him with deep suspicion. 'Do you? Why?'

'The right-hand-side bias,' he said mysteriously.

'What?'

Jay was bland. 'Tom Skellern's profile analysis.'

Zoe frowned. 'You mean that pointless test? What about it?'

Jay stopped and leaned on the wall, looking down into the busy canal. Dark gondolas jostled each other in duels for precedence. They just managed not to touch as the winner swept away with a flourish. Vaporetti chugged. People on the other bank strolled hand in hand. He propped his elbows on the river wall and locked his hands together.

He said, 'If you're interested in the PR business there's a spectrum of response. Male attitudes at the extreme left, female at the right. Most people are somewhere in the middle. But you particularly are hard on the right-hand side. Very girly.'

'Girly?' Zoe was revolted and did not try to hide it.

He smiled. 'Tom's score calls the category that you come into the Boyfriend's Dream.'

She tensed. 'Oh?'

'Sorry about that,' he said, unconvincingly. 'Touch of political incorrectness there. But the message is—you're all woman. And,' he added with an abrupt return to the prosaic, 'there won't be a lot of them at the conference tomorrow.'

'Then I'll be glad to fill in,' said Zoe between her teeth. *All woman!*

If only he meant it. And if only it was what Jay really thought, rather than the result of Tom Skellern's multiple choice questionnaire, she thought, depressed. If only it was what he thought after last night, in her arms!

She turned and leaned on the wall beside him, turning her head away. She had done her best to stay bright all day. But now she could not deny the emptiness between them any more.

Oh, he had made love to her, fair enough. He had said he would and he had kept his promise. More than kept his promise, she thought. There was warmth round her heart when she thought of the care he had taken of her.

But today, though he was trying, he was as far away as the moon. Zoe kept trying to work out why and she simply could not find the answer. He was not embarrassed, of course. He was much too sophisticated for that. And not emotionally involved, either. That had been implicit in the deal.

So what was it? Something was wrong; she knew it.

And then she remembered him saying, a lifetime ago, *'Once you've made up your mind to do something you don't want to, the best thing is to get it over with.'*

Well, it felt like a lifetime ago. But it had only been Friday night. Less than two days. And he had got it over, all right, hadn't he? At the time she had thought he was talking about her feelings. But now she realised he had been talking about his own.

He hadn't wanted to do it. But he had.

And, in doing so, he had caused her a little pain. He had not been prepared for that. Zoe had seen how it had shocked him.

Hell, she thought, staring out across afternoon Venice. I've made him ashamed of himself. He's never going to forgive me.

CHAPTER ELEVEN

THE rest of that day they walked, until Venice was swimming before Zoe's eyes.

Then Jay took her to some famous bar for a drink; then another, less famous, for jazz. They ate in a bistro. It was full and noisy, with families and a huge party of people who turned out to be gondoliers at the central table. Jay chatted to them in easy Italian and he and Zoe joined them in toasting the newest member of the group, for whom the dinner was being held.

When they left she nearly said, We're going to have to talk. We have to share a bed tonight and we have been walking round the subject all day.

But Jay got in first.

'They told me where the best club is,' he said. 'They're not as ageist in Venice as they are in London. They'll probably even let me in.'

They did. It was not so different from the clubs where Zoe danced at home. Maybe a bit smaller, and the drinks were different. More wine, less vodka. But the atmosphere was the same and so was the music.

She abandoned herself to the familiar intoxication of the music. There was nothing else to do. Jay was evidently quite determined not to talk. So she danced and laughed and waved her arms as if she were having the time of her life. And in the small hours of Monday morning, when her eyes were gritty with tiredness, he took her back to the hotel suite.

He did not put the light on. Instead, as he closed the door behind them, he said quietly, 'Zoe—'

She did not mind him not putting the light on. As long as he put his arms round her and took her to bed. Tonight she wanted to take the same care of him that he had taken of her.

Hell, be honest, Zoe. You want a lot more than that.

Yes, but I want that, too.

Jay said in a strained voice, 'Zoe, this virginity thing. I didn't understand. I should have thought harder.'

Why didn't he put his arms round her?

'What do you mean?' she said, her voice slurring with tiredness. And lust. Well, more lust than tiredness. Probably.

'I don't think it was an accident that you were a virgin.'

'What?' Her head reared up. Suddenly she was not tired at all.

'You gave me a line about how it was just chance—boy-friends in different places, friends getting the wrong idea. I don't think it was anything to do with that. I think you were exactly what you should have been.'

She was so hurt she could not speak. Could hardly move. Everybody in the world thought she was a hot babe. Every-body but one. Jay Christopher thought she was meant to be alone.

'I should never have interfered.' His voice rasped.

'Well, you should know,' said Zoe, equally harsh.

She heard him swallow in the dark. 'I know. I'm sorry. Not much point in saying that now. But I am. I wish—oh, *hell!*'

And he left her to sleep alone.

Long after she had gone to bed Zoe heard him moving around in the sitting room. He was ultra-quiet. But her ears were strained for sounds that would tell her what he was doing. And they did.

He sat for a long while. By the window, she thought. In the dark, certainly, because there was no light under the connecting door. Then he got up and she heard him move a large piece of furniture, gently, carefully. Arranging the sofa, she realised.

So he wasn't intending to come back to bed. He must really have hated last night, then. She had made him break his every rule. Even making him hold her through the night. No, he was not going to forgive that.

He was going to take her back to England, employ her for one more week at Culp and Christopher—and then she was never going to see him again. It was inevitable. Zoe knew it now, though she had been pretending to herself all day. Trying to pretend, anyway.

She closed her eyes. Sleep was a long time coming.

Jay came into the bedroom very quietly the next morning. He was barefooted and walked cautiously. But Zoe was already awake. She struggled up on one elbow.

She was not going to let him see how he had hurt her last night. She was *not*. Fortunately there was good old Performance Zoe to call on in times of need.

'Time to go and lecture the masses?' she asked brightly.

His smooth dark hair was tousled, and he had a red line on his cheek where his night on the sofa's piped cushion had marked him. Zoe felt an almost irresistible urge to stroke it away. She was shocked, and pulled the sheet up to her chin.

Jay sent her an inscrutable look. 'There's no need to cower,' he said coldly. 'I didn't jump on you last night. I'm not going to do it this morning. I've got work to do.'

He disappeared into the bathroom, leaving Zoe shaken. She had never seen the cold come off him in waves like that before. Was that what the people at Culp and Christopher meant when they called him the Ice Volcano?

By the time she had dressed in her smart trousers and jacket Jay had packed. His bags stood by the door: overnight bag, laptop computer, briefcase. He was wearing one of his dark suits. The shirt this morning was silver-grey. Beautiful, of course, but much more sombre than usual. Maybe that was what made his eyes look lifeless. No green, no hazel. Just dark pools of emptiness.

There was no sunshine this morning. The canal was wreathed in fog and the doors to the hotel terrace were closed. So they breakfasted rapidly in the suffocating formality of the restaurant.

They hardly spoke. Jay was going through his notes one last time. When he did speak he was conscientiously pleasant. But it was clearly an effort.

He can't wait to get rid of me, thought Zoe. She felt as if he had struck her to the heart.

And then he gave her a gentle smile that did not seem as if it was an effort at all. For a moment her heart rose.

'I thought you'd like your last ride in a gondola. I've ordered one to take us to the conference hotel. Shame about the weather, though.'

But he did not touch her. Her heart sank back to the bottom of the ocean again.

Jay dealt with the practicalities swiftly. He paid the bill.

'We'll take our bags with us to the conference. That way we can circulate as long as possible before making a bolt for the airport.'

'Good thinking,' said Zoe, working hard to play bright and interested.

His smile was twisted. 'Just another thing I've done before.'

The mist had the odd effect of concentrating sound. In the gondola, Zoe could hear the plop and swish of the gondolier's pole, the lapping of water against the low sides of the boat. Her breathing. Jay's. But of the other gondolas, which loomed out of the mist and then were swallowed up again, she heard almost nothing. As they moved towards the Grand Canal, though, she heard the machine gun fire of the Vaporetti motors. And the mist swirled and pulled apart, getting thinner and thinner.

She thought, *This is the last time we'll ever be alone.*

She took Jay's hand quickly, before she lost her nerve.

She said in fierce, rapid under-voice, 'I want to say—I'm really glad it was you. I won't ever regret it.'

And then the gondolier poled them out between two tall palaces. And the mist dissolved into little puffballs of bite-sized cloud and they were into thin sunshine.

'Zoe—' Jay sounded strangled.

But the gondolier demanded clarification of their destination—and then the laptop overbalanced—and then another
boat came dangerously close and a ferocious argument broke
out. And then they were there.

He helped her up the steps. And held onto her hand when
they were ashore, 'Zoe, we have to— I should have— Oh,
hell, this is terrible timing.'

Zoe looked up and saw a man coming towards them along
the canalside, hands held out in welcome.

'Jay. So good to have you. Come inside and meet everyone.'

Inevitably she slid into the background. Oh, everyone was
kind—and Jay was meticulous in introducing her—but she
had no role here. She could see it in everyone's eyes. They
were tolerant, even intrigued. But the message was clear:
she's just along for the ride.

Jay had her seated in the front row, though. He was doing
his best to pretend that she was a fellow professional,
thought Zoe, touched. The last thing he said to her before
he disappeared onto the podium was, 'Now, don't forget to
take notes. I want a proper post mortem on this speech.'

And her neighbour's smile said, as loudly as words, Yeah,
yeah, yeah.

Zoe set her teeth and applied herself to the foolscap notepad.

Jay talked well. Not a surprise, of course. He was always
fluent But this was different. He talked with knowledge and
wit and ease. But also with a seriousness that was almost
like passion.

He told the crowded room, 'Recently a friend reminded
me that what we call public relations a lot of our critics call
putting a spin on things.'

Zoe sat bolt upright. Jay smiled, straight at her.

'Not a high calling, you may think,' he went on. 'Not a
very laudable role. Let me tell you what I think we do. And
why it's important.'

There followed the stuff that she had researched. The statistics. The international examples. The anecdotes.

And then he said, 'When I first came into this business I was defensive. The press had stitched me up. I thought that what I was doing was giving people the tools to defend themselves against shallow and malignant journalism. But I have come to see that what we do is more than that. In our campaigns we are telling stories. We are reflecting the age back to itself. And in doing that—if we want to—we can reflect the best. Kindness instead of self-interest. Common humanity instead of hate. We are not just about selling things, ladies and gentlemen. We are about confirming values. In these dark days, that is important.'

He sat down to stunned silence. And then tumultuous applause. He did not take his eyes off Zoe's face.

Afterwards he was surrounded. The international delegates could hardly bear to leave him alone, it seemed. Four of them even insisted on accompanying Jay and Zoe back to the airport. In fact it was fortunate that they only had carry-on luggage or they would have missed the plane.

They whipped through formalities at top speed and were the last on the plane.

'What did you think of my talk?' said Jay.

But the noise of take-off was too great for easy conversation. And by the time they were airborne Zoe had thought better of saying, I thought you were talking only to me.

So she said lightly, 'It was great. You should have called it the death of spin.'

Her response did not please him.

'You and I,' said Jay grimly, 'are due a long talk.'

But the plane was not the place for it. Nor was the baggage hall. And when they got through customs and came out onto the crowded concourse the first person they saw was Molly di Paretti.

She blinked when she saw Zoe with Jay. But that did not stop her rushing over.

'Jay, bit of a crisis. We tried to get a message to the conference but you'd left. Barbara Lessiter has told a tabloid about your affair with Carla Donner. Banana is claiming that Carla only got her programme picked up by Sonnet Television because you're a director of Sonnet.'

Zoe stopped dead. His affair with Carla Donner? What affair?

She had never thought to ask about his private life. She had told him all about her own, spilled it out like the overgrown adolescent he clearly thought she was. It had not occurred to her that he might already be committed. He didn't *feel* committed.

But he wasn't saying, I'm not having an affair with Carla Donner. He was saying, exasperated, 'Banana Lessiter is a pain in the butt. Her eyelashes are bigger than her IQ.'

'We can't tell them that,' said Molly, walking rapidly beside him. She handed him a couple of sheets of closely typed paper. 'Sonnet are worried. An accusation like that could hold up their bid for American cable. They've got a press presentation tonight on the autumn schedules. We've planted a question. But you'll have to get a move on to make it. Car's here.'

'Good work,' said Jay, running hard eyes down Molly's list. 'Where's the presentation? No, don't bother. Better go straight there.'

They stormed through the concourse, talking hard. Zoe fell behind. Then slowed.

Finally she stopped.

Molly had talked about it as if everyone knew. Slowly Zoe accepted it. Jay was involved with Carla Donner! He probably thought Zoe already knew. Heaven help her, she would have already known, if she had had the wit to ask.

There had been plenty of rumours about his affairs in the office. Only she had never heard a name mentioned before. Now she had—Carla Donner was gorgeous and knowledgeable and as sophisticated as himself. Carla was the sort of woman he should have taken to Venice.

How stupid to think that Jay had been talking to her from the conference podium, thought Zoe. It was probably just another of his clever manipulative tricks. Find someone impressionable in the audience and play upon their feelings so they gave you all the feedback you needed.

'Zoe?'

She looked up.

Jay had come back for her. His eyes were still glittering with the light of anticipated battle and he looked harassed. But he was too well mannered just to walk off and leave her there, she thought.

'Are you coming?'

She swallowed, but her chin came up to the detonation angle.

'No, I don't think so. You've got a crisis to sort out. And I'm all dealt with, thank you,' she said clearly.

He looked astounded. 'Are you saying that's it? Thank you and goodnight?'

He sounded outraged, thought Zoe. She was pleased. That was the only thing that kept her from collapsing in the middle of Heathrow Terminal Two and bawling like an idiot.

'That's right. Thank you and goodnight,' she said, her eyes glittering as brilliantly as his own.

And before he could say a word she turned and bolted into the crowd.

Jay started to run after her. But he was just that half-second too late in setting off. The concourse was too crowded. He lost her before he had even taken a step.

He stopped. Took stock. Rushed out through the doors to see whether she was in the queue for taxis, but she was not there.

'Jay, come *on*,' said Molly, hopping from foot to foot beside an illegally parked limousine in front of the terminal building. The engine was running and a policeman was already approaching. 'The Sonnet press conference starts in forty minutes. We'll have to go like the clappers to get there anyway.'

He knew she was right.

He went.

It took hours. Every chance he could, he called Zoe on

his mobile. He left message after message but he never made contact.

Eventually he got a faraway female voice which said, 'Zoe? Oh, no, she's not here. She's gone to Venice.'

'She's back,' he said curtly. 'That's why—'

The phone was clearly taken out of the vague woman's hand. 'I'm Artemis,' said a voice very like Zoe's. It sounded brisk.

The sister.

He said rapidly, 'I took her to Venice but we—got parted at the airport. I really, really need to speak to her.'

'If she went with you to Venice you've probably had your ration,' said Artemis cheerfully. 'No idea where she is. You could try Suze Manoir.'

'Right.' Why hadn't he thought of that? 'Thank you.'

'If you see her, tell her I'm sorry.'

'What?'

'None us had realised how bad Mother is. Zo's been doing all the work and hiding it from us. Now we've realised we're having a family conference. My father, Aunt Liz, Harry and me. The doctor's in with Dad and Aunt Liz now. Tell Zo she's off the hook.'

'Thank you,' said Jay, with real gratitude.

He rang off and called Suze's mobile.

'Yes, she's here,' said Suze, before he had even mentioned Zoe's name. 'And I don't know what you've done to her, you jerk, but I've never seen her look like that. Don't come near us.'

He did not accept it, of course. He went straight to the Edwardian block. He did not get past the front door.

'Go away,' snapped Suze down the entryphone. 'She's sleeping. She looks as if she hasn't slept for a week. You'll have to wait until tomorrow. I hope you're proud of yourself you—you—you Bluebeard.'

No, he was not proud of himself. But for all sorts of reasons that Suze Manoir could not guess at. He walked through the summer night, trying to wrestle his thoughts into some sort of order.

Women said that they loved men so easily, and most of the time it was just baiting the trap for long-term partnership.

But Zoe was not angling for companionship. She had her family. She had all those damned boyfriends. Now she could go out with any of them and do whatever she wanted in the full knowledge that she started off with a clean slate.

At the thought of Zoe doing whatever she wanted with another man Jay stopped dead and looked round for something to hit.

But then he reminded himself—before they went into that damned conference hall she had said she was glad that it was him. And that she would never regret it.

Well, she was regretting it now, all right. All because of that stupid Lessiter woman—

He caught himself. No, that wasn't true. It was his own fault. If he had sacked Barbara as soon as she'd developed her crazy crush on him, if he had never given his luke-warm affection to Carla, this would never have happened.

Zoe waited. Why couldn't I?

Hormones, thought Jay grimly, had a lot to answer for.

But hormones were only part of what he felt for Zoe Brown. Though God knows how he was ever going to convince her.

'My love,' he said experimentally to the warm night air.

And realised he had said it before. Holding her. Thinking only of her and her heart racing beneath him.

It had not felt like an experiment. It had felt like truth.

Slowly the tension went out of him. He'd got a hard task ahead, sure. But he'd had things too easy for too long. This was going to be a challenge—and worth it. This was the most important challenge of his life.

'My love,' Jay said again. With certainty.

CHAPTER TWELVE

'I CAN'T go to work,' Zoe said, panicking. 'I can't face him.'

Suze did not dignify that with an answer.

Zoe pulled herself together. 'I mean—I broke all his rules. He said I'd be out on the hour if I fell in love with him.'

'Are you in love with him?' said Suze curiously, buttering toast.

'Yes,' said Zoe baldly.

Suze bit back a gleeful smile. 'Then you'd better go in and let him sack you,' she advised.

Zoe gave a wan smile. 'Get it over as soon as possible if you're afraid of it? You're not the first to give me that advice.'

'And you're not the first to be afraid of Jay Christopher,' said Suze comfortingly.

But Zoe looked surprised. 'Oh, I'm not afraid of him.'

'Now that,' said Suze, handing her her jacket, '*is* a first.'

But Jay was not available when Zoe steadfastly called Blonde Mark II for a slot to see the boss.

'Don't think he'll be available all day,' said Poppy, kindly enough. 'Merger talks. You can try dropping by before you go home. He might be finished then.'

So Zoe did not see Jay. She *did* see—and would rather not have done—the unbelievably beautiful Bharati Christopher.

'Miss Brown,' said the tall, exquisitely dressed woman, pausing by Zoe's desk. 'Abby told me that was who you were. I am Jay's mother.'

She held out an expensively manicured hand. Zoe shook it as if she were in a dream.

'Hello, Mrs Christopher.'

'May I invite you to lunch?'

'Oh, no,' said Zoe with genuine horror.

Bharati looked rather pleased. 'Then show me where your water cooler is.'

Zoe leaped to her feet. 'This way.'

Bharati sipped cold water out of a plastic cup with all the elegance she would have accorded vintage champagne.

'So you won't talk to him,' she said musingly.

'I—er—' Zoe pulled herself together. 'What do you mean?'

'I am on a shopping trip. So I stay at my son's house. He was back very late last night. And very chastened.'

'Oh,' said Zoe.

'You seem to have him tied up in knots,' said Bharati Christopher dispassionately.

'Oh.'

'And while I would, of course, prefer that he were not tied up in general,' she went on in her gentle, precise voice, 'you are the first woman to have got close to Jay for years. Perhaps ever.' She put the plastic cup in the bin provided with great care. 'Don't waste it.'

Zoe was speechless.

Bharati left with a faint smile.

Zoe threw her head back. *'Aaaaaarrgh!'*

But it confirmed her resolve not to go home until she had seen him.

Was his mother right? The first woman to have got close to Jay! Was it possible?

And what about Carla Donner? Zoe had gone through every newspaper this morning and there had been no mention of the television gardener, let alone Jay's affair with her. Yet would his mother necessarily know?

She was torn all day. There was work to do, but Zoe was working on autopilot. She hardly noticed what she was doing. She got odd looks from Molly, but she did not seem to have told anyone else that she had met Zoe along with Jay at the airport, coming back from their weekend in Venice.

Kind Abby asked her whether she was feeling all right, though. Clearly Zoe's distraction was showing.

'Look,' said Abby, as everyone else began to drift away at the end of the day, 'you haven't had anything to eat all day. You haven't been out of the building. What's wrong?'

But Zoe just shook her head. 'I—er—think I'll get some coffee,' she said uneasily. 'Poppy said there was always a pot on the go for Jay in her office.'

'Good idea,' said Abby, unsuspecting. She pushed her sunglasses on top of her head and hiked up her shoulder bag. 'Don't stay too late. It's a beautiful summer night. Everyone ought to be out looking at the stars.'

Fat chance, thought Zoe.

But she went bravely up to Jay's office.

Poppy had obviously gone. Her desk was tidy and nearly empty. The room was quiet, but the air was full of the luscious smell of Jay's favourite coffee. Zoe helped herself, skirted the man-eating plant and opened the door to his office. Jay's desk was equally clear.

She bit her lip. Looked as if he wasn't coming back tonight, then. She ought to go, but somehow she was reluctant to leave the place where he spent most of his days.

She wandered round the room, sipping her coffee, touching the surfaces, pulling books off the bookshelf, running her hands voluptuously down the upholstery of his chair, where his shoulders habitually rested. She brushed her cheek against the top of the tall chair.

'Jay,' she said aloud. All her longing was in it. All her love.

The door banged back. She looked up.

Jay stood in the doorway. She hardly recognised him. His face looked fleshless, as if he had been running. His eyes were concentrated and intent.

'So you're here,' he said in a still voice.

Zoe straightened rapidly. 'Thought I'd save you the bother of summoning me,' she said in a bright voice.

He frowned. 'Summoning you?'

'You're going to kick me out, right?' she said, quite as if she didn't care. 'After Venice? House rules?'

But her heart cried, Touch me. Love me.

'Oh, that.' He sounded almost bored. 'I suppose so.'

He *supposed* so?

'Well, don't give yourself a heart attack,' said Zoe, hurt. 'I'm sorry I have made so little impact on Culp and Christopher.'

He gave a snort of bitter laughter. 'Culp and Christopher? What about the impact you've made on me?'

She stared, clutching his chair like a shield. 'What?'

He was carrying a briefcase. He flung it away from him, into the corner of the room, as savagely as if he was launching a spear.

'Right. You're sacked. Satisfied?'

'The agency—'

'The agency will survive,' said Jay between rigid lips. 'I'm not sure I will.'

'Wha-at?'

He took a hasty step forward. 'I love you,' he said intensely. 'I never said that to anyone before. But I said it to you without even thinking.'

'You—did—not.'

'Yes, I did. I called you my love. What else do you think that was?' His eyes narrowed. 'Or do all your men call you that?'

Zoe decided that now was not the time to ask him to define his terms. She had never seen a man closer to breaking point.

'Well, if they did they didn't mean it.'

'Oh, God.' He sounded frantic. 'I don't know what to do about this. Your sister says I've had my ration. Susan Manoir said I'd hurt you. I keep thinking I'm too old for you—'

Zoe stopped hanging onto his chair like a lifeline and stepped round the desk.

'Why don't you ask me?' she said gently.

He shut his eyes. 'Will you marry me?'

She gave a soft laugh. His eyes flew open.

'Only on one condition,' said Zoe, hot babe incarnate.

His eyes questioned wildly.

She laughed softly and moved in close. 'You take me home and make love to me *now*.'

It was a perfect summer night. His room was huge and airy, windows open to the night-time sounds of birds and small animals. The moonlit breeze was cool on her skin, like a lover's breath.

I know what a lover's breath on my skin feels like now.

They had left their clothes behind them, in the hallway, on the stairs. Zoe trembled to his slightest touch.

There was only one doubt left in her mind.

'Why did you say that it was not chance that I was a virgin?'

He curved his hand round her neck, kissing her skin with moth wing dabs. Her lips parted and her breath quickened— and he relished it.

'Mmm?' he said, concentrating.

'Why did you say that it wasn't chance?'

He paused reluctantly, though his hand started to do wickedly enticing things to her nipple.

'Your family,' he said, surprised. 'When you told me about your mother it was so clear. You'd watched her collapse because your father left. You must have thought, This is grown-up stuff and I'm not ready for it. Perfectly sensible.'

'Oh.'

Zoe was not feeling sensible. She was feeling wanton and wonderful.

She said, 'I never thought of that. I just thought sex was mostly hormones and showing off.'

Jay gave a shaken laugh. 'And now?'

Zoe took hold of the wickedly skilful hand at her breast and carried it lower, to where they both had everything to discover.

'Now I know it,' she said coolly. 'And, oh, boy, have I got some showing off to do.'

But he made her wait. 'Not until you admit there's a little matter of love involved as well.'

He watched her eyes darken and nearly lost his resolve. But this was important. And he was good at physical self-control.

Her head fell back. 'Love…'

He stroked her so slowly that her eyes crossed.

'I don't know what love is,' she moaned.

'Yes, you do.'

He saw her bite her tongue as she tried to hold on to her senses.

'Okay, okay,' she said breathlessly. 'I fell in love with you at first sight. I thought you looked like a Mogul prince and I knew you were for me. I wanted you to make love to me, but I wanted you to talk to me and live with me and listen to me for the rest of our lives as well.'

Jay was humbled. He said so.

Zoe writhed. 'Good,' she gasped. 'I hope that's everything you want. Because I don't think I can hang on much longer…'

'Everything,' said Jay. 'Except maybe…'

Their bodies slid together in a slow, voluptuous locking. Somehow it took them into another dimension. He saw her eyes widen and widen as she realised it, too. For a moment he held her very still, looking deeply into her eyes. No reservations. No disguise.

Her lips parted. 'I love you.' She framed the words soundlessly, as if she were talking direct to his spirit. Her eyes were honest. All guards down now.

'Yes,' said Jay.

And took her on a journey he'd thought he knew by heart—and found he had never travelled it before.

Later they lay entwined in the dark. From his pillow they could see the fuzzy moon above the trees.

'What would you have done if I hadn't come looking for you?' said Zoe.

She could feel his smile against her skin. At once she detected teasing. She knew him so well now.

'What?'

Jay did not take his possessive hand off her naked waist. 'I was going to try and bribe you,' he said lazily.

'Don't believe it.'

Still keeping one hand on her, he stretched a long arm and extracted what he was looking for from a pocket in one of the garments on the floor. He flicked it across the bed.

'I spent today cancelling the merger. I thought I'd rather stay small and keep my self-respect,' he said. 'You taught me that. So I thought it would please you.'

It was a little velvet pouch. Zoe fingered it, but it was of less importance than what he was saying.

'I taught *you*?' She hardly dared to believe it.

'My darling.' He stroked her hair behind her ear. 'I love the way your curls cling to my fingers.'

'Electricity,' said Zoe impatiently. 'What do you mean, I taught you?'

'Love that electricity.' Jay gathered her close. For all the teasing laughter in his voice, Zoe knew this was serious. 'You saw right through my protective colouring right from the start,' he told her. 'Then, in Venice, you went further. You saw the man I'd forgotten was there.'

'Oh!' Her eyes filled. 'Oh, *Jay*.'

He unlaced the pouch. Stones fell out, heavy and warm and gleaming faintly in the darkness.

'Very useful, your not having any jewellery,' he said lightly. 'When we're old we can take up collecting rubies as a hobby. But for now—'

It was a necklace. She turned it over. In the light of the moon she saw the sheen.

'Do they solidify silk, somehow?' she said doubtfully.

He switched on the bedside light. The necklace was made of enamels—turquoise and rose and peacock and flame. The colours of his fantastic shirts. The colours of his imagination.

The colours of his life.

'Put it on for me,' she said softly.

His fingers were not entirely steady.

She ran her hands all over the compact and elegant body.

She had, she thought exultantly, the right now. She was his and he was hers.

She leaned over him, her hair catching the light. It was as soft as silk against that wonderful golden skin. They gave a sigh of exquisite longing at exactly the same moment.

'And now, my Mogul Prince, my darling,' said Zoe, 'love me.'